# FORTRESS OF THE LOST AMULET

TREASURE HUNTERS ALLIANCE
BOOK 1

MICHAEL WEBB

# ALSO BY MICHAEL WEBB

*The Shadow Knights Series:*
*#1 - The Last Shadow Knight*
*#2 - Rise of the Shadow*
*#3 - Shadow of Destiny*
*Prequel Novella - Shadow Knights: Origine*

*Treasure Hunters Alliance:*
*#1 - Fortress of the Lost Amulet*
*#2 - Legend of the Golden City*

Get a FREE prequel novella to the Shadow Knights series - Shadow Knights: Origine - by signing up for my mailing list at www.subscribepage.com/michaelwebbnovels

# PROLOGUE

Vicion Shepherd stared at the pommel of his sword, spinning its tip against the stone floor. When it stopped, he gazed down the unique scrollwork along the length of the blade—the blade that had taken the lives of hundreds, possibly thousands. He took in a deep breath before blowing the air out of his lungs and looking up. Dozens of men and women stared up at the dais, waiting. He felt the question hanging in the air. Would his sword take another life?

A man in the center of the room kept his head bowed. Chains held his arms behind his back. A red gash marked his forehead, surrounded by black and blue bruises that pocked his face. Despite his ragged appearance, the man was immense. Arms bulged beneath his ragged shirt. His thick neck sloped to massive shoulders.

Vicion stood. With his sword in hand, he descended the handful of steps to the waiting crowd.

"Please, My Lord, have mercy," a woman pleaded, tears brimming in her eyes. She stood to the side in a rumpled dress with her hands pressed together. "He's all we have." Two small boys peeked out from behind her, casting nervous glances at him.

Two guards with crossed spears kept the woman back.

"Your husband defiled the Viper's name," his advisor, Quinnell, spat, stepping toward the woman. "He spoke out against him in the city square."

The woman looked at her husband. "He's all we have," she repeated, her voice fading.

The others in the room watched and waited for the Viper's decision. Not known for compassion, Vicion sneered at the man in chains. *Have mercy,* he thought. A laugh escaped his mouth, and a smile tugged at half of his face. *Now, that's an idea.*

Vicion faced the crowd and held up his chin. "I will have mercy on this man," he said, holding his hands out, one still carrying his weapon. "I will not have him executed."

Gasps filled the room, and the people muttered to each other. The prisoner's head shot up, and his wife cried out with tears of glee.

Vicion held up a hand. "Instead, he will have the chance to earn his freedom."

The muttering diminished. The woman halted her celebration.

"He will fight in single combat. If he wins, he is set free. If he loses . . . he dies."

The man spoke up. "Who—who do I fight?"

Vicion took a step forward, staring back with an evil grin. "Me."

The man blanched, blood draining from his face. His wife's wail pierced the room. "My Lord," the man said, his massive muscles twitching, "how is that mercy?"

Vicion shrugged. "Would you rather be executed now?"

The prisoner's shoulders slumped.

"I thought not." The Viper turned to his guards standing nearby. "Release him and give him a sword."

Vicion walked to Desirien, who stood to the side of the room. His wife's silk gown curved down her body in luxurious folds. Her black hair cascaded off her shoulders in tight curls. A pouty look fixed on her face as she pulled him close.

"Do you have to do this?" Desirien asked, teasing her finger across his upper arm.

He chuckled. "No, but it's been so long."

"Do you have . . . it?" she whispered, her eyebrows raised.

He glanced to make sure no one was around. "Of course," he replied. He touched his chest, comforted by the object pressing against his skin.

Her lips pursed. "You said you'd stop wearing it. It's getting worse. You can't keep—"

"Hush!" he breathed, clenching his teeth. "It's my choice."

A metal scrape sounded behind him. Vicion turned. The man's chains were gone, and he stood alone. The others in the large room had spread out in a wide circle.

"Be quick about it," Desirien whispered in his ear, her breath tickling his neck.

A warm shudder rushed through him. He grinned as her eyebrows danced suggestively. "I will."

The room was silent as Vicion approached the prisoner. The bruised man stood taller by a hand and heavier by a wide margin. His arms were as thick as Vicion's legs, but the prisoner's legs were the ones shaking.

"You're a fine specimen," the Viper taunted. "Have some confidence."

The man held his sword before him with both hands. Vicion's blade whistled as it swung, cutting the air while he warmed up his arm. He settled into a crouch, standing just beyond the prisoner's reach, the object beneath his shirt thrumming a faint pulse.

He nodded. "Begin."

The man's sword shook. Sweat beaded on his forehead

despite having done nothing yet. With a roar, he stepped forward and heaved his weapon overhead. His guttural yell rang through the room as he pulled the weapon down with both hands.

Vicion didn't flinch, but casually held his sword up, blocking the blow with one hand. A resounding clang pierced the air, and the man recoiled as if he'd struck a stone wall. He backed away and shook his hand out. After a quick moment, he stepped forward again, leading with side strikes. The prisoner's strength was considerable. He flashed the sword on alternate sides, stepping in with wild power, yet each attack remained unfruitful, deflected by Vicion's firm hand.

"Come on!" Vicion shouted. "You can do better than that!"

Rising to the taunt, the prisoner rushed forward in a two-step lunge. He leaped into the air and brought his sword down in another overhead strike. His roar was deafening.

Vicion marveled at the bravery. *He would have made a fine warrior,* he thought. *It's a pity.* He stepped to the side, avoiding the potential killing stroke. Without giving the man a chance to shrink back, the Viper attacked. His sword struck the prisoner's with a deafening clash of metal, cleaving it in two.

With his mouth gaping, the man dropped the broken hilt and tried to scramble away. His wife resumed wailing.

Vicion ignored the distraction. He raised his foot and kicked the man's chest. A sickening crunch of breaking ribs filled the air, and the man's body flew backward, sliding across the ground to where the circle of onlookers parted.

Vicion wasted no time, but marched after the man. The prisoner writhed on the ground, clenching his chest and moaning in agony. When the Viper arrived, he scrambled to a sitting position, wincing in fresh pain.

"No one defiles my name and gets away with it," Vicion growled as he bent over. His hand wrapped around the prisoner's massive neck.

The man grabbed his arm with both hands, unsuccessfully trying to wrench it away.

Power flooded through Vicion's body. A warm surge of energy tingled inside as he pulled from the power of the object around his neck. The massive prisoner's body lifted. Extending his arm above his head, Vicion stared into the prisoner's eyes. *Scared. Helpless.* He laughed.

The man's legs flailed in the air just off the ground. His hands beat against Vicion's stony grip, but the lord merely scratched his chin with his free hand.

The observers had backed up, giving them plenty of space. The woman's wailing intensified but sounded distant to him. His eyes narrowed. With a sneer and a grunt, he tossed the man headfirst into the nearby stone wall. The woman's shriek covered the crack of the man's neck. His body fell in a limp heap, limbs contorted in a gruesome display of death.

Muttering resumed in the room, but the body remained motionless. Vicion turned to Quinnell. "Hang his body in the square. Let the people of this city see what happens when they speak against their lord."

His advisor nodded.

Vicion strode past the crying woman and her two children without batting an eye. His eyes locked on Desirien, waiting at the far side of the room, leaning against the wall.

Her grin grew as he approached. "No one can beat you," she said, taking his hand and leading him through a side door.

Vicion brought his other hand to his chest, pressing it against the Amulet hanging there. *That's right. No one.*

# 1

## 350 YEARS LATER

"You're sure this is the place?" Peter whispered. He grimaced at the high, crumbling stone wall above them. It was a familiar place, one Peter hurried by hundreds of times, never giving it a second look.

Rylan grinned with anticipation, having led the four friends to the narrow alleyway behind the wall. "The guy I followed came straight here from Banker's Row, opened a big fancy lock on the gate over there, and entered. Whatever he was carrying in that coin purse, I know there's more inside."

Peter nodded, his stomach growling with a deep ache.

"And you're sure we won't get caught?" Sephiri asked, chewing at the edge of her thumbnail. "Can't we just head back to the inn and earn some pintid playing gammit?"

"Gammit takes forever!" Rylan said. "I'm telling you, this will be worth it. We need it. Our parents need it."

Peter winced at the mention of parents. He glanced at Sephiri, but she didn't appear fazed by the comment.

"We won't get caught." Kira soothed her with a smile as she tied her blonde hair up into a ponytail.

Sephiri sighed in both agreement and defeat. "If you say so."

"I already said so," Rylan whispered. "This is a great idea."

"Your plans sometimes end with you stuck in the stocks for an afternoon," Sephiri said. "Kira's don't."

Peter stepped closer. "She's got a point. Let's get a move on. If we hurry, we might have time to make it to the tavern and get a proper dinner."

"Now that's what I'm talking about." Rylan grinned before kneeling and lowering his head.

Peter planted the soles of his worn boots on Rylan's broad shoulders, then steadied himself with one hand on the stone wall as Rylan exhaled and stood. Rylan was stocky whereas Peter was lean and tall enough to peer over the top of the wall.

There wasn't much to be seen behind it—a few dilapidated stables, a large old building, and a couple of guards talking to each other.

*What exactly are they guarding?* Peter wondered. *Just that building? A powerful gust of wind would knock it down.*

"Move left," Peter muttered.

Rylan grumbled but teetered to the left until the nearest stable blocked Peter's line of sight to the guards. He clambered over the wall, then dropped onto a large supply barrel near the wall. He froze at the sound of his boots hitting the old wooden lid, but the guards didn't stir. The barrel put him another short drop from the ground, and when he stood straight, he was tall enough to reach back over the wall and down the opposite side. Peter adjusted the coil of rope over his shoulder, hiking it higher.

Their system snapped into gear. Friends for years, the teenagers barely had to speak. Sephiri went next, up onto Rylan's shoulders, then grasping Peter's hand to get over the wall. Kira followed and landed gracefully on the barrel beside Peter. Side by side, they reached down and each pulled one of

Rylan's arms, his height assisted by a running start and kicking off the wall. With some scrambling and struggling, he fit his toes into the features of the wall and hauled himself up.

"All right," Rylan huffed. "Where do we think the stash is?"

"Wasn't this your idea?" Sephiri glanced around, shoulders tense.

"Well, yeah. It's not like I have a map of this place, though."

"Let's get in upstairs," Peter whispered, pointing to the balcony ahead. "You can boost us up. Less likely for the guards to notice that way."

"Ugh." Rylan's shoulders fell. "Again?"

Staying out of sight of the guards, the four repeated the process, clambering up onto Rylan's shoulders to sneak onto the building's second-story balcony. Sweat dotted Rylan's shirt as he hauled himself up last. He was the strongest of the four, but the climbing always took a toll.

Peter paused, crouched on the balcony, ears perked for any sounds of recognition while the four friends waited, motionless. Satisfied with the silence, he placed the coil of rope onto the balcony with a muted *whump,* then nodded over his shoulder at his friends. Pushing open the door to the balcony, he crept into the dark hallway behind it. There wasn't much to see: dust and cobwebs overhead, a few closed doors, floorboards that creaked under his feet. Peter grimaced as he tried to move in silence. *Where would the coins be stashed?* It looked more like an abandoned lodging than any kind of functional building. *Did Rylan imagine this guy and his coin purse?*

At the end of the hall, a light shone from beneath a heavy door. Not hearing any occupants beyond, Peter pushed it open but remained crouched in the doorway. A fire roared and crackled in the hearth behind a large dressing screen that divided the room.

"There," Rylan whispered. He peered over Peter's shoulder, then nodded toward a small table next to an armchair. The heavy bag of coins had been left as if dropped by someone as he passed.

"Um," Kira whispered, "guys?"

At the rear of their group, Kira grimaced at the door itself. A carving of a serpent wrapping around a skull displayed above the handle—the symbol of the Viper Syndicate.

Peter swallowed. A bit of thievery was one thing. Robbing the Vipers was another.

"We should go," Sephiri whispered.

"The pouch is right there," Rylan said. "Let me grab it real quick."

"No way," Peter said. "Seph's right—we should get out of here."

Rylan pushed past Peter. He entered the room just as another door opened next to the hearth.

Rylan dropped, cowering behind the armchair with eyes wide. Peter caught his terrified gaze and mouthed, "Get back here!"

Rylan shook his head. He pressed closer to the armchair, then cut his gaze to the bag of coins.

"Idiot," Sephiri whispered. "He's going to get us killed."

"The new land rates will go into effect immediately," a man said as he approached the hearth, his head and shoulders visible above the dividing screens. He peered down at something beneath him that commanded all of his attention. The man was tall with salt-and-pepper hair and small, dark eyes. Even from a distance, the firelight caught the gold detailing woven into his fine silk jacket. He stood straighter than his companions, two stocky lackeys who hung on his every word. "Inform the farmers about the increase tomorrow. See if you can't get them to pay up front."

A buck-toothed lackey laughed. "The Lord of Commerce already agreed to it?"

"Of course," the man drawled. "He didn't exactly have a choice."

"Garrett Razor," Kira whispered.

Peter's throat went dry. Not only were they in a Viper Syndicate facility, but their leader reviewed his plans next to them. *Great.* "Get back here," Peter mouthed to Rylan again before pointing to the floor at his feet. "Now!"

"And that will be enough to keep our coffers full?" the bucktoothed lackey asked.

"What about the loans?" the other man asked. "Are we increasing the interest rates alongside the land rates?"

Razor laughed, but it was a dark, humorless sound. "Not a bad idea. We'll see. Right now, we have bigger things to worry about." He smoothed his hand over papers on the table. "We're getting close. Close to something big. And once I have it in my hands, I won't need the Lord of Commerce at all. The Vipers will run Palenting."

"What do you mean?" a lackey asked. "Don't we already run the city?"

Rylan shuffled closer to the table.

"Don't," Peter mouthed.

"It's right there," Rylan mouthed back.

Razor scoffed. "Stoke the fire. I need better light." The men turned away while Razor's attention remained on the papers.

Rylan looked ready to pounce, tense and coiled like a spring. Peter's heart pounded. He slowly shook his head.

Rylan darted his hand out and snatched the bag off the table. The coins jangled in the pouch just as a log in the fire snapped and broke in the hearth, sending up a spray of sparks.

This was it, Peter was sure. Finally, Rylan's impulsiveness would lead to them getting in trouble, *real* trouble, not just a slap on the wrist from the local guards.

But Razor didn't move.

Rylan broke into a grin. Despite his irritation, Peter couldn't deny that a good meal with the money sounded great. The Vipers' leader sighed and turned away from the papers, arms crossed over his chest as he gazed into the roaring flames.

"Now!" Peter mouthed.

Rylan crept toward the door, staying low to the ground, as if that would keep him out of sight. He hurried forward, then grabbed the door handle.

Peter grinned. *We're going to make it!*

Rylan pulled the door open wider to slip back through— and the hinges creaked.

Razor whipped around. "Who's there!"

"Go!" Peter hissed. "Go, now!" He scuttled backward, nearly knocking Kira and Sephiri down. They jumped back, and Peter hopped to his feet.

"Get them!" Razor shouted.

The two lackeys stumbled out, eyes wide as they fumbled their knives out of the scabbards on their hips. Peter pushed his three friends down the hall. He stayed at the rear and faced the two lackeys. "Go!" he shouted to the others. "Get out of here!"

"No way!" Rylan said. "Not without you!"

The buck-toothed one sneered and lunged, knife forward in a sloppy overhand grip. Peter suppressed a grin. The man's unsure stance and flushed face suggested he didn't get the same amount of training Peter did in his spare time. He ducked under Buck-tooth's arm, then caught him in the gut with a hard punch. The lackey grunted in pain and dropped his weapon.

Kira rolled forward and snatched the knife with a whoop of victory. Rylan surged ahead and barreled into the other man's legs, low enough to knock him off-balance and send him careening to the floor.

"Peter!" Kira called. "Blade!"

Before Peter could turn and take the offered weapon, Sephiri's cry of, "Look out!" preceded Buck-tooth ramming into him, slamming his body into the wall. Dull pain throbbed through Peter's shoulder where it connected with the wall. He struggled against the lackey's bulk. The man worked his shoulder against Peter's neck, angling to cut off his breathing. Peter cringed and shoved back. *I'm going to kill Rylan for getting us into this—if the Vipers don't kill me first.*

Kira leaped forward, knife in hand, and slashed at the man's leg. The lackey cursed and reeled backward. Peter staggered away and stared. The man cried out and pressed his hand against the gash where a dark stain bloomed. Kira tossed the knife aside with a clatter against the floor, then grimaced and shook her hands out like she'd just touched a slug.

Rylan buried his fist in the other man's gut.

"Rylan!" Peter called. "Come on!"

The larger boy glanced over his shoulder. "Start down. I'll hold them off!"

Sephiri stared ahead, her body frozen and eyes wide.

Peter took her wrist and pulled her down the hall to the balcony. She kept up, stumbling as they rushed outside. Peter grabbed the rope he'd left there and wound it around the balcony railing. He tossed half over it, so it hung in two lines down to the ground. "Go!"

Sephiri touched the rail with wide eyes. "Peter, are you sure—"

"Go!" he insisted.

She winced, but took the rope in hand, shaking as she lowered herself over the edge. Kira went next. Rylan got a few more good blows in on the lackeys to hold them back then followed after her.

"You cocky little twits," Razor growled from the hallway. "You think you can enter Viper territory with no consequences?"

Peter took both sides of the rope in hand and leaped over the balcony. The rough fabric burned in his palms as he slid down and landed with a thump in the dirt. Rylan had already boosted Kira and Sephiri over the wall. Peter pulled the rope through the creaking balcony railing and left it in a pile as Razor rushed onto the balcony.

"Guards!" the leader of the Vipers shouted. "Guards! You useless morons! Get them!"

Peter's confidence grew as he charged forward, leaped onto Rylan's shoulder, and bounded over the wall. He reached down and hauled Rylan up and over as well, and then the four of them took off, sprinting through the narrow alleyways, with Sephiri leading the way.

PANTING AND EXHAUSTED, the four friends stopped running when they arrived at the city square. Despite the late hour, the gathering area still bustled with activity as people moved between taverns and played gammit under the dim lights of the torches. A string player busked by the fountain, filling the air with jaunty music. At the far end of the square, fine iron gates protected the entrance to the gardens, the Baron of Palenting's castle looming behind it.

Breathing heavily, Peter leaned against the wall by the fountain. "Well, it didn't go as planned, but at least we got some coins."

"About that." Rylan cringed, his chest heaving. "There was a lot of fighting and scuffling . . ."

"Rylan . . . ?"

"I may have, um, dropped it."

"Dropped it?" Sephiri asked.

"I got tackled!" Rylan threw his hands up. "It slipped out of my hands!"

Kira sighed and pinched the bridge of her nose.

"Awesome," Peter said. "Great call on that endeavor, Ry."

"At least we didn't get stabbed," he grumbled.

Peter laughed and grasped Rylan's shoulder. "Well, I guess you're right about that."

"Yeah, now we just have to worry about how the leader of the Viper Syndicate might want to stab us in the future," Sephiri said.

Peter waved a hand dismissively. "They're too busy to worry about people like us. They've got money to collect."

"Exactly," Rylan said. "Money we don't have."

"And whose fault is that?" Peter raised his eyebrows.

"Come on." Sephiri pushed her dark hair off her face. Her eyes were bloodshot, and her face pallid. "Can we not do this now?"

Guilt swept through Peter like a wave. *The fight must have scared her more than I realized.* It was easy for him to get carried away on nights like this. If things didn't work out, he and Rylan both had homes to return to, even if those homes were shabby and the cupboards were bare. For as long as Peter had known her, Sephiri had been on her own.

On her own, except for her friends.

"Seph's right," Kira said. "Let me buy dinner."

Groans all around. Even though it wasn't a significant expense for Kira, living as she did in the rich neighborhood of Paratill View, Peter hated depending on her to pay for them.

"Just for tonight," she said.

"You shouldn't have to—"

"I know," Kira said, silencing Rylan with a wave of her hand. "It's not a big deal."

"It's one thing to sneak some food from your family's kitchen," Peter said, "but buying us a whole meal . . ."

"I said it's nothing."

Peter sighed, his shoulders falling. A rumble ran through his stomach. "Guess that's what you get for hanging out with degenerates like us."

"Speaking of which, why do you even bother with us,"

Rylan asked. "Your parents don't approve, and you could have the attention of anyone in Palenting."

"I don't *want* to hang out with just anyone," Kira said, resting her hands on Rylan's and Sephiri's shoulders. "Everyone else I see only cares about appearance and money."

Rylan held up a finger. "Uh, I care about money."

Kira laughed. "Whatever trouble you three are getting into, I want to be there with you. I wouldn't have it any other way. Now come on, I'm hungry."

Peter followed with the weight of disappointment on his shoulders. If he could find the right target, with the right plan, and the right skills, he could change his life, his parents' lives, and his friends' lives in one night.

*Tonight wasn't that night.*

## 2

_____

Peter's feet pounded on the uneven cobblestones of Palenting. The late-suether sun had not yet broken the horizon, and the morning air was crisp, burning his lungs as he ran. In a few weeks, the season would change to wiether, and the cold of the morning would remain all day. His morning routine took him on a winding path away from his family's farm in Lowside, north past the bureaucrats' homes in Dulran Yard. He passed through the town square and turned west toward the artisan's shops in Brufec Heights. The streets were almost entirely empty, save for the workers leaving their homes, heading to their servant jobs on the wealthier northeast side.

When he made it back home, the sun was creeping over the horizon, turning the dark sky warm gray and glimmering over the sea far in the distance. He paused outside the threshold, catching his breath and wiping the sweat from his brow.

"Morning, Peter," Wynna said from across the road. "Already finished?"

"Not yet." Peter smiled at his elderly neighbor.

"You still practicing all that stuff my husband taught you?"

"Every day." He pointed behind the house. "About to go and work on it now. Trying to get it all in before I'm expected at the mason's shop."

"Right, you're still apprenticing, yes?" Wynna heaved the basket of chicken feed higher on her hip. She was a short, wiry woman, with a lined face and graying hair she wore cropped short. Across the road from Peter's farm, her property was substantially smaller.

Peter nodded. "I'm helping around the farm as much as I can, too. You know, if you need a hand with anything . . ." He glanced at the chicken feed.

Wynna smiled and shook her head. "I might be old, but I can still feed the chickens before I go to work. How are things for your parents?"

Peter pursed his lips. He didn't want to burden his neighbor with their family's woes. "Things are . . . fine. We're good." His shaking voice didn't convey confidence.

Wynna frowned. "Well, tell them I said hello."

Peter nodded and gave a wave, then hurried into the small barn behind the family house. The barn wasn't used for much more than storage. Peter's parents kept few animals, as the larger livestock became too much work as their health deteriorated. After their hens grew ill and died, they relied on agriculture. Amid the rusting farm tools and dusty yokes and harnesses, Peter stored a few heavy wooden training swords he and Rylan had carved together. They were roughly hewn and unbalanced, but it was better than no training at all.

He still remembered the cadence of Wynna's husband barking commands at him—watch his form, his power, his stamina. The retired army captain trained him for years, at Peter's request. The daily regimen wasn't easy, and it only served to push him harder.

Peter gripped the hilt of the sword and took a slow, steady breath. He widened his stance and held the weapon near his head, high up, pointed at his imagined opponent. With a flurry of movement, he dropped the blade, stepping and thrusting, settling into moves locked into his muscles from years of repetition.

If he'd had an actual sword the previous night, things would've gone differently. *Those Vipers wouldn't have known what hit them.* He pictured himself standing in the hall, sword drawn, as the lackeys stammered in fear before they turned tail and ran.

Instead, he was there, in the barn, swinging a stick around, already hungry despite the meager meal Kira had purchased the previous night.

He drew the sword down again. Strike. Strike. He imagined the blade clanging against a foe's arms and chest. The sword felt good in his hand. It felt right. It felt better than the mason's hammer or the rickety plow he used in the fields. This is what he was meant to be doing—training, adventuring, making a name for himself—not stuck on the south side of Palenting, stealing coins just to scrape by.

Only one more year until he was old enough to join the Rynorian army. The first thing new recruits did was move to Bromhill for training. Then they could be stationed anywhere in the kingdom. While his father cheered his training regimen to build discipline and strength, he discouraged any thoughts about him becoming a soldier.

Peter shoved the thoughts from his mind. The job sounded glorious, but the pay was virtually nonexistent. He couldn't leave Palenting until his parents were secure enough to survive without him, and that reality felt further and further away. *If only we'd hung on to the coins from the Viper compound. Then the harvest wouldn't be so . . . daunting. If it's not enough, what will we do?*

He pushed those anxieties down.

Peter ran through his swordplay drills until the golden

morning light poured through the window high on the eastern barn wall. With a sigh, he leaned the training weapon back alongside the others and linked his fingers behind his head, gazing up at the window as his heartbeat slowed. Gradually, his breath settled.

He made his way back into the small house. As expected, his father was up and stoking the fire in the wood stove. "Morning, Peter," he said. "Do your training this morning?"

"Yes, sir," Peter said. His father rolled his eyes at the honorific, but didn't push back. Peter took the poker from his hand and stoked the coals instead, knowing the angle wasn't good on his father's back that early in the morning.

Matthias Fairfield was a man of above-average height, a thick head of gray hair, and a spine that had recently begun to bow. Having just reached his sixties, his aches and pains seemed to increase daily. Being the stubborn son of a farmer that he was, he tried to hide them, but Peter always noticed.

"Saw Wynna this morning as well," Peter added.

"Early, hm? She must be back working at the library."

"Seems so."

"Jason?" called a weak voice from the back bedroom. "Is that you?"

Peter's father sighed and wiped his hands on a clean rag. "Let me help Gretchen out of bed. She's not doing well this morning."

"She thinks I'm Jason again," Peter said with resignation. Younger than his father by five years, his mother's mental clarity varied by the day, sometimes by the hour. Peter's resemblance to his late older brother sometimes knocked her off-balance. She could be having a fine day working in the house, and then when Peter came home from work, she'd lose her sense of time and place. Peter often thought it'd be better for his mother if he never saw her at all. "Why don't you wait until I leave? It'll be easier on her."

His father sighed, then stood at the entrance to the hall. He idly rubbed his neck, eyes closed. A flicker of pain rolled across his features at the motion. The farm work wore on him, even more so since Peter's mother wasn't able to help as much. And they didn't have money to hire any help.

When Peter was young, his older brother and sister helped with chores, but they both passed from the blue fever when he was two, leaving him as the only child in a family of three with two aging parents.

"Or I can skip work today," Peter said. "I can work the field so you can tend to Mother."

"You know you can't do that, Peter." His father sighed and rubbed his temple. "If you miss any more shifts, the mason might end your apprenticeship altogether."

"Would that be so bad though? I don't *need* to be a mason. It'd be better if you'd just let me work here on the farm for a bit. Then . . . maybe after a year, when I'm older . . ." His words faded. He didn't have the courage to mention joining the army.

"Peter." His father held him with his eyes. "You are smart and capable. You can do much more than working on a farm like this. Masonry will open up a lot of opportunities—chances to make better money than you ever would here." His father pressed his lips into a flat line then took a deep, steadying breath. "Plus . . . we might not have this farm for much longer if the land rates keep rising."

Peter stared at his father, eyes wide. Shock ran through him, icy cold. He'd known since he was a child that things on the farm weren't easy, but this was the first time his father had admitted things were that bad. *There's no way we could lose the farm. It's not possible. It can't be.*

He straightened up.

"You're nearly a man now," his father said. "There's no use in hiding it from you."

"What would we do?"

"Work elsewhere, I suppose." His father glanced down the hall.

How could his father work a waged job when his mother needed so much care?

"That's why it's best you continue the apprenticeship," his father said. "You need to build a career of your own."

"Yes, Father." Becoming a mason was the last thing Peter wanted to do—working in a crew of other poor souls to build the vast mansions, pubs, and bathhouses that peppered the north side. But if they lost the farm, he may not have a choice. Not if he didn't want his parents to end up on the streets. The life of a lowly soldier wouldn't earn enough. His vision of glory dimmed.

"There's breakfast on the table," his father said. "You should eat before you leave."

Peter glanced at the sparse table. "Is that it?" A bowl of thin gruel with a dollop of honey sat waiting.

"You need protein. I know. I'm sorry. We just don't have the money for it. I try my best, but—" His words faded.

Peter's gut twisted. "I didn't mean it that way. I know how it is. It's fine." As hungry as he was, the gruel wouldn't do much for him—and his mother needed it more. *I wish Rylan had held on to those coins. Maybe I can sneak a roll on the way from the baker in the town square.* "And I'll be fine. I'm not hungry."

"Son, we've had this conversation too many times before. Your mother and I don't need you to—"

A knock at the door interrupted the familiar argument.

His father answered it. "Oh, good morning, Wynna."

"Morning, Matthias," Wynna said. "My girls have been quite busy this week, and I can't use all these eggs." She held out a small basket, piled with brown and spotted eggs fresh from the coop.

Peter's eyes widened, mouth watering as he looked upon the bounty.

"Wynna," Peter's father said, "surely you can find a use."

"I insist." She pushed the basket toward Matthias, who hesitated.

Peter rushed forward and took the basket from her hands. "Thank you, Wynna. We can definitely use them."

She smiled. "I thought you might. A growing boy like you needs a lot of good food, right?"

Matthias grimaced and looked away, but Peter thanked her again. Wynna waved off his gratitude with a grin before crossing the dirt road back to her small home.

Peter immediately hung a small pot of water over the fire to hard boil a few eggs. It was something his mother liked to eat, and he could take one in his pocket to the mason's, too. It'd be a much easier workday with a little food in him. His mood had almost become something good when his father said, "We'll have to find something in the harvest to share with her in return. It's no small thing for her to provide us with food."

"She said the hens were overproducing," Peter said, his brow furrowed. "The eggs don't keep forever. Perhaps we can ask to take a hen off her hands."

His father sighed. "I doubt they're overproducing." He picked up an egg from the basket and rolled it in his palm. "These are small."

"What do you mean?"

"Wynna's struggling as well. Gerald passed away three seasons ago, and she has no one to help her now. The increasing land rates are likely hurting her even more than they're hurting us."

"But she has a job at the library, right?"

His father pursed his lips and paused. "Gerald was a good man. He was a brave captain in the army, and he loved Wynna very much."

Peter cocked his head, curious at his father's hesitation.

"He had a gambling problem though, which grew more desperate in his last year to feed his borrell spice addiction."

Peter inhaled sharply. "I had no idea."

"They kept it quiet. He worked up a sizable debt before he died, and Wynna's been working hard to dig out of it."

Peter looked at the eggs, an audible growl from his stomach filling the room.

"Go ahead," his father said, the water beginning to boil. "You need the protein."

With less enthusiasm, Peter plunked two eggs in the water.

"We'll have to help each other out if we're going to withstand these increases," his father hummed, more to himself than to Peter. "But first we need to get through this harvest."

"Did you talk to Gavin about seeing if we could borrow an ox?"

His father sighed. "I can't ask him for a favor like that. He's going to need them himself."

"Father, we won't be able to harvest in time without help. You can't get it all done."

"I've done it before." His father straightened, one hand on his lower back. "We'll be fine."

*Father was in a lot better health during those seasons,* Peter thought. There was no way he'd be able to do it by hand, especially with Peter spending his days at his apprenticeship.

"At least let me—"

"Peter. Your job is important. It will help you get out of this. I'm tired of having this same argument every day."

Peter was ready to keep arguing, but a hard knock on the door interrupted him. It was too firm to be Wynna.

His father cursed under his breath.

"Father?" Peter asked.

"Quiet." His father squared his shoulders, then opened the front door.

"Matthias Fairfield?" a man asked as soon as the door was

open. He was a small, skinny man with a serious, lined expression and a heavy book in his hand. He peered down his nose at the book, trailing his finger over the records. "I'm a clerk from the Department of Commerce."

"How can I help you?"

Peter took a step back, not because of the clerk, but because of the two tall, stern men behind him in studded leather armor with swords sheathed at their hips. *Why would the commerce clerk arrive with soldiers?*

"Our records show you're behind in your payments," the clerk said. "Substantially behind."

"I'm aware," his father said. "I've been to the Department of Commerce already this season to discuss—"

"I see that," the clerk interrupted. "You've been placed on payment plans and given multiple extensions."

"I just need a little more time."

The clerk pinched the bridge of his nose, as if the situation were nothing more than an irritating discussion of prices at the marketplace. "Mr. Fairfield, you've had plenty of time. The Lord of Commerce has instructed me to collect the full payment by the end of the day, or else we will seize your home and land."

Peter's heart dropped to his feet so fast it made him nauseous. "You can't do that!"

The clerk slid his gaze past Peter's father to peer at him, as if he hadn't realized Peter was there at all. "We certainly can. And if you can't pay, we must. This city doesn't operate on charity, you must understand."

"We're not asking for charity," Peter said, "just that Lord Dunn be reasonable."

The guards stepped closer to the doorway, posing like sentinels over the clerk's shoulders.

"Peter!" His father's voice boomed.

Peter took an unsteady step back. It'd been ages since his father had used such a sharp tone with him.

His father turned back to the clerk. "Please, sir. The end of suether is in two weeks, but we'll start harvesting today. The crops are close enough. We'll work straight through until it's finished, and have the crop sold by next Marketday. That should be enough to cover our debt."

"A third extension?" the clerk asked.

"Please." His father's voice was small, a stark contrast to the way he'd silenced Peter. "This will be the final extension we need. I swear it."

The clerk sighed. "Fine. One week."

His father's shoulders slumped with relief. "Thank you, Clerk, and please send my thanks to Lord Dunn."

"Save your groveling," the man said. "There will be no more extensions. And if you fail to pay your debts, no more mercy."

Peter swallowed hard.

The clerk turned on his heel and hurried away while the soldiers lingered. The taller of the two men grinned at them both, then struck Father with a solid punch in his gut.

"Father!"

Matthias doubled over with a groan, clenching his gut as he staggered backward.

Peter caught him with an arm around his waist, keeping him from collapsing. He glared at the soldiers, rage burning through him like wildfire.

"We'll see you in six days," the soldier said before turning and strolling away.

"Father, are you okay?" Peter helped him into a seat at the kitchen table.

"I'm fine." His face was pale, and his brow furrowed. He leaned against the table. "It's no worse than getting kicked by a mule."

"Getting kicked by a mule is awful," Peter noted.

His father laughed, but there was no humor in it. "Go to work, Peter. I'll start the harvest."

"At least let me go talk to Gavin about the ox."

"Please just listen to me." Exhaustion tinged his father's voice. "I'll have plenty of time to get it done. Go to work."

*Six days.* How were they supposed to pay enough of their debt to keep their home in just six days? Would the money from the harvest even be enough?

*I'm going to figure something out myself.* Peter nodded to his father, acquiescing even as the anger toward the soldiers and the clerk still boiled in his chest. *I'm not letting us lose the farm.*

———————

## 3

Peter cursed to himself as he hurried through the cobbled streets. The morning sun was high in the sky. He'd taken too long with his sword forms, and then lost track of time while the clerk was there.

Palenting hummed with morning activity. The town square filled with merchants already barking their wares: fishmongers, bakers, and seamstresses all layered their voices as they called out over the crowds. Peter peeled his egg and stuffed it into his mouth as he half ran, knocking against shoulders as he passed. His father was right—the egg was small. He was thankful for the protein, but it was gone after only a few bites. *If we'd planned better last night, maybe I'd be stopping to purchase a meat pie or a freshly baked bun, maybe a skewer.* His mouth watered at the scents as he hurried by.

He headed north, toward the Brufec Heights, where the mason's shop sat at the edge of the neighborhood. Jenkins wasn't one of the fine, well-paid artisans who built the homes and finery of the wealthy citizens of Palenting, but he did run a mid-sized crew of masons who built and repaired many of the taverns and shops in the city. If Peter did well in his apprenticeship, he would eventually be able to run his own business and have steady work bricklaying. It should be a relieving thought, but it hung over him like a storm cloud.

Peter burst through the door, huffing and puffing to catch his breath.

"There you are!" Jenkins shouted. He was a rotund, red-faced man, thick-armed with a bellowing voice. "You're late! Again!"

In the back, Rylan glanced up from where he kneeled by the workbench, fixing one of the brick molds. He cringed and threw up three fingers. Three out of ten for Jenkins' mood ranking. Not a great day to show up late.

"Sorry, sir," Peter said, "this morning, there was a bit of a complication—"

"No excuses!" Jenkins ripped off his apron and tossed it onto the workbench. "It's Marketday, and we're busy. I've got a big repair beginning next week, and we already have to be closed tomorrow and Prefinday. If you two want to get paid, you'll do what you're contracted to. Now take those molds outside and get to work."

"Yes, sir." Peter fought the urge to talk back. It would only cause more trouble. The only thing worse than working for Jenkins would be telling his father the mason had canned him for being mouthy.

Peter put on his heavy canvas apron, then followed Rylan out the back door of the shop. A low wooden fence blocked off the sizable outdoor workspace, surrounded by other shops and merchant buildings.

"I've already got the clay ready," Rylan said.

"Thanks. Sorry, I'm late." They set up the molds under the morning sun. The work didn't feel like an apprenticeship at all. Peter learned little about masonry by endlessly making bricks. Jenkins hadn't even let them onto a job site yet. Learning the construction portion of the job would at least hold a bit more interest.

"Rough morning?" Rylan asked.

Peter dropped clay into the first mold with his hands, then smoothed it down with a trowel. He bit back words about the clerk's visit. "Our neighbor came by, and I lost track of time."

"It happens." Rylan did the same with his own mold. For a while, nothing but the wet sound of clay dropping into the molds filled the air. Rylan sighed. "Your mother okay?"

"She's fine."

Rylan watched him for a moment, brow furrowed. Peter focused on the bricks. He didn't want to unload his issues on Rylan. His friend had enough of his own.

"Remember when my father disappeared at sea?" Rylan asked.

Peter glanced up. "Of course. You were, what . . . six?"

Rylan nodded. "I always missed him when he would travel to Kandis to work, but the money was good, and he came back every season . . . until the time he didn't. After his death, Mother tried to hold it together. That's when she started as a seamstress. I used to help her when I was little."

"Me, too, remember?"

"That's right." Rylan laughed.

"I used to hide in the—what did we call that thing?"

"The thing with all the colors." Rylan snapped his fingers together several times. "'The Fabric Castle!'"

"That was it!"

They both laughed.

"Anyway," Rylan continued, "she always said she was fine, but she wasn't. She missed Father, and I did, too. One night, years later, she finally broke down. She began to cry while she was stirring a pot of soup. I just sat there, not knowing what to do. Finally, I rested my hand on her shoulder, and the sobbing began. She leaned into me, soaking my shirt with her tears, and

I just hugged her. It took about an hour for her to settle, and when she did, we talked."

"About what?"

Rylan smiled. "About everything: sewing, girls, my future, food. She finally opened up about Father. She talked about how they first met and fell in love. She told me the ways I reminded her of him."

Peter smiled, his hand resting on the wet clay molds.

"It was one of best moments of my life—there with my mother, soaked in her tears."

"So . . . what does that have to do with bricks?"

"I know your mother's not doing well, and I want *you* to know . . . it's all right to talk about it."

Peter breathed out, his shoulders settling, and his body relaxing. "Thank you. I know. I know I can talk to you. You've always been there for me, and seriously . . . that means a lot."

"Best friends."

"Best friends." Peter smiled. "It's a good thing both of our parents pushed us into this apprenticeship."

Rylan raised his eyebrows. "Are you serious?"

"If we're going to be miserable, we might as well be miserable together."

Rylan laughed. "For now," he added. He leaned in and spoke in a low voice. "Only one more year."

Peter nodded. "You still running each day?"

Rylan's lips pursed. "Eh . . . not as much as I should."

"Come on, Ry. We need to impress them when we sign up."

"The army will literally take anyone though. It doesn't matter if I'm fast before we begin."

"But we don't want to be just any regular recruits. We need to stand out, so we can get the best assignments and most prestigious posts. That's why we train with the swords, now. That's why we condition our bodies."

Rylan bobbed his head and sighed. "I know. You're right. I'll get back at it."

Both boys shifted their attention back to the clay and returned to their monotonous tasks.

While he would eventually make a fine soldier, Rylan's broad shoulders and bulky frame proved useful for masonry work as well. He lugged the bricks and supplies around with ease. Peter kept up well enough, but his tall frame and lean form struggled when things got heavy. They both spent countless hours laboring under the sun, but Rylan's tanned beige skin was a shade darker than Peter's.

It was dull, repetitive, rhythmic work, and Jenkins was inside doing the more complicated tasks Peter thought he was supposed to be learning. It was easy to sink into his own thoughts as he formed the bricks. While calculating how much coin and food stores they would need to make it through the upcoming winter, a sneering voice jolted him out of his thoughts.

"Look who it is," the voice called. "Fairfield and Burton are playing in the sandbox again."

Peter closed his eyes, then took a deep breath. The day was already going poorly—so of course Ashton Dunn had to show his face.

Ashton hooked his arms over the fence and leaned down, grinning. His blond hair fell rakishly into his blue eyes, while two of his familiar friends stood behind him.

"We're working," Peter said. "Don't you have wine tastings to lurk at?"

"Oooh," Ashton said. "Peter has jokes today. No cold shoulder?"

"Beat it, Ashton," Rylan snapped.

"Better leash your attack dog before he hurts somebody, Peter." Ashton threw a grin at his two friends, who broke into dutiful laughter. Tanner and Hodge stuck to Ashton like barnacles, though Peter couldn't imagine why.

"You never can trust those types that grow up without a father," Ashton sneered.

"Go suck an egg." Rylan surged to his feet, and his hands tightened into fists at his sides. "Get out of here before I make you get out of here."

"Whoa," Ashton teased, hands up in faux surrender. "Dog's in a bad mood today, huh?"

"Don't," Peter muttered to his friend. The exhaustion he felt bled into his voice. He reached up and grabbed the back of Rylan's apron, tugging him back before Rylan did something stupid like vault the fence to land a few punches—something he'd been known to do.

"You should listen to your friend there," Ashton sneered at Rylan. "Sounds like Peter learned his place. Just like your father did before you."

Rylan surged forward, but Peter's tight grip kept him from reaching the fence. Ashton laughed, a high-pitched, mean sound, which set off his friends into peals of laughter. Ashton had been like that for as long as Peter had had the misfortune of knowing him.

"Cool it," Peter said to Rylan, straining to hold him back. "It's not worth it."

"Yes, it is."

"Go back to your mud there, Dog. Maybe it will help mask the stench of fish you've had since you were little." Ashton threw them a rude gesture, then wandered off, already recounting the jokes to his tittering friends.

Rylan returned to the brick making with a pinched expression on his face. "I can't stand that jerk! He thinks he's better than everyone else. Why do all those Paratill View snobs have to be like that?"

"At least Kira's different."

"That's true." Rylan's head bobbed. "I can't believe they grew up together. If she hadn't met us, do you think she would have grown up to be like him?"

"I think you're giving us way more credit than we deserve."

Peter was used to encountering Ashton and his stupid taunts. It was a regular part of his landscape, the same as shouldering through the town square or practicing his sword forms in the barn. It irritated him the way a mosquito did.

"Ashton needs to grow up," Rylan said.

Peter laughed. "You're one to talk, springing on them at the slightest insult."

"Hey!" Rylan threw a chunk a clay and hit him in the chest.

The rest of their shift passed in silence as they laid out clay brick after clay brick to cure in the sun. At midday, when the sun was high in the sky and blazing hot on the back of Peter's neck, they stepped inside for the sad excuse for a midday meal the mason provided. It was a thin, under-spiced soup, but it was better than nothing. His stomach already grumbled.

"All right, Peter," Jenkins said as he ladled their soup into the rough-hewn wooden bowls. "Eat quickly. I need you to make some deliveries for me."

"Sure," Peter said, frustration burning in his chest. *No break today—just a quick swallow of soup then some errand-boy work. At this rate, I'll never learn anything.* While he never intended to stay with Jenkins long term, he wished he could at least learn something useful during the time.

Jenkins slapped a tube onto the table hard enough to rattle their bowls. Rylan snatched his up to keep some of the precious meal from slopping over the edge. It was a small leather tube, tied closed, and when Peter moved to open it, Jenkins smacked his hand away. "This is important information," Jenkins said. "It needs to get to Commander Isert at the northern barracks this afternoon. You know of where I speak?"

"Yes," Peter said, perking up at the commander's name. His

runs took him all over Palenting, and he knew its ins and outs as closely as he knew the routines of his parents' farm. The barracks were on the far northeast side, at the edge of the city.

"These are plans for a new outpost to be built across the western mountains," Jenkins said, his chest puffing up. "Commander Isert commissioned them from an architect, and he asked me to estimate materials."

"Will we get to work on the job site?" Rylan asked.

"Mind your business, Boy," Jenkins snapped.

Rylan sighed and went back to his soup. Jenkins getting a new contract didn't mean Peter and Rylan would learn how to build. In reality, it was likely they'd be stuck making even more bricks.

Jenkins reached into his rucksack and fished out a handful of silver argen. He counted them, stuffed a few into a smaller pouch, then made some scratches on a sheet of paper. "Before you go to the barracks, take this to the bank at the town center and deliver it to Mr. Butcher, the head banker."

"Yes, sir."

Peter slurped down the rest of his soup, then stood. He put the pouch of coins in his pocket and took the tube in hand.

"Be careful with it," Jenkins insisted.

Peter nodded and left the shop with an unpleasant taste in his mouth from the soup.

# 4

The city's morning chaos had relaxed in mid-afternoon, as most people were working, and Peter took his time strolling. It was rare to be asked to do a delivery, and it was more pleasant than making bricks.

The clerk's words from the morning played over in his head as he walked through the city. Thinking about his family's situation left a sinking feeling in his gut, but the thought of visiting the bank gave him a trickle of hope.

*Maybe there's something this banker can do. Possibly we could get some of the debt erased, or get a new loan, or something.* All Peter had to do was charm him, tell him his parents' story, and surely the man would help out.

The bank overlooked the fountain in the town square. Made of the same white stone as the buildings of Paratill View, two statues of elegant falcons flanked its heavy wooden doors. For as long as he'd lived in Palenting, Peter had never been inside the bank. His family never had enough money to warrant an account there. He eased his way through the busy afternoon market, then up the stairs to the intimidating building.

He pushed the heavy door open. It closed behind him with a solid thunk, sealing out the familiar noise of the market and replacing it with a thick silence broken only by the scratch of pens from the desks at the far end of the room. The space was well-lit with polished floors. A vast, winding staircase led to an upper balcony lined with more heavy wooden doors. In his threadbare work clothes and heavy boots, Peter felt out of place. The bankers were all dressed in fine linen, with haughty, disinterested expressions, when they bothered to look at him at all.

Peter swallowed around the nervous knot in his throat, then stood up straighter and marched with purpose to the closest desk. "Hello."

The banker finished scratching on the parchment in front of her. "Do you have an appointment?"

"Um," Peter said, "I'm from Jenkins Masonry. I'm meeting Mr. Butcher."

"If he's expecting you," she said slowly, like Peter was stupid, "you can go directly to his office."

"Okay." Peter blinked.

"Upstairs," she said, long-sufferingly. "Where all the offices are."

"Right. Thank you." Peter climbed the elegant staircase to the second level, where the names of the bankers who worked in the offices embossed the doors. Peter found the one with Butcher's name, and then stood in front of it, gathering his courage.

His thoughts turned to the farm. If he wanted to save his family's property, he had to make Mr. Butcher like him. He had to be charming, capable, smart—all the things Jenkins seemed to think he wasn't. But he could do it. He could figure it out. *What kind of banker is named Mr. Butcher?* He imagined someone tall, severe, broad-shouldered and intimidating. He braced himself to have courage. He could do this. He had to do this.

Just as he raised his fist to rap on the door, it swung open.

"Oh!" the man across the threshold said. "Excuse me. I didn't think I had any morning meetings on my calendar."

"Mr. Butcher?" Peter asked.

The man in the office was short and stocky, with his jacket buttoned closed but straining to burst over the width of his belly. He fished out a pocket watch and grimaced at it. "Yes, that's me. What is it? Speak quickly. I'm in a hurry."

"I'm from Jenkins Masonry," Peter said. "Mr. Jenkins told me I should—"

"Ah, yes, the deposit," Mr. Butcher cut in. "Yes, yes, I can take that. You have the documentation?" He waved Peter into the round office. Bookshelves lined the room with a desk in the center.

Peter handed over the paper and the coin purse.

Mr. Butcher glanced inside the pouch, muttering to himself, then slid it into a drawer on the desk. Peter lifted onto his toes and craned his neck. Pouches similar to the one Jenkins had given him filled the drawer, some stuffed more than others. Mr. Butcher nudged it closed, then scrawled a signature onto the paper and handed it back to Peter. "Here you are, Boy. Take this back to your master." The banker corralled him toward the door.

"Wait," Peter said.

The banker moved with such urgency he nearly pushed Peter down the stairs.

"I was hoping, sir, for just a moment of your time, to discuss—"

"I don't have a moment to spare," Mr. Butcher said, descending the steps. "Especially not for craftsmen like Jenkins. It's only out of the goodness of my heart I deign to work with him at all." He rolled his eyes. "My time is better spent with clients whose endeavors actually turn a profit. Tell Jenkins he can come see me himself instead of hiding behind one of his scrawny little errand boys."

Mr. Butcher scurried out the front door. Peter stood in the center of the bank empty-handed.

*So much for that idea.*

At least he'd completed the delivery. Small favors. The clerk he'd spoken to upon entering raised her eyebrows at him. Defeated, he walked toward the front door and tugged it open. His heart dropped.

Ashton Dunn leaned against the falcon statue, legs crossed at the ankles. He fiddled with a rock, tossing it from hand to hand, like he waited for something. As soon as the door opened, he looked up with a smirk. "Hey, Peter," he said. "Fancy seeing you here. Stuck being the errand boy? Not like you'd have any business at this bank, what with the state of your family's coffers."

Peter let the door swing shut.

He took a step back into the bank. Sweat beaded at his temples. Running into Ashton out in the city often led to an unpleasant encounter—something he preferred to avoid.

He glanced around the bank. The woman at the desk sighed and pointed to a side door. Peter grinned sheepishly. *Looks like I'm not the only one who's had company waiting at the front doors.*

He rushed toward the side door, except when he opened it, Tanner was waiting. The larger boy grinned, then gestured with his arm, as if inviting Peter to step into his own butt kicking. *Yeah, no thanks.* Peter shut that door as well. Out of sight of the bank clerks, he rushed up the grand staircase, back to the offices at the top level. He hurried back to Mr. Butcher's office, and hoped that in his rush, the banker had been careless. *Yes!* He pushed the unlocked door open, then locked it behind him.

Only in the relative safety of the office did he exhale. At least there, Ashton and his lackeys couldn't get to him. Getting caught sneaking into a banker's office wouldn't be a great outcome, but he could explain. *Maybe if he comes back, Mr. Butcher will actually listen to me.*

He crept closer to the desk. Various papers covered it, and a thick stack of loan applications marked up with red ink sat in the center of the mess.

A farmer asking for a line of credit to buy seeds for the next harvest: Denied.

A young potter looking to start a ceramics business: Denied.

A mother with four children whose husband died in a fire: Denied.

*Someone in here has to be approved,* Peter thought. *At least one person.* The more he shuffled the papers, the more rejections he found, all from individuals and families from Lowside and Schuggec Row. *No wonder people are turning to the Vipers for money.*

He opened the desk drawer, and leather coin pouches stared back at him. His heart leaped.

A brisk knock sounded on the door. "Hello?" Ashton called. "Anyone home?"

Peter went still. *There's no way he knows I'm in here. He's just trying doors.* He didn't even breathe.

"Hello?" Ashton sing-songed. "Come out, come out!"

"What are you doing up here?" a woman's muffled voice asked sharply. "Do you have an appointment?"

"Um," Ashton said. "Appointment?"

"If you don't have an appointment, I have to ask you to leave."

"I'm Ashton Dunn, the son of the Lord of Commerce," he said. "I basically own this bank."

"Sure you do, honey," the woman said. "Why don't you go outside and have lunch by the fountain? It's a beautiful day."

"Wha—what!" Ashton stammered. "But—but there's someone here I'm trying to—"

"You just wait outside," the woman said. "Do you need me to get in touch with your father?"

"No!"

Their voices faded as they descended the stairs. If the staff of the bank had kicked out Ashton, there was no way Mr. Butcher would be amenable to finding Peter rooting around in his office uninvited. The pouches of money drew his attention again.

*I need this money. Father needs this money.* If it was just sitting here in a drawer, how much would they miss it? With a hint of remorse, he grabbed two bags and stuffed one in each pocket.

Out of the window behind the desk, he saw Ashton and Tanner trudge across the town square and duck into a nearby tavern. Only then did Peter creep out of the office and back down the stairs. With his head held high, he strolled outside as if he'd been there the whole time for an appointment, and didn't garner a second glance from the clerks.

Turning north from the square, he walked through the narrow, cobbled streets, calves burning as the roads inclined. The wealthy side of the city sat on a hill, with tall, polished buildings of fine white stone, slanted roofs, and decorative iron details over the doors and windows. To the west, the Dorthar Mountains rose like jagged teeth jutting from the horizon, dwarfing the dilapidated structure of an old abandoned watchtower.

Peter fiddled with the fastening on the leather tube. Whatever the outpost designs were like, there was no way they were as interesting as the old watchtower. Peter imagined himself as a soldier from years before, dressed in fine chain mail and leather armor, on lookout from the top of the watchtower. He pictured a sword on his hip and a bow in his hand as he kept a keen eye toward the mountains for the sign of an approaching enemy.

He sighed. Instead of a respected soldier dressed in finery, he was stuck running errands for Jenkins with his stomach rumbling and hands sore from making bricks.

A narrow, fast-moving canal separated the barracks from the rest of the north side. Peter lingered on the bridge, not wanting to finish the delivery and make his way back to the shop. Maybe he could convince Commander Isert to review the document with Peter. Perhaps he could pull off seeming like an actual skilled apprentice instead of just an errand boy. *I could tell him I helped with the estimates. He'll know I work closely with Mr. Jenkins. Maybe the commander will be impressed.* He pictured Isert clapping him on the back and saying, "What's a man like you doing working for a mason?" And then he'd tell Peter he had a special place for him in the army, and he'd offer him a job as an officer, and then—

"First the bank, then our side of town?"

Peter straightened up, cringing. "You followed me?"

With clean shoes clumping on the wooden bridge, Ashton stepped forward. "Lowsiders like you shouldn't be up here. Just because you're *friends* with someone who belongs here, doesn't make you worthy."

"Interesting isn't it? Kira's a friend of mine because she can't stand being around people like you."

Ashton's eyes narrowed.

"Anyway . . . I'm working." Peter took a step backward until a sharp bark of laughter alerted him to Hodge blocking the other direction.

"Looks like you're doing nothing," Ashton said. "Did you skip work to come up here and gaze into the wishing well?"

"I have a delivery—"

"Another delivery!" Ashton hooted. "Moving on up in the world!"

"Leave me alone." Peter was penned in on the bridge, with no way to escape.

Ashton's eyes gleamed with amusement. "I would, if you

weren't the one in *my* neighborhood. I can't let this kind of disrespect go unnoticed."

Peter rolled his eyes. "Disrespect. You're so full of yourself. Just because your father's the Lord of Commerce, that doesn't mean you own the entire city."

"Mm, that's where you're wrong. My family does own this city. And if you want to run your little errands, you need to show me some respect."

"Whatever." Peter turned away. He tried to shove past Hodge, but the larger young man just laughed and knocked Peter back with a hard shove in the center of his chest. Peter stumbled. Before he recovered, Ashton pushed him forward, so hard he nearly fell.

The frustration that glowed like an ember all day in Peter's chest burst into a roaring flame of rage. He was sick of rolling over whenever Ashton pushed him around, sick of ignoring him, sick of hoping Ashton would give it up. *He'll never give it up. As long as I'm an easy mark, Ashton will target me.* Peter shoved the tube in the waistband of his pants. His anger overpowered his good sense, and he whirled on Ashton.

Peter rushed forward, fists raised, and swung at Ashton's snide face. He was quick, but so was the blond, rich jerk, who reeled back so the punch glanced off his jaw instead of cracking across his nose. Ashton barked in surprise, then threw a wide punch of his own. Peter ducked under it and landed a solid blow in Ashton's gut. The grunt of pain Ashton expelled through his clenched teeth made Peter grin. It felt good to hit back for once.

"You little jerk," Ashton growled. He tried to grab him in a headlock, but Peter was too fast.

He wriggled out, stepped backward, and raised his fists again. "Try me," he taunted.

Ashton rolled his eyes. "You really want to do this?"

"Yeah." Peter shifted his weight, bouncing on the balls of his feet. "Come on. I can take you."

"No, you can't." Ashton stepped forward, sliding his thumb across his jaw.

Peter swung again.

He'd been stupid enough to think the spoiled son of a lord would fight him one-on-one. Ashton stepped backward with a grin as Tanner and Hodge jumped on Peter. Peter yelped as they shoved him forward again. Hodge landed a hard punch that Peter blocked with his shoulder. Surrounded, he curled in on himself as the blows rained down—punches on his shoulders, back, and arms where he protected his head. Someone kicked his legs, dropping him to the splintered wood of the bridge. Ashton's laugh rang out. A few lazy kicks landed on his back, more taunting than painful.

"That's enough," Ashton said. "You learn your lesson, Peter?"

Holding back a groan, Peter rose unsteadily to his feet. His head throbbed, and his body ached as if it were one enormous bruise, but nothing felt broken.

"Well?" Ashton twirled the leather tube in hand.

Peter cursed, hands flying to his waistband where the leather tube had been tucked not-so-safely. "Give that back."

"Why?" His long, knobby fingers toyed with the fastening on the tube. "Is this something important?"

"It's just a delivery. Give it back."

"A delivery, huh? Well, it's not wise for a delivery boy to cause trouble, is it?"

"Give it here, Ashton."

"I don't think so." Ashton smirked, pleased at his victory. "There are consequences for being careless with your work. Right?"

His friends murmured and nodded.

Peter's stomach lurched as Ashton tossed the tube over the

railing of the bridge. Peter rushed to the edge, as if he could catch it, but all he could do was watch, fingers clenched on the railing, as the tube splashed into the canal and disappeared.

"Good luck explaining that to your boss." Ashton laughed, then waved his friends over. They hurried off the bridge and back to Paratill View to do whatever the rich did for fun. Pluck the wings off butterflies, kick dogs, or knock over old ladies, Peter assumed.

He lingered on the bridge with arms folded on the railing. The water rushed by. Even if he slid down the steep sides of the canal, he didn't know how deep it was, and the plans would be waterlogged and ruined.

*So much for my new life under Commander Isert.*

He'd thought one day the hopelessness would stop feeling so heavy, but as he stared into the canal, it crashed over him anew. He lingered there, feeling sore, tired, hungry, and sorry for himself.

## 5

"He really threw the plans into the canal?" Rylan asked. "Just like that?"

"Yeah." Peter shoved his hands into his pockets, fingering the pouches hidden there. He had yet to tell Rylan about them or even take a peek.

Their workday was over, and the sun dipped near the horizon. The pubs filled with raucous patrons as Peter and Rylan plodded toward the southern neighborhood. "It was low, even for him."

"Seems like he's getting worse."

Peter shrugged. There was nothing he could do about it. All he could hope was that Jenkins' anger wouldn't linger throughout the week, leading to even more menial and backbreaking work.

As they walked, the loud pubs and fine structures closer to the town square gave way to the more familiar, creaky, old buildings they'd grown up in. Instead of heading back to the farms, though, they went west, to the even rougher edge of the neighborhood.

"Hopefully, Seph's already here, so she can do something about your eye," Rylan said.

"What's wrong with my eye?" Peter touched his brow and cringed at the throb of pain.

"It'll be swollen shut tomorrow." Rylan grinned. "Don't worry. It looks cool."

Peter prodded more at his brow, suddenly hyper-aware of the ache in his skull. Rylan winced and led the way through the familiar streets until the crumbling, small apartment buildings opened up to the overgrown courtyard outside the old Berregard Garrison.

The Garrison was the old army training center, and no one except Peter and his friends ever even considered crossing its brambled courtyard to its blackened doors. The people of Palenting were a suspicious type, and there were rumbles that the Garrison and the surrounding neighborhood were cursed. It wasn't a curse, though, it was just poor planning, which Peter understood the first time his curiosity led him to hop the walls as a kid.

According to the story, it was twenty years ago when the earth rumbled beneath the facility and rocked its stone foundations. It was already an old building, not as sturdy as the soldiers had thought. The tremors cracked the walls and caused the stone ceiling to rain down. Amid the chaos, the fire from the hearth spilled out and leaped toward the archery hay bales. Feeding on wood and straw, the roaring flames spread through the Garrison. Between the narrow entrances and the boulders crashing down, the soldiers couldn't escape. Many died—too many.

The Garrison was Peter's favorite place in the city. It was private, it was functional, and it was theirs. Theirs alone. Where others in Palenting saw the shadow of death on its smoke-stained, stone walls, Peter saw the memory of the brave soldiers who trained there. He saw the life he wanted to have—a warrior, respected and appreciated.

Inside, the only lingering sign of fire damage was the stained walls. Sturdy rafters still crisscrossed from wall to wall, but in the intervening years, half of the ceiling had collapsed. The remaining section kept the portion of the room beneath it mostly dry, but did little to aid warmth.

The straw that had once coated the floor had been swept out, and hard-packed dirt remained, dotted with hardy weeds that climbed the stone walls. Since he and his friends started meeting there, the four of them worked to make the Garrison a place to train, but also a place that was just their own. Rylan had hauled a table and a few mismatched chairs from abandoned homes and set them up by the fireplace. They'd collected training swords and a few steel blades—courtesy of Kira—and ropes hung from the strongest rafters for climbing practice. As soon as his feet hit the dirt, Peter felt better.

"There you are," Kira said without looking up. She notched another arrow on her bowstring. The *thwang* of the string releasing was as familiar as her voice. The arrow landed in the center of the target hung on the wall. "Old master Jenkins hold you up at the shop again?"

"Yup," Rylan said. "Thanks to Ashton."

"Ashton?" Sephiri asked, her attention focused on sharpening a set of throwing knives. "Was he causing problems again?"

"Ugh! I can't stand him," Kira added.

"Yeah, he and his jerk friends interrupted a delivery I was on," Peter said. "First, they waited outside the bank, then they followed me through the city. He tossed the plans I was supposed to deliver into the canal, and Jenkins got mad. He's docking my pay for a week."

"And we're going to be making so many bricks as punishment," Rylan groaned.

"What did he—Peter, your face!" Sephiri set the knives down and hurried over.

"It's fine," he said, waving her off. "I'm fine."

She took his face in her small hands and turned it to the side as she inspected him. Sephiri was the smallest of the four of them, with a slim build from years of undereating. Her skin contained a warm, dark complexion, and her long, brown hair was tied back in its usual fashion. Her lips curved into a familiar, concerned frown as she peered at Peter's face.

"It's nothing," he said.

"What happened?" Sephiri asked. "Are you hurt elsewhere?"

"Nothing's broken, if that's what you're asking. Just bruised up. I made the mistake of getting into Ashton's face when he had his friends with him."

"So they ganged up on you." Kira set the bow down. "How classy of them."

"Come sit," Sephiri said. "I've got something that will take the swelling down. You need to *see* to be able to be a mason."

Peter nodded. He didn't like to be doted on, but having a swollen eye would only cause more problems at work. He followed Sephiri to the table and pulled up a chair to sit across from her.

Rylan knelt on the battered fur rug in front of the cracked hearth and started a small, flickering fire. It wasn't cold in the Garrison, but the flames gave a welcoming light and a soothing warmth.

"We're hardly masons at all," Peter said. "We just put clay into molds."

"Be glad you don't have to attend polishing classes." Kira sat at the other end of the table and kicked her feet up onto its edge. Her pin-straight blonde hair was tied into a casual bun atop her head instead of the usual long braids or loose locks the wealthy girls wore. Her pale skin almost shone in the dim light. With her feet kicked up, the skirt of her fine blue gown rode up to reveal trousers beneath it. Sometimes, depending on how hard they were training, she'd even tie the skirt up at her waist. "I had to learn how to set a table for a four-course meal in the style the High Lords expect."

"We don't even have any High Lords in Palenting," Rylan said.

"That's what I told my tutor!" Kira threw her hands up. "You can imagine how that went over."

"What do High Lords even eat? Valcor meat?"

"Exactly," Kira joked back. "Raised for them in their magical creature farms."

"I should get a job on one of those. I bet it pays better than being a fake mason."

Sephiri reached into her bag and pulled out a small glass jar, then unscrewed the lid. An unfamiliar, sharp smell emanated from the jar.

"What is that?" Peter asked.

"Barkleaf balm."

"Where'd you get it?" Barkleaf fungus had remarkable healing properties, but it wasn't easy or cheap to come by. If Sephiri was nicking balms from healers, Peter was going to be both shocked and impressed.

"I made it."

"You made it?" Peter asked, stunned. *I shouldn't be surprised, though.* Sephiri wasn't strong like Rylan, a genius like Kira, or agile like Peter, but she had a variety of unique skills, and she cared.

"Yeah." She dipped her forefinger into the balm and then smoothed it over Peter's brow. "It's easy if you know where to find the fungus."

Peter didn't know where to find it. He didn't know anyone with that kind of knowledge, but he also knew better than to push and ask Sephiri too much. The more he pried, the less she offered. The three of them were the only family Sephiri had, but she rarely opened up to them. All Peter knew was that her parents died when she was young. He didn't know how, nor had he found the right time or way to ask. "Thanks."

"No need to thank me," she said. "Hope you got that jerk Ashton back."

"I tried," Peter said. "Not my best work."

"Next time, then." She dotted more of the balm over the bruise around his eye. It tingled cold on his skin and numbed the pain. "That should keep the swelling from getting too bad. It'll still look pretty rough for a few days, though."

"As long as I can see, I'm happy."

"Do you have any other injuries?" she asked.

"Just sore. Nothing bad."

Sephiri cast a dark look that suggested she didn't believe him, but then screwed the lid back on the jar and slipped it into her bag. "I have some of the fungus left. I can make some tea for us to keep here in case Ashton tries to pull something like this again."

"Thanks, Seph," Peter said.

She tugged at the thin leather necklace she always wore under her shirt—a familiar nervous tic. "Though it'd be best if you stopped getting into scuffles with him at all."

"I didn't plan it," Peter grumbled. "He started it. He may have gotten the jump on me, but . . ." A smile crept over his face as he pulled the two pouches from his pockets. "At least I didn't leave the bank empty-handed."

"Oh?" Rylan perked up. "What'd you get?"

"You robbed the bank?" Kira asked.

"I didn't rob the bank," Peter said. "I borrowed some things from the banker's desk, from an unlocked drawer in his unlocked office . . ."

"You totally robbed the bank!" Rylan said. "That's crazy!"

"All right, maybe a little," Peter said with a grin. "But they have plenty of money, and *we* could actually use it."

"You're right about that," Sephiri said.

Peter untied the first pouch and dumped it onto the table.

"Whoa!" Rylan's eyes widened. Pintid, tid, and even a few argen scattered onto the rug, catching the flickering light of the fire—every type of coin except gold sol.

*With this, maybe we can keep the farm.* Relief crashed over Peter like a wave. It wouldn't wipe out his family's debt, but it should help appease the clerk.

"What about that one?" Sephiri asked, pointing to the other pouch. "More coins?"

"Sol?" Rylan asked. "Please tell me we got some sol."

Peter turned over the pouch, and a pale-gray stone pyramid fell to the wooden surface.

Sephiri picked it up. Her brow furrowed as she examined the sides. The base of the object was the size of her palm. "There's nothing on it. It's smooth."

"Weird. Can I see?" Peter asked.

Sephiri tossed the pyramid to him. The stone was cool and heavy in his hands. He turned it toward the light of the fire, examining the sides the same way Sephiri had. As he did, he smoothed his thumb over the base and felt a small engraving.

"There's something written here." He leaned closer to read the carved writing. "'To gain the stone, you prove your worth. In ancient home it waits to test. Hidden in rock, in bone, in earth, death and dust await the rest.'"

"That's odd," Kira said. "What would an engraved stone be for?"

Rylan leaned closer. "Can we sell it? Do you think it's worth something?"

"I have no idea." Peter ran his thumb over the poem carved on the bottom of the pyramid. The rhyme circled in his mind as he set it down. *To gain the stone, you prove your worth. What stone? What worth? How old is this pyramid? Where did it come from? Why was it in Mr. Butcher's desk?*

Peter doled out the coins, evenly splitting the haul between Rylan, Sephiri, and him. Then, he tucked the mysterious pyramid back into its bag.

"Here." Rylan offered a few of his pintid to Peter. "Take this. Mother got some extra work this week, so we'll be okay."

"No, this is enough."

"Come on." Rylan dropped the coins into Peter's pile. "You already got your wage cut this week. Just take it."

With a sigh, Peter nodded. *I need all the help I can get.* "Thanks."

Rylan pushed himself away from the table. "You have the energy for a round or two?"

"Don't push him, Rylan. He got beat up today," Kira said.

"Sure I do." Peter tore his gaze away from the pouch with the mysterious pyramid, and stood. He was still sore, but he wasn't one to turn down a sparring match. "You might actually have a shot at beating me."

Rylan laughed sarcastically.

They picked their preferred training swords from the stash at the edge of the room and then stood across from each other with the wooden blades lifted. Rylan grinned and charged. Peter sidestepped, then moved to thwack Rylan across the back with the blade, but to his surprise, Rylan pivoted hard on the ball of his foot and blocked the intended hit.

"You've been practicing," Peter said.

"Maybe a little." Rylan grinned and swung his sword in a wide arc, which again, Peter hopped back and dodged.

"Nice, Rylan!" Kira hooted from her seat, which made Sephiri laugh brightly.

They sparred briskly, swords knocking together. What Rylan had in explosive strength he didn't have in stamina, and usually, Peter could win their sparring matches by dancing around until the larger boy wore himself out. The weight of the day wore on him, though, and Rylan managed a light smack on Peter's waist as he attempted to dodge.

"All right, all right," Peter said. "I'll call that a killing blow."

"Yes!" Rylan dropped his sword and threw his fists into the air. "Finally! I get a win!"

"I don't know," Sephiri said, "wouldn't you say Peter getting beat up is an extenuating circumstance?"

"Absolutely not!" Rylan crowed.

Peter shook his head, chuckling, and led Rylan back to the table. Kira had already unpacked a basket of food—crusty bread, venison jerky, and roasted verquash. Peter's mouth watered at the sight.

"Let's eat," Kira said. "I made the jerky, so you need to tell me how it is."

Kira visited the kitchen at her parents' estate mostly to pilfer meals for them, and Peter wasn't too proud to turn it down, especially when their nighttime thieving activities proved unfruitful. The jerky was delicious, and the four of them ate in companionable silence.

"What's going on with this verquash?" Rylan asked, poking at it. "Why's it roasted so fancy?"

Kira laughed and tossed a sprig of herbs into the fire. "The cooks are experimenting with some new dishes, and they deemed this one a failure."

"Doesn't taste like a failure to me," Sephiri said.

"That's why I offered to take it," Kira said. "My parents are hosting some big party tomorrow night, so everything has to be perfect." She took a bite of bread. "You know what? You guys should come!"

"To the party?" Peter asked with an eyebrow raised. "At your parents' house?"

"Sure, why not?"

"What's the party for?" Sephiri asked.

"I have no idea." Kira rolled her eyes. "Someone got promoted, or maybe someone is about to leave for a trip—something like that. You know what my parents are like. They can find any reason to have a party."

"Right," Rylan said with a frown, "and the three of us would fit right in."

"I don't have a dress," Sephiri said. "I don't even have a pair of trousers that haven't been mended at least four times."

"There's no way we'd be allowed in, Kira," Peter said. "But it's a nice thought."

Kira pressed her lips together. The awkwardness hung in the air between them. She straightened. "I can sneak you in."

"What?" Rylan asked. "Why?"

"For the food, obviously," Kira said with a wide, promising grin. "You think this is good? Wait until you see what they can cook up in the kitchen."

Peter perked up, interested. "You have a way to sneak in?"

"I don't know," Sephiri said, "What happens if we get caught?"

"Nothing," Kira said. "I'll get a slap on the wrist. It can't be any worse than that time my father caught me trying to break into the armory to take swords to bring here."

"Trying?" Peter said. "You actually did that."

"Sure, but it was the second time that I got caught," she said, chuckling. "I was overconfident."

Peter shook his head, laughing. The punishments Kira received were almost definitely worse than a slap on the wrist, and yet she kept taking risks for them.

"Why do you do all of this, Kira?" Peter asked. "The food, the swords, joining us on dangerous night missions? You laugh it off when we ask, but seriously. Why?"

Her grin dropped into a thin smile. "You know why."

The incident from eight years before flashed through his

mind. "Because of that night? We did what anyone would have done."

Kira shook her head. "You did what *no one* else did. It doesn't matter how much money any of those other idiots have, I'd rather spend my time with you."

"I'd like to try it," Sephiri said. "The party."

The three of them blinked at her, surprised.

"What?" Sephiri asked, shrugging. "I've never seen the inside of one of those fancy houses. I'm curious."

"Well, if she's in, I'm in," Rylan said. "I'll see how much food I can sneak out."

Kira raised her eyebrows at Peter.

"Well," Peter said, taking some jerky from the center of the table delicately as if it were the finest appetizer he'd ever had, "I have to admit, I'm swamped tomorrow night. I've got a bunch of other friends vying for my attention, and—"

The hoots and groans drowned out the rest of his sentence, which devolved into laughter as Rylan threw a hunk of bread at his head.

Sephiri waved goodbye as the boys and Kira left through the gap in the Garrison. She walked to the broken wall and pressed her hand against the aged stone, leaning her head through the space. Her friends' bodies grew smaller as they walked away. Peter's shaggy hair and loping gait brought a smile to her face.

"Peter," she breathed, her heart jumping. She sighed as he disappeared behind a curve in the buildings. A pang of longing filled her as the loneliness returned.

She slid her hand down the wall until the stone caught her eye. The soot stain remained. She touched it again. The grit of the rock scraped under her finger. She imagined the scene years before that caused the fire, then swallowed hard. A tear pooled in the corner of her eye, but she wiped it away.

Turning from the wall, Sephiri walked to the far end of the Garrison, where doors opened into several rooms. She entered the second one.

A small pallet of straw was pushed against the wall on the far side of the room. A threadbare blanket sat in a ball on top. She shook the blanket out and laid down. A thicker bundle of straw served as a pillow. The musty, pungent scent of mildew teased her nose. It hadn't rained in a week, but the dampness never seemed to go away. A partial roof blocked the sky from above her, while stars peered in from the opposite end.

Rolling to her side, a faded red scarf caught her eye where it was folded neatly on the floor. She reached out and grasped it. Tattered ends hung loose. Holes dotted the fabric where mice had tested it as a food source.

Sephiri held it to her chest, then closed her eyes and smiled. "I miss you, Mother. I miss you, Father." Her words, heard by no one, were too quiet to even leave the room. "I wish you could meet my friends." A smile tugged at her face again, and she laughed. "They're great. Rylan's hilarious, but a teddy bear. Kira's sweet and kind and *so* smart. And Peter . . ." Her smile grew. "You'd love Peter.

"I wish you could be here. Even though I'm around my friends all the time, I feel . . . alone." Her breath wavered. "They don't know. They don't know about . . ." Her words faded. "They wouldn't understand." Her eyes moved to the burn marks on the walls. "But you would." She touched the leather cord around her neck and traced it to the sealed vial at the end. "You understand all too well."

She grasped the vial and squeezed her eyes closed, pressing tightly as if it could push the pain away. Finally, she sighed, her breath creating a faint fog. She folded the scarf and set it back on the floor. Pulling up the thin blanket, she closed her eyes and waited for sleep to come.

## 6

Peter woke late on Postday morning, still bone-deep sore from the brawl. The sun slanted through the windows, falling in stripes on the floor of his tiny bedroom. Already, his parents were in the kitchen, speaking in low voices. He strained to hear the conversation, to get a read on if his mother were present or lost in the murky waters of her memory, but he couldn't make out the words.

He sat up, stretched his aching shoulders, then stood and peered at his reflection in the tiny mirror over his washbasin. He leaned close and drew his forefinger over his brow. There was no pain, no swelling, just some greenish discoloration—barely enough to warrant a second glance. *Sephiri's balm works.*

He ran his fingers through his shaggy, brown hair in a futile attempt to tidy it, then dressed in workwear. From his wardrobe, he pulled out his one set of clothing that could even be considered nice—plain dark slacks, faded from wear and mended a few times, and a simple cotton tunic. "Nice" was a stretch, but at least it wasn't brown and stained with oil and sweat like most of his clothes. It would suffice for that night. He stepped out of his bedroom and into the kitchen.

"Morning," he said. "How are things?" *How's Mother?*

His father adjusted the kettle over the fire. "Morning, Peter. Tea?"

"No thanks."

"Are you not with Jenkins today?"

Peter shook his head. "He has something going on, so I'm free—Prefinday as well. I'm able to help in the fields."

"On a day off?" his mother said. "You shouldn't have to work. You should go and have fun with your friends." She sat at the kitchen table with a piece of crusty bread and a smear of jam from last year's canning. A well-loved book sat open in front of her. Her silvery hair was loose to her shoulders, and she smiled as she spoke.

*So it's a good day.* Peter glanced at his father, who nodded subtly, as if he could read Peter's mind.

"I know, Mother," he said, "but we have a lot to do with the harvest."

"We're doing just fine," she said with a smile. "You enjoy your day off. You and your father can work in the fields tomorrow. One day off won't get us behind."

Again, Peter and his father shared a glance. His father pressed his lips together and returned his attention to stoking the fire below the kettle. So it was a good day, but she didn't remember about Peter's apprenticeship or the dire straits the farm crept toward. In some ways, that was a relief. It meant she wasn't worrying. Her days were better when she wasn't worrying.

"Okay, if you insist." Peter leaned over and gave his mother a brief hug. "You get some rest, too."

"It's what I'm best at," she teased.

Peter's heart clenched at her smile. Good days were hard in their own way. They were a brief glimpse into the life they used to have when Peter was younger—when the farm hummed along, and his mother wasn't sick.

Peter grabbed a crust of bread from the table and a boiled egg to go with it. He leaned and whispered in his father's ear, "I'll be out in the field."

His father nodded, knowingly. "I'll be there in a moment."

Peter spent most of the day laboring with his father. Together they harvested a large portion of grain, bundled it, and loaded it on the cart for transport. In the afternoon, his father finally shooed him away, insisting he could handle the rest.

After cleaning up and changing into his nicer clothes, Peter made his way to the Garrison, where he met Rylan and Sephiri. As soon as the sun lowered close to the horizon, the three traveled north toward Kira's home, passing people on their way to the taverns.

The Lancasters lived in Paratill View, high on the hill, in the heart of the wealthy neighborhood. Peter had run past the Lancaster home countless times. It was a four-story white stone building with enormous glass windows and multiple balconies. Even though he'd been friends with Kira for years, he could count the number of times he'd been inside on one hand. Approaching the front door always filled him with trepidation, like he expected one of the Lancasters' servants to pop out and shoo him away. Since Kira's father was the head of the merchant's guild, and her mother the curator of the Palenting Museum, they could afford a *lot* of servants.

"Psst!" Kira hissed. She peered from behind the house. "This way!"

"That's a relief," Rylan whispered. "I was worried she expected us to just walk in."

They followed Kira as she hopped the low fence surrounding the small back garden. Overhead, the balcony doors hung open, and the sounds of conversation and music filtered out into the cool night.

Peter looked up. "So, what do we do? Boost up to the balcony?"

"That's where the guests are having cocktail hour," Kira said. "Us climbing over the railing might raise an eyebrow or twenty. The cellar's easier." She turned to Rylan and nodded toward the storm doors where she had stopped. "Can you get that?"

Rylan grunted as he heaved the heavy wooden handle of the cellar door. It clattered open, and the four of them stood stock-still, waiting for someone to burst onto the balcony or out of the door to the garden.

No one did. Kira sighed and pushed a strand of hair off her forehead. "All right. This way." She pulled her fine silk skirt up around her waist, revealing her trousers beneath, and tied it up with practiced ease.

Kira descended the stairs first, then Rylan, Sephiri, and Peter. "Grab the door," Kira whispered.

Peter cringed. *Nothing like being locked in a cellar to start the party.* He grasped the rope on the door and heaved it closed, enclosing them in near darkness. Moonlight flowed in from a narrow window leading to the garden, giving Peter just enough light to not accidentally knock Sephiri down the stairs.

"Whoa." Rylan paused in front of a shelf of dusty wine bottles. "Is this up for grabs?"

"Ha!" Kira laughed. "You think my father doesn't have the staff take inventory?"

"Ooh," Sephiri teased. "The *staff.*"

"The good stuff's upstairs," Kira said. "Meaning food. Up this way." She waved them to the other side of the cellar, then opened a narrow door—too narrow to be intended for a person.

"What is that?" Peter shuffled up next to her and stuck his head into the doorway, peering up the dark chute.

"It's a dumbwaiter."

"A what?"

"A pulley system. So the kitchen can bring things up and down." She peered up the chute. "It's really old and has been broken for years though. This is our way in."

"You're kidding," Sephiri said.

"What about those?" Rylan pointed to a set of actual stairs, leading up on the other side of the cellar.

Kira shook her head. "It opens into the main hall. We could easily be seen."

Sephiri laughed, a loud, bright sound. Her eyes widened as she slapped her hand over her mouth to muffle it. "So this is how you get back in when you sneak out? How do you open the cellar door?"

"I can open it." Kira raised her chin. "But why should I when Rylan is here?"

Rylan flexed. Sephiri rolled her eyes and thwacked his shoulder. Rylan grabbed his arm and made a face like a horse had kicked him.

"All right, who's hungry?" Kira stepped into the chute. It was so narrow she could press her feet and hands to either side of the chute then shimmy her way up.

"That's the method?" Rylan asked.

"Yeah." Kira's voice was strained as she moved upward. "Think you can do it?"

"Well, obviously. But maybe I should go last, just in case I, um . . ." He mimed a falling motion with his hands. Sephiri and Peter hid their laughter behind their hands.

Sephiri went next, mirroring Kira's technique and moving with graceful ease up the chute. Peter followed, pressing his feet hard into the rough sides of the chute. He pushed with his hands, creating the needed tension to creep upward. One foot, then one hand, then the other foot, then the other hand—he moved upward like a spider. It wasn't a long climb, but his muscles burned from the exertion. Beneath him, Rylan climbed with his back pressed to one side and his feet to the other.

"Don't fall on me," Rylan grunted.

"No promises," Peter muttered.

Kira pried open the dumbwaiter door at the ground level of the house. It opened into a dim room. She climbed out of the chute, disappearing above. Then her hand appeared and wrapped around Sephiri's arm to help her up. Peter braced himself, then when Kira's hand reappeared, he grasped her wrist and climbed out himself. As soon as his feet were on solid ground, he reached down with Kira to grab red-faced Rylan before he lost his grip and tumbled back down into the cellar.

With a heave, they hauled him up onto the floor. He lay there, sprawled out. "I never thought I'd miss boosting all three of you up over walls," he grumbled. "That's a lot easier than this."

Peter turned his attention to the dark room. "Where are we?"

"Ground floor kitchen storeroom," Kira whispered. "The kitchen connects everywhere. This way."

The kitchen bustled with activity. Well-dressed staff placed small, colorful snacks on fine silver platters and poured white wine into elegant glasses. Peter paused in the doorway, but Kira strode in with no concern. She waved a hand at the rest of them where they lingered in the storeroom.

The staff seemed used to Kira's antics. A cook threw a distracted wave in their direction, but no one said anything as she continued up the servants' staircase at the far end of the kitchen. Peter and the others hurried to catch up.

They bounded up the narrow set of stairs, then another. Sounds of the party filtered through the walls as they made their way to the fourth floor. Anticipation and anxiety tightened Peter's throat. He imagined himself stepping into the party atmosphere, charming the pants off the wealthy artisans and soldiers. Maybe the Lancasters knew Commander Isert. Maybe he could still impress him.

*Don't be ridiculous.* The thought rose unbidden. *You'll be lucky if you get a good meal and don't get caught trespassing.*

At the fourth-floor landing, Kira opened a window and climbed outside.

"Um." Sephiri cringed. "Is this really what we're doing?"

"Guess so." Peter followed out of the window and onto the narrow sill. A blast of wind hit him, rustling his hair and whipping the hem of his shirt. Ahead, Kira pressed to the wall, creeping along a decorative ridge jutting out a hand's width.

"Don't fall." She grinned as she shuffled sideways.

"There has to be a better way to do this," Peter mumbled as he followed.

Below him, the garden was a tiny square of green. He swallowed down his nerves and focused on the cool stone against his back instead of the dizzying fall beneath him. He was used to running through Palenting on foot, clambering up walls and onto roofs, hopping over the gap between buildings, but moving at such a slow, careful pace made his heartbeat pick up. Ahead, Kira stepped gracefully from the ridge down onto a balcony.

Kira extended her hand, and he grasped it and hopped down after her. As soon as he was on steady ground again, he collapsed against the railing and exhaled. Sweat beaded at his temples. *This meal better be worth it.*

"I'm good," Sephiri said. She scurried across the ridge with ease, like she crossed a bridge over a canal and not a four-story drop. She smiled as she hopped down onto the balcony.

"Not afraid of heights, I guess," Peter said.

"What?" Sephiri teased. "Are you?"

"I am," Rylan said as he stepped out onto the ridge. "Guys, I definitely am."

It took some goading, whispers of encouragement,

breathing exercises, and a few explicit bribes of the exquisite snacks the staff carried around, but Rylan made his way across the ridge and landed heavily on the balcony. He sat down and leaned against the railing. "Why are we doing this again?"

"Because it's fun," Kira said.

"And the food," Sephiri added.

A heavy velvet curtain partitioned off the balcony from the rest of the party. Peter pushed it aside, the fabric feather-soft against his fingers. Behind the curtain, the party was in full swing. The fourth floor was a vast, open space, with polished stone floors and high, vaulted ceilings. Lit with torches along the walls and fine chandeliers hanging from the ceiling, the room contained a warm, flickering glow. A string band played a jaunty tune in the corner.

Peter knew the Lancasters were rich, but he hadn't realized they knew what appeared to be every person in Paratill View. Women in elegant silk gowns and fine jewelry filled the room. Men dressed in slacks or military finery milled about in small groups, discussing whatever the rich and powerful discussed, with pauses to sip wine and take measured bites of tiny sandwiches and fruit that made Peter's mouth water.

"Wait here." Kira untied her skirt from around her waist and smoothed out the wrinkles, then pulled down her hair so it fell loose around her shoulders. "I'll get some food."

"We should've just gotten some in the kitchen," Rylan said, still pale-faced and leaning against the railing.

"And miss the party? No way." Kira grinned, then swept aside the curtain and disappeared into the crowd as smoothly as a fish in a river.

---

## 7

Kira kept her chin up, taking purposeful steps toward the tables on the far side of the room. Dresses twirled past her while couples danced, arms locked together and faces impassively staring anywhere except at their partners.

Her eyes darted around the room, taking care to steer clear of anyone who would draw her into conversation. A young man named Donovan caught her eye from the bar. He held a drink up and nodded at her with an oily grin. *Ugh*, she thought, averting her eyes and making a slight course correction to stay clear.

She made it to the food table and chose a plate, then piled food on, grabbing a few of everything.

"Is that what you're wearing?"

Kira spun, sending grapes rolling off the edge of the plate.

Rosalyn Lancaster stood before her in a floor-length red dress with a plunging neckline. Her hair was pulled up in a twisted bun, and dangling crystals hung from each ear. The stern look on her face rarely showed itself at parties.

"Mother! There you are." She cringed at the waver in her

voice. Glancing down, she noticed the scuffs on her dress where she'd climbed up the dumbwaiter. "It's . . . I like this dress."

"We're the hosts, and we need to look presentable." She scoffed and took the plate from Kira's hands. "And these parties aren't for you to stuff yourself. Eat on your own time. You should mingle with the guests." Her eyebrows lifted, and her mouth pulled into a grin. "I noticed Donovan is here."

Kira's face soured. "No, thanks."

"What do you mean? I thought you and he were a nice pair. Didn't you go out with him a lot?"

"You *forced* me to go out with him *once*." Kira kept her voice low. "We took a walk through the castle gardens."

"That sounds lovely—"

"He brought a parasol . . ."

Her mother's brow furrowed. "He probably cared about your skin."

"For *himself*," Kira added. "Not for me. All he talked about was the new coat he was having tailored and how he wished the women of this city would—I'm quoting here—'learn to cook better.' Later, he invited me to come watch him hunt." She scoffed with a twinge of disgust.

"Kira!" The hushed rebuke was louder than Kira liked. "You can't go around blowing off potential suitors. His father is the head of the banker's guild. He would make a fine match."

Kira scoffed. "What about you?" she asked, trying to change the subject. "Why are you over here?"

Her mother pursed her lips. "Me? I'm—" She glanced over her shoulder. "I'm trying to avoid Cathleen Dunn."

Kira laughed internally. *Oh, the irony.*

"She's simply awful—always wearing those gaudy dresses and pointing out how wealthy they are. I can't stand talking to her."

"Isn't her husband the Lord of Commerce, Mother? Isn't it

good to make connections with a powerful family like that?" She fought to hold back a smirk.

Her mother's mouth formed a tight line. A flick of her eyes told Kira that someone approached. "It's her," her mother muttered. "Maybe she won't—"

"Rosalyn!" a woman's voice called from over Kira's shoulder. Her mother's face transformed into a beaming smile. "Cathleen! I'm *so* happy you could come."

Kira turned. Cathleen Dunn's dress *did* make an impression. Blue lacework and white gemstones around the neck left no doubt as to its significant cost. Her long, brown hair fell in luxurious curls, giving her a casual but glamorous look.

"Your dress is absolutely stunning," Kira's mother said. "You always have the best taste."

Kira rolled her eyes.

Cathleen returned the smile. "Thank you. Alonzo's job takes good care of us." She turned. "Kira. It's nice to see you again."

Kira nodded and offered a faint smile. "Mrs. Dunn."

Cathleen looked over her shoulder and beckoned with a hand before turning back. "My son's here tonight as well. I'm sure he would love to see you." Her smile faltered as she looked Kira up and down. "I see you've gone for the, uh . . . casual look tonight."

Kira cocked her head while a contented smile remained on her face. "I like this dress. It's comfortable, and the way I see it is . . . people should like me for who I am, not for what I wear." The conversation paused, but Kira held her chin high, refusing to back down from her confident pose.

"Ah, here he is," Cathleen said, stepping to the side.

Ashton Dunn arrived, and Kira's friendly smile turned into a flat line. A thick layer of pomade shellacked his blond hair flat against his head. His crisp, white shirt buttoned tight around his neck, and a dark-blue suit hugged his body. His smile showed off straight, white teeth.

"Mrs. Lancaster, thank you so much for inviting us here tonight," Ashton said. "This party is incredible, and *you* look amazing."

Kira's mother held her hand to her chest and giggled. "Thank you, Ashton." She nudged Kira. "Such a gentleman."

Ashton turned to Kira, holding the same smooth grin. "Kira, you look . . . beautiful as well."

"Ashton," she replied, fighting to keep her tone pleasant. "You are . . . here."

"I ran into one of your friends yesterday."

"I heard," she said, her teeth clenching. "He mentioned you ganged up on him with your friends, and beat on him for no reason."

"Kira!" her mother scolded.

Mrs. Dunn's eyes grew until Ashton burst into laughter. "Oh, Kira! That's great." He turned to her mother. "Don't worry, Mrs. Lancaster. She's only teasing. We're all friends from when we were young." He took a step toward Kira and touched her lightly on the arm. "Can we talk for a moment?" He angled his head to the side.

Kira kept her jaw clenched but followed Ashton out of earshot of their mothers.

Ashton dropped his voice low. "What is your problem?"

"My problem is you," Kira replied. "You think you're better than everyone and can do whatever you like. Peter was—"

"And you don't?"

Halted mid-sentence, Kira's jaw dropped. "What do you mean?"

"You think you're better than everyone here. You spend your time gallivanting with your friends, doing . . . whatever you like. What do you see in those poor losers?"

"I'd rather be in their company than yours any day."

He narrowed his eyes during a half-pause. "Is this because of that time in Dulran Yard?"

She clenched her teeth together, her heart rate increasing.

"Kira, that was like ten years ago."

"Eight," she spat, her jaw set.

"Come on. We were kids. We were fooling around."

"Fooling around?"

"Yeah."

"By pulling my dress off?"

"You had that other stuff on under it."

She crossed her arms. "That's not the point. You pushed me down. You and your friends threw mud on my clothes and in my hair and then laughed."

"Hodge was the main one laughing."

She punched him in the chest. "And you were the one who ripped off my dress."

Ashton shifted his feet, his words gone.

"There were, what . . . ten of you standing around gawking? If Peter and Rylan hadn't shown up and run you off, what would have happened next, Ashton?"

"Nothing," he muttered after a tense moment. "Like I said, we were only fooling around."

"Peter covered me with his cloak."

Ashton laughed. "You mean his long, tattered rag?"

"They didn't even know me, but they made sure I was safe and walked me home. On their worst day, they're better than you on your best."

Ashton sneered. "Do your parents know how much time you spend with them?"

Kira swallowed but didn't answer.

"Do they approve of who you're growing up to be?"

"Do your parents approve of you?" Kira retorted. "What about your father? I hear he's very understanding."

Ashton blanched.

Kira glanced around the room. "Maybe we should find him and get his thoughts on beating up poor people when they're out trying to work."

Ashton swallowed hard. "He wouldn't care." His words shook, and his eyes flitted around.

Kira stared for a long moment. "You're probably right. He wouldn't."

Ashton stepped forward, pointing a threatening finger at her. "Stay out of my business, Lancaster." With a curl of his lip, he turned and walked away.

"Wow." Sephiri peeked out from behind the curtain, shoulder-to-shoulder with Peter. "Looks fun, doesn't it?"

"I don't know if fun is the word I would use," Peter said. "What do these people even talk about?"

"Art, probably. Art, and music, and poetry."

"Maybe military strategy. Trading old war stories."

"Or bragging about their children."

"Comparing the sizes of their gardens and stables."

Sephiri laughed. "Yeah . . . it's just one big room full of people talking about horses."

"That sounds right." Rylan stood and wriggled his way between them, peering through the gap in the curtain. "Think we're dressed well enough to get in there?"

"Maybe you two could, but do you see those gowns?" Sephiri sighed and looked down at her own trousers. "I don't even look as nice as the servants do."

"Aw, c'mon, we could get at least half a dance in before we got kicked out."

A nervous wave rushed through Peter at the mention of dancing.

"Don't be ridiculous, Rylan," Sephiri said with a hint of laughter in her voice.

Peter stepped away, leaving Sephiri and Rylan to admire the crowd. He leaned against the balcony and gazed out over the horizon. A cool breeze rustled through the trees below. In the distance, moonlight spilled over the mountains, silhouetting the peaks and the top of the old watchtower. Peter sighed. Usually, breaking into a party and getting a free meal would lift his mood for a few days, but as he gazed out toward the watchtower, he felt a dull ache. *What am I even doing here? I'm stuck on the edge of a world I'll never be a part of. Again.*

"What do you think, Peter?" Sephiri asked.

"Huh?" He turned around. "Think about what?"

Sephiri glanced over her shoulder, peering through the gap in the curtain. "Rylan thinks he can pass as a military recruit and get his hands on the fancy snacks."

"Kira's getting us food."

"I bet I could, though," Rylan said. "I look responsible."

"You're too short," Sephiri said.

"What? Height has nothing to do with military capability!"

"If you get caught and put in the stocks, I'm not breaking you out again," Peter said.

"Aw, come on. The stocks' lock is so easy to pick, and I won't get caught."

Before Rylan's hunger could drive him to behave even more recklessly than usual, Kira slipped back through the curtain with a platter stacked with tiny, fancy-looking foods: finger sandwiches, cheese on tiny toothpicks, sliced fruit, even chocolate. "I better not go back out there," she whispered.

"Finally." Rylan dropped to sit on the balcony floor and gestured for Kira to set the plate of food between them.

Peter took one of the small sandwiches from the plate and leaned against the balcony wall, seated with his legs stretched out in front of him. He was always hungry, and always appreciative of a free meal, yet the sandwich didn't taste any better than ones he'd had before.

Sephiri sat next to him and plucked a berry from the plate. "You okay, Kira?"

She looked pale. Peter snapped to attention. "Did something happen out there?"

"Nothing happened." Kira didn't take any of the food for herself, just pulled her knees up to her chest and glanced toward the curtain. "But I didn't realize my father invited him."

"There you are, Joseph!" a low voice boomed.

Sephiri dropped her berry.

"That can't be—" Peter whispered until Kira shushed him.

"Razor," she mouthed with a nod.

Still chewing his sandwich, Rylan stared wide-eyed at the curtain separating them from the leader of the Viper Syndicate. There wasn't even a door between the balcony and the room behind it. It was just the plush velvet curtain. If Razor decided he wanted a breath of fresh air, the four of them were done for.

"Garrett," another voice said. "I trust you're enjoying the festivities?"

Peter raised his eyebrows at Kira. "Your father?" he mouthed.

She nodded, frowning.

"I always do," Razor said. "You Lancasters are the finest hosts in Palenting. Tell me, have you considered my proposition?"

Mr. Lancaster chuckled. "You'll have to remind me which one, Garrett. I've got a lot of proposals that come across my desk."

"From our conversation," Razor said, clipped, "at the tavern. I still see great potential for us to work together."

"You're always suggesting such things," Mr. Lancaster said, good-naturedly with an air of condescension. He spoke to Razor like he was a rambling street urchin, not the terrifying leader of the Vipers who took the fingers of debtors who couldn't pay him back. "The Lancaster estate is quite comfortable with our current investments, and—"

"This is different," Razor hissed. "The Vipers are close to grasping an object of immeasurable worth—far beyond the coffers of the Lancaster estate. With this item, the power of the merchant's guild would be limitless. Beyond anything either of us could ever imagine."

"I see. Then why would you wish to involve me at all? The Syndicate is not known for its inclusiveness."

"I'd like to change that."

Peter grimaced, picturing a false smile on the man's face.

"You see," Razor continued, "you have a connection to Mr. Butcher."

"The banker?"

Peter's ears perked at the familiar name.

"He has something I need," Razor continued. "Something that will help me obtain an object I seek, and I'd like you to convince him to give it up. I'll share the wealth of power coming to me."

A steady beat drummed in Peter's chest, growing more rapid by the moment.

"Razor." A thump, as if Mr. Lancaster had clapped his hand onto Razor's shoulder. "You have to understand my confusion here. Why would you need someone like me to connect you to Mr. Butcher when you're already working with the Lord of Commerce himself?"

Razor said nothing.

"You can't believe I haven't heard about the Syndicate's pressure. I'd love to know the details, though. How did you convince the lord to raise the rents so drastically, driving people to come to the Syndicate for loans?"

"It's mutually beneficial. It's good for the coffers of the city in the short-term, and good for the Syndicate's coffers in the long-term."

"And is it beneficial to those ousted from their homes?" Mr. Lancaster probed. Razor didn't reply. "But why would you even ask? Surely your goons over at the Syndicate are capable of breaking into a bank to steal something you want."

"It may come to that, but I'd like to draw less attention. If he were to *give* it away, less eyes would be in our direction. Considering what I pursue, that's something I greatly desire."

"What do you pursue?"

A long pause filled the air. Peter strained his ears, unsure if the men remained.

"This is about lost treasure, isn't it?" Kira's father asked.

Rylan's eyes grew wide, and Peter tensed.

"I heard merchants talking. Someone was looking for a mythical artifact or something. Is that what this is about?"

A gasp escaped Peter's mouth that he quickly stifled with his hand. Kira's inquiring eyes bored into him.

"But why would . . ." A soft laugh issued from Kira's father. "You don't want Lord Dunn to know about it, do you? Oh, Garrett. I remember when you first stumbled into this city. You had nothing, but you tried *so* hard to get everyone to respect you. I was there with Lord Holcomb when you petitioned him about appointing you as head of that . . . crime task force idea you had." Another laugh. "I've never seen him laugh so hard."

A silent pause followed.

"That was right before you formed the Viper Syndicate, wasn't it? Tell me Garrett . . ." Shuffling steps indicated the bodies on the other side of the curtain grew closer. "Was it his rejection that led you to create your own . . . group of friends? Ones that only liked you because of the money you wrung out of others and gave to them?"

"Don't push me, Lancaster. You would be wise to take advantage of this opportunity. When things change in this city, think about whose side you want to be on. It would be a shame if something happened to you . . . or your family . . . and the Vipers weren't there to protect you."

Kira's eyes widened.

"Don't you dare threaten me, Razor."

"What's your answer?"

A tense moment hung in the air, broken by a soft laugh from Mr. Lancaster. "You are a snake," he said cheerfully. "Have fun looking for your treasure, but leave my estate out of it."

"You're a fool." Razor's voice was low and cold. "You're soon to regret this."

"Right, right. Have you had a bit too much wine, Garrett? I believe it might be best if some of my staff escorted you downstairs."

"That won't be necessary."

Footsteps indicated Razor's departure. Mr. Lancaster sighed, then muttered to himself, "Now, where did my daughter go?"

After a moment of silence, Peter delicately pulled the curtain aside enough to peek out. Both men were gone. Only then did he exhale hard. He slumped down and tipped his head back as his pulse raced.

"What was that about?" Rylan asked. "What's this treasure —this 'item of immeasurable worth?'"

"Father doesn't seem very worried," Kira said. "The Vipers are always planning schemes like this."

"I don't know." Sephiri picked at the fruit on the platter. "I don't think we should underestimate him."

"What is an item that could give you that much power, though?" Rylan asked. "Don't the Vipers have enough power?"

"Some men never have enough power," Kira said. "I know the type."

Peter's arms tingled. His throat felt dry, and his vision spun.

"He sounded serious, too," Sephiri said. "Rylan, did you see anything on that table in the Syndicate building?"

Rylan shook his head. "I was a little focused on not getting caught and stabbed."

"What about the banker? What would Razor need from a random banker?"

Kira leaned forward. "He said the banker had something he needed. Something to get to the thing he actually wants."

"That's a lot of help," Rylan muttered. "The bank has a thing he wants to get to another thing that he wants." He bit into a sausage link, and his face lit up. "These are good. Can we get some more of these weird little things?"

Kira laughed and stood. "Sure, but if I end up pulled into a conversation with my father and some suitor he wants to marry me off to, it's your fault."

Rylan nodded solemnly. "It's a price I'm willing to pay."

"Hey," Peter finally said, his weak voice turning the other heads. "The banker—Mr. Butcher."

Rylan leaned in, his eyebrow quirked. "Yeah?"

Peter swallowed to clear his dry throat. A clap of thunder rumbled in the distance, signaling an approaching storm. "He was the banker I visited."

Kira's eyes steadily grew, but Rylan's forehead pinched.

"The banker's office where I . . ."

Rylan's confused look shifted, and he sucked in air.

"The pyramid," Sephiri breathed.

Peter nodded. "I'll bet that's what Razor's looking for. The pyramid is the item that leads to the treasure."

## 8

All four friends labored to breathe when they burst into the Garrison. Peter wiped the sweat off his brow and grabbed the leather pouch from the table. He scrambled to untie the clasp. Silence fell over the four of them as he pulled out the stone. The smooth, gray pyramid held new interest in light of the information they'd just heard. He ran his eyes over it, hoping something might make more sense.

"To gain the stone, you prove your worth." Sephiri's eyes narrowed. "What stone is it talking about?"

"I have a bad feeling about this," Kira said. "We should take it back to the bank. We don't even need to say anything. We could just leave it in front of the door."

Rylan held up his hands. "Hold on a second! We should probably try to figure out what it is, first? Right?"

Peter turned it over, hoping to find something he'd missed. "Treasure sounds great, but . . . if Razor is involved . . ."

"Exactly!" Kira reached for the object, but Peter blocked her with his free hand.

"Hold on," he said.

"We're talking about the Viper Syndicate. It's not worth the risk!"

"What about Butcher?" Sephiri asked. "What do you know about him?"

"My father's worked with him for years," Kira said. "But I don't know much more than that."

Peter flopped down onto a chair and leaned forward, staring at the object. "He's a jerk. He barely spoke to me. He said he doesn't enjoy working with Jenkins because his work isn't 'profitable.' And it looks like all he does is reject loans."

"What do you mean?" Kira asked.

"He had a big stack of them on his desk. All rejected. Seems like no one who actually needs money can get it from the bank."

"I bet that's great for the Vipers," Sephiri said.

"Exactly what I thought," Peter agreed.

Rylan leaned forward. "What about the pyramid?"

Peter shrugged, rubbing the engraving again. "He didn't say anything. We only spoke for a moment."

"So, what would he use it for?"

"It's got to be the poem," Sephiri said. "Hidden in rock and bone and all of that."

"Where would we start?" Peter mused. He leaned so close his eyes could barely focus on the chiseled words.

"Peter," Kira said sternly.

Peter looked up, shaken out of his reverie, and tightened his grip on the pyramid.

"Don't you agree?" she asked. "That we should return it?"

"I don't know," he said. "Don't you think it's kind of odd that I just happened to pick it up?"

"It's a coincidence," Sephiri said. "I'm with Kira. I want nothing to do with Razor and his business."

"But it says you have to prove your worth," Rylan argued.

"Razor wouldn't be able to do that, but maybe we could. And we can't let him get the stone, whatever it is."

Kira laughed. "How do you know that? Have you been on any quests for lost artifacts recently?"

"Well . . ." Rylan sputtered. "It's just obvious. Razor's a mean little snake. If he figured out this riddle and then got his hands on the stone, who knows what he might do with whatever sort of power he'd get?"

"That's a good point," Sephiri added.

"What's the stone?" Peter asked.

Rylan shrugged. "I don't know, but if Razor is looking for it, it has to be something important . . ."

"Yeah," Peter agreed. "Something really important."

"Which is why we should not get involved," Kira said. "Right?"

Peter sighed and slipped the pyramid back into its pouch. "Right."

"Good. So you'll take it back to the bank?"

"I guess."

"Ugh." Rylan rolled his eyes. "Kira, you're no fun."

"If it weren't for me, you'd be in the stocks a lot more often," she said. "Stealing from a banker is dangerous enough. Having something like this in our possession is asking for trouble."

"What do you think, Seph?" Rylan asked.

Sephiri was quiet, gazing into the flickering fire as the other three argued. She had a familiar, thoughtful look on her face, like her mind was elsewhere as the conversation rolled by. The three of them waited for her to speak. After a long moment, she plucked a pintid from the pile and flipped it over her fingers. "I don't think we should have it, but I don't think Razor should, either."

"Razor won't have it if we take it back to the bank," Kira said. "They know what they're doing there."

"Apparently not, since Peter walked out of there with it in his pocket," Rylan noted.

Overhead, the sky rumbled, the oncoming storm close.

"Just give it back, okay?" Kira stood up with a sigh. "I need to return home. They're going to wonder where I went. Do you promise you'll return it?" She looked down the bridge of her nose at Peter, frowning.

"I'll take it back," Peter said. A strange tug pulled at his chest as he spoke. The weight of the pyramid felt promising in his palm, like something within it reached out to him. The thought of returning it to the bank felt wrong.

But Kira was the smartest of them, and the rest were wise to listen. If they got caught with that thing, whatever it was, they'd end up in a lot more trouble than just an afternoon in the stocks.

"Good," she said. "I'll see you guys tomorrow after work? Fountain?"

The three of them murmured their agreement. Kira hurried out of the Garrison, scrambling over the rocks that led through the opening.

"This stinks," Rylan muttered. "We never get to do anything fun."

"You have a weird definition of fun," Sephiri said.

"The bank's closed by now," Peter said. "Might as well go drop it off and be done with it."

They pulled their cloaks on. Peter exited the Garrison with his friends at his heels. It was quiet in the streets, with conversation filtering out from a few taverns as the evening melted into night. Rylan walked ahead of them, humming as he tossed a pintid up and caught it.

The thunder rumbled again. Rain fell in fat droplets.

Sephiri walked alongside Peter, chin dipped down with a focused gaze. She tugged her cloak tighter around her body. "Do you really think we should return it tonight?" The delicate lilt of her voice was barely audible over the raindrops. "Just leaving it outside the bank? What if someone else picks it up?"

Peter tucked his hand into his rucksack and touched the soft leather of the pouch. If it were a key to something powerful, like Kira thought, maybe it was unwise just to drop it where anyone could pick it up.

*You just want it for yourself, Peter,* he thought.

He did. He couldn't explain why. The weight of it felt right in his hands and in his bag.

"Hey!" Rylan called over his shoulder. "Something's happening! Hurry!"

Peter took Sephiri by the hand so he wouldn't lose her as they shouldered their way through the crowd gathering in the town square. They caught up to Rylan and followed as he pushed through the growing crowd with ease. Around them, people whispered and gasped.

"What is it?" Rylan asked. He bounced on his feet, ignoring the puddle splashing beneath him as he tried to see over the person in front of him.

Peter was tall enough to rise on his toes and see over the crowd. Bile rose in his throat. "We need to go."

The doors of the bank stood open, and the bodies of Mr. Butcher and two other clerks sprawled lifelessly on the stairs leading to the town square. One was the woman who had directed Peter upstairs, and he didn't recognize the other.

*Who would do something like this?*

All three had their throats cut, and the blood mixed with the rain, running down the steps in a fluid stream. Peter closed his eyes and turned away. "Seriously. Let's go."

Movement caught his eye. A tall man with salt-and-pepper hair walked slowly away from the crowd, his movements conspicuously casual. He wore a black jacket with the collar popped up, but Peter recognized the profile of his face. *Razor!* Peter's legs wobbled, and his stomach churned.

Sephiri remained standing stock-still, staring at the bank stairs, wide-eyed.

"Seph," he said, forcing himself to action and jerking his head in the opposite direction.

"Right," she said, dazed. She didn't move, though. Peter took her hand again and pulled her away from the scene.

"Was that the guy?" Rylan whispered as they hurried out of the town square and back toward their neighborhood.

Peter nodded, pushing his wet hair back. "Razor did it," Peter whispered. "I saw him walking away."

A thick silence filled the air. The pyramid in his rucksack felt heavier than ever, and the anticipation he had felt turned to dread. Kira was right when she said it was serious—but it was more so than any of them had imagined.

Whatever the pyramid was, the Vipers wanted it enough to commit murder.

Peter took a deep breath. "We can't let this fall into the wrong hands," he said resolutely. "We should keep it. We have to figure out what it is."

"Yes!" Rylan pumped his fist in the air.

Sephiri elbowed him and threw a stern look in his direction.

A sheepish look covered his face. "Sorry. I know—the bodies and everything—it's terrible." A trace of a smile crept back on his face. "But still . . . it's an adventure!"

9

---

The next afternoon, after another long day at the mason's and hours of silently considering what the stone pyramid was for, Peter and Rylan met the girls in the town square. Someone had cleaned the steps of the bank, and patrons went in and out of the building as if nothing had happened.

Peter perched at the edge of the fountain with Rylan, while Sephiri lingered at a nearby vendor stand. It was odd, seeing life go on as normal when the stairs dripped blood less than a day before. No one in the town square seemed curious. *Did things like this happen in Palenting a lot, and I just never noticed?* He wore a loose hood, keeping his face angled away from the bank in case anyone might remember him from his visit.

"Hello?" Rylan nudged Peter with his toe. They sat side-by-side on the fountain's edge with a spread of gammit between them. "Your move."

Peter dropped two cards. After a moment to think, Rylan drew four of his own, swearing under his breath as he did so.

Sephiri sat down next to Peter and nibbled the garront skewer she purchased from a vendor. She looked pleased, having purchased it with the coins they'd split, not having to mooch off Kira as they often did. "So, is the clerk of commerce leaving you alone?" she asked.

She offered the skewer to Peter, and he shook his head. "I don't think so," he said. "I told Father the extra coins were bonus pay from Jenkins. He was grateful, but apparently, there's still a lot of debt. More than I realized."

"I still have most of my share. Would that help?"

He laughed, but there was no humor in it. "I wish. The entire amount would have barely made a dent. Plus, Father would be suspicious if I mysteriously showed up with another pile of coins. Thanks though."

"Well . . . it was better than nothing, though, right? And at least your father accepted the help."

"That almost makes me more worried," Peter admitted. "He never wants to depend on others."

"Hey, watch it!" Kira said as she approached. A young boy crashed into her legs, knocking her off-balance. Her shawl slid off her shoulders, and she scrambled to catch it before it fell into the dirt.

The boy just laughed, gripped the hilt of his sword made from a stick, and charged back toward his friend. "Face me!" the boy shouted at his friend. "The Shadow Knights will strike you where you stand!"

His companion, just as small and covered in dust and dirt, lifted his hand and brandished a smooth rock like a weapon. "You can't beat the Amulet of Power!" he cried. "I'm invincible!"

The kids ran at each other. One stick thunked against the skewer vendor's cart, making him shout half-heartedly after them. Unfazed, the kids ran laughing into an alley off the town square.

Kira rolled her eyes as she approached. "Did you see that? He nearly knocked me down!"

"You got a stain on your dress," Rylan said.

"What!" She grimaced, looking down at the hem of her linen dress. "Ugh, my tutor's going to kill me."

"He almost knocked you all the way over," Rylan said. "That would've been funny."

"Shut it, Rylan." She pointed at the cards. "You're about to lose this round. I've got next."

"I'm not losing!" he exclaimed. His frown proved she was right.

At Peter's side, Sephiri went still. "You okay?" Peter asked.

She took another bite of her skewer. "Do you have the pyramid with you?" she whispered.

"Yeah."

Kira and Rylan argued over the next best move in their game, which looked like it was about to devolve into actual fighting. Peter's brows pinched, and he swatted Rylan's shoulder. "Hey, let's take a break."

"Fine," Rylan agreed. "I was about to win, anyway." He noticed the change in tone. "What is it?"

The three friends scooted closer, creating a small pocket of privacy around Sephiri amid the busy town square. "I've been thinking about something," she said. "About the item we found."

"Do you know what it is?" Kira asked.

"No," Sephiri said. "But . . . when I was a little girl, my parents told me stories from centuries ago. Stories passed down from my great-great-grandparents. Stories of a stone that could grant the one who held it certain powers."

"You mean the Amulet of Power?" Peter asked in a whisper. "Like that boy playing pretend? You think it's real?"

"I don't know, but my parents thought it was real. They believed someone was going to find it soon—someone who was worthy."

Everyone's eyes fell on Peter. He set his hand on his rucksack, feeling the shape of the pyramid beneath the well-worn leather. "You think this is the way to find it?"

"It might be," she said. "Which would explain why Razor was so intent on finding it, and why he would kill the banker."

Kira's neck extended, her eyes wide. "I heard about that. You don't mean . . . ?"

Peter nodded. "The dead man was Mr. Butcher. We saw his body and Razor walking away from the scene."

Kira paled and fell silent.

"We decided to hold onto . . . the object . . . until we could figure out more about it."

"If the Amulet of Power is the treasure, and this is a guide to find it," Sephiri said, "we can't let Razor get his hands on it. We can't. With that kind of power . . ." She trailed off, her gaze fixed on the ground.

After a pause, Kira nodded slowly. "We need to figure out what it is."

Peter's mouth twitched up at the corner. "How can we be sure of what it is, though?"

"Well . . ." Kira said.

"Please don't say go to the library," Rylan moaned. "Please."

"I think we should try the library first."

Rylan groaned.

THE PALENTING LIBRARY was an immense building in Paratill View, just east of the town square and the baron's castle, built of smooth dark stone with stained glass windows and decorated doors. Kira led them inside, shoving the heavy door open with an easy familiarity. Peter had never been inside the library. After finishing the city's meager version of school for poor kids, he spent his time working, not reading.

"Whoa," he whispered. The door fell shut with a clunk behind them. "This place is enormous."

The library was three stories, with vaulted ceilings and immense windows. Neatly arranged and close together, the shelves were taller than Peter and Rylan combined, and stuffed full with books of all colors and bindings. A well-lit desk sat in the center of the room where a librarian scratched notes, hunched over a large open book. Peter thought they'd be asking her for advice, but Kira grabbed his sleeve and tugged him forward.

"This way," she whispered. "I know where the good stuff is."

"Good stuff?" Rylan whispered back. "It's all books!"

"Shh!" Sephiri pushed Rylan forward, and the four of them scurried along the edge of the library, following Kira to the back.

The back of the library was quiet and dark, with dustier shelves and dim lanterns. It looked like visitors typically stayed near the front to access the novels and poetry. The books in the back were bigger, thicker, and bound in leather with faded titles like "A Complete History of Norshand" and "Compendium of Plant Life in Feldor". Peter's head ached just looking at them.

Kira removed her shawl and draped it over a chair at a small table along the edge of the room. "Plan of action. We're looking for history books. What range do you think, Seph?"

"I heard it existed when Norshewa was known as Norshand, and they controlled Terrenor," Sephiri said. "So focus on ancient history."

"Thrilling," Rylan said. "Ancient history. Awesome."

The four of them split up and drifted into the stacks. Peter wandered in the dark, dusty aisles, squinting at the book titles. He grabbed whatever he saw that seemed related to ancient history and potentially legendary amulets, having little idea of what such a book would look like. He pulled volumes until he had a teetering stack of a dozen in his arms, high enough that he could barely see over the top. He staggered back to their table and dropped his finds with a thunk.

"Nice," Sephiri said, already poring over the yellowed pages of one she gathered. "What'd you find?"

"Um, some stuff about military history," Peter said. "I think. And something about architecture? I don't know. They look old."

Sephiri tilted her head, but then nodded. "I'll sort through them."

Kira and Rylan returned with books to add to the piles. Rylan used Peter's strategy, grabbing as many books as he could carry, whereas Kira had been more discerning. Sephiri went to Kira's books first.

In silence, they searched the piles. They rifled through the pages, scouring for anything that might reference the Amulet of Power or a similar totem. They grabbed books from the heaps until they spread out across the table, open to various maps, illustrations, and rambling narratives.

"Check this out." Rylan nudged Peter's shoulder. "This one's got war illustrations. Did you know Feldor used to wield these big, crazy maces in battle?"

"Whoa," Peter said, "let me see!"

"I thought I heard voices back here."

Peter slammed the book shut, as if caught red-handed. As soon as he saw the librarian, his tense muscles relaxed. It wasn't the woman from the desk—it was Wynna, his neighbor, pushing a rickety cart full of books to be reshelved.

"Good day, Peter," she said. "It's rare that I see people your age back in this part of the library."

"Hello," Peter replied. "Yeah, we um . . . thought we'd give it a try."

Wynna smiled. "What are you four researching?"

"Um," Sephiri said. "History."

"History, hm?" Wynna stepped closer and peered at the

books stacked at Sephiri's elbow. "Ah, I see you found the old history of Terrenor written by Elwith Eanith. You know, most people thought he was a hack."

"That's right," Kira said, "though some scholars suggest there might be more value in his work than he's received credit for. I thought he might have some info on . . ." She trailed off, her eyes widening.

"Info on what?"

Peter flinched, his hands turning clammy.

"On . . . um, the migrations. From Norshewa to Tarphan."

"You're interested in migration patterns?" Wynna smiled at them. "All four of you?"

"I love travel," Rylan said. Peter stepped on his foot, and Rylan coughed to cover his grunt of surprise.

"Eanith was one of the few scholars to write about the Amulet of Power," Wynna said. "Most others write it off as a myth."

Kira glanced at Peter. He pressed his lips together.

"Oh, really?" Sephiri said, her voice wavering. "That's interesting."

Wynna glanced between them, then straightened up with a smile. "Let me pull a few things from the archives room for you. I've got some good books about migration, as well as some other things that might interest you." She left the cart in the hall and strode between the aisles to reach a heavy-looking door.

"That's where they keep the rare books," Kira said, "the really old stuff."

"She might suspect we're looking for it," Rylan said. "Is that safe?"

"I don't think she has a reason to be suspicious," Peter said. "Plus, she's my neighbor. She helps my family out sometimes."

"We're just curious," Sephiri said. "That's all."

"Right." Rylan grimaced. "Librarians are supposed to

support education and all that, right? We're just getting educated. It's fine."

Wynna returned from the rare books room with a small, thin book, bound in red leather. "Be careful with this. It's the only known copy of this Eanith text."

"Whoa," Kira said.

Wynna smiled. "There must be something in the air that's got everyone curious about Eanith. Some men were in here just yesterday researching the mythical Amulet."

"Oh?" Peter kept his tone light, even as his heartbeat hastened. "That's interesting. Did you, um . . . did they use these books as well?"

"No, they weren't interested in help from us," Wynna said. "Between you and me, I'm not keen to help a rude patron. They were definitely not friendly. Eanith was an excellent writer, though. I think you'll enjoy this work."

"Thank you," Peter said.

"I'm sure I will," Kira said. She stared at the red book with her eyes wide, not unlike the way Rylan would look at a spread of roasted boar.

Humming, Wynna pushed her cart back into the stacks, leaving them alone with the books. Rylan nearly knocked down his stack of books in his eagerness to sit next to Kira. "What did she mean?" he asked. "Not friendly? A group of men? You don't think . . . ?"

"Yeah, I think so," Peter said. "Had to be the Viper Syndicate. Who else would try to get information about the Amulet?"

Kira opened the book gingerly.

"That just means we have another thing they'll want," Sephiri said.

"But they don't know this book exists!" Rylan said. "If this Elmer guy—"

"Elwith," Kira said.

"If he knows what he's talking about, this could help us figure out what the pyramid thing is."

"Or they could catch word that we're in here looking for information and start hunting us," Sephiri said.

"That won't happen." Peter met Sephiri's unsure gaze. "I won't let it happen."

Sephiri raised her eyebrows at the seriousness of his voice, but then nodded.

*I don't know if I can keep that promise,* Peter thought, *but I'll do everything I can to try.* The pyramid in his bag felt heavier than ever. If it was the key to the Amulet of Power—if it were even real—then there was all the more reason to keep the Vipers far away from it.

"Listen to this," Kira said. "'The Amulet of Power was formed from a unique crystal found in the Straith Mountains. The crystal is said to have provided unique qualities.'"

"Qualities?" Rylan asked. He leaned closer. "What qualities?"

Kira continued to read. "'The crystal acts as an amplifier, magnifying the holder's personal traits to their highest capacity.'"

"So it doesn't give you powers," Sephiri said. "It just improves the skills you already have."

"You're out of luck, then, Peter," Rylan teased.

Peter shoved him in retribution.

"'As of this writing,'" Kira continued, "'the Amulet has been lost for a century. Attempts to discover records or remains of it have proven unsuccessful.'"

"When was it written?" Peter asked.

Kira flipped to the front of the book. "In 409."

"Ugh." Rylan flopped forward onto the table. "That's two hundred years ago. If they couldn't find it then, and no one has found it by now, this thing is definitely not real."

"Is there any mention of the weird pyramid we found?" Peter asked. "Did he write about that?"

"I don't know," Kira said. "This book doesn't have a table of contents or anything. I can't just flip to the 'weird pyramid' section."

"Back again, sirs?" Wynna's voice rang through the library, conspicuously loud. "Can I assist you with any research today?"

"As I said yesterday," a cold, familiar voice snapped, "we do not require your assistance."

"Razor," Sephiri whispered, her eyes wide.

"We need to get out of here," Peter said. "Let's move. Kira, take the book."

"What? This is from the rare books room! She said it's the only copy—"

Peter grabbed the book and stuffed it into his bag, ignoring Kira's slack-jawed expression. "We need to move, now."

"We really shouldn't—" Kira whispered.

Peter took her by the upper arm and all but dragged her into the stacks. "It's a book," he whispered, "and we can't let Razor get it."

Rylan and Sephiri hurried after them, then all four cowered in the narrow aisles as heavy footsteps approached the table they'd just left. The rumble of the book cart accompanied them.

"Ah, I'm sorry, I haven't had a chance to clean this table off," Wynna said. "Students, you know, they always leave such a mess. Here, I can take you to a table in the back—"

"That's enough," Razor said. Peter peered out from behind the shelf, keeping the other three behind him.

Razor waved Wynna away dismissively. He was dressed in plain, dark silk, heavy boots, and no jewelry of any kind. The sneer on his face sent a shiver through Peter's bones. It was the type of expression that would part a crowd in the town square without a word. The two lackeys with him seemed more interested in intimidating Wynna than in looking at any of the materials on the table.

Razor drummed his fingers against the stack of books. "Interesting." He picked up the Eanith history book Kira had initially pulled and turned it over in his hands. With a sudden movement, he straightened and looked around the library.

Peter jerked backward, out of view, and held his breath.

"I believe someone else might be curious about the same topics as us," Razor said.

After a moment of silence, Peter peered around the corner again.

The Vipers' leader stalked around the table to the chair Kira had used. He picked up her shawl draped over the back and ran the fabric through his fingers. He turned to his men. "Go ask the librarian who used these books. Now."

Razor sat in the chair Kira had vacated and opened the abandoned Eanith book, peering at it closely as if he could see who had pulled it from the shelves by the fingerprints on the pages.

"There's a side door," Kira whispered. "This way."

The four friends crept through the stacks, moving as quickly and quietly as they could.

Footsteps sounded nearby. Kira froze, and Peter stopped behind her. "What—"

"Sh!" Kira hissed.

Peter held his breath. Blood pounded in his ears.

The head of one of the Viper lackeys bobbed above the next shelf, glancing around. He reached the aisle and stopped, checking in each direction.

*If he comes this way, he'll see all four of us,* Peter thought.

Kira's eyes grew wide.

The man stood motionless. Finally, after a long pause, he turned in the opposite direction, walking away from their aisle.

Rylan exhaled in Peter's ear.

Kira creeped forward and peeked around the shelf as the man's footsteps faded. She turned back to the rest. "Quickly," she mouthed, waving them forward. She ran in a crouch one aisle down to the narrow side door.

Peter followed, hurrying on his tiptoes with an eye on the Viper's back as the man walked farther away. Thankful for the silent hinges, he jumped through the door, followed immediately by his other friends.

In the alley behind the library, Peter slumped against the wall and exhaled hard. He tipped his head up and gazed at the slow-moving clouds in the afternoon sky. His pulse still pounded as he caught his breath. *That was close. Way, way too close.*

# 10

"Let's get out of here," Peter said. "We can review the book back at the Garrison."

"Sounds good," Rylan said. "I need to work on some sword forms and get some energy out." He marched through the alley and back toward the town square, but before he could step out into the main street, Kira grabbed the back of his collar. Rylan sputtered in confusion, and Kira shushed him with a hiss.

"Look," she whispered.

Peter peered over her shoulder. Just around the corner, at the front of the library, two men with dark expressions and narrowed eyes stood scanning the town square.

"You think they're with Razor?" Peter whispered.

Kira nodded. "We'll have to go the long way."

"The long way?" Sephiri asked.

"Yeah, around back, toward Brufec Heights."

Sephiri winced. "Do we have to?"

"Well, yeah, unless you want to get caught by Vipers."

Kira led the way, taking them west, away from the town square. The mountains loomed above the city. As they walked, the buildings grew shabbier.

"Yikes," Rylan said. "I see why few people come this way."

A makeshift gallows sat outside an abandoned workshop. Hanging from the gallows, three bodies swung by their ankles in the faint breeze, knocking against each other. Lifeless arms dangled with a missing finger on each hand. The wind brought the stench of the rotting corpses in their direction, and Peter covered his nose. A few crows perched atop the wood, their cries shattering the delicate silence. The few people who moved about the streets ignored the scene. The dried-out flesh and tattered clothes showed they had been there a few days. A sign propped against the gallows: *Viper Debtors*.

"They can't do that." Kira stood in front of the gallows, gawking. "They can't just—just leave people out here like this!"

"Clearly, they can." Sephiri pulled at her sleeve. "This is why I didn't want to go this way. Please, let's just go."

"Something bothering you?" A man in a torn jacket stepped out of the doorway of the workshop. He pushed the sleeves of his coat up to his elbows and clenched his fists, revealing the tattoo of a skull and serpent on his forearm. "You got a problem with these pieces of filth hanging here?"

"Um," Rylan said, "no, we were just—"

"Shut up," Kira hissed.

"Just passing by." Peter ripped his gaze away from the gruesome scene. He nodded to his friends. "Come on." He led them southward, away from the bodies, though something in his spine itched like their lifeless eyes still watched them.

"Is he following us?" Kira asked. "Are we gonna be the next 'examples?'"

"We should stay closer to the center of town, if we can," Sephiri said. "We're too close to the edges. This is where the Vipers get away with roughing people up for extra money."

Peter glanced over his shoulder. The man hadn't followed

them—but he still moved quickly. "This has been happening a lot?"

Sephiri nodded, but offered no details.

"I don't think we should risk it." Kira glanced around, checking the nearby alleys for any more lurking Vipers. "I agree with Sephiri."

"We could take them. Especially if it's just one or two." Rylan balled his hands into fists, glancing around the same as Kira, but with a lot more eagerness in his grin.

"It's never just one or two," Sephiri said.

Peter glanced between each of them. "We should play it safe. East it is."

They took the extra-long way, zigzagging back through the narrow alleys. As they approached Dulran Yard, where the cobbled road widened and improved in quality, Peter led his friends onto the main road. The Vipers would be less likely to cause trouble where all the bureaucrats and government officials of Palenting lived and worked.

"Well, hello there," a voice called. "What are you rats doing in this part of town?"

Peter closed his eyes and exhaled hard through his nose. *Really? Now?*

Across the street, Ashton, Tanner, and Hodge sat at a table outside a tavern with far too much food spread between them. Ashton grinned and stood up, then gestured for Tanner and Hodge to do the same. Hodge heaved a sigh at their soon-to-be-abandoned meal, but obeyed.

"We're in a hurry, Ashton," Kira said. "Go back to your dinner. Maybe you'll choke on it."

Ashton stormed across the street, shouldering through the pedestrians and mules and earning a few disdainful glances for his aggression. Tanner and Hodge stumbled after him.

"Nice work, Kira," Peter muttered.

"He's being a jerk. We shouldn't let him walk all over us."

*Easy for you to say. He didn't beat you up a few days ago.* Peter sighed and stepped in front of Kira and Sephiri. "Ashton, do we have to do this now?"

"Do what?" Ashton smirked. "I'm just saying hi." He tugged at the strap of Peter's rucksack. "What do you have today, huh? Doing more errands for the boss again?"

Peter shoved Ashton's shoulder hard. "It's none of your business."

Ashton stumbled backward and knocked into Tanner behind him. He sneered and straightened up, his expression dark with renewed anger. "Protective, huh? Give it here."

*Maybe I should. Maybe I should let Ashton get beaten up by the Vipers for having the pyramid in his possession.* Peter tightened his grip on the rucksack. He glanced around the street at the flow of people, but no one paid them any mind. Hodge looked over his shoulder at the tavern, where their food waited untouched.

Rylan stepped closer. "Beat it, jerk!"

"Seriously, Ashton, stop it," Kira said.

"Shut up, Lancaster," Ashton snapped. "Again, I find you hanging out with these poor losers."

"I'd much rather hang out with them than you." She lifted her chin.

"And that's why your family reputation is tanking. Your parents are embarrassed that you spend all your time with these urchins. I said *give me the bag!*" He yanked on the rucksack. Peter stumbled forward, then caught his balance.

"And I said beat it!" Rylan lunged forward, fists raised. Sephiri grabbed him by the shoulder and wrenched him back before he could tackle Ashton.

"Don't," she said, "it's not worth it."

"Seph's right," Kira said. "Ashton will just go crying to his father as usual."

"I don't need my parents to deal with you," Ashton growled. "We'll handle it ourselves. Hodge, grab Rylan."

"But my food . . ." Hodge said.

"Are you serious?" Ashton whipped around to pin Hodge with a glare. "You're worried about a cheap tavern meal?"

"It wasn't cheap, it was five pintid!"

Peter ducked, wrenched the bag from Ashton's grip, then grabbed the drawstring on the boy's fine canvas trousers and tugged. The waistband loosened.

"What are you—" Ashton started, then kicked at the crouched figure.

Peter tumbled backward onto the cobblestone. He had his bag, though, pulled close to his chest as he grinned at Ashton's confused expression. Then Ashton's trousers dropped. Rylan burst into hysterical laughter, which set off Peter, too, guffawing behind his hand at the sight of Ashton's patterned underclothes and spindly legs.

"You jerk!" Ashton tried to retreat, but the fabric caught around his ankles and made him stumble. He fell backward onto the muddy road. Even Tanner bit back a laugh.

"Sorry, Ashton." Peter stood and brushed the dust off his pants. "We told you we were in a hurry."

Ashton staggered to his feet, his back covered in mud. He groaned as he tried to brush the worst of it off before pulling his pants back up. "What are you waiting for?" Ashton snapped at Tanner and Hodge. "Get them!"

"Come on, let's just eat," Hodge said. "We'll get them later."

Peter scurried off, laughing as he and his friends jogged toward Schuggec Row.

"That was great!" Kira said.

"Did you see his face?" Rylan agreed. "He was as red as a beet!"

"Do you think they'll leave us alone now?" Sephiri asked.

"Almost definitely not," Peter admitted. "If anything, he'll just be angrier next time he tracks us down."

"We can handle him." Rylan punched his fist into his hand.

They reached Schuggec Row and slowed to a walk as they ambled through the familiar empty streets, passing dilapidated buildings and shops.

Kira sighed. "If we fought back for real, you know he'd go crawling to his father."

"I don't think it's worth it," Peter said. *Things are hard enough for Father right now. If the Lord of Commerce intervened, we'd definitely lose the farm.*

"Well, he sucks," Rylan said.

They clambered over the rocks at the edge of the Garrison wall. As soon as Peter's feet hit the ground, familiarity fell over him like a blanket, and for the first time since he was in the library, he took a deep breath. He leaned against the cool stone wall. Rylan hurried forward to start a fire in the hearth while Kira dropped into a chair at the table and kicked her feet up. She sighed and pushed her hair off her forehead. "You still have everything, right?"

Peter nodded, then opened his rucksack, just to be sure. The pyramid weighed down the bottom of the pack with the delicate red book on top. "Got it. Do you think Razor figured anything out from the materials we pulled?"

"I doubt it." Sephiri leaned against the wall next to Peter. "It seems like all the books we pulled treat the Amulet like a myth, or don't even talk about it at all. It was all stories and illustrations, not anything based in history. I think Wynna gave us the only useful book."

"I hope so," Kira said. "I hope there's not something we missed. I wish we could go back."

"Not going to happen." Rylan picked through the training swords leaning against the wall, then selected one of the steel ones and tested the sharpness of its edge. "We should stay far away from that place if we don't want Razor to know we're doing the same research."

"Can I see the book?" Kira asked. Peter fished it out of his bag then handed it over. Sephiri moved to join her.

Peter pulled the pyramid out again and turned it over in his hands. He examined it for any seams or symbols he might've missed, but there was nothing. Just smooth stone and the inscription at the bottom. What did the riddle mean? *To gain the stone, you prove your worth . . .*

Rylan busied himself sharpening the steel blade of the sword. "Let me do this, then we can run some forms."

"Sure." Peter turned the pyramid over and over in his hands, distracted.

"Don't sound too excited."

"Is there anything in the book?" Peter asked, looking at the girls.

"Give me a minute." Kira leaned over the book, just as she had in the library. "I'm a fast reader, but not that fast."

Peter pushed off the wall, then strode across the room to join them at the table. He tossed the pyramid and caught it as he walked.

"Careful with that," Sephiri said.

"I'm careful. Plus, it's a rock." As Peter spoke, the pyramid bounced awkwardly off his fingers and tumbled to the ground.

"Peter!" Sephiri leaned over the table, eyes wide.

The pyramid bounced across the floor and landed in a shallow puddle. Peter rushed to grab it, but as his fingers neared the water, he stopped and gasped. "Whoa."

"What is it?" Kira asked. "Did you break it?"

"No, it's—" He kneeled on the ground, his heart pounding. "It's changing."

"Did you say changing?" Rylan rushed over. "I thought it was solid!"

"I did, too. Look at this." Peter turned the pyramid in his hands, and all four leaned closer.

Where the water had touched the pyramid, new details

revealed themselves. One side showed an icon of a tower, another a wave cresting, and the third a serpentine line. "What's that?" Rylan asked, pointing to the line.

"The other two are objects," Kira said. "Maybe it's a river."

"What's that?" Sephiri pointed to a thin line visible near the base, about a finger's width from the bottom. "Do you think . . . ?"

"It's not solid." Peter gripped the pyramid in both hands and, hoping he didn't break anything, twisted it firmly.

Something inside clicked. The top twisted, then lifted up and off, revealing a divot carved into the center of the base. Within the divot was another description, carved inside a triangular border. "'Seek the Shepherd's Pride,'" he read.

"What does that mean?" Rylan asked.

The four remained in stunned silence for a moment. Peter touched the divot gently, tracing the inscription. "I bet the Amulet fits here. It's not just a way to find it. It's a way to keep it safe."

"Seems like it works, since you dropped it," Sephiri said.

"Good thing you did, though," Rylan said.

Peter turned the base over, and his eyes widened. "Do you think it's part of the riddle? Hidden in rock?"

"I don't know. I wonder if there's anything else in the book about the other parts." Kira stood up. She stared up toward the open sky and bit the tip of her tongue between her teeth as she thought. "The other 'bone' and 'earth' have to be related to getting the Amulet itself. Unless we're reading too much into it, and this was just a coincidence." She rushed back to the table to return to the book. "The Shepherd's Pride . . ." she muttered to herself.

"It doesn't seem like whoever made this is big on coincidences," Sephiri said.

Peter nodded. "It has to be intentional."

"Can I look?" Sephiri asked.

Peter handed the pyramid over. Sephiri joined Kira at the table, peering at the icons as Kira buried her nose in the Eanith book. She turned the pyramid in all directions as if it might reveal more unknown secrets, but none came. With Kira sucked into the book, Peter wandered to the ropes hanging from the rafters. *Looks like we might be here a while.*

He was right. After a half-hour of silence, Kira threw her hands up and shouted, "Ugh!" She moved to slam the book closed, then caught herself and closed it gingerly. "I need a break. This is dense. Eanith likes to ramble."

"Anything good yet?" Peter called from halfway up the rope, his arms burning with the exertion.

"I need to clear my head." Kira stood and stretched her arms over her head. She grabbed her bow and quiver. *Thwok, thwok, thwok.* A few arrows landed in quick succession near the center of the target.

Sephiri remained at the table, closing and re-opening the pyramid. She sighed. "This is such a strange inscription. What is a shepherd even proud of?"

"His flock," Rylan said as he huffed and puffed through a set of push-ups. "Which means we're out of luck."

"Right," Peter said. "If this was made with the Amulet, then it's at least three hundred years old."

"And sheep don't live that long."

"Eanith's book has so much information in it." Kira strode across the floor and gathered her arrows from the target. "I get why people stopped taking him seriously. The book feels like it's half gossip about high lords and their families, and half speculating about the future of Norshewa."

"With stuff about the Amulet peppered in?" Peter gripped the rope in hand and began to climb it again. The rough canvas burned his palms, a familiar sensation. His muscles ached as he hauled himself up, touching the beam the rope wrapped around, then lowering himself back down.

"Seems like oral histories more than anything. He repeats stories other people told him about the Amulet."

"That's the same way it was passed down in my family," Sephiri said. "Little was written. I heard about it as a bedtime story more than anything else."

"A bedtime story?" Rylan asked. "What else did they tell you?"

Sephiri pressed her lips together as she picked up the book and flipped through the pages. "Not much. The tales weren't about the Amulet itself. They were about my ancestors, people generations ago, but I never thought anything of them. They were just stories."

*Thwock. Thwock. Thwock.* Three more of Kira's arrows hit the target. "What kinds of stories?"

Peter's feet hit the floor. He squeezed his upper arms, massaging out the tension from the climb. He had the same questions as Kira. *What did Sephiri know about the Amulet?* But he burned with even more curiosity about who had told her these stories. He knew so little about her history, about her family. What connections did she have to the Amulet?

"Nothing too interesting," Sephiri said. "The same stuff Eanith writes about. Stuff about how the Amulet amplifies existing abilities."

"Sounds interesting to me," Peter said.

Sephiri shrugged, still focused on the book. "They're just stories. We should focus on figuring out what these clues mean before Razor somehow does."

*Thwock.* "And he got my shawl."

Rylan hopped up from his push-ups, eyes wide. "I forgot about that. Do you think he recognized it?"

"I don't know." Kira crossed the width of the Garrison and gathered her arrows. "It's got the Lancaster crest sewed into the corner."

"He knows your family," Peter said. "Will he recognize it?"

"I'm trying not to think about it. Ashton was right about one thing. My father does not like it when I get mixed up in things."

"You mean . . . with us," Peter said.

She sighed and spun an arrow in hand. "He thinks I should focus on my finishing classes . . . so I can become a suitable candidate for marriage."

"Marriage!" Rylan stared at her. "Already?"

"Not if I have anything to say about it. Father doesn't like Razor, though. I can't imagine he'd give him the time of day if Razor asked about finding my shawl in the library."

"We should be more worried about Razor knowing it at all," Sephiri said. "We saw what he did to the bankers."

The memory made Peter shiver. The freshness of the bodies on the steps of the bank was different from the dried-out corpses hanging from the gallows, but both were the work of the Vipers. *Will that be us, next?*

"Do you think Butcher even knew what he had?" Kira asked.

"I don't think so," Peter said. "It was just stuffed in a drawer. If he knew, wouldn't he have kept it locked up?"

"Butcher is such a weird name for a banker," Rylan said. "It's like if Jenkins' name was Swordsman or something."

Peter paused with his hands on the rope, poised for another ascent. "Wait." His pulse thudded as an idea came to him.

Kira met his eyes with a matching wide-eyed expression. "Butcher."

Peter rushed over to the table. He brandished his open hands, and Sephiri handed him the pyramid with her head tilted. "What is it?" she asked.

"Seek the Shepherd's Pride," he recited, peering at the inscription. "Shepherd is capitalized. It could be . . ."

"A name," Kira agreed, "not an occupation. Shepherd is a person. Gah! How did I not think of that sooner?"

Kira and Rylan rushed to the table, peering over Sephiri's and Peter's shoulders.

"Have you seen the name Shepherd anywhere in the book?" Kira asked. "Even just an offhand mention? I didn't. But if . . ." She chewed on her lower lip.

"What?" Peter asked. "What is it?"

"I'm not sure. It sounds familiar. Maybe we covered it in school? I can't remember."

"They sure didn't in our school. We didn't even discuss history," Sephiri said. She pushed the book aside, and Kira grabbed it. "What about this, though?" She tapped the pyramid on the side with the icon of the wave. "There's a lot in the book about the land. Maybe there's something in connection to the coastline or the Isle of Paratill? Or something about a tower?"

"A tower," Kira repeated. "I think I remember something about a tower."

She thumbed through the book. Peter's heart pounded as he waited. He itched to shove closer and peer at the book himself, but Kira had the best eye for research. If she said she had seen something in the book, she'd find it again.

"A-ha! Here. Look at this."

Near the back of the book, a map, drawn in delicate ink, covered two pages. The map illustrated the Rynor coastline, from the coastal city of Kandis, all the way to the southern city of Marris. It illustrated the winding rivers and dense forests between them, as well as the Dorthar mountain range and the larger Straith Mountains to the west. Palenting nestled in the Dorthar Mountains, and Kira leaned close to peer at the tiny illustrations. "Look. It's tiny, but it's there." She pointed to an illustration of a tower, which was labeled with even smaller precise handwriting. "'Palenting Watchtower,'" she read. "'Built in 395 by the Rynorian merchant Ambrose Shepherd.'"

"There's our Shepherd!" Sephiri shouted, a grin on her face.

"The old watchtower?" Rylan asked. "The one in the mountains? No one's used that place for years!"

"If Shepherd built it himself, it probably was his pride." Excitement sparked in Peter's chest like flint striking a rock. "Going to the watchtower is the first step to finding the Amulet!"

"Rylan's right, though," Kira said. "That place is rotted where it stands. I think this is the right location, but I doubt we'll find anything there—or even if the Amulet is real."

"You're the one who figured out the riddle!" Peter said.

"I just don't want us to get our hopes up too much. This is from hundreds of years ago."

"The Amulet was always a story to me," Sephiri said quietly. "But if it's real, we can't let Razor get it."

"Plus, it'll be fun," Rylan said. "I've always wanted to check that tower out."

"We'll go tomorrow. Rylan and I are off work again." Peter nodded to himself, unspooling the plan in his mind. "We'll meet in the square and make our way to the tower." He took the pyramid in hand and clicked it back into place. The small icons —the wave, the tower, and the winding line—remained visible. He smoothed his thumb over the tower.

*We figured it out. This is going to work.*

11

---

"Man, you stink," Tanner said, waving his hand in front of his nose.

"Shut up!" Ashton punched him in the arm as they passed through the gate to his family's home.

Hodge muffled a laugh. "He's right. You really do."

Ashton inhaled and winced. *They're right. Stupid Fairfield idiot.*

The house guard nodded as the three boys crossed the lawn of the Dunn estate. Lanterns lit either side of the stately double doors ahead, and a glow behind the windows indicated someone was awake.

"You think your parents are still up?" Hodge asked.

The boys slowed on the steps. Ashton stopped with his grip on the bronze handle.

"Can we still get to the whiskey?" Tanner asked.

Ashton huffed. "I don't know. Stay quiet." He pulled the door open, entering first.

The marble entryway glowed with a flickering lantern hanging in the hall. The kitchen with its supply of liquor lay at the far end of the house, but he had to pass his father's office to get there. Even from down the hall, he could see the light through the crack at the bottom of the office door.

Everything was silent, except for his own breathing echoing in his ears. Ashton kept his feet light to avoid drawing any attention. He slowed at the door to the office. Tanner and Hodge crept behind him. They understood the importance of remaining undiscovered.

"Ashton!" A slurred pronunciation of his name bellowed through the heavy office door.

Ashton inhaled sharply, and a watery feeling ran through his gut. He looked at the other boys with his shoulders drooped. After taking a deep breath, he pushed open the door.

Alonzo Dunn leaned forward in his chair, staring down at the desk. His left hand held a stack of papers while his right swirled a glass of dark liquid. His thick brown hair and beard gave him a wolf-like appearance, but the ruddy complexion of his face made him seem almost comical.

Ashton wasn't laughing.

His father's gaze drifted up. His eyes were narrow, jaw sharp. "Where've you been?"

The words felt like an accusation. "I've—we've been out," Ashton fumbled, risking a glance at his friends.

"You—" His father's nose wrinkled and he recoiled. "Ugh! What is that smell?"

Ashton dropped his head. "I, uh . . . fell in some mud."

"Look at me when I speak to you." The words were hard, spoken quietly but with an edge.

Ashton jerked his head up. He tightened his jaw. "I'm sorry, sir."

His father took a large gulp then set the glass down. The chair scraped as he pushed it back and stood. He rounded the corner, his boots clunking across the floor. Ashton took a half-step back.

Alonzo's face formed an eerie smile. "You *fell* in mud, did you?" He traced his hand in the air while he spoke in a sing-song cadence.

"It was Peter Fairfield," Tanner said.

Ashton's head jerked to silence him with a glare. *Too late.*

His father turned.

Tanner took a step back and swallowed hard. "It was, sir. Peter knocked him down. It was completely unprovoked."

Alonzo's eyebrows raised. "Really?"

Ashton caught the patronizing tone, but his friends would not have.

"That's right," Hodge added. "Peter pulled his pants down and caused him to trip into the mud."

"Hodge," Ashton hissed. He clenched his teeth and stared down his friend.

Alonzo held a hand to his chest and laughed heartily. "What's this? He *pulled* your pants down and *knocked* you into the mud?" His face looked frozen in a laugh. "In the center of town?"

No one replied to the rhetorical question.

"In front of other people?"

Ashton's eyes dropped to the floor. *Smack!* A white-hot pain radiated across his face.

His father's hand retracted, curling into a fist. He lunged close. "Look at me when I'm speaking to you!" Spittle flew from his father's lips, striking his face from a breath away. The laughing expression was gone, replaced by a venomous curl of his lips.

"I've worked all my life to build up the Dunn name. You do nothing but lounge around the city, spending my money and boasting about how great you are. Well, let me tell you something, Ashton." He drew close again, shouting, "You're! Not! Great!"

Ashton bit down on his teeth to keep the tears back.

"You're an idiot son who spends all his time with his stupid friends. Our *dog* would be a better representation of our family name than you."

Alonzo stumbled back to his desk and picked up his glass.

Ashton didn't dare take his eyes away again.

His father took another drink, the dark liquid dripping down his beard. "If Peter Fairfield can embarrass you so easily, maybe *he'd* do a better job of carrying on the Dunn name." He returned to the door and rested his hand on it. "Get out of my sight."

Ashton flinched as the door slammed closed. A hollow feeling filled him. His mind was hazy and numb.

"Man . . ." Hodge whispered. "I'm sorry."

His friends' faces drooped, filled with discomfort and pity.

Ashton bristled. "Get out."

He spun on his heels, leaving the gaping mouths behind. Fury quickly replaced his feelings of inadequacy. *Peter Fairfield is going to pay for this.*

LATE MORNING on Prefinday was cool and sunny. The cloudless sky allowed the sun to beat against the pale stone of the Palenting town square, but the light breeze kept the air comfortable. Peter met his friends as promised. Kira brought enough lunch for the four of them—crusty bread with jerky and hard cheeses wrapped in paper—and Rylan carried a short sword in a scabbard. Peter didn't expect they'd come across any Vipers at the watchtower, but carrying the sword made Rylan puff his chest out in a pleased way, so Peter just smiled.

"All right," Peter said as they walked west toward Brufec Heights. "The watchtower is not too deep in the mountains, so it should be—"

"I know how to get there," Sephiri said.

Peter paused. "Really?"

Sephiri nodded. "Yeah. There are some paths I can lead us through."

"Paths? To the watchtower?" Kira asked.

"They're not used anymore," Sephiri said. "But it's handy, you know. Knowing the terrain, having places to hide." She shrugged.

"Hide from what?" Rylan asked.

Sephiri glanced sidelong at him. "Might be Vipers, if we're unlucky."

Peter met Rylan's eyes but said nothing. That wasn't what either of them were asking. *Had Sephiri been hiding out in the mountains? From whom? And why? Was that part of how she'd survived on her own?* The thoughts made Peter's gut twist. Things weren't easy at the farm, but at least he hadn't spent nights alone near a rickety old watchtower.

"All right," Peter said. "Let's go. All of you, keep an eye out for Vipers. We can't have them following us to the tower."

Peter led them through Brufec Heights to the edge of town, and then Sephiri took the lead as they climbed the balds outside Palenting. The base of the mountains were an hour's hike away over sloped, easy to traverse terrain, but the climb grew more complicated when they arrived.

The watchtower stretched high above them, up a steep slope. For all his time in Palenting, Peter had never been that close to it. Nestled against the dark stone of the mountains, the structure was built with clay brick similar to the ones Peter and Rylan spent their days molding behind Jenkins' shop. The roof looked caved in, and the entire structure contained a faint tilt. It was taller than any of the buildings in Palenting, with immense open windows. Determined ivy crawled up its walls and over the bare sills.

To get up to the tower, they had to climb up rocks. A lot of rocks.

Kira grimaced at the jagged boulders jutting from the rocky

soil at the base of the mountain. "Really?" she asked. "This is how we get up there?"

"There's an easier way," Sephiri said. "Follow me."

Half an hour, one bramble-filled path, three stumbles, and two skinned knees later, Peter set his toes into the edges of a boulder and hauled himself to the top. He reached down, taking Kira's hand and helping her up.

"This is the *easier* path?" Kira paused, catching her breath, red-faced and flushed from the scrambling.

"It's the easiest one I've found." Sephiri looked like she had done nothing harder than a few minutes of light jogging. Sweat clung to her temples, but her brown eyes shone with excitement. "Everyone okay?"

Rylan heaved himself up onto the boulder. "Yup," he said through labored breaths. "Dandy."

"Rest for a moment," Sephiri said. "That was the hard part, but we're almost there."

They sat at the top of the flat boulder. From there, Palenting looked like it could be an illustration from Eanith's book, with its low buildings, pale stone, patchwork farms and the distant coastline.

"Are you sure?" Rylan glanced around. Nothing surrounded them but rock, like they nestled against the mountain itself with no watchtower in sight.

"Yep, I know where we are." Sephiri smiled. "Here, eat some jerky."

"We brought jerky?"

Peter chewed on some food as he gazed out over the balds. They ate in silence for a few moments, and Peter regained some much-needed energy. He leaned back, weight on one hand. "Do you think it's really up here? The Amulet?"

"I don't think it's real," Kira said. "I think it's a myth."

"You were willing to climb all the way up here without thinking it's real?" Rylan asked.

"It's more fun than polishing classes," Kira said.

"Fair."

"Why would the pyramid exist if the Amulet isn't real?" Sephiri asked.

"It doesn't say it's for the Amulet," Kira said. "It just says to seek 'the stone.' Could be anything."

"What do you think, Peter?" Rylan asked.

"I don't know," Peter admitted. "It seems to fit, you know, that the pyramid was made alongside the Amulet."

"It does," Kira said. "I just don't want us to be disappointed if it turns out to be a myth—or a dead end." She looked pointedly at Peter.

"I won't be disappointed." It sounded like a lie, even to his own ears. "Like Rylan said, it's fun regardless."

"Just fun?" Sephiri asked.

"Is it more than that for you?"

Sephiri nodded. "I want it to be real." Her voice was small. "I want it to be real so badly. All the stories my parents told me . . . I never thought it was something I might see in real life, you know? Like it was just a legend. But if it's real, if it's something we can find . . . I feel like I owe it to my family to try." She blinked hard, then wiped at her eyes.

"I want it to be real, too," Peter said. "If it's real, and it does what you say it does, this could change everything for us. And for me."

"You mean the trouble with the farm?" Rylan said.

"More than that. It could be a way out of Palenting." He looked up toward the mountains and the clear sky. "If it gives us some kind of powers, maybe we can get out of here."

"And do what?" Sephiri asked.

"I don't know. Travel. Adventure. See more of Terrenor. Make some money. The stuff we've all talked about doing together."

"Anything besides being a mason!" Rylan agreed.

Peter laughed, then stood up. "Yeah. We should do something exciting. Like this!" After basking a moment in wishful thinking, he shook off his desires of getting out of the city and on his own. There was no point in thinking about that yet. They didn't even know if the Amulet was real—or if they'd be able to get to it before the Viper Syndicate did.

Kira nodded. "Let's get to this tower. I don't want to scramble down these boulders after dark."

They packed up the remainder of their lunch and looked to Sephiri for direction. She grinned and waved them toward the narrow trail that wound into the mountains. Peter followed, eager to finish the trek.

He rounded the sharp corner behind the boulder, and then stopped in his tracks. "Whoa."

"Told you we were close," Sephiri said with a grin.

The tower soared overhead, so close that when Rylan barreled into his back, Peter nearly crashed into the foundation.

"Watch it!" Peter said.

"Whoa," Rylan echoed.

"We really were close," Kira said.

The building loomed, dark and covered in winding ivy. Even in the clear, crisp mountain air, the smell of decay was unmistakable: the wet scent of rotting wood, dirt, and even the creatures that lived inside. Peter grinned. "Let's find a way in."

"How about we try the door?" Kira pointed to the side of the tower.

A wooden doorway stared back, barely accessible behind a few large boulders. Half-buried in the dirt, they stacked atop each other like the remains of a landslide. *Was that what made the tower unstable?* "We can probably get in through a window."

"I don't think we should try to climb it," Sephiri said. "This whole tower is rickety—I don't want to do anything that might cause it to collapse on our heads."

Peter squeezed past the boulders and to the door. Chains crisscrossed the front, padlocked with an immense rusted lock. "Window might be our only option." He looked up. The closest windows were past the range of their usual boosting method. *A few of the rocks jut out. Maybe I could climb up the wall then—*

"Scoot." Rylan butted in. He grabbed a large rock from the ground and rammed it into the rusted lock. The lock groaned. He grinned, then struck it again, hard enough that the whole door shook. Peter glanced up. The tower still stood unmoved. With a clank, the lock snapped and fell off the chain.

"Ta-da!" Rylan said.

"Nice job," Peter said, chuckling.

"Yeah, I could see you trying to figure out how to climb this thing, and I really didn't want to do that," Rylan stepped backward. "You can go first, though."

"Chicken," Peter teased. Rylan didn't deny it.

Peter pushed the old wooden door open, fighting the groan of the hinges.

Sunlight filtered through the windows, but not enough to dispel the shadows inside. The dusty wooden floor contained determined weeds pushing through the floorboards. "It's safe," Peter called over his shoulder. "Come look at this."

Sephiri, Kira, and finally Rylan stepped into the tower.

"Creepy," Rylan muttered. "Please don't tell me we're going up those stairs."

In the center of the tower, an immense wooden staircase wound in a tight spiral. The stairs looked just as rickety and rotted as the rest of the tower. "Yeah," Peter said, "we're going up them."

"What is all this?" Sephiri asked, peering at the walls. "There are runes or something written here."

"I thought you knew this place!" Rylan said.

"I've never been inside," Sephiri said. "You saw the lock on the door."

"What do you mean, runes?" Kira asked. She hurried to Sephiri's side and inspected the bricks. "It looks like the symbols from the pyramid. But there are others, too—something that looks like a mountain range. This one is a wave inside a little triangle. I don't know what this one—ahh!"

Kira's sharp scream cut off her own questions as a rat dashed over her foot. She leaped backward and rushed to the door, then stood in the doorway bouncing on the balls of her feet and shaking out her arms like rats covered them. "Gross, gross, gross!" she squealed.

"It's just a rat," Sephiri said. "Look, he's curious." The rat sat up on its back legs, nose wiggling as it peered toward them.

"Ew," Kira moaned. "They're so gross. I hate rats. I hate them. Can we go upstairs now, please?"

"You'd rather climb those stairs than be around a little rat?" Rylan asked. "Seriously?"

"Yes, seriously," Kira said. "Either we go upstairs, or I wait outside."

Peter bit back a laugh. "You wouldn't last a day on the farm, Kira. Our tomcats can hardly keep up with the mice."

"Mice are fine," she said primly. "Rats are different."

"All right, all right. Let's go upstairs." Peter led the way up the winding stairs. He took his steps carefully, avoiding the worst of the rot and gripping the banister in case the wood gave out under their feet. The wood groaned as they ascended. His breath grew labored at the endless rise.

"How old do you think this wood is?" Sephiri asked, interrupting the silence with a catch in her voice.

"Assuming they're the original steps . . ." Kira began.

"Which they look and smell like," Rylan added.

"They have to be three hundred years old."

A loud creak of wood echoed in the tower until Rylan's heavy breath covered it up. "I'm not sure they're going to hold me," he said, tromping dutifully along.

Peter looked ahead. *Only a dozen more steps to go.* He leaned over the side to see the distance they'd traveled. The drop made him dizzy. He took another step, pressing down to test the wood. "You'll be fine. Even though it's old, it—"

A shattering crack filled the air as the step under Peter gave way. His stomach lurched. He tried to yell, but his lungs didn't work. The banister ripped from his hand, and he scrambled to grab on to anything solid. His side slammed into the next step while his body fell through the gaping hole.

He braced himself for the free fall to the distant floor below, but a firm hand wrapped around his forearm.

"Got you!" Rylan shouted.

Peter's fall halted. His feet dangled over air, and his body twirled, holding on to nothing but Rylan's arm. He used his free hand to grab the next step and, after great exertion on both their parts, collapsed onto the steps.

He panted, his heart racing. "Thank you, Rylan."

"You were saying something—before you fell. Something about the steps being fine. What was that? You broke off at the end there."

Peter punched him playfully, and Rylan grinned back.

"I'm glad I was here."

"Are you all right?" Sephiri asked, leaning in on the narrow stairs.

Peter nodded. "Yeah, I think I'll be fine . . . as long as my pulse will settle again." He breathed out, long and slow, and looked ahead, past the gap in the stairs. "What do you all think? Should we try to continue up? Or head back?" His stomach twisted at the thought of turning around when they were so close, but he had no desire to lead his friends into danger.

"We're almost there," Rylan said after a pause. "Let me go first. If I can make it, you all can."

Peter nodded, reluctant but relieved.

Rylan stretched his leg over the missing step and gingerly

tested the next board. A loud creak made Peter's hands sweat. Gradually, the larger boy shifted his weight forward. While holding the railing with white knuckles, he continued on, past the gap.

A collective sigh of relief exhaled at the same time from the girls. Peter looked over his shoulder and shrugged. "I guess we're next."

They took turns crossing the broken stair, waiting for each other and ready to assist in case anyone else fell through. Thankfully, there were no more incidents.

At the top, the stairs ended at a small wooden platform, which was in only slightly better condition than the stairs themselves. Framed with white stone like the buildings of Palenting, the eastern window was larger than every other window in the tower. In an undulating shape, it still had some glass intact. The tower was so tall that, through the window, the blue sea glimmered in the distance.

For a moment, Peter imagined himself as a soldier again, posted in the watchtower, standing serious and alert like a sentinel. Maybe it'd be wartime, and he'd be tasked with guarding both the mountain pass and the coast—to alert the city of any approaching enemies. Maybe he'd see them in the pass, send the message, and then rush down the stairs, sword drawn to stop the enemy where they stood.

He sighed. *Nice thought. I can't even get a commander to look in my direction.*

"This is something. Look." Kira pointed up to an inscription carved into the white stone above the window. "'He who looks to the sea will find what he seeks,'" she read. She placed her hands on the windowsill and gazed out toward the waves. "I'm looking out to the sea. Am I supposed to see an amulet?"

"It says *he*," Rylan said. "Let me try."

Kira rolled her eyes and stepped aside. Rylan placed his hands on the sill and squinted out the window. He looked left and right. "Nope. Just ocean. And Palenting. The farms look like quilts from this far away."

"The waves," Sephiri murmured to herself. She stared up at the window, and her gaze traced the shape of it. "I saw this downstairs."

"What?" Peter asked. "What do you mean?"

"This way, come on!" Sephiri said brightly. She hurried back down the stairs on feet so delicate, they were nearly silent. Peter moved more slowly, mindful of the creaks and the groans. *How does she move so lightly? It's like she barely put any weight on the steps at all.* A faint breeze stirred the air inside the tower, lifting dust from the ancient surfaces and clouding the air.

He made it down to the ground level of the tower without collapsing the stairs. Kira and Rylan did, too, though Rylan was quite pale in the face.

"Look," Sephiri said. "This one's different from the rest of the inscriptions."

Peter stepped closer and peered at the runes Kira and Sephiri had examined earlier. There were so many, they seemed to cover the wall. They followed a regular pattern of the same six in a row, but where she pointed, one was different. The wave icon appeared on many of the bricks on the wall. But it was the only one placed inside a triangle.

"It's different," Peter said.

"Exactly," Sephiri said, a grin growing on her face. "And it's the same icon as what's on the pyramid. It has to mean something, right?"

"The pyramid's pretty much a triangle," Rylan said. "Right?"

"Yeah. And the inscription inside was inside a triangle, just like this." Peter ran his fingers over the relief of the icon. The brick wiggled under his light touch. "Weird." He touched a few others, but all the other bricks held firmly in place. He placed his fingers back on the wave and pushed.

The brick slid backward with a clunk. Then another clunk sounded, and another. Two seams appeared in the brick wall.

The wall now looked like a door.

Peter stepped back and wiped the dust off his hands. Excitement sparked in his chest while his eyes lit up. "Well. I think we found something."

## 12

P eter placed his hands flat on the door and pushed. Above them, the entire tower groaned, like an animal awakening after a long hibernation. He stilled, eyes wide and breath caught in his throat as he waited for disaster.

None came. He exhaled, then glanced back over his shoulder.

Sephiri nodded. Kira stared upward, eyes wide in fear. Rylan was paler than ever.

Peter pushed again, but this time, the door didn't budge. He groaned with the effort of it and dug his feet into the ground, pushing with all his might, but it didn't give. "Come on," he insisted. "Help me."

"Are you sure this is a good idea?" Rylan asked. "This tower doesn't seem stable."

"It was constructed with this hidden passage in mind," Peter said. "It'll be fine." *I hope.*

Rylan looked unconvinced, but he stepped forward. Kira and Sephiri did, too, and the four of them stood shoulder-to-shoulder with their palms on the door and pushed.

Slowly, and with a low creak, the thick door opened. Above

them, the tower groaned in tandem, but stayed standing. Peter exhaled.

"Whoa." Rylan squinted into the darkness revealed behind the door. "Where do you think it goes?"

"Down, it looks like." Peter stepped gingerly over the threshold. The door revealed a small foyer with an earthen floor and walls built of the same red stone as the tower. Then, stairs. Stairs winding down, down, into deep, still, dense darkness. A torch was mounted on the wall, dusty with disuse. Peter pulled it down and shook the cobwebs from it. Spiders crept over the wall where the torch had been. "Looks like whoever built this wanted us to go down there."

"How deep do you think it goes?" Sephiri asked.

"I believe we're about to find out," Kira said.

Peter lit the torch with flint from his pocket. Flames leaped to life, casting the walls of the tunnel in flickering, shadowy light. The stairs wound deep into the earth, in a spiral opposite to the one leading up. He swallowed, suppressing a minor flare of anxiety. *I wonder what's waiting for us.*

"Let's go," he said, finally. "Seek the Shepherd's Pride, remember?"

"I don't know what there is to be proud of down there," Rylan said. "You first."

Peter brandished the torch and descended.

The stairs were hard-packed earth and wood, dug into the ground. The deeper Peter went, the smaller the tunnel got. His nerves were on edge, his muscles tense. He imagined himself creeping down a massive beast's gullet, and a shiver ran up his spine. The air grew damp and musty—still, like no living thing had been there for an age. It was so quiet that his gentle foot-steps seemed ear-splitting. They descended for several minutes until the ground flattened out into a wide, circular room carved from dirt. Sephiri traced her forefinger along a thick tree root jutting from the wall.

"Earth," Peter said. "Remember what the clue said? 'Hidden in rock, in bone, in earth.'"

"Yeah, and 'death and dust await the rest,'" Sephiri said. "Remember that part?"

"There's something written here," Kira said. "Peter, light, please."

A long stone dais spanned the center of the room with a small stone tablet resting atop. "'Knowledge and words are given freely,'" Kira read, "'but neither the tablet nor the coins are yours to take.'" She traced her finger over the words carved into the dais itself, in a circle around the stone tablet.

"Coins?" Rylan craned his neck and peered over the dais. "Whoa, yea! Not just coins—sol! Gold sol!"

Peter pushed the torch into Kira's hand and then joined Rylan looking over the dais. He gasped at the sight. It wasn't just a few gold sol. It was an enormous bag, the size of Rylan's head, so stuffed full of sol the glittering coins spilled from the top of a canvas bag. The bag waited at the bottom of a shallow pit. Peter's head spun. He'd never seen so much money in one place. *With that kind of sol, Father could pay off all the rest of our debt. We could fix up the broken equipment so we wouldn't fall behind on harvest and payments again. We'd be able to take care of Mother. And then there'd be some left over, too, plenty for Rylan and Sephiri.* Excitement rushed through him, washing away his thoughts of the Amulet and replacing them with the real, tangible sol right in front of his eyes.

"I can totally reach it," Rylan said. "Climbing out of that pit will be a snap."

"Don't even think about it," Kira snapped.

"What?" Peter asked. He straightened up. "It's right there."

"The inscription explicitly says not to take the coins."

"Um." Sephiri tapped Kira on the shoulder. "I don't think we're the first ones to come down here."

"Huh?" Kira's gaze followed Sephiri's. She gasped, then took a stumbling step back as she held the torch up high.

Peter looked up. Overhead, two skeletons stuck to the ceiling, pressed into the dirt and staring down at Peter as if he were beneath them in the grave. Thick, sharp spears jutted down and poked through the skeleton's ribcages, keeping the piles of bones in place.

"Who do you think that was?" Rylan asked. "They were here a long time ago." He clambered onto the dais and then pulled his sword off his hip again.

"Don't," Kira hissed. "Leave them alone."

"I'm testing something," Rylan said. "We'll see if it triggers a trap or anything like that. I bet since these guys already got the worst of it, we'll be fine."

"There's something more on the tablet, too," Sephiri said. "Listen to this. 'The Amulet is power for any who wear the flame upon the sea. Finding it takes strength of many. The Shepherds' Sword will hold the key.'"

"Get down, Rylan," Kira hissed.

"A sword?" Peter gazed at the gold sol in the pit as he pondered.

"Maybe more people had nice swords back then," Sephiri said. "Do you think it's in the watchtower?"

"Rylan!" Kira said again. Rylan shuffled to the edge of the dais. Kira grabbed the edge of his tunic and tugged. "Stop it!"

"I'm just seeing something." Rylan grunted through gritted teeth. "Almost . . ." He stretched as far as he could, sword out, and nudged the sheathed tip against the closest skull.

With a crunching sound, the skull detached from the skeleton and dropped into the pit. The four fell silent as the skull thumped into the dirt and rolled toward the pile of coins. Peter held his breath, waiting for any kind of sound, or for the spears still in the ceiling overhead to drop into the pit.

"See?" Rylan said. "Nothing. We can grab them and then come back to the tablet. No problem."

Kira exhaled and then pressed her palms to her forehead. "That's not what the inscription says. It says we have to leave the tablet and the coins here."

Rylan shrugged. He hopped off the dais, but didn't look convinced.

Peter wanted the sol so badly his mouth watered. *Kira's right, though. We have to leave it. It's not worth the risk.* Still, part of him wanted to try. There had to be a way to get a few of the sol—enough to wipe out his family's debt.

"Okay." Kira leaned over the tablet again. "This is the next clue, I guess. What does it mean to 'wear the flame upon the sea?' Seph, have you ever heard of anything like that?"

"I don't think so," she said. "Could it be a lighthouse or something? A flame over the sea?"

"How do you wear that, though?" Peter asked. *We'll figure this out*, he thought, *then I'll get a few sol before we leave.*

"That isn't the most important part, though," Sephiri said. "It says the key to finding it in the first place is the Shepherd's Sword. Did anyone see a sword anywhere in the watchtower?"

"We would've seen it," Peter said. "There's nothing here but stairs and rats."

Kira shivered. "Don't remind me." She held the torch closer to the tablet. "But it says Shepherds'. It's not just a single Shepherd—it's many Shepherds."

"Good thing you're here," Peter said. "They didn't just carve it wrong?"

"I doubt it," Kira said. "Everything about this place is intentional. Maybe it means a sword that belongs to the Shepherd family. If Ambrose Shepherd had the wealth to build a tower like this, he probably comes from a pretty accomplished line. There might be someone else in his family who had a famous sword or something."

Peter nodded. "We can check Eanith's book. Maybe he has some other people listed."

"Probably," Kira said. "Ugh. It's going to be a nightmare to find in the book, though. It's like he wrote that book with no plan for how to—"

Metal clinking interrupted Kira's words. Peter leaned over the dais again. Rylan lay on his belly with his sword extended toward the coins. He bit his lower lip in concentration as he wiggled the canvas bag closer to him.

"Rylan!" Kira said. "Don't!"

"Almost," Rylan muttered. "I almost got it . . ."

"Nice!" Peter said. Kira smacked him on the shoulder. Peter grimaced and rubbed his arm. "What? I know a few sol don't make a big difference to you, but for the rest of us, it could help a lot."

Kira's face fell, lips parted in a stunned expression of genuine hurt before she scowled at him. "It's not about the money." She pointed at the skeletons. "It's that I don't want my friends to end up like *that*."

"I didn't mean it like that," Peter said. "It's just—with the stuff at the farm, if we can just a get a handful—"

"It's not worth it." Sephiri's voice wavered. "The inscription—"

"I won't take the entire bag," Rylan said through gritted teeth. "Just a few."

"I don't think how many you take matters," Kira said.

With a triumphant grin, Rylan hooked the edge of his sword into the canvas. With slow, careful precision, he lifted the bag from the pit. The spears in the ceiling quivered, then dropped with a sharp and sudden thunk. The skeletons fell with a stomach-turning rattle, bursting apart on impact with the earthen floor. Arm bones rolled one way, leg bones another, scattering like marbles. Then the spears lifted back up, out of the dirt, and slotted back into the ceiling where they came from.

"Yes!" Rylan hugged the bag to his chest, grinning like a small child with a brand-new toy. The sol spilled out of the bag, overstuffed and pouring out from the canvas and over Rylan's arms like water. "I got it! Look at all of this! Peter, we're set for life!"

Peter's eyes widened. He couldn't believe Rylan had pulled it off. It didn't seem real. The sol in his arms was *theirs*. "You did it! You beat the trap."

"I told you." Rylan grinned at Kira. "We're all gonna be as rich as Lancasters, now. We can throw our own parties, with our own fancy cheese plates, and I'll get a brand new sword, and Peter can pay off the farm, and Seph can get dresses like yours, and—"

"Shh," Sephiri said. "You hear that?"

"I hear my future," Rylan said with a smile, his eyes closed as he cradled the bag. "It sounds like a hired string band, playing something fun and jaunty as my private chef wheels in a cake . . ."

"Shut up," Kira snapped. "Listen."

A low rumble sounded from the earth above them. It grew louder and louder. The ground under his feet quivered as if there were an earthquake, except the tremors came from above. Dirt fell like snow from the ceiling, and the bones in the pit clattered against each other.

"We need to move," Peter said. "Now! Go!"

A powerful tremor rumbled through the room, and the earthen floor shifted like an ocean swell. Sephiri stumbled and fell with a shocked cry. Peter ran to her side, grasped her wrist, and hauled her back to her feet. Behind them on the dais, the tremor knocked Rylan backward. He nearly tumbled into the depression, but Kira grasped his leg and kept him from falling. The canvas bag spilled from his arms and back into the pit. The sol cascaded out, clattering amongst the bones. Rylan shouted. "No!"

Another tremor rocked the room. "No time! Let's go!"

Peter pushed Sephiri in front of him, guiding her toward the stairs with his hands at her waist to keep her from falling. She moved deftly, so fast Peter could hardly keep up. They took the stairs two at a time. Rylan and Kira scurried up behind them with Kira waving the shuddering torch.

"Faster!" Rylan shouted from below. "Oh, man! Faster!"

Cracks appeared in the ceiling of the stairwell above them as the earth caved in. A crashing noise bellowed in the darkness behind, blowing their hair forward with a whoosh of musty air. Peter pictured the dirt below collapsing in a wave, chasing them as they ran up the stairs as fast as possible. *Almost there!*

Light spilled through the doorway ahead where the circular ground floor of the watchtower waited. Sephiri leaped over the threshold, and Peter stumbled through behind her. He reached back and grabbed Kira's hand, then Rylan's, pulling them up as the rest of the earthen staircase behind them collapsed.

Peter dusted dirt off his face and clothes. He panted for a moment until another tremor rocked the tower. Overhead, the wooden stairs creaked and then snapped. Rotten wood rained down on them, and Peter shouted as he rushed toward the door. His feet halted. His breath left him. The boulders they squeezed past on the way into the tower had shifted and blocked the only exit.

"It's collapsing!" Peter shouted over the rumble of the tremors and groaning of the brick. "We need a way out!"

He looked frantically around. Stones blocked the door. The roof and stairs above them crumbled, dropping debris. The brick walls would fragment soon. *The windows!* If they hurried, they could reach them before the stairs were completely gone. Rylan was as white as a sheet, and his eyes were red from the dust as he cried out, "I'm sorry . . . about the coins! I didn't think—"

"Not now!" Peter shouted. "The window!"

They needed to climb up the stairs. It would take time, but they had enough time—they *had* to have enough time—he couldn't think of any other option. The skeletons buried in the pit in the basement lingered in his mind. *That could be us.*

With an ear-splitting crunch, an immense crack traveled up the side of the tower like a lightning bolt. The walls split and swayed for a precarious moment. Peter held his breath. *Maybe it won't fall.* His stomach lurched as the walls crashed toward each other, slamming together and raining bricks like hail.

Time seemed to slow down as reality hit him. *There's no way out.* No sol. No Amulet. No new life. Just four more skeletons under a pile of rubble in the Dorthar Mountains. *Sorry, Father.*

Jolting him from his trance, Sephiri grabbed him and Rylan and tugged them close to Kira. Sparks jumped down her skin like flint striking to light a torch. Her dark eyes washed out to pale, and her hair swept back as if caught in a breeze. She swept her hands overhead in a wide arc.

Stillness fell like a sheet. Sephiri stood a pace ahead of them, arms raised. Peter looked up, and his breath caught. It was as if he were underwater, looking through the surface at the world above. In their bubble, it was quiet. Even the rumbling of the tower was muted, dulled, like cotton filled his ears. He stared wide-eyed as the bricks slammed into the shimmering air above them and bounced off. Rylan and Kira curled toward Peter, cowering away from the falling detritus.

Sephiri hissed in exertion. She dug her heels into the ground, palms up. Sparks danced over her skin, streaming from her hands like water, skittering down her arms and falling to the shifting ground where they disappeared.

*What is happening?* Peter wondered, in awe and terror at the same time. *How can she do this?*

Great beams in the walls collapsed, falling with the bricks. One immense wooden joist slammed into the air Sephiri held in place, and the impact rippled across it. Sephiri made a sound like she'd been struck and stumbled backward toward Peter. He rushed closer, steadying her with a hand on her shoulder. Another beam crashed, and another, piling down with bricks and rocks with nowhere to go. Sephiri groaned, her knees wavered.

"Seph!" Peter cried out.

Another rumble sounded, louder this time, another tremor under their feet. Sephiri collapsed, and then there was nothing but shouting, chaos, terror, dull throbbing pain—

And then darkness.

———————

## 13

"Peter . . . Peter!"

*Ugh. Too early. Don't want to get up. Don't want to run before work. Head hurts. Maybe I'm sick. Too sick to go to work.*

"Peter!"

Peter groaned. *Five more minutes.*

"Hey . . . hey, wake up," someone said.

*Didn't sound like Mother.*

"Wake up!"

Peter's body ached as if he were one immense bruise. He wasn't in his bed—he was on the ground, with a rock in his back and his arm under something heavy. His ears rang, and his head pounded. With some effort, he opened his eyes a sliver. Sephiri, Kira, and Rylan all leaned over him: Sephiri pallid, Rylan with dirt on his face and in his hair, Kira flushed with a minor cut high on her cheekbone. Behind them, blue sky waited high above.

The tower had collapsed.

"My arm," Peter groaned.

Rylan leaped to attention, then hurried to lift the beam pinning Peter's arm.

With the pressure relieved, Peter wriggled his arm out and cradled it to his chest as dull pain throbbed through him.

"Is it broken?" Rylan asked. "Peter, is it broken?"

Peter exhaled. *Why does he sound more scared than me?* Peter peered at his arm. A shallow gash oozed in his forearm, but nothing seemed broken. It just ached. Everything ached. "I'm all right," he said, his voice raspy. "Just a scratch. What about you all? Anyone hurt?"

The three of them shook their heads. "We're okay," Kira said. Everyone moved stiffly, with grimaces that suggested similar aches and pains. But everyone was talking and walking, which was better than Peter had feared.

"Seph," Peter said, the sound of her name bringing an eerie stillness. "How did you . . . ?"

"Later," she said, her eyes flitting between them. "I'll explain when we're back to the Garrison. We should go if we want to get back before dark."

Peter was too exhausted to argue. He nodded.

Peter followed Sephiri over the wreckage of the tower, with Kira and Rylan behind them. He creeped over the bricks and shattered beams, careful not to upset anything rickety and tumble down again. They made it out of the wreckage and back to the flat boulder where they'd had their lunch just a few hours before, and sat back down to dress their wounds before the hike back. Sephiri pulled her barkleaf balm from her bag with quivering hands. Kira took the jar from her, unscrewed it, and then smoothed some on Sephiri's wrists where angry, red scrapes marked her.

"I didn't realize it'd bring down the whole tower," Rylan said quietly. He favored his left foot, like he'd twisted his ankle. "If I'd known—"

"None of us knew that would happen." Sephiri closed her eyes as Kira applied the balm.

"You all right?" Kira asked.

Sephiri nodded, her face peakish. "I'm okay."

"I thought we could get around it," Rylan said, his eyes averted and head drooping. "I'm so sorry. I really wanted that sol."

"It's buried treasure now." Peter sighed at the thought. All that sol, a life-changing amount of money, buried so deep underground beneath all this wreckage. They'd never get to it even if they tried.

"Don't be so greedy next time," Sephiri said, but there was no anger in her voice—just exhaustion. "Remember what the pyramid said? 'To gain the stone, you prove your worth.' I think this was a test."

"A test we failed," Rylan said.

"We?" Kira shot back.

Peter's head hurt. He didn't have the energy to listen to Kira and Rylan fight. He waved a hand as if dispelling the argument before they could have it. "We got the next clue, didn't we? It's not a total bust."

"'The flame upon the sea,'" Kira said. "'Finding it takes the strength of many, the Shepherds' Sword will hold the key.' Or something like that."

*Lucky Kira has such an excellent memory.* "The Shepherds' Sword," Peter said. "That's what we have to find next."

"Let's finish cleaning up," Sephiri said. "This collapse is going to attract some attention. And I don't think we want to be here when others show up." She nodded in thanks to Kira for the help with her wrists.

"You and Rylan get a head start," Kira said, looking at Rylan's hurt ankle. "I'll wrap Peter's arm, and we'll catch up."

Sephiri nodded, handed her rucksack to Kira, then helped Rylan shuffle down the trail. Kira pulled a clean cloth from

Sephiri's bag and a small canteen of water. She rinsed the worst of the dirt from Peter's arm. He hissed through his teeth with pain from the cool water, but Kira just tutted and kept going.

"Sorry about what I said," Peter said, "underground . . . about the coins not mattering to you."

Kira said nothing as she wound the cloth around Peter's arm.

"I should've stopped Rylan," Peter continued. "You were right about the warning on the tablet. I was just thinking about my parents. I wanted the coins badly, too."

Kira sighed as she tied off the bandage just tight enough to stop the bleeding. "I know," she said. "And you were right, too. I know my family's well off. You know I'd do more to help if I could."

"I know," Peter said. "We'd all be a lot skinnier if you didn't feed us, that's for sure."

"Yeah, well, enjoy it while you can," she said. "Once Father marries me off, I'll probably be shipped off to Felting or Tarving or somewhere across the Straiths to improve his business relations."

It was Peter's turn to say nothing. He often forgot that Kira had a whole slew of her own problems. They were unlike the ones Peter faced, but they were problems just the same. Just as Peter wished to get out of Palenting and adventure as a soldier, maybe Kira aspired to keep her adventures here.

"All right," she said. "That should be good enough for now. You okay to walk?"

"Yeah, I'm fine." He pressed against his arm. "It really is nothing. What about you?"

"Fit as can be," Kira said with an exhausted grin.

Sephiri led them toward Palenting, off the usual trail. As Sephiri had predicted, a scouting mission of soldiers on horseback made their way across the balds as the sun neared the horizon. The four friends lingered in the tall grass, far enough away to remain unnoticed as the soldiers thundered by.

"Will anyone know it was us?" Rylan whispered.

"I don't think so," Peter said. "The tower was so old it looked like a breeze might knock it down. It's just a structural collapse."

"We hope," Sephiri said.

"Yeah," Peter agreed. "We hope."

Once the horses thundered past, they kept moving, traveling as fast as they could with Rylan's twisted ankle. It was nearly dark by the time they made their way back to Palenting and into the safety of the Garrison.

Kira started a fire in the hearth while Rylan stretched out on the fur in front of it with a groan. Sephiri knelt at his side and checked his ankle again, prodding the swelling. Rylan hissed and grimaced. "It doesn't look broken," Kira said. "Just pulled something, most likely. Take it easy, and you should be okay in a few days."

"I hope so," he grumbled. "I've got to go back to work."

"So much for our early retirement, huh?" Peter said, wistfully thinking of the buried coins. He sat at the table and leaned back with a sigh. His whole body hurt. Exhaustion weighed on him like the bricks of the collapsed tower.

"We got a clue, though," Kira said. "We can still find the Amulet."

"Right," Rylan said. "Since we didn't get crushed to death."

Peter's eyes fell to Sephiri, and Kira's and Rylan's followed. Sephiri glanced around at them, then pressed her lips together. Rylan scooted back on the rug, making space for her to sit on the fur as well. She turned her gaze to the crackling fire and tugged her knees to her chest.

"That was real, right?" Peter asked. "You really did that?"

It seemed like something from his imagination. Or something he'd made up after an unexpected knock to the skull. Rylan and Kira stared at her, too—they'd seen it as well.

"It was like a dome," Rylan said. "A dome, but invisible. Stuff just bounced off of it."

"Like you were manipulating the air." Kira poked at the fire.

Silence hung over the Garrison for a long moment, broken only by the warm crackle of the fire in the hearth. *This will be like every other time I've asked her about her past,* Peter thought. *She won't tell us anything. She never does.* It bothered him, like a splinter deep in his palm, that Sephiri could do something as incredible as what she'd done in the tower and had never even mentioned it. They were friends—how could he know so little about her?

Sephiri took a deep breath and exhaled it out. Her gaze remained on the fire when she spoke. "My parents died when I was ten."

Peter's breath caught in his throat, like the smallest sound would spook her, the way it would a tentative stray cat.

She nodded around the Garrison. "This was them."

Rylan's eyes widened. "They died in the Berregard Garrison fire?"

"That was twenty years ago," Kira said. "How is that possible?"

"Guys," Peter said, with an edge of sharpness.

Sephiri caught his eyes and her lips quirked up in a small show of gratitude. "They were soldiers, both of them," she continued, her gaze growing distant as it returned to the fire. "Twenty years ago, they got lost on a mission. The Straith range is so big and wild. They ran out of water. It grew cold, deep in the mountains, so they found a small cave to stay in." She paused with her lips slightly parted. "In the cave was a spring. Mother always said it was the most beautiful spring she'd ever seen in her life. The clearest water, cold and refreshing, rushing from the depths of the earth. Like it waited for them. Both

Mother and Father drank from the spring, then refilled their canteens."

Peter and the other two listened with rapt attention. Even Rylan was silent.

"After drinking the water, they felt different," Sephiri said. "Mother sensed the breeze—like they were connected. She could tell it where to go and what to do, even helping her to be lighter on her feet."

Peter thought of Sephiri on the stairs of the tower, her steps silent despite the creaking rotted wood.

"Father understood the mountain range better," Sephiri said. "He could discover paths he hadn't seen before and find their way out with ease. He said it was like the stones in the mountains told him where to go." She pulled her knees a little closer to her chest. "When they made it back here to the Garrison, their commander punished them for getting lost. Corporal punishment. He wanted to make an example of them to the other soldiers, so he pulled Mother aside to lash her."

She swallowed.

"Was she okay?" Kira breathed. "Your mother?"

"Father begged the commander to stop," Sephiri said. "But he wouldn't. Mother was tough, Father always said, and hard to break, but the lashings were brutal. He got mad."

"Mad," Rylan echoed.

"Yeah. Mad. And his power brought the Garrison down."

Peter's eye widened. "Like the tower?"

"Sort of," Sephiri said. "He could manipulate stone. He didn't know it at the time, but that was his power. His anger activated it—grabbed the stones out of the walls and ceiling and pulled it down, killing the commander. The hearth broke open and caught the hay bales on fire. After that, it was out of control."

"Whoa," Kira said.

Peter swallowed hard, looking at the large crack in the hearth. "What happened to them?"

"They ran then hid," Sephiri said. "They left Palenting for a few years, until the constable stopped looking for them. When they returned, they kept a low profile. Eventually, they got married, and then had me. When I was a young girl, they told me stories about the Amulet, which gave special powers to people. I thought it was just that—bedtime stories. I didn't know they had powers of their own until I turned ten. That's when I found out I had something, too."

"It just showed up?" Kira asked.

Sephiri nodded. "My parents called it the Source. I could control the wind, like Mother. I didn't tell them the power had shown up, though. I was playing with my friends who lived near us, making little tornadoes out of the dust. I didn't realize it was special. I was just a kid." She closed her eyes and propped her chin on her knees as she spoke. Her brows pulled together. "I didn't know I was supposed to hide it."

Peter's heart sank to the floor. "Someone was still looking for your parents."

Sephiri nodded. "Rumors started about what I was doing." She paused. "Mother heard the soldiers coming at night. She pulled me out of bed and told me to go to the neighbors' house and hide in their storm cellar. She said no matter what I heard, I was to stay in the cellar until dawn. I remember how dark it was. And how cold. I plugged my ears, but I could still hear the screaming."

"Seph," Peter murmured. "I'm so sorry."

Sephiri cleared her throat and shook her head like she was shaking off the memory. "I came out at sunrise, and I've been on my own ever since. I moved in here not long after. It was the only place I could find with any semblance of shelter."

"Who killed them?" Kira asked. "And why would they do that?"

"Kamael Holcomb, the Lord of Defense for Palenting." Sephiri's words were distant, straightforward, like she explained a fairy tale instead of the death of her own parents. "He was afraid of what he didn't understand. Or wanted revenge. Or both."

"How long after that was it when we stumbled into you here?" Peter asked. "A year?"

"Around two."

"And we never had any idea." Kira shook her head. "I'm so sorry, Seph. I wish you would have told us."

Silence fell over them again. Sephiri sniffed hard, then cleared her throat and stood. She was unsteady on her feet, rocked to one side, and her eyes lost focus. Kira jumped to her feet faster than Rylan with his twisted ankle and caught Sephiri by the shoulder. "You okay?" she asked. "What happened?"

"It's fine. I'm fine. Just a little dizzy."

Kira walked her to the table and sat her down next to Peter.

"Maybe she needs some food," Peter said. "Do we have any left?"

Kira pulled out the remains of their lunch and handed some jerky to Sephiri.

She took a grateful bite. "Sorry," Sephiri said. "It's normal. I don't use the power a lot, and after I do, I'm always weak for a while. It'll pass."

"Is that what happened in the tower?" Peter asked. "You passed out?"

"I think so," Sephiri said. "I don't remember. I keep it hidden, so I was out of practice. There was so much weight to hold up . . . I could only do it for so long."

"You saved our lives," Peter said. "We owe you."

"Don't tell anyone about it," Sephiri said. "Please." She kept her gaze low as she took another bite of her jerky, like she waited for bad news.

"Of course we won't," Kira said. "We never would. We wouldn't risk anyone finding out."

"Definitely not," Rylan said from where he remained in front of the fire. "I think it's cool, for what it's worth. I wish I had powers like that."

Sephiri glanced up. The furrow in her brow smoothed out.

"Totally," Rylan said. "Do you get to choose what you get? If I found the spring, could I be like, 'thank you Source, please give me fire powers!' and then get them?"

Sephiri laughed, bright and sudden, then hid the sound behind her hand. "I don't think that's how it works."

"So it's more like the Amulet is supposed to be, right?" Kira asked.

"Mother and Father always thought the Amulet was real because the stories seemed so similar to what they had experienced," Sephiri said. "Mother assumed the same power created it, whatever that power was."

"If that's true," Peter said, "then we definitely can't let Razor get it first."

"Razor with power like Seph's . . ." Kira said, her voice trailing off. "He'd be able to intimidate my father a lot better, that's for sure."

"He'd do that to everyone. That's why he's so intent on getting it." Peter drummed his fingers on the table. "He'd run Palenting." The thought made his blood run cold. *Would he come for Sephiri, too? Could he know about her?*

"I need to think." Kira stood and strode across the Garrison to her bow and arrow. She spun an arrow over her fingers, then notched it into the bowstring and let it fly to the target. *Thwock.* "Remember what the tablet said?"

"'The Shepherds' Sword will hold the key,'" Peter recited. "Any ideas on what it means?"

"The Shepherd's Pride related to the tower icon." Kira

loosed another arrow. "The wave led us to the underground passage. Maybe the Sword is connected to the squiggly line."

"A snake," Rylan said. "Maybe the symbol is a viper."

"Did the Vipers exist when the Amulet was made?" Peter asked. "Is that in the book?"

"More research," Rylan moaned. He flopped flat onto his back again. "I'm so sick of research."

*Thwock.* "Would you rather a tower collapse on your head again?" Kira asked.

"I'd rather have a cool power like Sephiri to prevent tower collapses."

"That cool power is called paying attention to obvious warnings."

"Come on, Peter," Rylan said, "wouldn't you want an amazing power?"

"Who wouldn't?" Peter asked. "Imagine how much easier farm work would be if I were crazy strong. I could harvest all by myself."

"Wow, think big," Rylan said.

"You'd really want to risk it?" Sephiri asked. "Having a power that could get you killed?"

"There are a lot of things in Palenting that can get you killed," Peter said. "At least if I had power like you, I might make a difference somehow. Like you did today at the tower."

Sephiri flushed and stared down at her lap. Hair fell from behind her ear and covered the side of her face, blocking a faint smile.

A warm feeling rushed through Peter's chest. His pulse quickened. He was struck with the sudden urge to reach for her, but instead, he cleared his throat and stood. "So, um, Kira, was there anything in the Eanith book about swords?"

*Thwock.* Kira set her bow down and retrieved her arrows from the target. "Tons," she said. "Everyone had swords back then."

"So, where do we start?" Peter grabbed a few throwing knives, then stood next to Kira and took turns with her. For every arrow she loosed, he threw a knife with his uninjured arm. His accuracy was not as good as hers, but at least the blades stuck into the target. "Back at the library? Or should we ask a blacksmith if they know anything?"

"I've got an idea," Kira said.

"Please, no more libraries," Rylan said.

"So you know how my family funds that museum in Paratill View?"

"Yeah, of course," Peter said, "but I've never been there."

"Mother is the curator. It's right near the center of the neighborhood. There's a lot of stuff there, old armor and weapons and stuff—we can see if there are any swords that were owned by Ambrose Shepherd or someone related to him. We should all go on Weekterm."

"They'll let us in there?" Things in Paratill View were not technically closed to people from Lowside, but getting turned away was often to be expected. Especially to people like Peter—dirty, with patched-up clothes and empty pockets.

"With me, you will be," she said. "Father will be thrilled. He's always telling me to"—her voice dropped into a teasing, low imitation—"'pay more attention to our storied history.'"

"At least in Paratill View, we'll only get beaten up by Ashton instead of Vipers," Rylan joked.

"Seph can protect us," Kira teased.

"About that." Sephiri stood up from the table, steadier on her feet. "You all say you'd like to have special powers." She paused, scanning the room as the others leaned forward. "Were you serious?"

## 14

P eter chuckled, a nervous laugh while he pondered her question. "Um . . . yes, I was serious."

"My parents looked for the spring again," Sephiri said, crossing the room to where an intact, moss-covered staircase led up to a wide balcony on the west side. "After I was born, father went back into the Straith Mountains to find it again. Mother didn't want him to, but he insisted. He couldn't get it out of his mind."

Peter and the others followed her up the stairs as she talked. A breeze hit him as he stepped onto the balcony that looked across the city. The backlit Dorthar Mountains rose in the distance, conspicuously missing the outline of the watchtower.

"Did he find it?" Rylan asked as he hopped up the last stair, stubbornly refusing Kira's help. Kira still had her bow over one shoulder and a few arrows in hand.

"Nope." Sephiri folded her arms over the banister of the balcony and gazed out toward the mountains. "He went back a few times. He thought his power, the connection to the stone, would guide him back to the spring, but no matter how hard he looked, he never found it again. It was like the cave disappeared. But . . ." She touched the thin leather strap around her neck.

"But the canteens," Peter said, leaning next to her, watching her intently. "You said they filled up their canteens."

Sephiri nodded. "They saved some of the water."

Kira and Rylan leaned against the wall of the balcony behind them, silent.

"After my powers showed up and my parents knew they were in danger, they told me everything. Then . . . they gave me this." Sephiri tugged the leather strap of her necklace. It fastened to a small vial, wrapped in leather and sealed with a wax-covered cork.

"The Source," Peter whispered.

"They said it was mine to do with what I wanted. I could pour it out and forget all about it, or I could save it." She turned around, her back to the balcony rail. The four of them faced each other in a small circle, with the waxing moon shining high above. The breeze brushed over Peter's skin, but his goose-bumps came from something else entirely.

"Are you sure you want it?" she asked.

"Uh, yes," Rylan said, staring at the vial. "Absolutely."

Peter pushed down a shiver of nerves. *What would it feel like? What would it do?* He nodded.

Kira bit the tip of her tongue between her teeth and furrowed her brow. "Are you sure this is how you want to use it?"

"No," Sephiri said with a small, self-conscious laugh. "I'm not sure. But . . . you three are my family, now. And I'm—" Her voice broke, and she rubbed one hand over her eyes. "I'm tired of doing this alone."

"You don't have to," Peter said. "I'll do it. I want a power. And it'll be easier to stay safe if we're all protecting each other."

"I'm in," Rylan said. "Kira?"

Kira swallowed, pushed a stray bit of blonde hair off her forehead, and then nodded once. "I will, too."

"What's it like?" Peter asked. "What does it feel like?"

"I don't know," Sephiri said. "I never drank it. I was born with it."

"I hope it doesn't hurt," Rylan said.

"Is there enough for all of us?" Peter asked. "That's all that's left of the water?"

Sephiri nodded. "Just a few drops for each of you. But that's all it should take."

"I hope I get flame control." Rylan closed his eyes and tilted his face up to the moonlit sky. "Please, please, flame control."

Sephiri tugged her necklace over her head, then pulled a small knife from her pocket and sliced through the wax sealing the vial. She uncorked it and handed it to Peter. "Just a few drops," she said.

Peter nodded. Despite its small size, the vial felt heavy and cool in his hand, as if the promise of power was a tangible weight. He lifted it to his lips and tipped a few drops into his mouth. He handed it to Kira—*don't want Rylan to chug all of it in excitement.*

Then he waited. For what, he wasn't sure. Pain? Sensation? Sparks dancing over his skin like Sephiri's in the tower?

But there was nothing. He felt the same.

Kira sipped a few drops, and then Rylan the rest before handing the vial back to Sephiri. She held it in her open palm for a long moment, then tucked it into her pocket. "Do you feel anything?" she asked.

Peter shook his head, then watched Rylan and Kira to see if they felt something different.

"Not yet." Rylan bounced on the balls of his feet. "How long do you think it takes? I'm ready. I really think I'm gonna get flame powers. I just know it."

Peter was about to give up and wander back downstairs

when an odd tingle grew in the center of his chest. He rubbed his palm over his sternum.

"I feel it, too," Kira said. She held her hand in the same place.

"Something's happening," Peter said. "It's working."

Rylan shook out his arms and grinned. "It's definitely working."

The sensation expanded, sharpened, until it was like tiny pinpricks against his bones, starting from his ribs and radiating outward. Goosebumps rose on his skin, and his heart raced as the Source worked. *What will it be?* He stared at his hands, half expecting to see sparks, but they looked as they always did: callused and dirt-streaked. *What power will I get? Will I get a power at all?*

As quickly as it had come on, the sensation ceased.

"What?" Rylan asked. "What happened? Where'd it go?" He patted himself down. "It just stopped. Why did it stop? Did we not drink enough?"

"Hush." Kira stepped closer to the balcony rail. "I can . . . Hmm." Her quick eyes darted around the landscape. She tipped her chin upward as the breeze rustled her hair. "I can tell what's changed."

"What is it?" Peter asked. "You got something?"

"It's odd." Kira pulled her bow off her shoulder and gripped it in hand. "It's like I can see further."

"You got better vision?" Rylan said with obvious disappointment.

"No, it's more than that. Look." She nodded toward a skinny tree growing determinedly on the balds, far enough away that the trunk looked no wider than the edge of a pintid. "You think I can hit that?"

"No way," Rylan said. "You're good, but you're not that good."

Kira notched an arrow into her bow and drew it back. She

sighted down the length of the shaft, pausing for a moment before she let it fly. The arrow soared through the air in a perfect arc. All four watched, holding their breaths as it approached the target. Too far away for them to hear the thunk, it landed dead center in the tree. Peter had to squint and lean over the railing to even see it.

"I'm that good now." There was no braggadocio in Kira's voice—she sounded awed as she stared at the tree. "The wind, the arc of the arrow, the tension needed. It just makes sense. With the Source, my brain works better now. A little faster."

"It's enhancing your best traits," Sephiri said. "Kira's always been smart."

"Now you're even smarter," Peter said. A new twitchy, tingling sensation crawled over Peter's skin. It wasn't like the initial feeling of the power entering him. It was a different, more familiar feeling—like he was antsy, over-energized. He bounced from foot to foot to resist the urge to pace.

"So that means no flames for me." Rylan flexed his arm, then kneaded the muscle of his bicep. "But I have an idea of what I've got."

"Ready to pick up boulders, huh?" Kira asked.

"How'd you know?" Rylan squawked.

"I don't need Source intelligence to figure that one out."

"What about you, Peter?" Sephiri asked. "Do you feel any different?"

Peter chewed his lower lip, then stared back out toward the arrow stuck in the distant tree trunk. "Hey, Kira. Do you want your arrow back?"

She shook her head. "It's so far away, it'd be too much trouble. I'll just grab a few more from home next time I'm—Peter?"

Peter gripped the balcony railing and hopped over to the other side, glanced down, let his feet dangle, and dropped. It was a far drop—longer than he'd normally take—but the antsy feeling racing in his muscles told him it'd be fine. He landed softly on the balls of his feet, then grinned up at his friends staring slack-jawed from the balcony. "I'll get it for you," he said. "Just a second."

He turned on his heels and ran.

He'd spent a lot of time in his life running. Every morning, he ran through the streets of Palenting, and he ran from Ashton and his friends when they tried to catch him and cause trouble.

*This feels different.*

The earth was spongy under his feet, pliant, like the ground itself propelled him forward. His blood sang with energy, and the wind chilled his lungs. He moved so quickly he felt he could leap from the ground and take flight. The speed thrilled him. He broke into laughter as he charged across the balds all the way to the narrow tree. Pausing for only a moment, he snatched the arrow then ran back just as fast.

He raced inside the Garrison just as Kira, Rylan, and Sephiri descended the stairs. He spun the arrow over his fingers, basking in their stunned expressions. "Did you see that? I'm fast! And I think there's more to it, I still feel like I can do stuff like . . ." He glanced around the Garrison and then rushed to the ropes hanging over the rafters. "Like this." He grasped the ropes in hand as he'd done many times before, but this time, it was easy to climb, even with a bandaged arm. It was like his body already knew what to do. He swung from one rope to another, hanging next to it with ease, then scrambled up to the top of the rafters they tied to. Easy as anything. He grinned down at them, lounging on the beam like a cat.

Below, Rylan wormed his fingers under one of the big slabs of rock from the damaged walls. With a grunt of exertion, he rocked the slab of rock where it sat in the dirt. Beetles skittered out from under it, and he yelped in surprise, leaping back. The rock fell back into the indentation in the dirt with a whump. "I can totally lift it," he said as Kira laughed. "I just don't want to disturb the bugs. And my ankle still hurts."

"Peter!" Kira called. "Come back down!"

"All right, all right." Peter eased his way back down the rope. Gone was the familiar rope burn on his palms and the ache in his shoulders from the climb. He felt light on his feet, still buzzing from the run. He considered going for a run again when a wave of exhaustion crashed over him.

"Oh." Kira pinched the bridge of her nose. "Oh, I see."

"Feeling it?" Sephiri waved Kira over to the table. "Come on, sit down. All of you."

Peter sat in front of the fire. He'd been so full of energy moments before, but he was suddenly worn out, like he'd hauled bricks at Jenkins' all day. "This happened in the tower, didn't it?" he asked. "It's why you passed out?"

"Yeah," Sephiri said. "Exerting a lot of power at once always comes with a crash. It doesn't last long, but it takes time to recover. Food helps."

"But, wow!" Kira propped her chin on her hand, elbow on the table. "It worked. Seph, it really worked."

"It's hard to believe," Rylan said. "I guess this means . . . the Amulet is real."

"Even if we don't find it, it was probably real once," Kira said.

"Do you think the Amulet will do anything different if we use it?" Peter asked. "Since we've all had the Source?"

Sephiri shrugged. "No one knows. Everything I knew about it was just myth. Rumor."

"All I know is that we need to find it." Kira stood up, unsteady on her feet just as Sephiri had been. "I'm going to review the Eanith book again tonight. Maybe I'll see something I missed the first time, now that I have the Source."

"Something about the Sword?" Peter asked.

She nodded. "Or anything that might give us a lead on the Amulet. I'll let you know what I find tomorrow. Meet me at the library?"

"I thought we were going to the museum on Weekterm," Rylan pouted. "Not the library again!"

"We should give the book back," Kira said. "Hopefully Wynna won't be too mad at us. She might have another good resource for us, too, now that we know what we're looking for."

Rylan groaned. "Peter, you go, and I'll cover for you at Jenkins'."

Kira rolled her eyes. "It won't take long, I promise."

The four of them parted ways outside the Garrison under the light of the moon. Palenting was quiet as Peter made his way back to Lowside to catch some sleep before he had to start another familiar workday. Tomorrow would be different—tomorrow he'd still have the sparking feeling of the Source in his chest. A secret. A secret that could change everything.

And the Amulet felt closer than ever. *The Shepherds' Sword.* He looked toward Paratill View. On the hill, the fine buildings stood in silhouette, quiet in the deep darkness of night. Was the weapon up in one of those dark buildings just waiting to be found? Peter's palms itched for it, to grasp a hilt and swing it overhead like he did in his fantasies.

*We're going to find it. I'm sure of it.*

## 15

The next morning, Peter met Sephiri and Kira at the town square. Rylan, as promised, headed to Brufec Heights to keep Jenkins appeased. Kira carried the red book, and Peter had the pyramid in his rucksack, just in case. They made their way back to the library. Kira offered them fresh breakfast rolls as they walked, and one for Peter to take to Rylan, too.

"How do you feel today?" Sephiri asked. "Any different?"

"Slept like the dead," Peter said as they climbed the steps to the library.

"I can definitely read faster," Kira said. "But I didn't find anything else in the Eanith book."

"Hopefully, Wynna will have something to help," Peter said. "As long as she doesn't ban us from the library for stealing a book."

"It's borrowing," Sephiri said. "That's what libraries are for."

"Um, sort of," Kira said.

Peter shouldered the door open and peeked inside.

In the early hour, the library was quiet. Wynna sat behind the circular desk in the center of the room, sorting a large stack of books. As Peter approached, she looked up and grimaced, then glanced over her shoulder. "Now's not a good time."

"Huh?" Kira asked. "It's the library."

"You should go," Wynna said.

"We've got to return a book," Peter said.

"Ah," Wynna said. "The one you stole?"

"Borrowed," Kira said. "But, yes, that's the one."

Wynna sighed and beckoned with her hand. "This way." She checked over her shoulder again and then guided the three of them through the winding stacks and around the edge of the library to the archival room. She unlocked the heavy door then ushered them inside. "Hurry, hurry, please." She closed the door behind them. The room was even dimmer than the rest of the library, with books on low shelves and glass cases lining the walls around a single long table in the center of the room.

"Wow," Kira said with awe, rushing to a case. "I didn't think you allowed patrons in here."

"We don't," Wynna said. "Touch nothing."

"I'm sorry about the book," Peter said. "We were in a hurry to leave last time and didn't realize we'd left with it."

Kira pulled the red-bound Eanith book from her bag and offered it sheepishly to Wynna.

"I know you were." Wynna took the book back with a frown and smoothed her hand over the cover.

"Why are we in here?" Sephiri glanced toward the door behind them. "Are we hiding?"

"There's someone here in the library researching the same topics you were," Wynna whispered. "I think it'd be best if you avoided him."

Peter's eyes widened. "He's here now?" *Razor?*

"All citizens of Palenting have equal access to the library," Wynna said. "And he is well within his rights to use our facilities, but I'd rather not have more trouble and mess on my hands. You understand me?"

"Of course," Kira said.

"We need your help again," Peter said.

Wynna blinked at the three of them. "More research, I assume? More research that will lead to trouble?"

"Have you heard of the Shepherds' Sword?" Peter asked.

Wynna's brow furrowed. "The Shepherds were a big family. I'm sure they had a vast armory."

"But was there a specific one?" Kira bit her lower lip. "Maybe one that was famous? Or had some kind of rumored power? I didn't see anything about it in the Eanith book, but we wondered if there might be any other records that might mention something."

"What are you kids looking for?" Wynna asked. Her eyes narrowed.

Peter glanced over at Sephiri and Kira. Kira shrugged, and Sephiri pressed her lips together.

"We think the Amulet of Power is real," Peter admitted in a quiet voice. Wynna had always been kind to him, and she'd been the one to find the Eanith book that led them to the tower. If anyone would know where to find the Sword, it'd be her. "Between what Eanith wrote, and some things we've found, I think we can find it. But we have to figure out what this Sword is, first."

Wynna's eyes widened. "What did you find in that Eanith book?"

"It's more than that," Kira said. Peter nudged her, and she shut her mouth.

"You kids don't need to be involved in all of this." Wynna took the Eanith book, unlocked one of the locked glass cases, and slipped the book inside. "You should take the information you found to the army commanders or the baron. If something like that is real, it needs to be put into safekeeping—not be the subject of a wild goose chase." She threw Peter a sidelong glance. "It's too dangerous."

*The city leaders getting their hands on the Amulet could be just as dangerous as the Vipers getting it,* Peter thought. "We can't trust anyone," he said.

"Please," Kira said. "Do you know of any sources? It's just research."

"Last time you said it was about migration." Wynna sighed. "But all right. I don't know of any resources off the top of my head, but I'll look. If I find anything, I'll pull it aside for you. Until then, keep your noses clean. All three of you."

Kira led them out of the archive room, around the edges of the library, creeping through the stacks to avoid any other patrons. "So much for that."

"Who was she trying to hide us from?" Peter craned his head over the stacks. "Do you think he's still here?"

Sephiri tugged at his shirt. "Get down! The last thing we need is to run into Razor now."

"Do you think it was him?" Peter crept toward the back of the library, where they started their research what felt like ages before.

"I don't care," Kira hissed. "Let's get out of here."

"Let me check." Peter ignored the whispered demands of Kira and Sephiri as he creeped toward the back of the library, light on his feet, with just a tiny spark of Source speeding him up. If Razor were back there, Peter wanted to know what he researched, and if he'd gotten any leads.

At the table in the back of the library, an unfamiliar man leaned over a scroll unfurled over the width of the table. His skinny arms braced against the surface. He stared at the parchment while small glasses slid down his nose. *What is he looking at?* Peter crept closer, craning his neck from where he stood on his tiptoes to see over the shelves.

It looked like an architect's drawing—building plans. He squinted. *Is it the Palenting Watchtower? Did they find something, or are they just looking into it after the collapse?* His nerves eased.

Maybe this was just a bureaucrat, here to do the requisite examination to discover the structural weakness that led to the collapse.

Then the skinny man looked up. Tattooed just under his collarbone, visible under the loose neckline of his shirt, was a skull and serpent.

*Viper.*

"What are you doing back here? Beat it!" the man snapped. His eyes narrowed as he leaned forward. "Hey, aren't you . . . ?"

"There you are, Will!" Kira rushed forward and grabbed Peter by the nape of his neck like he was a misbehaving puppy. "I told you to stay close to me. Didn't you hear me?" She turned a blinding smile to the Viper. "Sorry, sir, my cousin here is just so curious. He's always getting into people's business despite how much we tell him to mind his own—isn't that right, Will?"

"Um," Peter said, "sorry."

"I know you," the man said, his eyes narrow. "You're the Lancaster girl."

"Ha!" Kira said brightly. "That's nice of you to say. She's so pretty. I'm honored you would mix us up. Come on, Will, let's get home." She tightened her fingers around Peter's wrist and all but dragged him away.

"Wait," the man said. "Both of you, stop there."

"Sorry," Kira said, "in a bit of a hurry!"

The man moved to the other side of the table, leaving his materials behind. Shoot, Peter thought. *He's going to follow us.*

A window high in the library clattered open. A gust of wind swooped into the room and caught the parchment on the table, sending it and some loose notes cascading off the table. The man swore and rushed to snatch them off the floor.

"Go!" Kira said. They ran to the side door. Sephiri caught up with them along the way. Her eyes paled from the wind she'd summoned.

They slipped outside and hurried away, hustling west

toward Brufec Heights through the narrow streets instead of regrouping at the town square. At the corner near Jenkins' shop, Peter finally stopped and glanced over his shoulder to see if they were being pursued.

"You're as bad as Rylan." Kira bent over, resting her hands on her knees as she caught her breath. "That could've ended badly. And thank you, Sephiri. You saved our butts. You feel okay?"

"I'm fine," Sephiri said. "It wasn't much."

"He was looking at plans of the watchtower," Peter said. "Do you think the Vipers made the connection?"

"No idea," Kira said. "But the tower just collapsed. I can see why they might think that was suspicious."

"You can't do stuff like that, Peter," Sephiri said.

The sternness in her voice surprised him. "Like what?"

"Just barrel into situations like that," Sephiri said. "It's too dangerous now. For all of us."

"You sound like Wynna," he said, guilt curling cold in his chest.

"We have to be careful from now on," Sephiri said. "The closer we get, the more dangerous it's going to be. If the Vipers know what we're up to, they'll do anything to gain the knowledge we have."

"And now another one of their lackeys knows what we look like," Kira said.

Peter sucked his teeth. "Yeah, I guess so. And he called you the Lancaster girl."

"He might tell Razor he saw us," Kira said.

Sephiri nodded. Her eyes were their usual dark brown again, and fatigue lines marked her face. She said using the Source in a small capacity was fine, but clearly it still had an effect.

"We'll be careful," Peter promised. "And thanks—both of you."

Kira waved a hand dismissively. "Just another day on the job," she teased. "Go to work. See you at the museum tomorrow? You promise you won't be reckless and cause trouble?"

"Cross my heart."

"All right. Come on, Seph, let's get lunch." The two girls linked arms and strolled off like nothing had happened, heads tilted together as they chatted. Peter watched them walk away, guilt still sour in his throat as he headed into Jenkins' shop.

## 16

Aﬅer another long day of hauling bricks, Peter trudged home in the dim light of early evening. He resisted the urge to tap into the Source and speed up his pace. Rylan, to his shock, agreed with Kira that he'd been foolish to sneak up on the guy in the library. But Rylan also admitted he probably would've done the same thing.

By the time he made it home, the sun was low on the horizon, and his house was dark. He stepped into the kitchen, listening for any sounds. "Father?"

"Jason?" his mother called from the bedroom. "You're home late."

Peter pressed his eyes together. He didn't want to explain to his mother that Jason was still long dead. "Busy at work," he said. "Do you know where Father is?"

"Oh, that old dog. He said he'd be in the fields until dark. Can't seem to get that man to stop working." She laughed fondly, making her sound young. "Go get him and tell him to come in, will you?"

"Sure. Be right back."

Peter hurried out of the house and toward the fields. *Father's still working? This late?*

His father was deep in the field, reaping grain by hand with a scythe. Perspiration poured from his brow. Sweat and dirt stained his linen shirt from long hours of harvest. An old lantern hung on a post at the edge of the field providing barely enough light to see. "Father!" Peter called as he hurried into the field. "What are you doing?"

His father looked up, then offered Peter an exhausted smile. He leaned heavily on the scythe, then wiped his brow. "What does it look like, Son?"

"I thought you were going to borrow oxen." Peter stared wide-eyed at all the grain left in the field, and the bundles of reaped grain stacked up in a nearby wagon. "You've been harvesting all this by hand?"

"Gavin lost one of his oxen to illness this year. He doesn't have any to spare. It would've been nice, sure, but we can't count on our neighbors to carry us through."

"That's not what I meant," Peter started. "You said you were in good shape. I believed you were farther along. I could've been helping you. All day yesterday, I—I didn't realize . . ." His words faded as the gravity of his father's situation settled on him. *He won't finish in time. He won't have the money he needs.*

His father sighed and pinched the bridge of his nose. "It's about dark now. I'll finish tomorrow. With some luck, this harvest will be enough to cover our bill—enough to keep the farm, at least."

"They're coming on Marketday, Father! You're going to harvest and sell the rest of this in a day?" Peter stared at the grain still standing tall in the fields.

"I'll do what I can. We should head back inside, now, though. It's getting too dark for my tired eyes."

"Mother thinks I'm Jason again."

His father leaned the scythe against the wagon of reaped

grain. "She's having a good day otherwise. Just play along over dinner."

Peter's throat tightened. *I don't want to pretend to be my brother. She should recognize me. I want things to go back to how they were before the debt—before the sickness. Back when things were easy.*

Despite his exhaustion from a long workday at the mason's shop, Peter shook his head. "Let me work a bit out here. I can see well enough with the lantern."

After a long moment, his father heaved a sigh and agreed. "All right, Son. Not for long, though, you hear me? It's Weekterm tomorrow, and you need your rest as much as anyone else."

The lack of argument made Peter antsy. If his father wasn't pushing back on Peter stepping in after a workday, he might be a lot more desperate than he let on. "Of course."

"We'll leave some stew on the fire for you," his father said. "Make sure you eat something."

"Yes, sir. Father?" Matthias turned around and paused. "What will we do if we don't get the money we need from the harvest?"

His father frowned. He paused for a long moment and looked at the field. Finally, he turned back to Peter and nodded his head. "We'll get it."

Peter watched as his father walked back toward their house. The older man favored his left leg with his back rounded forward. In the dimming light of the early evening, Peter surveyed the field. There was a lot of grain to reap, but the pile in the wagon was substantial. *Maybe Father's right. Maybe this will be enough to get the clerk off our backs for long enough for me to find the Amulet. Long enough to make sure we never have to worry about coins again.*

As the sun dipped below the horizon, the flickering flame of the lantern lit the field just enough. He gripped the smooth handle of the scythe and began the rhythmic work of the harvest: slice, gather, bind, add to pile, repeat.

He worked until the sun dropped well below the horizon. The field glowed with the orange flicker of the lamp and the white light of the waxing moon. His eyes hurt from squinting, and his shoulders ached from the repetitive swinging of the scythe, but it was easier than normal. Without even knowingly using the Source, he felt better, stronger, and more resilient. At the pace he moved, he hoped his father wouldn't have to spend all the next day trying to finish in time. He grinned. *We might do this after all.*

"Look what we've got here, boys. This is going to be even easier than I thought."

Peter whipped around, surprised to hear a sneering voice cut through the silence and his circling thoughts. His stomach lurched.

Ashton scowled at him in the cleared area of the grain field, like he owned the place. Dressed in dark cotton, he blended into the dark night, as did Tanner and Hodge behind him—as if they'd planned their outfits.

"What are you doing in Lowside?" Peter snapped, already suspecting the answer.

"Just wanted to pay you a visit," Ashton said. "You thought you could get away with that little stunt you pulled? That there wouldn't be any consequences?"

"Stunt?" Peter echoed. "You mean when you dropped your pants in the middle of Dulran Yard?" He grinned at the memory. It didn't surprise him that Ashton had shown up for revenge, but it had been worth it.

"It's not just a game," Ashton spat with surprising vitriol. "You don't get to humiliate me like that in the middle of Palenting. My father is the Lord of Commerce! People talk—not that you would know anything about that." His gaze burned with disdain. "You wouldn't know anything about building a reputation. You're stuck here in Lowside. For people like me, reputation matters."

"You started it." Peter crossed his arms over his chest. "I just defended myself. If you minded your own business, this wouldn't happen."

Ashton reached into his pocket and pulled out a small folding knife. He flicked it open, and the blade gleamed in the fluttering light of the lantern. "I mind my business. And I take care of my business."

Peter took a stumbling step back. Ashton had caused a lot of problems in the past, but he'd never pulled a knife or spoken with such undisguised fury.

"Whoa," Hodge said, "Ashton, are you sure—"

"Shut up!" Ashton snapped.

Hodge shut up. His face paled as he caught eyes with Tanner. They both looked unsure, but held their ground at Ashton's sides. Peter kept his eyes trained on the blade in Ashton's hand, but no cold fear rose in his throat—nothing like what might've happened even a few days before. He wasn't scared. He felt like he was dealing with a spooked horse, a creature that might act unpredictably and cause annoying problems. But nothing he couldn't handle. He'd handled Ashton before. He'd handled the Vipers. And now the Source sparked in his chest.

"Go home, Ashton," Peter said. "I'm sick of fighting with you."

Ashton barked a laugh. "Cute. You think you can tell me what to do?"

"I've got work to do," Peter said. "Go back to Paratill View and tell your father you robbed a poor kid again. Would that finally make him proud of you?"

Ashton's eyes burned with rage.

*Oops,* Peter thought. *I think that hit a nerve.*

Ashton lunged forward, knife in hand and blade out. He

slashed wildly like he attempted to bushwhack his way through the brush.

The Source sparked through Peter, bringing with it a new rush of energy and clarity of vision. Ashton swung the blade in a high, messy arc, but it was as if it happened in slow motion—like Ashton dragged the blade through molasses. Peter ducked under it easily, sidestepping the attack, and Ashton lost his balance with the force of the blow. Ashton whirled on him and tried again, stabbing forward with the knife, but again it was so slow. *How is he moving so slowly?* Peter sidestepped that one, too. The movement put him in a perfect position to swat Ashton upside the head, or even land a strong punch right in his ribs. But he didn't. It felt like cheating. It was easier to just move again, out of the way, when Ashton slashed at him.

"How is he doing that?" Tanner said.

"Help me!" Ashton shouted. "Hodge, get him!"

Hodge lurched forward, reaching for Peter. The lumbering brute was even easier to dodge than Ashton. Peter spun toward Tanner, and dodged his attempted grab, too. He couldn't suppress the grin spreading on his lips. *This is so easy. How is this so easy?* Faint sparks tickled his skin as he moved, dodging a punch, a grab, hopping over a kick. It took all his self-control not to laugh in Ashton's face. *If he thought dropping his pants was embarrassing, this has to be worse.*

Soon, Ashton was red-faced and huffing with exertion. The knife fell from his hands and into the dirt after a clumsy swipe. Before he could retrieve it, Peter snatched it up. He offered it back to Ashton, handle-first. "Try again?"

Ashton glared at him, angry as a spitting cat. "I don't need that to kick your butt."

Peter shrugged. "Sorry. Just trying to help." He felt good, light on his feet and buzzing with energy. Ashton, Tanner, and Hodge all panted as they labored to catch their breaths, sweat beading on their foreheads and staining the underarms of their dark shirts.

Ashton shouted and then lunged at Peter again. Peter side-stepped, bouncing, so he was behind Ashton and in front of Hodge. Ashton whirled around and charged forward, shoulder first, aiming to plow into Peter and knock him to the ground. But Peter was still too quick, and he hopped to the side. Instead of careening into him, Ashton's shoulder rammed into Hodge's solar plexus and sent him stumbling backward.

Hodge cried out, and Ashton tumbled down into the dirt next to him. They narrowly avoided bashing their heads into the rickety wooden post holding up the lantern. Peter suppressed a laugh. *This is almost too easy.*

Ashton scrambled to his feet. He turned to face Peter, and Peter smiled as he prepared to dance around another sloppy attack.

But Ashton stood still. The anger on his face morphed into a mischievous look, sending an uneasy feeling through Peter. The rich son of a lord pulled the lantern off the post.

Peter's eyes widened. "Ashton . . . don't—"

With a wicked grin, Ashton tossed the lantern into the field, as casually as if he tossed a pebble into a lake.

"No!" Peter shouted.

The lantern shattered. Oil spread, and brought with it the flames, and then the flames licked the edge of the unharvested grain and caught.

It happened so fast—like an explosion. The dry grain burst into roaring orange flame, spreading wild and uncontrolled over the field that even Peter's Source speed couldn't follow. His heart stopped. His breath caught in his throat, and he stood frozen and wide-eyed as the harvest burned in front of his eyes. Burned, and burned, and burned.

"Come on!" Ashton spat. "Let's get out of here!" He turned on his heel and ran, not even waiting to see if his friends were behind. Tanner took off after him. Hodge stumbled backward briefly, staring at the flames licking toward the sky before he followed.

The heat seared Peter's skin. Sudden sweat broke through his stunned stillness, and he leaped into action. He rushed back to where he had been reaping grain, but the flames were already there, too. A wall of fire belched smoke as it destroyed the crops. *Just have to get to the wagon,* Peter told himself, glancing at the vehicle piled high with valuable harvested grain. *Need to get it out of there.* He staggered closer, shirt pulled over his nose and mouth to block the worst of the smoke from creeping into his lungs. Dizzying exhaustion spread through his body. Was it the smoke? The adrenaline crash? Or did he use too much Source to teach Ashton a lesson?

*Should've just punched him when I had the chance,* he thought. *Should've done something. Too busy showing off.*

He grabbed the handles of the wagon and tried to drag it closer to himself, but it wouldn't move. He pulled again, and again—*why isn't it moving?* The fire creeped closer. If it caught the wagon, there'd be nothing left. Nothing at all. No grain. No money. No farm. His eyes burned from the smoke as he heaved the wagon.

"Peter!" his father called. He rushed forward with a rag wrapped around his nose and mouth. He grabbed Peter by the back of his shirt and wrenched him back, away from the fire. "Get back!"

"Father, the harvest!"

His father stopped and scanned the scene. Moving quickly, he reached down and grasped the handle of the scythe, hauled it out from where it had fallen under the wheels, and tossed it aside.

The fire roared, growing closer by the second. "Come on!" Peter yelled. "Help me move it!"

He and his father both grabbed a handle and pulled. The wheels fought against them but began to turn.

"That's it! We can do it!"

The wagon rolled—too slowly. His father caught a faceful of smoke and devolved into a fit of coughing. The progress halted. Only a few more turns of the wheels, and it would be free of the field and the danger from the soon-to-be-burning crops. The fire continued to grow.

Peter strained at his handle. "Come on! Help me pull!" His father grabbed his handle again. Peter's feet dug into the soft earth. He moved, one step at a time. The acrid smell of burned grain filled the air. The blaze was only an arm's length away from the dry wood of the wagon. The wheels turned. A groan escaped Peter's lips as he pulled with all his strength. "One more good pull!"

A lone flame jumped from the field to the back corner of the wagon.

"No!"

The flame spread in an instant, consuming the dry harvest and the wooden boards of the wagon itself.

Peter's father dropped his handle and grabbed Peter by the upper arm, hauling him toward the house.

Peter didn't resist. He was stunned. *It's gone. It's all gone.*

"Your mother is filling buckets," his father snapped. "Go get some. We'll get this under control."

Blinking from his haze, Peter rushed toward the house and fetched the water his mother had left on the porch—there was no time to converse. He was sooty, sweaty, and covered in dirt. His body ached, his heart raced, and his chest burned. But when his eyes prickled, it was not from the smoke.

The harvest was destroyed. All they could do was contain the spread of the fire.

*What's the point?* Peter thought as he hauled a bucket closer.

*We'll never get ahead. Something will always go wrong. We'll lose the farm. We'll lose everything.*

Even with the Source filling him, everything at the family farm got worse. Every time he thought he was about to get ahead, something else went wrong. As he and his father worked to put out the fire, Peter's exhaustion weighed heavier and heavier on him. All he wanted was to have the freedom to strike out—to leave Palenting behind, knowing his parents would be safe and happy on their farm so he could start his own life. *I'm not meant to be doing this,* he thought as he shoveled dirt onto the smoldering ashes of their grain field. *I'm meant to be out in the world. Adventuring. Traveling. Rising in the ranks as a soldier. Doing anything but this.*

But how was he ever supposed to escape Palenting when every day a new weight tied to his ankles, dragging him down? With a burned harvest, they'd never have enough to pay off the clerks. They'd lose the farm. They'd lose everything.

*And it's all my fault.*

---

## 17

Despite the exhaustion from using the Source and putting out the fire, Peter hardly slept. He skipped his morning training and dragged himself out of bed long after the sun had risen. Even though it was Weekterm and the rest of the city would take the day off, they had a lot of work to do. He dressed and cleaned up as best he could. Soot remained under his nails, despite scrubbing in his room's basin.

As he cleaned up, low voices sounded in the kitchen. It didn't sound like his mother, and it was too quiet to be someone from the city. And no one from the commerce office would come to the house on Weekterm. *Who would come to see us so early? Wynna?*

Peter stepped out of his room and down the hall into the small kitchen. He expected to see Wynna or another one of his neighbors asking about the fire, but to his surprise, it was Kira, Sephiri, and Rylan seated around the rough-hewn table.

"Oh," Peter's father said with surprise. "I didn't realize you were still home. I told your friends you were likely out running."

"Skipped it this morning." Peter rubbed the back of his neck. "Too tired."

"That's good," his father said. "You don't rest enough as it is. I'm fixing some eggs right now, and there's bread and butter on the table. Your friend, Kira, brought it."

Kira flashed a tender smile from her seat.

The kindness in his father's voice only made Peter feel worse. His father should be furious, chewing him out for taunting Ashton and encouraging the fight. Anger would make sense. The calm, sad acceptance was worse. "I'm not hungry."

"Of course you are. Sit down."

"What happened?" Sephiri asked. "You weren't at the museum this morning. Then in the town square, people talked about a fire in Lowside late last night. And we saw . . ."

"Yeah." Peter sank low into the chair. "It's not looking good."

"It'll be fine," his father said. "I'll speak with the commerce clerk. We'll figure something out. It'll be all right."

"How?" Peter asked.

"Let me worry about that." The tension in his father's shoulders made Peter doubt the veracity of his words. He set his elbows on the table and pushed the heels of his hands into his eyes.

"How did it start?" Sephiri asked, her eyes soft.

"The lantern," his father said. "I never should've let you work under that lantern's light. You could've been killed."

"It wasn't just the lantern," Peter said. "Ashton and his friends showed up."

"Ashton?" Rylan asked. "He showed up *here*? At your house? Is he crazy?"

Peter nodded. "He was angry with me and wanted to teach me a lesson, I guess. He had a knife."

"A knife?" Rylan repeated, his eyes huge. "Getting pushed around is one thing, but come on!"

"Yeah, and so we were fighting, and I . . . well, I thought I was winning. But I guess I egged him on a bit. He got angry, and then instead of trying to fight me, he grabbed the lantern by the field and smashed it."

He caught Sephiri's eye. She ducked her chin in acknowledgment. Kira sighed. *They know what I mean. They know I used the Source.*

"You should report them to the authorities," Kira said. "This is a lot more than Ashton just being an irritant around town."

"We should beat him up," Rylan said. "Teach him he can't just get away with stuff like this! I mean, he destroyed your entire harvest!"

"The last thing you kids need to do is get involved with the Dunn boy." Peter's father set a shallow bowl of boiled eggs on the table to cool.

"Mr. Fairfield, you can't just let him off the hook!" Kira said.

"We have to, Kira," Peter's father said. "Ashton's father is the Lord of Commerce."

"What does that matter?" Kira huffed. "He caused all this damage. There has to be something we can do."

"We owe money to them," Peter said. "And Ashton already hates me. No one would believe us. Ashton will just deny it, and everyone will believe him."

"You kids don't need to get involved with things like this. I'll take care of it. What's this about going to the museum?"

"They can go without me," Peter said. "I'll help clean up."

"We can all help," Rylan said. "Ashton's always after all four of us, not just Peter. I feel like it's sort of my fault, too."

Sephiri and Kira nodded in agreement. "Yeah, we can help. It'll be faster with all of us."

Peter's father sighed and shook his head. "Absolutely not. It's Weekterm."

"But you'll be working," Peter said.

"I own this farm," his father said sternly. "With your mason jobs, you'll make your own careers away from here."

*Unlikely,* Peter thought sourly to himself. *We're not learning any masonry. We're just brick makers. I'll be stuck as a day laborer, unable to leave this town.*

"Go to the museum," his father insisted. "It's been too long since you've been in school. Go learn something. That's a good way to spend your Weekterm."

Peter's three friends looked to him to decide.

With eyes on him, he stood, his body aching with soreness. He selected a piece of bread from the plate and took a bite. It was warm. Its scent filled his nose, and his taste buds celebrated. He stepped to the door and slid on his boots.

"I love you, Father, but . . . I'm going to work for a bit." He turned to his friends. "Sorry, but I'll catch up with you all later." Without waiting for a response, he exited the door and headed toward the field.

The morning air held on to its chill as his feet crunched across the ground. The acrid smell of charred grain filled the air the closer he got to the field. He picked up a shovel on the way, then stood at the edge of their land, surveying the work to be done. Wet ash, dirt, mud, and charred remains filled their property. *This is going to take some time*, he thought, his shoulders falling.

Footsteps approached from behind. He spun. Sephiri stepped up with a sweet smile on her face. She gathered her hair and tied it back with a ribbon. Rylan came next, using a hoe like a walking stick. Kira took short steps as she tied up the hem of her skirt, keeping it out of the dirt.

His father arrived last, carrying a shovel of his own and shaking his head. The smile on his face told Peter everything. As much as he insisted Peter go, he was thankful for the help.

"All right then," Peter said. "Let's do this."

. . .

WITH A GROAN, Peter dropped his load of charred grain onto the wagon. He turned and leaned against the remains of the wooden vehicle, sweat dripping from his nose and arms. He scanned the field. They'd worked hard for three hours straight, and the work was nearly done. Barely a handful of useable grain survived—not enough to even put a dent in their debt.

"You didn't have to do this," his father said, stepping up and handing him a jug of water.

Peter drank, letting the cold water flow down his throat, replenishing the fluids he'd lost. He smacked his lips and returned the top to the jug. "I know I didn't . . . but I could."

"Your friends . . . they're something else."

Peter smiled. Sephiri finished gathering a pile of burned crops. Kira pulled on the hoe, digging into the ground to mix in the charred soil. Rylan approached the wagon with his arms filled. Soot smeared his cheeks and forehead.

"How'd you stay so clean?" Kira asked, leaning on the hoe and staring at Peter.

"Me?" Peter asked, looking down at his clothes. Ash and dirt stained his shirt, and his hands looked nearly black.

"What do you mean?" Rylan asked as he dropped his load on the pile. "He looks pretty dirty to me."

"Not compared to you, he doesn't," Kira said. "I'm talking about his face."

"I tried not to touch it," Peter said. "I figured if I—"

A clod of charred debris hit him in the side of the head, jerking his attention. Sephiri stood a short distance away. Her body swayed over her pile of burned scraps. She moved another clod from her left hand to her right while a mischievous grin tugged at her face.

Peter's jaw dropped. "Did you . . . ?" Peter looked between his other friends. Kira covered her mouth with her hand, stifling a laugh, and Rylan only stared with wide eyes. "Oh, no," Peter said, turning back to Sephiri. "That's not going to fly."

He fumbled in the cart, finding a small piece of rubble then flicking it toward her. Sephiri ducked, her joyous laugh bouncing over the field. Her other clod whizzed toward him, hitting the center of his chest.

"That's it," he said, turning around and scooping what he could from the cart. Kira and Rylan both scurried to grab handfuls of charred projectiles.

Sephiri lobbed ash-covered loads from her stash. Rylan ducked behind the wagon wheel, but Peter left the safety of the vehicle, charging at her with a yell and a smile.

Sephiri yelped and ran. Peter threw handful after handful at his fleeing foe, running after her as she snaked across the field. Most of the loads missed, but a few found their target, bouncing harmlessly off her back.

A root snagged her foot, and she cried out as she fell to the ground. Peter drew up short, his desire to attack replaced with concern. When she rolled over on her back, laughing hysterically, his worried expression turned playful again. He held the rest of his debris in the air, dangling it over her prone body with both hands.

"You thought you could attack me with no retribution, huh?"

Her laugh settled, her infectious smile warming his heart. She closed her eyes and held her arms apart. Her grin invited him to do his worst.

With a chuckle, he tossed his handful to the side and bent over to extend her a hand. "That was just mean," he said as he helped her up.

She shrugged. "I didn't want Rylan showing you up as the more dedicated worker. That's all."

"I thought you all were here to help *clean* this mess?" Peter's father said with a laugh. "But seriously . . . thank you all. I couldn't have done this without you."

"Peter would have done the same for us," Rylan said, "without question. We're here for him and for you anytime."

"I'm serious when I say . . . I can take care of the rest," his father said, nodding his head as his look bounced between the four friends. "Please, enjoy the rest of the day before it's gone. I insist."

Peter took a deep breath. "All right. Kira, will your mother still be at the museum? Is it too late?"

"She should be there," Kira said. "We *might* want to clean up first, though."

## 18

A fter a period of time at the nearby stream and using a few rags to scrub their faces and arms, the four friends made their way across town toward the museum. They finished the bread and eggs from breakfast as they walked, wandering through the town square and north into Paratill View.

"Your father mentioned something about being able to take care of his payments with the city," Sephiri said. "Is he right?"

"I don't know." Peter sighed. "He doesn't tell me anything."

"Well . . . hopefully we can figure something out at the museum," Kira said. "We'll find out what the Shepherds' Sword is and be one step closer to the Amulet."

Peter nodded. He didn't know how finding the Amulet would help him save the farm, but he didn't know what else to do. He had to believe it would fix things. Somehow. *It's the only idea I have.*

"Did you at least get Ashton back?" Rylan asked.

He bit back a smile and shrugged. "Maybe a little. You should have seen him trying to stab me. I was dancing all around him and his pals." He chuckled. "It *was* pretty funny."

The museum was tucked a few blocks away from the library. It was a large and impressive building, built of the finest white stone with elegant decorative columns and a heavy wooden door. Kira bounced up the steps like she owned the place.

Sephiri and the boys were more hesitant.

"Come on," Kira said. "Mother's expecting us."

"That's what I'm worried about." Rylan tugged at the collar of his ratty cotton shirt, still damp from sweat and tinged with ash. "Are we even going to be let in?"

"The museum is public," Kira said. "Anyone's allowed in."

"That's what they say," Sephiri said. "But I've never been inside."

"Me, neither," Peter said. The museum was just another one of the many impressive buildings in Paratill View to which he wasn't privy. He couldn't imagine ever being allowed in without Kira to guide them.

"Plus, it's Weekterm," Kira said. "There won't be many people here. Quit being shy, this is our best bet to figure out where to go next."

Peter sighed and started up the stairs.

"Peter, wait," Sephiri said.

He turned around. Sephiri pulled the sleeve of her shirt over her knuckles and rubbed something at his hairline. Her dark eyes focused on a spot, and she bit the tip of her tongue between her teeth in concentration. Peter stood still, ignoring the odd swoop in his chest as she worked.

"There," she said, stepping away. "You can't go in there looking like a chimney sweep."

"There's only so much I can do about it." Peter grimaced at his sooty nails. "I should go to the bathhouse."

She held up her hands, showing the identical black nails. "I think we could all use that."

Kira pushed the heavy door open and waved them inside. Rylan, cringing, motioned for Peter and Sephiri to go first.

The museum was quiet and still. Sun streamed in from a skylight high above, while lanterns along the fine stone walls added even more light. Peter grimaced as his shoes tracked dirt across the dark, polished wooden floors. The museum contained four stories, each with rooms built off the main lobby, filled with things Peter had only heard about. It contained animal life, recreations of old architecture, armor, weaponry, textiles, paintings, sculptures . . . things that defined life in Terrenor through the years. Overhead, in a winding path around the skylight, an enormous skeleton of a sea serpent hung with its jaws open. The wealthy citizens of Palenting funded the museum, and the Lancasters were high on the list. Kira's mother worked as the museum curator.

"There you are," Mrs. Lancaster said, calling from down the hall. "I wondered if you four chose to spend your day gallivanting in Schuggec Row instead." Her shoes clacked on the floor as she approached.

Just being near her made Peter straighten his posture. Mrs. Lancaster was tall and elegant. Her silvery-blonde hair was pulled into a low, tight bun that made her sharp features look even more dramatic. Her navy silk gown looked finer than anything he'd ever seen Kira wear. Golden embroidery even matched the rings on her fingers. *I'd get in trouble for just breathing on her, if I met her anywhere else.*

"Sorry, Mother," Kira said.

"Gah! You're all filthy!" Mrs. Lancaster held her hand to her chest. Her eyes danced between the four kids.

"It's my fault—" Peter began.

"It's no one's fault," Kira said quickly. "We all worked on the Fairfields' farm this morning. We tried to clean up, but . . ." Her words faded.

"You should have seen us a bit ago," Rylan said with a laugh.

The stern expression on Mrs. Lancaster's face did not crack. "You're lucky it's Weekterm. Otherwise, I'd shoo all four of you out." She turned to her daughter. "And you are going home to change immediately after this."

Kira nodded.

Mrs. Lancaster's shoulders relaxed, and she sighed. "But it's my pleasure as curator to introduce curious young minds to the history of Terrenor. Just . . . don't touch anything. We'll start here on the lower level, which is an exploration of the natural flora and fauna of the various kingdoms. This way."

Mrs. Lancaster led them into the first room on the ground floor, which was a recreation of a cave filled with stuffed bats, lizards, and glimmering crystals. Fake ones, Peter assumed, even as his eyes widened.

"Here we have an accurate rendition of the depths of the Straith Mountains," Mrs. Lancaster began. "As you can see, the makeup differs from the stone we're familiar with from the Dorthar Mountains. The difference can be traced to thousands of years ago . . ."

"Hey," Rylan whispered as they leaned over the railing by the recreation, peering at a stuffed bat clinging to a stalactite. "Did Ashton really show up with a knife?"

"Yeah," Peter whispered back. "He was furious. I've seen him annoyed plenty, but nothing like that."

"Guess we've got another thing to be worried about, then. And he really burned the field on purpose?"

Mrs. Lancaster led them out of the cave room and into the next one, a lush forest setup. Her droning voice was easy to tune out.

"I was messing with them," Peter admitted. "Using my speed to dodge them. Ashton got mad when he couldn't catch me. He had this stupid grin on his face when he smashed the lantern. He knew what he was doing."

"I didn't think he'd sink that low," Rylan murmured.

"I should've known, though. I should've just let them beat me up so they'd leave me alone." He sighed. "But what's the point of even having the Source if nothing good ever happens?"

"You didn't get stabbed," Rylan said. "I'd count that as a good thing."

"Boys!" Mrs. Lancaster snapped. "Pay attention! This way, to the coastal exhibit."

Sephiri and Kira threw them a look.

"I know enough about the coast," Rylan muttered. He looked a little sheepish. "Father would never shut up about the wonders of the sea." His expression pinched, and he was quiet as Mrs. Lancaster explained the currents on the coast of Terrenor and the formation of the Isle of Paratill.

Mrs. Lancaster led them up the stairs to the second level of the museum, where she talked them through the sculpture hall with its white stone carvings of tall men and women brandishing swords and grappling with beasts. Stories that should've been exciting—like narratives of soldiers beating the odds and saving their cities from certain doom—were flattened into monotony by the dry tone of Mrs. Lancaster's voice.

The third floor contained furniture replications. Peter considered jumping off the balcony when Mrs. Lancaster explained the history of chair glue. Finally, they climbed the stairs to the fourth story.

"And here we house our collection of ancient armor and weaponry," Mrs. Lancaster said.

Peter perked up.

"The Palenting Museum has a vast collection of historical material from all over Terrenor, both original and recreations."

"What's over there?" Rylan asked, pointing to the far end of the hall, where two armed soldiers in leather armor guarded an enclave. The men yawned, looking bored as they watched the five of them.

"Ah, that's one of the prized acquisitions of the museum," Mrs. Lancaster said. "Well . . . acquisition is the wrong word. It's on loan from the capital. Step closer."

Peter hurried to the enclave with Mrs. Lancaster's heels striking the wooden floor behind them. The guards stepped to the side, hands clasped behind their backs but still in easy reach of the swords on their hips. Glass blocked off the enclave, and behind it sat a pedestal with a fine black silken pillow displaying four sparkling jewels. Shades of rich blue, red, green, and purple glittered behind the glass. Peter's eyes widened.

"The Jewels of Bromhill," Mrs. Lancaster said. "Gifted to the King of Rynor by the people of Kandis in the year 406, they expressed gratitude for the slaughter of the valcor that wreaked havoc along the Rynorian coast, devouring livestock and children alike."

"I thought valcor weren't real," Kira said.

"It's just the story of the jewels," Mrs. Lancaster said. "To have them here in Palenting on display is a great honor."

"Whoa," Rylan said. "What's over here?" He scurried into the room next door to the gems.

Peter followed. The room was full of weaponry: full suits of armor, both steel and leather, mannequins armed with javelins, knives, maces, and swords. So many swords. It wasn't really a room, though—the walls didn't reach the ceiling, acting more as dividers than walls. Vaulted above them, large wooden beams of the rafters and the fine bones of the sea-serpent skeleton looked down on the display. Peter and Rylan caught eyes, nodded, then went to opposite ends of the room. A tiny placard marked each suit of armor, displaying where the armor and weapons were from.

*Shepherd. Shepherd. There has to be a Shepherd in here*

*somewhere.*

"Of course, the boys aren't interested in the jewels," Mrs. Lancaster said, entering the weapons room with Sephiri and Kira.

"This is an amazing collection, Mrs. Lancaster," Sephiri said. She beelined to a beautiful hand-carved bow.

"These are the kinds of things we always have on display." Mrs. Lancaster's voice contained an edge of annoyance. "The rarities in this museum are much more worth our limited time."

Peter caught Sephiri's eyes, then nodded his head back toward the jewels, hoping she'd get the hint to lead Mrs. Lancaster away.

Sephiri wrinkled her nose.

"Please?" Peter mouthed.

Sephiri sighed, stuck her tongue out at Peter, and then turned from the bow. "I'm not so interested in these things," she said. "What were you saying about the jewels?"

"Ah, I knew we had a woman of taste in here." Mrs. Lancaster led Sephiri back toward the jewels. "Come, I'll show you the best way to identify the differences between them."

Kira, Rylan, and Peter all darted to different parts of the room. "Anything?" Peter whispered.

Kira stared up at the rows of armor. "There are a lot of swords."

"Well, gotta start somewhere," Peter said. Nothing he found had any special labels—just swords in various states of disrepair, handmade, used in battle, lost and forgotten.

"There must be something," Kira said. "Keep looking."

Nearby, Mrs. Lancaster droned on and on. *Yeah, I owe Sephiri one.*

"Peter!" Rylan motioned for them. "Kira! Look! Look here!"

They hurried over. Rylan stood before an imposing set of leather armor and a long sword mounted on a stand. It shone in the dim light, its carved wooden hilt oiled and gleaming. Tiny engraved letters ran down the blade itself.

"'Sword of Vicion Shepherd,'" Rylan read from the placard below the sword. "'Known as the Viper, he was famous for his formative skill on the battlefield, and his fearless defense of the city of Palenting.'"

"The Viper?" Kira said. "No way!"

"As in the Viper Syndicate Viper?" Peter asked.

"It doesn't say," Rylan said. "That's all it says."

"It has to be," Kira said. "This must be the founder of the Syndicate."

"But then why wouldn't they have the Amulet?" Rylan asked. "It belonged to the Shepherds."

Kira tapped her chin. "We need to find out how Vicion was related to Ambrose. There has to be a family tree somewhere. Something."

"There's something written on the sword." Peter leaned over the railing separating them from the sword. "It's so small, though."

"There is?" Rylan turned back to the sword and leaned over, too. "You're right! There's an engraving! Kira, can you read this?"

Peter gripped the rail and raised up onto his toes, trying to lean as close as possible. If he could just make out the writing on the blade, maybe it'd lead them to the Amulet's hidden location. *Just a little closer . . .*

"Peter Fairfield!" Mrs. Lancaster snapped. "No leaning over the railing!"

Peter stumbled backward, caught his balance, and then turned to grin sheepishly at Mrs. Lancaster. His pulse pounded. "Sorry. Just trying to get a closer look. There's some cool stuff here."

"That's quite enough in this room," Mrs. Lancaster said. "Come. Across the way, we have a fine collection of ceremonial crowns used years ago in Norshewa. Their origin stories will fascinate you."

The four of them followed Mrs. Lancaster into another section of the fourth floor. Peter tuned out her narration, as his attention was behind them in the armory room. He buzzed with excitement. *We found it. We found the Shepherds' Sword.* It was so close, but so impossible to get to. There had to be a way. The next clue had to be the writing on the blade. Peter was sure of it.

"Questions about any part of our collection?" Mrs. Lancaster threw a dark look at Peter and Rylan. "Not pertaining to the armory?"

"This was so great, Mrs. Lancaster," Sephiri said. "Thanks for showing us around."

"Yeah," Peter agreed. "Really fun. Thank you!"

They hustled back toward the stairs down to the main floor. "Kira, head home to clean up," Mrs. Lancaster called. "Mr. Hayes is bringing his son for dinner!"

Kira cringed as they burst out of the museum and back onto the street.

"Bringing his son, eh?" Rylan teased. "Kira's got a date!"

"We'll see how long he lasts in conversation," Kira muttered. "The men Mother chooses know nothing about history or archery or anything fun. They just want to talk about how rich their parents are."

"What do we do now?" Sephiri gazed back up at the top floor of the museum. It was midday, and the sun was high in the sky. "How are we going to figure out what's written on the sword?"

"I've got an idea," Peter said. He followed Sephiri's gaze up the exterior of the building. Windowsills and decorative sconces made a path from a balcony to the roof.

"I think I do, too," Sephiri said.

*After getting into the Viper Syndicate, this will be a snap.*

## 19

A s soon as the house had quieted for the evening, Peter crept out of bed. His parents were sound asleep. His mother might stir, but it'd take the house collapsing to wake his father, especially after all the cleanup work he had done during the day.

Outside the house, the burned field was clear. The wet scent of ash and soot sat thick in his nostrils. Guilt chewed at him as he hurried past the field and into the barn, where he grabbed two coils of rope and slung them over his shoulder. *Feeling guilty won't fix anything*, he thought to himself as he tied his boots tighter. *But the Amulet might. If anything, I could sell it. That'd at least make enough to keep the farm.*

With his ropes secure across his chest, Peter headed toward the town square. In the depths of the evening, the town was quiet, save for a few pubs at the edge of Lowside still humming with drunken gammit games and drifters with nowhere else to go. At the town square, he met Rylan, Sephiri, and Kira, all dressed in dark clothes and grinning nervously. All three were silent—nothing needed to be said.

They made their way back into Paratill View. Lit by dim

lanterns mounted high above the streets, there was no activity on the streets. The stillness heightened Peter's nerves, and he hitched his ropes higher on his shoulder as they stopped next to the wall of the museum.

"We'll have to move quickly," Kira whispered. "We're in plain view out here."

"There's no one around," Rylan whispered back. "We'll be fine. Better to do it right and not fall."

"I'm great at not falling," Sephiri said with a smile. Her voice had an edge of renewed confidence, a tone Peter wasn't familiar with. But it was nice. It suited her. *Must've been difficult hiding her power all this time.*

"Everyone remember the plan?" Peter whispered.

The three of them nodded.

"Let's move fast," he said. "In and out. They'll never know we were here."

"They really can't," Kira whispered. "It'll be worse than the stocks if we're found out." Even in the dim light, she looked pale.

"Don't worry. We're quicker than ever, remember?" Rylan grinned and nudged his shoulder against Peter's. "Especially this guy."

Kira didn't look convinced, but she nodded.

"Ready?" Rylan asked Sephiri.

She nodded. Peter took off a coil of rope and handed it to Sephiri. She looped it over her shoulder just as Peter had worn it. Rylan knelt down and laced his fingers together, creating a small platform. Sephiri placed her foot in the cradle of his hands and set her hand on his shoulders. She looked up toward a balcony, her dark hair falling down her back like a wave over the rough coil of rope.

"I don't know about this," Kira murmured with her arms crossed over her chest.

With a burst of energy, Rylan stood and flung his arms up,

sending Sephiri flying as if she weighed only a handful of feathers. Peter stepped back, staring slack-jawed as Sephiri soared upward. Sparks flashed on Rylan's arms from the use of the Source. A gust of wind rustled Peter's hair as Sephiri dropped onto the high balcony light as a feather. There wasn't even any sound of her feet hitting the stone. It was as if she'd floated up there, like a leaf on the wind.

"Told you," Rylan whispered.

"We're not out of the woods yet," Kira whispered back.

The three of them could only watch as Sephiri peered up at the exterior of the museum. She stood for a moment, hands on her hips, surveying the situation with the coil of rope over her shoulder. She squared her shoulders, then grasped one of the decorative sconces on the outside of the museum and climbed.

White stones jutted out of the wall of the museum, but it wasn't made for climbing. Peter's breath caught in his throat as Sephiri made her way upward. She was the best one to climb, of course, considering that she might control a fall—but that was a big maybe. Sephiri set her fingers in the small gaps in the stone and her toes on the decorations as she crept upward, spider-like.

As she neared the roof of the museum, her toe caught on a decoration. Beneath her foot, a stone sconce split and crumbled. Her foot cut out, and her grip tightened on the hold above her as she lost her balance. Kira gasped and slapped her hands over her mouth. Peter took a step forward, heart in his throat— as if he could do anything if she fell. The stone sconce tumbled down, clattering against the wall of the museum, bouncing off the railing of the balcony, then into the street. The crashing sound split the quiet evening like a clap of thunder.

With a hand holding on to the wall, Sephiri pulled her body into a shadowy depression.

"This way," Kira hissed. She grabbed Rylan and Peter by the sleeves and hauled them around the corner and into the narrow alley between the museum and the administrative building next to it.

"What?" Peter asked. "But Seph—"

"Shh!" Kira hissed. She pressed herself closer to the wall, eyes wide.

Peter peeked around the corner.

The door to the museum creaked open. An irritated-looking guard stepped out. He wasn't one of the leather-armored guards Peter had seen guarding the Jewels of Bromhill —this looked like just a regular citizen of Palenting, dressed in plain linen with a club on his hip. He could've been someone relaxing in a Lowside pub. The guard saw the sconce in the street, then stepped forward and nudged it with his toe. He glanced around. Peter jerked backward, holding his breath as he stared up at the dark sky.

"Nothing out here," the guard called. "Another one of those useless decorations came off. I keep telling the Lancaster woman she needs to get a mason out here to knock off the rest before they take a guest out, but no one listens to me, right?"

The door clanked shut. After a long moment of silence, Peter peered around the corner again.

The guard had taken the crumble of stone inside, and the street was empty. Peter stepped back out from the alley and peered up toward the museum roof.

As he looked up, Sephiri emerged from a shadow and hauled herself onto the flat roof of the museum. Peter suppressed the urge to cheer. *She did it!*

She peered down over the edge, grinning as she removed the coil of rope from her shoulder. Peter gestured for her to move to the other side of the roof, near the alley. The last thing they needed was for the guard to come back out and see the rope dangling as they climbed.

Sephiri nodded and shuffled away, disappearing from view.

Peter returned to the alley, where Kira and Rylan waited, staring up at the roof. Kira looked even more nervous.

"That was way too close," she whispered. "We should ditch now and try again later."

"No way," Rylan whispered. "She made it all the way up there! This might be the only chance we get."

"Especially if they take off the decorative stone," Peter said. "That's our only way in."

Kira chewed her lower lip. "Fine. But we need to move fast. Really fast."

"We will," Peter promised.

The rope dropped, the extra length landing with a thump in the alley at their feet. Sephiri peered over the edge of the roof and waved.

"It's on," Rylan whispered.

Rylan went first, then Kira, and Peter brought up the rear. With the rope, it was easy enough to climb the flat wall of the museum. Soon enough, all three crested the edge and stood safely on the roof.

Sephiri pulled the rope up. "I heard someone talking below," she whispered. "Who was it?"

"A guard," Kira said. "I don't know how many patrol inside, but we need to be careful."

"This is good." Peter inspected the wooden beam around which Sephiri had tied the rope. "This will work. Nice, Seph."

The skylight rested in the center of the roof. Peter grabbed the rope, still tied to the beam, and moved to the window. The moonlight shone down. With the dim light, he peered through the glass and down into the museum. It was shadowed inside, and still, with no movement from the guards. *Maybe they're on break,* he thought to himself. *Maybe they don't patrol at all.*

He unlatched the skylight and slowly lifted it up. The hinges creaked, the noise making him cringe. Kira poked her head through.

"Anything?" Peter asked.

She shook her head.

He lowered the skylight panel to the roof. Then he fed the rope down slowly so the extra length coiled onto the rafter below the skylight. "Let me go first," he whispered.

Kira swallowed. "You're sure about this?"

Peter nodded with a grin. "We're so close." He took the rope in hand, then climbed through the opening. Navigating the descent was easy, but he took extra care to ensure he didn't disturb the immense sea serpent skeleton winding around him like the bars of a cell.

His feet touched down on the rafter. There was still no movement on the ground floor of the museum far below. He motioned for the other three to join him, carefully managing the excess rope as they lowered onto the rafter.

"Keep watch," Peter whispered to Sephiri. "Tap the rafter if you see anything."

She nodded. Peter shuffled across the large beam, making his way toward the armory room with Kira and Rylan behind. The rafter ran the width of the entire museum. When he arrived over the weapons, the faint outline of the Shepherds' Sword shone back. It was right there, almost within reach. *All we have to do is grab it.*

He set the second coil of rope on the rafter, then tied it around his torso in a secure harness. Confident he could drop from the rafters without hurting himself, he worried both about the noise it would make and how he would get back up after retrieving the sword. Kira checked his work, pulling at the knots at his shoulders and waist, then slipping her fingers under the rope to test the tightness. She nodded with approval.

"This is gonna be so cool," Rylan whispered.

"As long as you don't drop me." Peter peered down over the rafter into the room. "All right, you ready for this?"

Just as Peter was about to lower off the rafter, footsteps sounded up the stairs. He froze.

"I'm telling you," a guard said, "half the stuff in here is junk, anyway. If it weren't for the jewels on display, they wouldn't even need a patrol."

"Can't believe you're complaining about having a job," the other guard said. "And an easy one, too!"

"In the middle of the night?" the guard said. "They could at least put me on day duty."

"You talk too much. That's why they won't."

The two guards arrived in the armory room, bickering with each other as the four friends froze on the rafter directly above them. Peter's heart pounded as he stared down, too still to even blink.

A faint squeak pierced the air, and he risked a glance in its direction. Kira's eyes were wide, staring at the rafter where a rat wiggled its nose at them. She pressed her hands hard to her mouth and scooted backward, away from the rat and closer to Rylan, looking like a shriek fought to escape her lips.

*Not now,* Peter thought, his heart dropping. He waved a hand at the rat to scare it off. *If it gets any closer, Kira's going to lose it.*

A gust of wind rushed by them. The rat toppled onto its side before it turned and scuttled away along the rafter. Kira dropped her hand and exhaled.

On the other side of the rafter, near Rylan, Sephiri's eyes paled. A hand extended in the direction the wind had blown. Peter ducked his chin in thanks, and she returned the gesture.

"Sorry," Kira mouthed.

Beneath them, a guard scoffed loudly. "I'm not getting into this again with you," he said. "It's your turn to watch the jewels. I'm going back downstairs."

"Fine," the other guard said. "When I get promoted to daytime guard, you'll be jealous!"

With a wave of his hand, the first man left for the stairs. The remaining guard idled by the Jewels of Bromhill, looking bored but standing in the hall outside of the armory room.

"Let's do it," Peter whispered.

"Seriously?" Rylan stared over at the guard. "He's right there!"

"We just have to be quiet," Peter said. "This might be the only chance we get."

Rylan sighed and nodded. He took the rope in hand, then looked at Kira. She looked more horrified than ever, but nodded and grabbed the rope as well.

Peter lowered himself until he dangled from the rafter by his arms. Rylan and Kira held their end of the rope, and the harness tightened painfully around his body. Exhaling his breath, he released the rafter. Rylan and Kira lowered him while he kept his focus on the sword displayed below.

There wasn't much distance to cover. All he had to do was drop, grab the hilt, and have Rylan and Kira haul him back up. Then they could climb back up to the roof and sneak out just as quietly as they'd gotten in. It would be like they'd never been there at all.

The guard near the jewels sighed and muttered to himself. Peter couldn't see him from where he dangled, but he could hear the man's breath. All the guard would have to do would be to glance around the corner.

*Faster,* Peter thought to himself. *We're so close.*

He reached down toward the sword. It was only an arm's length away, maybe less. He leaned, tipping forward in the harness to better cover the distance. The rope dug into his shoulders, but he ignored the sting. *Just a little closer.* He bit the tip of his tongue between his teeth. His fingers brushed the polished wooden hilt.

"Yeaugh!!" A shrill shriek broke through the silence.

Peter gasped as the rope went slack. He hit the ground

behind the railing of the armory with a thud, face-first. The shock of the fall made him dizzy as he staggered to his feet, standing in the armory display. Overhead, Kira's hands covered her mouth again, pale and terrified as a rat scampered away again. Rylan stared down at Peter, wide-eyed.

"H-hey!"

Peter spun. The guard rounded the corner. The man sounded more shocked than anything else, unsure of how to deal with an actual intruder.

"Who are you?" the man asked.

Peter looked down. The Shepherds' Sword displayed beside him. Without hesitation, he pulled it out of the stand. Over half as tall as he was, the steel blade glimmered in the moonlight. He swung the weapon at his side, slicing through the rope that attached him to the rafter above.

"Alert!" the guard shouted. "We got a thief! Get up here!"

Peter jumped over the rail out of the display, sword in hand. The guard took a step back, hand on the club at his hip, wide-eyed.

Rylan dropped from the rafter, landing with both feet on the floor with a thump so loud it rattled the armor on display. He looked up at the guard, hands balled into fists.

"Two thieves!" the guard shouted. "Two of them! Drop that sword!"

Peter tightened his grip at the hilt. It wasn't how he had hoped this would play out, but at least he had the sword. He wasn't giving it up now.

"Can't do that," Rylan said to the guard before leaning toward Peter. "Let's go, now!"

"Hey!" the guard shouted. Rylan shoved past him, out of the armory and into the hall, knocking the man aside with a firm push to his shoulder. Rylan's strength sent the guard sprawling head first into the wall. He collapsed in a groaning heap.

Peter turned toward the stairs as the second guard thundered up. "Stop!" the other man shouted. "Stop right there!"

Rylan stepped backward, returning to the armory with a grin. "Come and get us!"

"What are you doing?" Peter asked as he followed.

The guard rushed in after them. "Hand over that sword. Now."

"I don't think so," Rylan said. He grabbed the guard by the straps of his leather breastplate, then lifted him up off his feet.

"Whoa!" the guard shouted, limbs flailing. "Put me down!"

Rylan turned and hurled the guard into the armor display. The man crashed into the steel suits, and the pieces rained down on him in an endless clatter.

"Go, go, go!" Peter said, chuckling as he pushed Rylan out of the room and toward the stairs again.

The other guard had gathered himself to his feet. He shook his head, looking unsteady. Rylan feigned slamming into him again as they passed, and the guard dropped to the ground of his own accord. The two boys thundered past and descended the stairs with rapid feet.

On the ground floor, they pushed the front door open into the quiet, dark night. A quick check around the corner revealed the girls dropping from the rope in the alley.

Kira was as white as a sheet. Sephiri grinned as she caught Peter's eye.

"We got it," she said. "We really got it."

Inside the museum, a bell rang. It was a loud, ear-splitting gong of a bell that would wake up the entirety of Paratill View.

"Uh-oh," Rylan said. "That can't be good."

## 20

"We better run!" Peter held the sword close to his body and took off, resisting the urge to tap into the Source to hasten his pace. He made sure his friends were close behind as they rushed southward, winding through the narrow streets as lanterns flickered to life at the loud sound of the gong.

"Run ahead!" Sephiri shouted, giving Peter a small push. "We'll meet you at the Garrison. Don't get caught."

"You're sure?" Peter asked.

Voices yelled in the distance. "The authorities," Kira said. "They'll be looking for the sword. Go!"

Peter gripped the hilt. He exhaled, then let the sparking power of the Source dance down his limbs, from the center of his chest down to the tips of his toes. He sprang forward off the balls of his feet and ran.

The city sped by in a blur. Peter barely felt his feet on the ground, rushing forward on instinct and power. He arrived at the door to the Garrison in the space of a few breaths, so quickly he careened into the rockfall outside. He stumbled to a stop, sword still in hand, then scrambled over the boulders to enter.

Only when he was inside the Garrison did he exhale and let his shoulders slump forward. He stumbled to the table and dropped the sword atop it with a clatter. Exhaustion rushed over him. He dropped to his hands and knees on the fur by the hearth and stayed there for a few moments, panting. The Source crash and the adrenaline slump hit simultaneously. Yet even as sweat dripped from his temples and nose onto the fur beneath him, he grinned.

*We did it. We got it.*

The Shepherds' Sword was in their possession. The next clue to the Amulet. Soon, they'd have the Amulet itself, and it would solve all their problems.

Peter sat up only to flop over onto his back and stare up at the starry night sky. The moon was nearly full, and its light flooded the room. His chest still heaved. As much as he itched to look at the inscription on the sword, he'd wait. *We should all see it together,* he thought. *We all worked for this.*

As long as they didn't get caught by the authorities.

He shoved that fear aside. Sephiri knew her way around the neighborhoods, and Kira could smooth-talk them out of anything. Rylan was the only one in danger, anyway—the guards hadn't seen the girls.

He took a few more deep breaths. By the time he'd regained some of his energy, and the worst of the exhaustion had passed, anxiety creeped back in. *How much time has passed? How long would it take them to get here? Should I go back to the town square? What if Rylan is already in the stocks?*

As if on cue, a familiar voice shouted, "Peter!" Rylan poked his head through the entrance. "Are you okay?"

Peter dropped back onto the fur with a relieved laugh. "Yeah, I'm good. What about you guys?"

Rylan, Kira, and Sephiri hurried over. They were sweaty,

breathing as heavily as Peter had been, but Rylan and Sephiri grinned. "We're fine," Sephiri said. "We avoided all the guards."

"They're so loud," Rylan said. "It's like they want you to know they're coming."

Kira's pinched expression cracked, and she buried her face in her hands. "I'm so sorry," she said, the wail muffled into her palms. "That was all my fault."

"What happened?" Peter asked.

"The stupid rat," she said. "I thought it was gone. We were lowering you down, and I felt something furry on my ankle. The rat was *right there!* I thought it was going to bite me! I'm so sorry!"

"At least I wasn't higher up," Peter said.

"It was kind of funny when you landed on your face," Rylan said.

Peter swatted him. "My nose still hurts."

"Ugh," Kira groaned, "this was supposed to go smoothly. In and out like we planned. I ruined it."

"It's all right," Sephiri said. "I should've paid more attention, too. I should've expected the rat to come back."

"It's no one's fault," Peter said. "We got the sword. That's what matters." He hauled himself to his feet and picked up the sword from the table. "Ready to see what it says?"

"You haven't looked?" Rylan asked.

Peter grinned. "I waited for you guys."

"Yeah," Rylan laughed. "Because you need Kira to figure out the riddles. Come on, let's see it!" He practically vibrated with excitement.

Peter brought the sword over to the table, gleaming under the light of the full moon. He traced a finger over the carved hilt, where it ended in the shape of a snake's mouth open around the blade. *What was Vicion Shepherd like?* He imagined him tall and broad-shouldered, in leather armor, snarling as he brought the sword in a high arc over the head of some faceless, cowering enemy. The Viper himself. *Did he use the Amulet? Was it part of his skill on the battlefield?*

*Could that be me, too?*

Peter traced a finger up the center of the steel blade. He swallowed around the sudden tightness of anticipation in his throat.

Then he gripped the hilt and turned the sword over.

The four of them leaned in, nearly knocking their heads together.

"What's it say?" Rylan asked. "Peter, what's it say?"

Peter leaned closer. The engraving he'd glimpsed in the museum was just that—an engraving.

A decoration.

There were no words at all.

"What?" he asked, as if the sword could explain itself. He rubbed the pad of his forefinger over the engraving, like the movement would reveal hidden letters. "It doesn't say anything."

"Triangles." Kira knocked Peter's hand away. "It has to be connected to the Amulet somehow."

"What are we supposed to do with that?" Rylan asked.

"It's like in the watchtower," Sephiri said. "The triangle marked the door. It's a sign that we're on the right path. Somehow."

Peter flopped onto his back. All the anticipation he'd felt lifted away like steam and left in its place a gaping hole of disappointment. "What path is that?" Peter asked. "It's just decorations. It means nothing."

"I don't know," Kira said, her voice unsure. "Maybe it means something. There are five of them. That could be a clue."

"It's not." Peter had no proof of it, but he could feel it. Sense it. "It's just a sword."

"A cool sword," Rylan said morosely.

"But it's the Shepherds' Sword," Kira said, like she couldn't believe it. "This has to be the right thing. There has to be something there."

Peter got to his feet again and grabbed one of the steel training swords and the whetstone. He drew the blade across it, just for something to do. "The Shepherds' Sword will hold the key," he muttered. They had the sword—so where was the key?

*I never should've gotten my hopes up. We did all that for nothing. Now we'll have the authorities looking for us, but we're back to square one.*

"What do we do now?" Sephiri asked. "If the sword's just a sword, how do we figure out how to get to the Amulet?"

Peter kept sharpening the training sword, seated away from the other three. He tuned out the curious murmurs of their voices as they took turns inspecting the weapon and running their fingers over the hilt and the triangles carved into it. Soon, his blade gleamed under his hand, and he had no reason to keep running it over the whetstone. With a sigh, he stood and leaned the blade back against the Garrison wall with the other swords. "Let's get home," he said, gazing up at the moon high in the sky. "It's late. Rylan and I have work at Jenkins' tomorrow."

"You don't want to keep looking at this?" Sephiri asked, holding the sword near the fire.

"What is there to look at?" Peter asked. "There's no clue. We've got nothing."

Kira sighed. "We'll figure it out, Peter. There has to be something here."

"Just stash it somewhere safe, okay? I'm going home."

"Peter!" Sephiri said. "Wait!"

Peter was already climbing over the rockfall and out of the Garrison. The disappointment sat in his chest like a stone. All he wanted was to crawl into bed and catch a few hours of sleep before he had to get up at dawn for another workday—the same workday he always had . . . that he *would* always have.

· · ·

PETER WALKED BACK to Lowside with his hands stuffed in the pockets of his trousers. His muscles ached from the climbing and running, and his skin burned from the rubbing of the rope harness. The sky already lightened with the threat of oncoming dawn. He'd be lucky if he got two solid hours of sleep before he had to start his day.

The road narrowed as he approached the farm, and Peter sighed as the wet-soot smell of the burned field drifted through the air even before he reached the fence surrounding the property. His feet dragged as he made his way to the front door. He pushed the door open, moving quietly as to not wake his parents in the back bedroom.

"Peter?"

Or who he thought were in the back bedroom. He turned around. "Father?"

His father walked down the road as slowly as Peter had. He looked as exhausted, too, hunched with one hand rubbing up and down his forearm. He raised his eyebrows at Peter. "It doesn't seem like you're heading out for your run."

"You're out late," Peter said, deflecting. "Everything okay?"

"Where were you?" his father asked. "Not out causing more trouble, I hope."

*Understatement.* "No, I was . . . I was going to get back at Ashton and his friends for what they did to us."

"Peter," his father said with his forehead pinched, "tell me you didn't."

"No, I chickened out," Peter said. "They hang out late in a tavern in Brufec Heights." The lie spilled out so easily that it made Peter feel guilty. Better that his father think him reckless with bullies though than to know he'd broken into the museum.

"You leave those boys be," his father said. "It's all taken care of."

Peter's eyebrow quirked. "What? What do you mean?"

His father led him into the house. His shoulders looked tense, and his expression dark as he lit the fire in the kitchen and cleaned up the few dishes still scattered on the kitchen table from dinner.

"What happened?" Peter asked.

"Shh," his father said. "Your mother's asleep."

"What do you mean it's taken care of?"

"Matthias?" his mother asked. "Is that you?"

"Yes, dear. It's still early." His father threw Peter a stern look, then hurried down the hall to tend to his wife.

Peter stood alone in the kitchen with the fire crackling. What did his father mean, it was taken care of? *Did he go to Lord Dunn and argue our case? Are we getting a break?*

*Are we keeping the farm?*

All of Peter's plans to help keep the farm secure had failed, but maybe his father had figured it out.

From down the hall, his father grunted in what sounded like pain.

"Matthias!" his mother cried. "What happened to you?"

Peter rushed down the hall to the back bedroom his parents shared. As soon as he appeared in the doorway, his mother sighed and waved her hand at him. "Peter, can you take your father into the kitchen and help him clean this up?" she said. "He can't go out into the fields with a wound like that. It's not safe."

Peter's heart swelled at the clarity in his mother's gaze and the ease with which she recognized him. "Right. Sure, Mother, I'll help. What happened?"

His father stood up straight, his palm over his forearm. "It's nothing. Just a minor wound from clearing the field."

"Go clean it up, Peter," his mother said. "Use the water in the kitchen."

"Come on," Peter said. His father followed him back down

the hall, almost sheepishly, his hand still pressed over his forearm.

"What is it?" Peter dipped a clean rag into the basin of water on the counter. "Did something happen?"

"I can take care of it," his father said. "Don't you need to head out on your run if you want to finish before work?"

"I'm skipping the run today." Peter tried to draw the injured forearm to him, but his father resisted.

"Here, give me that." His father reached for the rag. Peter held it away, staring. Finally, his father lifted his palm from his forearm.

Peter saw what his father had been hiding. His eyes widened. "Father? Is that . . . ?"

A small, bright pink burn marked his father's forearm. A brand. A fresh brand—fresh enough to still be shiny, raised, and blistering. Even through the swelling, the shape of a skull wrapped in a serpent showed against his skin.

"It's not ideal," his father said, "but it's the only way to keep the farm."

"A Viper loan?" Peter stared at the brand, his blood running cold.

"It's a temporary solution. After the next good harvest, we'll pay it off." His father ran the cool rag over the brand, grimacing with pain.

"Temporary," Peter echoed. He pictured the bodies swaying from the gallows near Schuggec Row. *What is the point of keeping the farm if Father has to pay with his life?* "But Father, the Vipers—"

"This wasn't my first choice. When you're grown, you'll understand. Sometimes we have to sacrifice for the people we love." He looked back toward the bedroom. "Your mother isn't in a state to leave this farm. We'll figure out what to do next. We always do."

"How much is the loan? What do we owe?"

His father shook his head. "It's not for you to worry about."

"But it is, Father! The Vipers won't just come after you. If you can't pay, they'll come after Mother . . . and after me. You haven't just doomed yourself, you've doomed us all!"

"That's not going to happen. Trust me."

Peter took a deep breath then sighed, letting his pulse settle. A wave of remorse washed over him. "Father, if—if the field hadn't—"

"Peter, stop." His father straightened and pinned Peter with a stern look.

"It's a valid question." Guilt bubbled in his chest, crawling into his throat like bile. "If I hadn't gotten the field burned up, would we have needed the loan?"

"It's not a valid question because what's done is done. Look forward, not backward." His father's expression softened. "Get some sleep. You can't miss another day at Jenkins'."

Peter slunk to his room. It was nearly dawn. He'd barely get a full hour before he'd need to leave for work.

---

## 21

"We hid it before we left," Rylan whispered to Peter as they pulled another box of ancient masonry tools from Jenkins' back room. Today, their assignment was not masonry, but to clean and sort all the tools Jenkins had neglected for years. "It's still in the Garrison."

"Thanks," Peter said. "I don't think it's any use to us, but it's best if we don't get caught with it."

"Yeah, a priceless artifact from the museum in our possession? Not a great idea," Rylan whispered.

"Shh," Peter hissed. "Let's just get through today, and then we'll figure out what to do."

They settled into their work, cleaning and polishing until their eyes crossed.

Hours later, when most of the tools sparkled and shone, a harsh, unfamiliar voice called, "Mr. Jenkins?"

Peter looked up. A guard in polished, unblemished leather armor stood in the doorway to the shop. He was a broad-shoul-dered, stern man with dark hair and beady eyes like a hungry possum. He swept his cloak over his shoulder and sneered.

"Constable Eastling." Jenkins' eyes were big and watery, a

fake grin plastered on his face as he scurried from his desk to the front door. "What an, um, unexpected delight. What can I help you with on this fine morning?"

"I'm here for two of your apprentices," the constable said.

"My apprentices?" Jenkins asked. He whipped around to face Peter, and his eyes narrowed. "For what reason?"

"City business." Constable Eastling unfolded a piece of paper. "Peter Fairfield and Rylan Burton? Are they with you today?"

"Boys," Jenkins said through gritted teeth. "You heard the constable. Off you go."

Peter pressed his lips together and stood. "Constable, what's this about?"

"We'll discuss it at the courthouse. Come with me, please."

Constable Eastling led them out of the mason's shop and into the busy streets of Brufec Heights. Peter rubbed his wrists as he followed behind. *They know. They know we have the sword.* He glanced around as they walked toward the alleys. *Should I make a break for it? No—that'd only make me look guilty. How could they know?* His heart raced. *At least we're not restrained. That has to be a good sign, right? Unless they're just giving us a last taste of freedom before they lock us up.*

The constable walked at a swift, military pace, one that had Rylan and Peter scampering to keep up. He didn't even bother to look back and ensure they followed, he just surged forward, moving through the crowds.

"This is bad," Rylan whispered. "This is really bad."

"Shh," Peter hissed again.

They crossed the town square. Ashton, Hodge, and Tanner lounged by the fountain. *Do those guys even do anything during the day?* Peter thought sourly. Ashton's eyes widened when Peter passed, but then his face split into a cruel, delighted grin. He waggled his fingers in a teasing wave. Tanner broke into a laugh, then nearly tipped backward into the fountain. Hodge caught him, but then threatened to shove him backward again. A minor scuffle ensued with Ashton leaping off the fountain rail to chew them out.

"Morons," Rylan muttered.

"He looked surprised," Peter said. "Do you think they knew about this?"

"They don't know anything," Rylan whispered back. "They just cause problems."

"Pick up the pace, boys," Constable Eastling said over his shoulder. "I'm on a tight schedule today."

"Yes, sir," Peter said, hustling to keep up.

Constable Eastling led them through the town square, across from the bank to where the courthouse stood. Less imposing than the bank, the building was still intimidating. White stone made up the walls. Heavy double doors waited ahead with a statue of the founder of Palenting in front of them. The constable nodded at two guards who pushed open the doors.

Peter had never been inside the courthouse before—which was luck more than anything else. The authorities dealt with the more serious crimes in Palenting—the major robberies, assaults, and the occasional bodies that turned up on the edges of Lowside. They didn't have time to deal with riffraff like Peter and his friends. At least, they never had before.

The inside of the courthouse was plain but well-kept, with polished wooden floors and a sturdy intake desk in front of another set of doors. Constable Eastling brushed past the desk and led them down a narrow hallway to another heavy door. He pushed it open. "Wait in here."

"Sephiri?" Peter stared wide-eyed into the small holding room where his friend waited. He ran in. "What are you doing here?"

"I don't know." Her red-rimmed eyes proved she'd been

crying. "A guard found me near Schuggec Row and brought me here. No one has told me anything."

The room was small, but not uncomfortable. A few chairs and couches filled the room with one small table. Another door set into the far end of the room, but no windows decorated the walls. Peter sat on the couch next to Sephiri, and Rylan dropped into a chair.

"They didn't tell us anything either," Peter said. "Just showed up and brought us here."

"They would've said something if . . ." Sephiri trailed off. She cast her eyes down.

"I think so," Peter whispered. If anyone knew they were behind the theft of the sword in the Palenting Museum, they wouldn't be in a holding room like this. They'd be in a cell. Or worse.

Constable Eastling opened the door again. "Peter Fairfield. Come with me."

Peter nodded. As nervous as he felt, he refused to show it to the constable.

Constable Eastling led him further down the hall, through yet another heavy wooden door. *This place is like a maze.* Peter was about to ask where they were going when the constable shut the door behind them.

"Mr. and Mrs. Lancaster?" Peter said.

Kira's parents sat in two fine, well-upholstered chairs next to an immense wooden desk. Constable Eastling dropped into the leather chair on the other side. He sighed and gestured for Peter to take the third empty chair, next to Kira's parents.

He risked a quick look at the Lancasters. Kira's mother, who had looked put together in the museum, appeared unkempt now. Her silvery hair was loose, and she dabbed a handkerchief to her nose and mouth. At her side, Mr. Lancaster looked stern and cold, with deep bags under his eyes.

"You're familiar with the Lancasters, then?" the constable asked.

"Um, yes."

"He's friends with our daughter," Mr. Lancaster said coolly, his voice laced with disapproval. "Kira's kind-hearted. She had invited Peter and the others to the museum."

"For what reason?" the constable asked.

The Lancasters stared at Peter.

*This is an interrogation*, Peter realized. He gripped the arms of his stiff-backed wooden chair. "What happened?" he asked. "Where's Kira?"

"We're hoping you can tell us," the constable said. "When's the last time you saw her?"

"What?" Fear shot through Peter like a lightning bolt. "Is she—is she okay? Where is she?"

"Just tell me when you last saw her." The constable dipped his pen into the inkwell, then held it over the parchment on his desk, his gaze flat as he waited for Peter's answer.

"At the museum. We were all there together. And then when we finished, we all went home—I went to Lowside. She stayed in Paratill View . . . I assume."

"And you didn't see her after that?" the constable asked.

"No. I went to sleep. Then I went to work this morning."

Constable Eastling didn't look convinced. "You didn't see her at all after the museum?"

"No!" Peter nearly shouted. He couldn't tell them he'd been with her later that night. *What happened?* He tightened his grip on the arms of the chair. "Please, will someone please just tell me what this is about?"

"The Lancasters reported the incident to us this morning," Constable Eastling said. "Their daughter's bedroom was upturned and damaged. Kira is missing, and someone left a note in her chambers." He slid a sheet of parchment across the desk, and Peter still had to crane his neck to see it. "It says, 'Bring—'"

"I can read," Peter snapped, causing the constable to flinch.

He returned his gaze to the note and muttered as he read. "'Bring the sword to us by midnight, or she dies.'" Beneath the demand, a familiar stamp turned his stomach—a skull with a serpent wrapped around it.

Mrs. Lancaster burst into sudden tears, muffling the sound into her handkerchief. "They've got my baby!" she cried. "My Kira!"

"We'll find her," Mr. Lancaster said, keeping his hand on his wife's knee. "We'll find her, and she'll be just fine."

"Do you know what they mean by this sword?" the constable asked.

Peter shook his head. He felt if he spoke, he might throw up. How had the Vipers found out so quickly? Had they been following them? Did they find something about it in their research? And how did they know—

"They left this with the ransom letter as well." Constable Eastling set a fine silk scarf on the desk. "Have you seen this before?"

"That's Kira's," Peter said, swallowing hard. "Her scarf. She —she thought she lost it."

"Any idea why the Vipers would include this with their ransom note?"

Peter shook his head again as his heart thudded. It was the very scarf Kira left in the library. Had the Vipers recognized the family crest? Had they realized what their research related to? Peter thought they were well ahead of the Vipers—but it seemed like the group had been snapping at their heels the entire time.

"It's an interesting coincidence," the constable said. "Just hours after you and your friends completed your visit to the Palenting Museum, someone stole a sword from the collection."

"Is that the sword the Vipers want?" Peter asked. He met the constable's eyes despite the stomach-curdling nerves.

"Why don't you tell me," Constable Eastling said, his eyes like daggers. A tense silence filled the room.

Peter fought to keep his voice firm. "I didn't hear about a break-in. Who did it?"

"The guards are under questioning."

"Admit it was you!" Mrs. Lancaster wailed. "Give us the sword so we can get my daughter back!"

"I didn't do anything!" Peter insisted. He couldn't risk getting caught with the sword—not when he was so close to finding the Amulet. If he ended up locked in a cell, there would be no one to keep the Vipers from getting it first. "I don't know what you're talking about!"

"All right, both of you," Constable Eastling said, "cool down. I don't need any yelling in my office. Peter, come with me."

Peter nodded. He was sure he would be thrown in a cell for the night, or locked in the stocks, but Constable Eastling walked him back down the hall to the holding room. He motioned for Peter to sit, then summoned Rylan.

"Everything okay?" Sephiri whispered after Rylan left.

"No." Peter's entire body thrummed with nervous energy, and his stomach tied up in knots. "Kira's missing."

Sephiri's eyes widened. "What do you mean, missing?"

"Vipers kidnapped her."

Sephiri's eyes flashed white, and the room felt colder as a wind rustled at his ankles. As quickly as the sensation arrived, it dissipated. Sephiri took a deep breath and closed her eyes. When she opened them again, they were their familiar deep brown color.

*How long had she been hiding reactions like that?*

"We have to find her," she said.

"I know. As soon as all three of us get out of here, we will.

Just don't tell them anything. I insisted we didn't see each other after leaving the museum. Make sure to back me up."

She nodded.

"Let's hope Rylan says the same thing."

They sat side-by-side in nervous silence until Rylan returned. The constable took Sephiri next. Rylan mimed zipping his lips, and Peter nodded with a weak smile. He could always count on his friends.

After what felt like hours, Sephiri returned. Constable Eastling lingered in the doorway and pinched the bridge of his nose. "The three of you can go," he said. "We'll send notice if we need any additional information. And if anything comes to mind that you forgot to inform us"—he narrowed his eyes while sustaining a long, awkward pause—"don't hesitate to speak up. Understood?"

"Yes, sir!" Peter leaped to his feet and hurried out of the courthouse with Rylan and Sephiri behind him.

In the town square, the sun shone brightly on the busy crowds. "What now?" Rylan asked. "We can't just go back to work. We have to find her."

"Let's go back to the Garrison," Peter said. "We'll make a plan."

"We can't," Sephiri said.

"Why not?"

"What if someone follows us? Constable Eastling clearly believes we know something. They might wait to see where we go. Them—or the Vipers." Her voice dropped even lower as she spoke through her teeth. "And we *know* what's at the Garrison."

Peter looked over his shoulder, then gazed around the square. Ashton and his friends had left. "All right. Somewhere else then. I don't want to run into Ashton again. Let's stay away from Brufec Heights and other places they hang out."

"That's everywhere," Rylan said. "This sucks. It feels like the walls are closing in on us."

"I know where we can go," Sephiri said.

"Where?" Peter asked.

She sucked her teeth. "Just . . . promise you won't make fun, okay?"

Sephiri led them south to Schuggec Row, walking the familiar streets that led to the Garrison. But instead of heading to their hangout, Sephiri led them down a winding alleyway running like a stream between the crumbling and abandoned workshops and taverns.

"Here." Sephiri stopped in front of a three-story stone building. "We won't be bothered." She pushed open the splintering wooden door and led them inside.

Peter's footsteps were soft on the hard-packed earthen floor. Inside, a fire roared in an enormous hearth beneath a huge, steaming cauldron. The room smelled delicious, of cabbage and braised garront. An old woman stood hunched behind a narrow bar, pouring ale from immense barrels. Rickety tables filled the room where men and women played gammit and smoked pipes.

"Sephiri," the woman said with a smile. "Here for some lunch?"

"If you don't mind," she said. "I brought my friends, too."

"The more the merrier." The woman was short, with thinning hair and one eye clouded over into blindness. She slid three bowls to Sephiri. Peter reached into his pocket for a pintid, but the woman just laughed and waved a hand. "None of that, young man. A friend of Sephiri's is a friend of mine."

"But—our meal—"

"Shh," the woman said. "Eat. It's a beautiful day. Why don't you go upstairs and enjoy the sunshine?"

"Thanks, Yani," Sephiri said. Peter followed her to the immense cauldron, where Sephiri ladled out generous portions of rich-smelling stew into each of their bowls. Carrying her steaming bowl, she led them up the narrow staircase, walking carefully to keep her stew from sloshing out.

"What is this place?" Rylan asked.

The roof was flat but lush, with a well-tended rooftop garden. Raised vegetable boxes grew all kinds of produce beneath wooden trellises covered in lush ivy. A few people ambled around watering the produce, poking at the dirt and checking the leaves for pests, but overall it was quiet. Sephiri led them to a small table near the edge of the roof, where they could overlook Schuggec Row and the Dorthar Mountains beyond the city.

"Seriously," Rylan said through a mouthful of soup, "this place is amazing. How have we never been here? Is this a restaurant?"

"It's like an inn," Sephiri said. "Yani downstairs runs it. She knew my parents, so she helps me out sometimes."

"Helps you out?"

"I stay here occasionally," Sephiri admitted. She looked embarrassed to even say it. "There are rooms on the second floor, but I try not to impose on her too often. It's not much, but sometimes I need an actual bed and a warm meal."

"Right," Peter said. It was easy to forget that Sephiri had no place to call her own. He knew she spent most nights in the drafty Garrison, and that she picked up odd jobs in Lowside and Schuggec Row—but nothing permanent. "Thanks for bringing us here. We can talk here, right?"

"Yeah. Especially up here. Much worse conversations happen here than anything we're dealing with." She took a sip of the stew. "What did the constable ask you two?"

"When the last time was that I saw Kira," Peter said.

"Me, too," Rylan said. "We all just said the museum, right?"

Peter and Sephiri nodded.

"And he asked me if I knew what they meant by the sword," Peter added.

"Same here," Rylan said.

"He asked me if I had any connection to the Vipers," Sephiri said. "If they offered me money for information about Kira." She grimaced as she stared into her soup. "He thought if anyone was involved in the kidnapping, it was me."

"What? That's ridiculous!" Rylan exclaimed. "She's our friend! Why would you be involved at all?"

Sephiri shrugged. "I'm just a street kid, I guess."

Peter shook his head. His stomach soured at the idea of the constable grilling Sephiri alone. "We can't count on the constable to figure anything out. We'll get her back ourselves."

"How?" Rylan asked. "They want the sword."

"The sword's a dead end," Peter said. "Why even hang on to it?"

"Unless it's not," Sephiri said. "What if it is the key and we just haven't had time to figure it out?"

"Maybe that's true," Rylan said. "Maybe the sword is our only shot to find the Amulet."

*And the Amulet's my only shot to save the farm. The farm . . . the Viper loan.* Peter sighed. "Kira would've figured it out if the sword were the key." He wasn't sure if he believed it—but he didn't have any other options. "What do we do instead? Just hang on to the sword? The note said they'd kill her."

"They won't do that," Sephiri said. "Even the Vipers aren't stupid enough to get on the Lancasters' bad side."

"Are you sure?" Peter asked. "What if we keep the sword and they go through with the threat? We've all seen what they do to debtors. Why wouldn't they go through with this threat, too?"

Silence fell over the three of them. For a moment, they sipped their stews and looked out over Palenting.

"It doesn't feel real," Sephiri said. "All of this."

"Do you think she's okay?" Rylan asked quietly.

"She has to be," Peter said. "She's fine. I know it." He couldn't entertain any other option.

"We should've been more careful," Sephiri said. "I didn't think the Vipers would stoop to this level."

"Constable Eastling said they broke into her house and took her." Rylan stared into his stew. "That would have been terrifying."

"She's tough," Peter said. "Tougher than the rest of us."

"So what do we do?" Sephiri asked.

"Trade the sword," Peter said. "We can't risk the Vipers living up to their threat. It's not worth it."

"Plus," Rylan added, "if we really want the sword, we can get it back. We broke into their headquarters once. It can't be that hard to do it again."

Sephiri nodded. "Especially now. Last time we broke in, it was without the Source."

Peter nodded with a grim smile, then took a deep breath. "Tonight. We'll go to their headquarters just after sundown."

Doubts and worries rolled around in his mind. *What if she's hurt? What if we're too late? What if she's not at the headquarters at all? What if the sword is the key, and we didn't figure it out?* He thought of his father with the brand on his forearm. *What if Razor gets to the Amulet before us?*

---

## 22

In the cool of night, as soon as the sky darkened with the moon yet to rise, Peter, Sephiri, and Rylan approached the gates of the Viper Syndicate headquarters. Peter had the sword wrapped in rough linen, strapped across his back and beneath a cloak as they moved through the streets of Palenting. The last thing he needed was to be stopped by a curious guard and have the stolen sword discovered.

Instead of clambering over the fence as they had done previously, Peter rapped his knuckles against the wooden gate.

A skinny, gap-toothed guard appeared behind the wooden rails. "What do you want?"

"We're here to talk to Garrett Razor." Peter's voice sounded a lot steadier than he felt. "It's about Kira Lancaster."

"Talk?" the guard asked, narrowing his eyes. "Razor's not interested in talking."

Peter swept his cloak aside, then tapped the hilt of the sword where it showed at his shoulder. "We brought what he asked for. We're ready to talk."

The guard raised his eyebrows and then stepped aside.

With a clank, the gate unlocked and swung open. "It's a shame," the guard muttered. "Thought we might get a fun show this evening."

Peter's stomach turned, but he said nothing. *Stay focused. Get in. Get Kira out.*

The guard led them into the headquarters, through the front door, unlike the last time they'd been inside. The unfamiliar ground floor was as dark and dusty as the upper levels they'd broken into, with narrow hallways and cobwebs collected in the rafters. Sephiri stuck close, and Rylan brought up the rear. Peter followed the guard into the heart of the building. Each door they passed and henchman they saw increased his unease, but the crackle of the Source comforted him. It gave him confidence that he could handle anything Razor threw at him.

The guard opened a plain, dark double set of doors. "Sir?" the guard said. "You've got visitors. Claim they've got the sword."

"Oh?" Razor's voice said with a teasing edge of disbelief. "Bring them in. Let's see if they're lying."

The guard shoved Peter over the threshold. He stumbled, surprised by the sudden push. After catching his balance, he straightened up and squared his shoulders. Fear crawled up into his throat, but he pushed it away.

The dusty and dark room belied the appearance of a dining hall. It was long and wide, with hardwood floors layered in threadbare rugs and old furs. A fire roared in the hearth, and two cobwebbed chandeliers hung from the rafters, casting the room in a flickering yellow glow. Four Viper guards stood at the far end of the room, flanking two heavy wooden doors.

At the head of the dining table, Razor sat alone, lording over an impressive spread of food: roast pheasant, a suckling pig, crusty rolls of bread, roasted root vegetables, and fresh greens. Razor sneered at Peter and took a long gulp of wine from an immense goblet, staining the corners of his lips. He leaned against the sturdy back of his chair and raised his eyebrows. "So," Razor said, "You received my message?"

"Where's Kira?" Peter snapped.

"Patience," Razor said. He took another slurping drink. "Show me the sword."

"What do you want with it?" Peter asked. Sephiri and Rylan stood shoulder-to-shoulder with him, but Peter kept his gaze locked on Razor.

"That's not what we're here to discuss," Razor said. "Show it to me."

"Do it," Sephiri whispered. "It's not worth fighting about."

It wasn't. Peter knew that. Yet anger still burned in his chest at Razor's lazy posture and the gratuitous spread of food. This would feed Peter's family for weeks—but it was all just for Razor himself to devour like a glutton. It turned his stomach.

*What would he be like with the Amulet under his control?*

Peter reached over his shoulder, gripped the hilt of the sword, and drew it from its makeshift scabbard. The blade gleamed in the flickering light. Peter tightened his grip on the hilt, the carved wood textured against his palm. The weight of the sword felt good in his arms. He was loath to give it up—to hand such a gorgeous weapon over to someone like Razor. He spun it in hand, a deft maneuver, the blade slicing through the air. "Bring Kira out."

Razor stood from the table. His eyes widened, as if he hadn't believed Peter would have it. He strode closer. Sephiri and Rylan both took a small step back, but Peter held his ground despite a shiver of fear running down his spine.

"So," Razor said, low, "it's true. You found the Viper's Sword."

"We did. Now let Kira go."

"How did a bunch of fools like you get this sword, I wonder?" Razor reached for the sword, and Peter pulled it close to his body, out of reach. "And for what reason?"

"We're poor. We steal to survive. It's just a sword, but it means nothing to us."

Razor chuckled. "Is it related to the 'research' you did in the library?"

"It doesn't matter."

"Oh, I think it does." Razor turned and strode back to the table. He pulled a leg of roasted pheasant from the spread and took a bite. Then he snapped his fingers. "Bring out the girl," he said, muffled through the bite.

"Disgusting," Rylan muttered.

A guard left through a door at the far side of the room, revealing only darkness behind it. He emerged a few moments later, hauling Kira behind him.

Sephiri gasped, then covered her mouth with her hand.

Kira's eyes blazed with anger as she stumbled over the layered rugs. Razor pulled a chair from the table, and the guard shoved Kira into it. She wore a plain linen dress—a nightgown. They'd taken her from her bedroom. Dirt covered her bare feet, and rope bound them loosely, providing just enough slack to walk. Her hands were tied together in front of her body. Her blonde hair was a mess, spilling over her shoulders unlike her usual smooth braids or high ponytails. She sneered at Razor with pure vitriol in her eyes, like an angry cat, but the fabric tied around her mouth kept her silent.

*How dare he treat Kira like this?* More than anything, Peter wanted to bring the sword down on Razor's head. But with the guards on the far wall, and the man still behind him, that wouldn't end well for any of them. Still, he tightened his grip on the hilt. The Source crackled within him, begging to be used. *It'd be so easy. Just one well-aimed strike.*

Razor chuckled. He set his half-eaten pheasant down and

stood behind Kira. He slid his hands over her shoulders. She shuddered then thrashed, trying to shake off his hold, but Razor only tightened his grip.

"You know what I think?" Razor asked. "I think you four seek the Amulet of Power."

"That's ridiculous," Peter said. "Everyone knows the Amulet is a myth."

Razor chuckled. "Funny you would say that, considering the books you pulled at the library. You see . . . I *am* searching for the Amulet of Power, and I've been reading similar materials. And wherever I look, it seems like you four always show up as well. Care to explain how that might be?"

"We don't have to explain anything," Peter snapped. "We came here to make your exchange. I'm offering the sword. Let Kira go."

"It's an interesting thing," Razor said. "What does this sword have to do with the search for the Amulet? Regardless of its purpose, I'm always happy to bring a Viper artifact home. I can't help but wonder, though. If you were merely thieves, you would've gone for the Jewels of Bromhill. Why the sword?"

Peter said nothing.

"The Amulet is another artifact that should be home with the Vipers," Razor continued. "And I intend to bring it back."

"It never belonged to the Vipers," Peter said, "and it never will."

Razor laughed, low, and squeezed Kira's shoulders. She wrinkled her nose, still squirming under the touch. "Is that what those silly books told you? If that were true, what would lead you to take the Viper's sword?" He chuckled again, causing Peter to sweat. "But what does it matter? The Amulet is within my reach. And once it's mine, I'll be able to make the changes this city—" he caught himself "—this *kingdom* needs. Tell me, Peter . . . what interest do you four have in the Amulet?"

"To keep men like *you*—"

Sephiri stomped on Peter's foot. He hissed and then coughed to cover it up. Sephiri glared at him.

Peter swallowed. "You think we want to be farmers and masons, always indebted to people like you? Our families deserve better."

"People like you are always so shortsighted," Razor said. "You want money? Better homes? Meals like this?" He gestured at the spread of food across the table. "You don't need the Amulet for that. Tell me what you know, and once I have the Amulet in my possession, I'll ensure you're set for life."

Peter froze, blinking several times. "Why should I believe you?" he shot back. "When have you ever kept your word?"

"You should be grateful I'm even discussing this with you at all, Boy." Razor spat the sentence like it tasted bad in his mouth. "The Amulet will be mine regardless of your agreement or not. If you want your families to survive the transition, you'd best get on my good side now." He slid his hand into his pocket and withdrew a small knife. He kept his dark gaze pinned on Peter as he pressed the flat of the blade to Kira's throat. Her eyes widened, and she went still. "Now, give me the sword."

"Stop that!" Peter shouted. "Untie her first!"

"It appears we're at an impasse." Razor teased the flat blade over Kira's throat.

She pressed her eyes together, tears rolling down her cheeks.

"Give the sword to my guard, then I'll untie her," Razor said.

"How can I trust you to do that?" Peter asked. His hand shook as he gripped the sword. "Set her free, then your guard can have the sword."

Razor sighed. "Or maybe I'll just *take* the sword and keep her for myself." He removed the knife from her throat, but then wrapped his hand around her neck instead. He leaned close, nose brushing her temple. "She's a pretty one. I might want to get to know her better."

Kira whimpered.

"Stop that!" Peter stepped forward, sword held up and ready to attack.

Guards drew short bows off their backs with lightning speed, notching arrows aimed at Peter. Others stepped forward, drawing swords from scabbards at their hips. Razor returned the knife to Kira's throat before Peter could take another step. They were surrounded.

"Another step and all four of you die," Razor hissed.

"Peter, just hand it over," Rylan whispered. His voice wavered.

Peter sneered at Razor. With a cry of disgust, he tossed the sword with a clatter onto the table. The heavy blade sent a plate of rolls to the floor, and a carafe of wine spilled across the wood and dripped off the edge.

"Now, was that necessary?" Razor straightened up, tucked the knife back into his pocket, and strode to the middle of the table. A pleased smile grew on his face as he picked up the weapon. He gripped the hilt, then bounced it, checking the weight. "Nicely balanced. Well-made." He held it up and peered at the hilt, then traced the shape of the snake's mouth around the blade. "Wielded by the Viper himself."

"We gave you the sword," Peter said. "Now let Kira go."

Razor acted like he didn't hear him at all. Instead, he turned the sword over in his hands, examining the blade. He drew his thumb over the triangular symbols. "How does this connect with the Amulet?" he snapped. "What did you find?"

"We found the sword," Peter said. "And now it's yours. The deal's done."

"Tell me what you know," Razor hissed. "This connects to the Amulet. How?"

The guards maintained their arrows pointed at them.

"You know everything we know," Peter spat. "The sword's yours. Now release her!"

Razor sighed and shook his head. He slammed the sword back onto the table. More dishes clattered to the floor. "You think this deal means anything if the sword is worthless?"

"It's not worthless," Peter said. "You said it yourself. It belonged to the Viper. Isn't that something you wanted?"

"I want the Amulet!" Razor roared.

Peter reeled back a step, stunned by the ferocity in his voice. Sephiri and Rylan steadied him with hands on his shoulders and back. Still seated in the chair, Kira closed her eyes tightly and struggled against the ropes.

Razor cleared his throat, then pinched the bridge of his nose. "You think I'll trade the Lancaster girl for something useless? You think I'm a fool?"

"We held up our end of the deal," Peter said, his voice shaking.

"Forget the deal," Razor hissed. "Victor! The girl!"

The largest guard sheathed his sword and stepped forward next to Kira with an evil grin. Snapping into action, he wrenched her out of the chair and slung her body against the table.

"Leave her alone!" Rylan yelled, gritting his teeth next to Peter.

The guard pressed down on her bound arms, pinning her hands to the wooden surface. He pulled a large hunting knife from his belt and spun it in his fingers. Finally, he gripped the hilt and held it point-down, hovering over Kira's fingers. She cried out, the sound muffled against the fabric gag as she stared in horror at the knife.

"Your friend has ten fingers," Razor said. "That gives you ten chances to change your mind. Here's your first chance. What do you know about the Amulet's location?"

The question hovered in the air between them. Peter's pulse raced, thumping in his ears. His eyes darted around the room.

The guards kept their arrows directed at them and their swords at the ready. The big guard stared hungrily at Kira's hands, waiting for his cue. Kira looked at Peter, her wide eyes brimming with tears.

"Well?" Razor prompted.

The bow from the guard behind Peter creaked. He imagined the string stretching farther. After a deep breath, he exhaled.

Sephiri squeezed his shoulder.

"Wrong answer!" Razor yelled. He turned to Kira. "Cut it off!"

With a surge of energy, Peter barreled backward, quick as a bird with his Source power. He slammed his shoulder into the chest of the guard behind him, knocking the man off-balance as he loosed his bow. The arrow flew toward the ceiling and stuck into the rafter with a *thwack*. Peter dropped low and wrenched the short sword off the guard's hip. The man shouted and reeled backward, trying to notch another arrow.

Razor roared in fury, and the other guards loosed their arrows. Rylan shouted, dropping into a crouch to avoid them, but the arrows never arrived. Midway to their targets, a force field of wind stopped them in mid-flight, then launched them backward toward the opposite walls.

Sephiri stood with her hand raised, eyes pale. She drew the surrounding air in a protective bubble. It remained for a moment, like a breath—just long enough to protect them from the arrows.

In a rush of motion, Peter whirled around and knocked the guard back with his sword. The man yelled and grasped his leg from where a gash of blood spurted across the floor.

Amidst the commotion, Rylan sprang to his feet and barreled forward with all his Source-infused strength. He targeted the biggest guard, Victor, who backed away from Kira with a look of terror on his face. Bones crunched and a hollow thud filled the room from the collision. The guard flew across the room, careening into two other men behind him along the back wall. All three collapsed to the ground, but Rylan was on them, knocking one unconscious with a blow to the temple then brandishing his fists at the other two.

"Get them!" Razor howled. "Get them all!"

The leader of the Vipers charged toward Peter, but Sephiri blew him back with a sudden gust of wind. Razor fell to the ground. He sat, frozen, with a bewildered look on his face.

Sephiri darted forward, grabbed the abandoned knife on the table, and cut Kira's bindings and gag. Before Peter could reach her, Kira was already on her feet, eyes blazing with anger. She grabbed a bow off an unconscious guard and slung the quiver of arrows over her shoulder. She notched one and shot it with instinctive ease. The sharp arrowhead buried deep into a guard's shoulder just before he could strike Rylan.

"Let's go!" Peter shouted.

With a rush of wind, Sephiri blasted open the double doors behind them. Peter sprang to Kira's side and looped her arm around his shoulders. She exhaled with a grimace but staggered to her feet, weak and exhausted. Sephiri shoved them and Rylan forward into the hall.

Peter pulled Kira's weight, struggling to help her move as fast as possible down the dark hallway. Shouts echoed behind them. Sephiri turned and sent a blast of wind up the corridor. Peter glanced over his shoulder to see silhouettes of Vipers blown off their feet with their weapons flying from their grips. The doors, pushed by the wind, slammed closed.

At the end of the hall, they rushed out of the headquarters and into the courtyard. Rylan charged forward first, barreling into the gate with his shoulder and knocking it off its hinges. Angry shouts filled the air behind them.

"This way!" Sephiri called. They ducked into an alley and

moved as quickly as they could, considering their rapidly increasing exhaustion from using the Source.

"Stop right there!" a stern voice down the cross-street called into the night.

*Constable Eastling.*

## 23

They skittered to a stop in the darkness of the narrow alley. Rylan collided into their backs, nearly knocking them down. Guards rushed by—not Viper guards . . . Palenting guards, led by the constable himself. They ran in a straight formation to the headquarters of the Vipers Syndicate with their swords drawn, moving past the alley without seeing the four of them concealed by the shadows.

The Vipers had a new foe to contend with. The four friends exhaled in unison. They were safe for the moment.

"They're looking for me," Kira whispered.

"Should we go to your house?" Peter asked.

"No," Kira said. "The Vipers might look for us there."

"She's right," Sephiri whispered. "Both the Vipers and the constable will be."

"I need to sit," Rylan said, slightly choked.

Kira nodded in agreement. She slumped against Peter.

Peter caught Sephiri's eyes and raised his eyebrows in question. She ducked her chin. She was fine—she still had energy. *Will it get easier for us?* Peter wondered. Maybe in the future, using the Source wouldn't drain them so dramatically.

"Here . . ." Peter knelt down, pushing away the thought of his own exhaustion. "I'll carry you."

In any other situation, Kira would never agree to such a thing, but being kidnapped and nearly having her fingers cut off gave her a change of heart. He bent down so she could jump up on his back, and she hooked her legs around his waist.

"Let's get back to the Garrison," he said. "We'll recoup there."

Peter led them through the quiet streets of Palenting, taking side streets and alleys in case any Vipers or guards were out on the prowl. Inside the Garrison, the four of them collapsed onto the furs in front of the hearth. Peter pulled some bread and jerky from their stash, and they all tore chunks off and ate in exhausted silence.

"Well," Rylan said after a long moment of silence, "at least we made it out, huh?"

Kira rubbed at her wrists. Sephiri's gaze tracked the motion until she inhaled sharply. "Come here," Sephiri murmured. She pulled her barkleaf balm from her bag, then took Kira's hand in hers. Both of Kira's wrists were rubbed red and raw. "This looks bad," Sephiri said. "How long were you tied up?"

"The whole time," Kira said. "Those jerks."

"Are you okay?" Peter asked. "Did they hurt you?"

"I'm all right," she said with a sigh. "They stuck me in a room and left me alone. It wasn't comfortable, but it was okay. Just a bunch of empty threats."

"They told you what they left in the note?" Rylan asked.

"No," Kira said. "I figured it had to do with the sword though. I wish I hadn't left that shawl."

"They said it was the sword or your life," Peter said.

Her eyes widened, then she swallowed and turned her gaze back down to her wrists, where Sephiri rubbed the balm into the reddened skin. "You think they would have?" she asked. "Would they have killed me if they didn't get it?"

"I don't know," Peter said. "Razor seems serious about finding the Amulet though."

"Did you catch what he said?" Sephiri asked. "He intended to bring the Amulet *back*. When has he owned it before?"

Rylan clicked his tongue. "He must've misspoken."

"I don't know." Peter leaned back onto his hands and tipped his head back, gazing up at the night sky. "That seems like a weird slip."

"When would he have owned it before?" Kira asked. "It's been missing for ages."

"Maybe he meant it the same way he talked about the sword," Sephiri suggested. "Was there anything in the Eanith book about the Amulet once belonging to the Vipers?"

"The Vipers didn't exist when Eanith wrote the book," Kira said. "Did Vicion Shepherd found the Syndicate?"

"I don't think any of that matters." Rylan chewed thoughtfully at the end of a stick of beef jerky. "What does it matter if the Vipers once controlled the Amulet if we never find it? Knowing where it was doesn't help us find where it is now."

"And we don't have a lot of time," Peter said.

Kira looked up at him, and her brow furrowed in concern. "What do you mean?"

"My father took out a Viper loan."

"It's that bad?" Kira asked. "Don't they give you time to pay it off?"

"Some," Sephiri said. "But you can't trust them."

"He says it's the only way he could keep the farm. But . . . what if Razor finds out he's my father? He'll use the loan to get back at me."

"The Vipers always find a way so you can't pay it off," Rylan said. "They invent some loophole or terms or fake rules. A loan with them is for life."

"I know." Peter raked one hand through his hair. "They'll never let Father off the hook. It's only a matter of time until he demands the money back. And if he can't get it . . ." He couldn't make himself say it, but the fear weighed like a stone in his gut. *He'll end up like the debtors we saw hanging off the gallows. Maybe Mother, too.* He swallowed hard. *Maybe me.*

"Sounds like Ashton," Rylan muttered. "Just another idiot bully."

Peter huffed a bemused laugh. "Except Ashton can't destroy my family's farm."

Sephiri raised her eyebrows. "Isn't that exactly what he did already?"

"Oh, right." Peter laughed for real, then flopped onto his back. The laughter was contagious, and the other three joined in. In the midst of tragedy, the moment of levity lifted his spirits after the harrowing experience at the Vipers' headquarters. The air was crisp in his lungs, the stars glittered above, and Rylan started a fire in the hearth. Peter sighed. *How are we going to find the Amulet? Every lead is just a dead end. Are we just biding our time until Razor finds it first?*

*But Razor sounded just as lost as us.*

*Where do we even go from here?*

Kira stood up, rubbing her wrists. She walked to the shelves by the hearth where Peter's rucksack with the pyramid inside was stashed among their snacks, books, balms, and other detritus in the Garrison. She sat back down on the fur and opened the pyramid, murmuring to herself as she reviewed the clues again, as if they might reveal some further secrets. "In ancient home it waits," she repeated, and smoothed her thumb over the engravings.

"It's waiting for us," Peter said. "But if we can't figure out the 'key' then how are we supposed to find the 'ancient home'?"

Rylan wandered over to the training swords. He picked one up and swung it around a few times, running through a few sword positions. "I can't believe Constable Eastling thought we were involved in the kidnapping. When I was a kid, I used to think he was cool."

"What?" Peter asked. "You knew him?"

"Oh, no, not really." Rylan swung the sword around his head. "My father did, a little. They grew up together. Before he became a constable, Eastling worked down south and got a reputation for defending the trade routes, busting bandit skulls. They called him the Sword of Palenting. But then he became a constable instead of a commander and got all lazy and snide like he is now." Rylan scoffed. "It's a shame. Commander Isert needs to knock some sense into him."

"What did they call him?" Kira asked.

"The Sword of Palenting." Rylan paused in his practice and looked at her, head tilted. "It's a common term in the army for guys who are outstanding fighters."

Kira stood up so fast that she wavered on her feet. "It's not an actual sword."

"What?" Peter asked. He and Sephiri stared at her. "What do you mean?"

"The clue in the watchtower. It's not Vicion Shepherd's sword. It was capitalized. It's a title."

An icy-cold wave hit Peter, washing away his exhaustion. He stood up as well. "You're right."

"Rylan!" Kira said, bouncing on the balls of her feet. "You're a genius!"

"What?" Rylan asked. "What are we talking about? What's the sword?"

"Vicion Shepherd himself." Peter nodded. "Remember what it said in the museum? He was known for being a warrior. He's the sword of the Shepherd family."

"But he's dead," Sephiri said. "How do we figure out what the key is if he's dead?"

"In ancient home it waits," Kira murmured again. "Where's this ancient home? There must be records somewhere."

"More research," Rylan groaned. "Awesome."

THE FOUR FRIENDS caught a few hours of sleep beside the roaring fire in the Garrison. Peter woke at dawn when sunlight shone through the open roof, falling in golden beams over his face.

Rylan groaned as he roused, rubbing his eyes. "Already?"

"Yeah, already," Peter said. "Can you go to Jenkins' and let him know I'll be late for work today?"

"Oh, no," Rylan said miserably. "We have work."

"Yeah." Peter glanced at Kira and Sephiri, still asleep on the furs. "I'm going to walk Kira home before I make my way over."

"I get the rest of the jerky, then," Rylan muttered, taking a chunk of meat off the table. He clambered out of the Garrison, waving over his shoulder as he hopped down off the boulders and onto the street.

Kira and Sephiri both looked exhausted when they finally woke. Kira's face drooped while dark rings hung beneath her eyes. Peter smiled to see the raw skin on her wrists was already healing. Sephiri yawned, stretching while her disheveled hair stuck in all directions.

The three of them made their way first to Yani's place, where the innkeeper offered them breakfast and even a kettle of hot tea. Too tired to climb the stairs to the rooftop, they sat around one of the rough-hewn wooden tables inside. The room was nearly empty. The only other person eating breakfast was a haggard older man sipping at his soup.

"Do you think the Palenting guards are still looking for you?" Sephiri asked.

"Probably," Kira said. "I'm sure my mother's losing her mind."

"Definitely," Peter said. "At least, she was when they questioned us."

"They're never going to let me out of the house again," Kira said with a groan. She folded her arms on the table and rested her forehead against her stacked forearms. "She's going to be worse than ever."

"What are you going to tell them?" Sephiri asked. "If you say we had the sword, we're all going to get in a lot of trouble."

"I won't say anything about that," Kira confirmed.

"Do you think the constable's men arrested any Vipers?" Peter asked.

"Doubt it," Kira said, her voice muffled into her arms. "The Syndicate owns half of Palenting at this point. Eastling probably asked some polite questions, then left when Razor said he wasn't involved."

"You can just tell them you got away," Peter said. "Since it's not like anyone cares."

That hung over them for a long moment as they ate their breakfasts. Peter stared into his bowl at the thin broth, the gamey meat, the wilted vegetables. He recalled Razor's spread in his headquarters, different even from the meals he'd seen in the Lancasters' home. The constable only cared about finding Kira because of her parents' standing—they'd do nothing to help Peter's father if the Vipers changed the terms of the loan. They'd do nothing to help Peter if Razor came looking for him.

*I'm on my own.*

"I'll walk you back to Paratill View on my way to Jenkins'," Peter said. "In case any Vipers are still lurking around."

"We need to get to the library," Kira said. "After you're done with work, I guess, but—I mean, I can't imagine my parents will let me out of their sight. They'll probably lock me in my room."

"We shouldn't go during the day at all," Sephiri said. "What if Razor has someone posted there waiting to see if we come back to research?"

Kira pursed her lips. "Hmm. Good point."

Peter glanced at the man at the nearby table, who continued sipping at his soup.

"But we still need to go there," Kira insisted. "How else are we going to find out what the clue means by 'ancient home?'? I know there's something there that will tell us where to go."

"We'll go," Sephiri said. "We just need to go when it's closed. It'll be safer."

After they ate, Kira and Peter left Sephiri at Yani's. He walked with some trepidation toward Paratill View, but his anxiety was misplaced. As soon as they were at the front door to the Lancaster home, Mrs. Lancaster opened the door with a gasp and burst into tears. She swept Peter into a hug tight enough to crush his ribs, squeezed his cheeks, and then rushed Kira inside. It all happened in the space of less than a few seconds, and then the door slammed shut, leaving Peter standing dazed on the porch.

Whatever story Kira concocted to explain her absence and return, at least she'd be the only one keeping the story straight. Peter stuffed his hands into his pockets and turned away. Before he left through the gate, the door to the house opened again, and someone called out.

Peter turned. A female servant jogged down the steps with a small sack in her hand. "Here," she said, shoving the sack forward.

Peter accepted it, and the servant hurried back to the house without another word.

He opened it and smiled. Some bread, dried meat, and cheese stared back at him. Below the bread, a few copper coins jingled together. *Her mother's attempt to thank me.* Appreciative of the gift, he exited the gate. He needed to get to Jenkins', where he expected to get chewed out for being late. Again.

## 24

"Give me a second," Kira whispered as she knelt in front of the side door to the library.

"Where did you learn how to do this?" Rylan whispered back. He held the lantern close enough to shine the orange light over the heavy lock.

"When I was younger, my parents used to lock my window," Kira said. "And now they're doing it again, but this time to keep people out instead of me in. Just a little more . . . there!" The lock clicked, and she pushed the door open.

Peter held his breath, half expecting an alarm bell to ring or a posted guard to rush forward with a lantern and a blade, but there was only silence and darkness within. The first step Peter took over the threshold onto the hardwood floor echoed into the rafters.

"What are we looking for?" Peter whispered.

"Records." Kira took the lantern from Rylan.

Sephiri grabbed another off the library wall and lit it. The warm light fell in flickering beams across the library but seemed to cast more shadow than light.

"Close the dampener," Kira said.

Sephiri closed the shades on the side, matching Kira's actions on her own lantern.

"Do you know where they are?" Sephiri whispered.

"Of course I do." Kira threw a grin over her shoulder, her eyes glittering in the light. "This way."

The records section of the library was up a narrow staircase on the far back wall, leading to a short balcony overlooking the main chamber. The entire back wall of the balcony was lined with shelves stuffed full of nothing but scrolls.

The sheer number of scrolls gave Peter a headache. How could they find anything notable when all the scrolls looked the same?

After a few minutes, Kira whispered, "Yes!" to herself. She pulled three scrolls from the shelves and then motioned for them to scurry back down the stairs. They made their way to the table in the back, where they'd initially done their research. Sephiri and Kira set their lanterns down, and Kira unfurled the first scroll.

"What is this?" Peter asked. The scroll was faded and fragile with age, full of dark, winding script.

"Bank records," Kira said. "These are the ones from the years Ambrose Shepherd was alive. If we can find out where he lived, that could be the 'home' where the Amulet waits."

"That's smart," Sephiri said, her voice almost awed. "Hand me one. I'll look, too."

The four of them pored over the records. Peter stared at the tiny script until his vision swam. It felt like hours, though from the burning of the lanterns it couldn't have been longer than the time to mold a half-dozen bricks.

"Here!" Sephiri said. "Kira, look!"

Kira scurried over and pressed her shoulder to Sephiri's. The two of them leaned over the scroll Sephiri had in hand. "Here it is," Kira said. "Ambrose Shepherd—buried in the Solaris Crypt with the rest of the Shepherd clan. His last place of residence was . . . the Watchman Manor, where he lived alone."

"The Watchman Manor. Of course. Because he built the watchtower." Peter said. "That's in Dulran Yard, isn't it? Or it was, right?"

"Yeah," Kira said, "as long as it hasn't been demolished. No one's lived there in forever."

"That's where it is," Peter whispered. "It has to be." A tiny flame of hope flickered in his chest again. *We have a lead. This could be it.*

"Now this is an unexpected sight!" a scratchy, high voice called. Peter reeled backward and nearly fell, the voice snapping him out of his focus on the documents.

Wynna marched into the back room, no lantern in hand, her mouth twisted in a scowl and a wild expression in her eyes.

"Um," Peter said, "we're just—"

"More research, I assume," Wynna said with a grin that didn't quite reach her eyes. She sighed, and her shoulders dropped. "Don't worry. You're not in trouble. I understand why you'd be less than keen to come during working hours. But you could've just asked to use the library off-hours. I would've been happy to give you access."

"Sorry, we were in a hurry," Kira said. "I needed to see these scrolls. I didn't even think to ask."

"I can't be angry about eager young researchers," Wynna said, her stern face cracking.

"How did you know we were here?" Sephiri asked.

"I always know what's going on in my library." Wynna waved her hand. "What are you looking for here?"

"I think we found it," Peter said. "Where Ambrose Shepherd lived."

"We think the Amulet might be hidden there," Kira said. "It's been abandoned for so long. There's a chance Shepherd could've left it there."

Wynna nodded, then tapped one gnarled forefinger to her chin. "You're looking for the history of the Shepherd family?" she asked, her eyes lighting up. "I might have something to help you. Follow me." They began to roll up the scrolls, but Wynna waved her hand. "Leave them! What are librarians for? Come on, this way."

"To where?" Peter asked as he followed her through the stacks toward the other end of the library.

"The private archives," Wynna said. "Library patrons aren't allowed down here, so don't tell anyone."

"The Eanith book was so helpful," Kira said. "Is it another one of his histories?"

"Something similar." Wynna knelt and tugged a small throw rug aside, revealing a dusty trapdoor beneath. She gave Rylan a look, and he scurried forward. He grasped the heavy iron handle and hauled the door up, revealing a dark staircase beneath.

"The library was built many years ago when the city was still at risk of siege," Wynna said. "It holds our most sensitive information, including some things the librarians would rather the Palenting guard not know." A grin grew on her face as she leaned forward. "Information is power, and sometimes we have to keep it to ourselves."

Wynna took the lantern Rylan offered, then descended the stairs.

Peter hurried behind her, trying to keep the smile off his face. A private archive? *No wonder we haven't found much in our own searches.* "Do you know the records well?" Peter asked. "Have you seen anything about Vicion Shepherd?"

"The Viper himself!" Wynna said. "I believe there might be some oral histories included, if memory serves. But it's been quite some time since anyone has looked through these materials."

"Come on." Peter nodded over his shoulder and gestured

for his friends to follow. Sephiri grimaced at the dusty state of the stairs as she descended, with the others right behind.

Peter hurried to keep up with Wynna. Whatever information she had on the Amulet, they needed it if they were going to move forward.

The stairs led down to a long, low-ceiling hallway tunneled deep into the earth. Wynna's lantern swung as she led them down the passage. At the end of the hallway, a heavy wooden door waited with an iron handle. Wynna opened it and ushered them toward the dark room inside.

"Peter, wait." She touched his shoulder as the others passed by. Wynna reached into the pocket of her linen trousers and pulled out a slim book bound in dark, cracked leather. "Take this. It may help."

Peter frowned as he took it. The book was light and felt like it might disintegrate in his hand. "Thanks . . . but . . . you just happened to be carrying it with you?" He slipped the book into his pocket.

"For my own research," she said, her hushed voice carrying an odd tremble. "I was, um . . . returning it to the archives."

The comments felt forced, and a tingle ran down Peter's spine.

Wynna closed the heavy door behind them. As she pulled on a metal ring, her sleeve rode up and something caught Peter's eye. On her forearm, near the crease of her elbow, her skin contained a small, dark scar.

A skull. A skull with a serpent wrapped around it.

Peter's stomach turned. His breath caught. "Wynna," he said, voice shaking, "is that—"

"It's about time," a deep voice called from the dark room. "I didn't want to wait all night."

A lantern roared to life, illuminating Garrett Razor seated at a large, plain table in an earthen room. Men flanked him at every side—dozens of them, more than Peter had seen even at the Viper headquarters. They crowded in the room like statues, swords drawn, and sneering gazes fixed on Peter. At Razor's side sat the haggard man in a cloak—the man from Yani's.

Behind him, Sephiri gasped, and Rylan swore under his breath. Fear crawled into Peter's throat, thick and slimy and blocking his breath.

*How could I have been so foolish?*

"How lovely to see you four again," Razor said coolly. "You're a frustrating bunch to keep up with." Titters of laughter rang through the crowd.

*Dealing with a handful of Vipers at the headquarters was one thing, but this . . .* Peter despaired. *Where would we even go? We'd never make it back to the library.*

His friends edged closer to him. Kira glanced toward the ceiling and the walls, as if searching for a way out. Rylan grimaced at Razor, his hands balled into fists at his sides. Sephiri stared ahead, resigned.

*I should've been more careful. I shouldn't have blindly followed along.* He'd been too excited to have a lead, and to have someone he trusted helping him. *I can't trust anyone. Not where the Amulet is concerned.*

Razor stood with a sigh. He withdrew the sword from the scabbard hanging on his hip. The Viper's Sword. The clue that led nowhere. "It's funny." Razor drew his finger up the steel blade. "I thought you had something when you uncovered this sword in the museum. I was almost impressed. Certainly surprised by your speed." He stared at Peter. "As well as that odd gust of wind. Strange happenings." Razor walked forward, holding out the sword. "How did you do that?"

Peter glanced at Sephiri, but her jaw was locked tight. He swallowed the dry feeling in his throat.

"Odd gust?" Rylan said. "What are you talking about?"

Razor leaned in, narrowing his eyes.

"Are you suggesting we can . . . control the wind?" A soft

laugh escaped from Rylan. "I'm sorry. I'm not laughing. It's just—"

"No matter!" Razor roared. "Whatever trickery that was, it won't save you now. The sword is worthless. I need the Amulet." He grinned, a predatory look that sent an icy-cold jolt of fear down Peter's spine.

"Old Ames here said he heard some interesting discussion at Yani's," Razor continued. "And here I thought he was going deaf!" More titters of laughter echoed around the room, each chuckle like a wasp on Peter's skin.

*Nowhere is safe. We never should've been talking in Yani's. I should've known the Vipers have ears everywhere.*

"I was especially excited to hear of your plan to sneak into the library. Wynna was more than happy to help us out."

Wynna balked. "I wasn't—Peter, I'm so sorry. If I didn't agree, I was going to lose my home."

"Your home, which you've been able to keep thanks to the graciousness of the Vipers." Razor waggled a hand at her. "Come here, Wynna."

Wynna cringed and stepped forward. "Our deal is completed now, right? This paid my debt?"

"Of course. I'm a man of my word." Razor wound his arm around Wynna's shoulders and tugged her close to his side. She grimaced and tensed in his hold. "You've paid your debt to the Vipers, and your help was invaluable."

Her arms shook. Peter's teeth clenched as he watched helplessly.

Razor sneered. "And by invaluable, I mean . . . no longer needed." With a twitch, he dragged the steel edge of the sword across her throat.

Peter jerked his head away, his heart racing as she gurgled her last breaths.

Sephiri gasped and clasped her hands over her mouth, and Kira choked back a terrified cry. Razor dropped Wynna's lifeless body to the ground like a sack of potatoes, blood pooling beneath her. He handed the red-stained sword to the man at his side, and the Viper wiped it clean on his cloak.

Wynna had only ever been kind to him. She helped his family whenever they needed it most. The book in his pocket felt suddenly heavy. Even as she'd betrayed Peter, she'd given him something to help. Despite turning on them, she didn't deserve to die like that. His father didn't deserve that fate. Nor did his friends.

The fear squirming in his throat melted down to his gut. He stood up straight. "What do you want?"

"Tell me what you know about the Amulet," Razor said. "Now."

"We don't know anything," Kira said. "We don't even know if it's real!"

"Don't lie to me!" Razor roared. "I no longer have patience for your ridiculous games. I know you discussed the Amulet's location at Yani's. Tell me what you know, or I'll strike you down where you stand."

Peter squeezed Kira's arm. She pressed her lips together and said nothing else.

"We know where it is," Peter said with a sigh. "We figured it out."

Razor's eyes lit up, like a starving dog presented with a leg of lamb. "You have the location?"

Peter nodded. "We haven't found it yet, but we believe we know where it is."

*And we still don't know what the "key" is. Even if they find the Amulet, Razor won't be able to get to it. We still have time.*

## 25

In the depths of the Palenting night, Razor led them out of the hidden underground chamber and onto the silent streets. Their hands were bound in rough rope, and they walked in a huddle, surrounded by a handful of broad Viper guards with sneering faces and more than a few scars. The group headed east.

In the shadow of the baron's castle, the far eastern side of the city was almost entirely abandoned. Destroyed in a siege before Peter was born, it had never been rebuilt.

"I haven't been back here in years," he whispered. He gazed up at the wall, where lanterns flickered but no guards walked in the late hour.

"We shouldn't be back here at all," Sephiri whispered back. Her shoulder bumped against Peter's as they hurried over the rough streets. The abandoned buildings watching over them created an ominous atmosphere. Roofs had collapsed and walls spilled inward. Conditions were worse than the scruffiness of Schuggec Row or even Lowside. No one lived there. And yet, Peter still felt watched from the darkened windows and empty doorways.

The Watchman Manor lay at the edge of Palenting. The baron's castle loomed overhead, but the manor in its disrepair seemed to melt into the forgotten farmland behind it. It was a three-story home, made of dark stone. The roof had caved in, and the immense windows were boarded up with sturdy pieces of wood covering each opening. Ivy crept up the walls of the building, as if the land tried to draw it deep into the earth.

"Halt!" a voice called.

A crow burst from the collapsed roof of the manor with an earsplitting cry. Peter stumbled back in surprise, knocking into Rylan, who was as still as a statue.

"Halt!" the voice shouted again. From beside the manor, a young Palenting guard in fine, brand-new leather armor and a red cloak rushed forward. He rubbed his eyes, then stumbled over his feet as he approached the Vipers. "Halt! Patrol! This area is, um . . ." He swallowed as he glanced between Razor and the imposing Vipers. "Um. It's off-limits to citizens of Palenting. So if you could just, um . . . be on your way . . ."

"Son," Razor said coolly, "are you new to the Guard?"

"Um, sir," the guard said, taking a step backward, "I'm on the night patrol, so if you'll just be on your way—"

"Your little night watch is secondary to the needs of the Viper Syndicate." Razor sneered. "And I'm not in the mood to explain things you should already know."

The guard paled. He looked back toward the wall, then frantically around him, but no other guards leaped from the shadow to his rescue. Razor's hand moved as quickly as a fish leaping from a wave. He drew the sword from his scabbard and drove it through the guard's leather armor like butter. The guard hit the ground with a thump, unmoving, as blood oozed from the wound on his chest.

"I'm not in the mood for distractions." Razor sheathed his sword. "I want that Amulet. Now!"

Peter's heart pounded as he moved away from the guard's

fallen body. Razor grew angry—wild-eyed and impatient. He might take his anger out on them next.

Razor strode to the wooden door of the Watchman Manor. Heavy chains locked with an immense iron padlock criss-crossed the dark wood. Razor scoffed, then slammed the hilt of his sword against it.

The lock didn't budge. He frowned and did it again.

The lock clanked against the wood but didn't break. It was sturdy—well-kept, despite its age. The walls were crumbling, but even as the Vipers searched, with the boarded-up windows, they couldn't find any easy entrances into the building.

"So?" Razor asked. He whirled around, eyes containing a simmering rage. "Do you have a key?"

The four friends exchanged glances.

*Could this be the key we needed?*

"I can unlock it," Kira said, holding her arms up. "But you'll have to untie me."

"We can manage a lock," Razor said.

"Please. I can do it." Kira held her arms out farther.

The closest Viper to her glanced at Razor, who huffed and nodded. The man cut her bindings, and she rubbed her wrists with a pinched expression. Then she knelt in front of the lock, pulled her lock-picking tools from her pocket, and got to work.

"Get a move on," Razor hissed.

Kira nodded, her attention focused on the lock. She was unflappable, despite having Razor standing over her, sneering. He kept one hand still on the hilt of his sword, like he might bring the blade down on Kira's back at any moment.

But he wouldn't do it. He'd had plenty of chances to kill them so far. As far as Razor knew, he needed all four of them to get the Amulet. Peter pressed his lips together. Despite that reality, he felt like a cow being herded through a gate to go to the butcher. If the Amulet was in the manor, and if they could access it, what would Razor do to them once it was in his hands?

The lock clanked open. Razor shoved Kira back, threaded the chains through the handles, and yanked the door open.

Peter walked in behind Razor, still flanked by Viper guards. The door opened into a grand entrance hall. Despite the age and state of ruin, the interior of the Watchman Manor was beautiful. The floors were white stone, coated in dirt and cracked by audacious plants insisting on growing. In the back, the collapsed ceiling had brought down the wall as well, opening half of the manor to the cool night air. The ocean was barely visible on the horizon. Crumbled stones lay in piles around the perimeter of the building.

The entrance hall still contained the detritus of what looked to be an extravagant social life. Plush but rotting couches sat against the walls, and fine wooden cabinets stood open and half-collapsed by age. From one of the few remaining rafters, a chandelier hung askance. Portraits lined the wall, the painted visages obscured by dirt and mold. At the far end of the hall, something rustled. Kira squeaked and stepped closer to Peter.

"Oh, yeah," Rylan muttered, "there'll definitely be rats in here."

"Where's the Amulet?" Razor demanded. "You've claimed it's here. So where is it?"

"'In rock, in bone, in earth,'" Peter whispered. "Where could it be?"

"There are plenty of rocks around," Sephiri said, her head on a swivel. "Are there bones in here?"

"Look at that door." Rylan gestured with his bound hands to a door at the far end of the entrance hall, nearly blocked off by the collapsed ceiling. "Is that ...?"

"You're right." Peter's nerves dissipated, replaced with an anticipatory thrill as he hurried to the door. The carving was faded but still visible against the dark wood of the door. The icon of the watchtower within the window frame. The same one they'd found in the tower itself.

"This way." Peter pushed the door open.

Behind the door was a circular room built within a tall, narrow turret. The roof was still mostly intact, and soared three stories overhead, ending in a pointed ceiling. The rafters rotted, and a steep, narrow staircase led to a window in the roof. A fountain made of a pile of smooth rocks sat in the center of the room—so large it took up most of the space.

"Rock," Sephiri whispered.

"It's like they built this room just for the fountain," Kira murmured.

The fountain had a large, circular base filled with muddy water and algae. Rocks built up from the water's edge, rising to a plinth where a beautiful but frightening sculpture of a ram reared up on its back legs, locked in battle with a raging wolf. The ram, with its horns down and gaze focused, drove its front hooves toward the wolf's chest while the wolf was off-balance, its jaws open and tongue flapping.

Overhead, a drop of water fell from somewhere on the roof. It landed atop the wolf's head, then slid over its jaw, rolled down the pile of rocks, and into the still water. The four looked up, and another drop fell.

"Find the Amulet," Razor sneered. He barreled into the room, hand on the hilt of his sword. "Where is it hidden?"

"It might be in here," Kira said. "In the rocks . . . or the water." She wasn't looking at the fountain, though. She looked at the wall behind it.

Peter's gaze followed hers. A small painting was mounted on the wall behind the ram, not much larger than a dinner plate. Painted in muted grays and browns, it contained a streak of fading gold near the bottom and a yellow sunbeam that cut through the center of the painting. *What's so interesting about that?* Peter thought. *Some sort of landscape?*

"Well, look for it!" Razor drew his sword, filling the room with a shriek of metal. "All of you!"

Peter plunged his hands into the dirty water along with the other three. His bound hands knocked rocks and slimy wood, the sensations making him grimace. He sifted through the pile of loose rocks, finding nothing but a stone base behind them. He caught Sephiri's eye and shook his head minutely. *It's not here.*

Razor roared in anger, then swung his sword in a wild arc. Peter gasped and ducked, nearly dunking his face in the water. The blade struck the statue with a clang. The ram teetered on its podium, then tipped over. It slammed against the edge of the fountain and shattered. Pieces fell into the water while the head of the ram clanked across the floor and slid to a stop. Undeterred, Razor knocked over the wolf as well, destroying it, then paced like an angry dog over the wreckage. "If the Amulet isn't in the fountain, then where is it?"

Peter racked his brain. Where would it be? If not behind the rocks—in earth? Is it buried? Under the foundations of the manor somewhere? How could they possibly find it if that were the case?

Razor grabbed Sephiri roughly by the arm. He hauled her close and wound his arm around her neck. Sephiri gasped. Her eyes widened, and she clawed at his forearm as he pressed against her windpipe.

"Let her go!" Peter shouted. He tugged at his bindings, but only rubbed his skin raw against the rough rope. He longed to use the Source to fight, but his bound hands would remain a challenge. Plus, there were too many Vipers.

Razor stared Peter down as he loosened his arm. Wrapping his hand around her neck, he squeezed, forcing a strangled cry from her throat. With a rough shove, he sent her sprawling forward, slamming into the edge of the fountain.

Rylan was at her side first. He helped her stand and guided her to the far side of the room, while Razor watched, chuckling to himself.

"Find the Amulet," Razor said, "or one of you will die . . . tonight."

*There has to be a solution,* Peter thought. *Where is it? It has to be here. Is there a key? Is it buried? Or underwater? There must be something—*

Kira gasped. Her eyes widened, and she turned her gaze to the roof.

"You remember what the Eanith book mentioned," she said to Peter. "The Amulet was hidden 'over its earthly home.'" Her words carried a curiously heavy emphasis.

"Uh," Peter muttered. He didn't remember that in the book at all—*wouldn't I have remembered something that important?*

"Yes!" Sephiri said forcefully while pointing. "Yes, that's what it said! Kira, do you think . . . ?"

*Kira's planning something.* Peter nodded. "Right . . . yes, I remember."

"Over," she said. "Over its earthly home. It's on top. It's on the roof! Come on!"

Kira rushed toward the rickety stairs and charged up. Rylan hurried behind with Sephiri and Peter at the end of the line. Sephiri looked weak. Peter kept his hands up as they ran, gentle at her back in fear that she might fall backward. The stairs were in even worse shape than the spiral staircase in the watchtower. They moved quickly while the wood creaked under their feet.

The stairs ended at a wide window that led nowhere, and a narrow sill perched over a three-story drop. Peter stepped out onto it, dizzy as he peered across the farmland below.

At the base of the stairs, Razor shouted at his men to stay with them, and several of them worked their way up, tentative at the echoing groans. The Viper in front was halfway up when his foot burst through a step. The whole turret creaked.

"I'm getting flashbacks," Rylan said, his voice low. He plastered himself against the wall. "Guessing the Amulet isn't up here, is it?"

"Seph," Kira whispered, "can you do it?"

Sephiri nodded.

"You're sure?" Kira asked.

"Get up there!" Razor shouted. The lead Viper crossed the broken step and hurried upward.

"They're almost here!" Rylan called.

Kira grasped Rylan and Sephiri's bound hands, and Peter held on to Sephiri's arm.

Peter's pulse pounded. The climbing Viper was only a few steps away. He gulped then started, "Three, two, one—" His heart leaped into his throat as he jumped off the roof, dragging the other three with him.

## 26

Peter held tight to Sephiri. He plummeted through the chilly night air, voice trapped in his throat. He closed his eyes. Falling. Falling. *This is going to hurt.*

But then, he slowed in midair as wind rushed from the ground and cradled him like a hammock. He opened his eyes. He hovered just off the ground with his three friends doing the same, exchanging wide-eyed looks as they floated, hands clenched and clothes blowing in an upward gale.

Sephiri's eyes were completely white, as if covered in a thick fog. Her hair floated, and her body quivered, she exhaled, and all four dropped to the ground in a heap.

Peter scrambled to his feet, his legs wobbling. "We need to get out of here," he urged. "Now!"

Kira and Rylan jumped to their feet, but Sephiri was still.

"Seph!" Kira yelled. She grasped Sephiri's shoulder and shook. "Seph, get up!"

Voices sounded in the manor. Razor shouted, his rage audible through the stone walls. Peter had no time to feel fear. He knelt down, grabbed Sephiri's limp arm with his bound hands, and hauled her onto his shoulders. "Let's go!"

They ran south, back into the winding streets of Palenting, leaving the manor and the Vipers behind.

"Is she okay?" Kira asked as they clambered into the Garrison. "Is Sephiri all right?"

"I should've carried her," Rylan said. "Sorry, Peter."

Peter lowered Sephiri onto the fur in front of the hearth. "Can you get her some water?"

While Kira cut their bonds with a dagger, Rylan grabbed a canteen from the corner and brought it to Sephiri's lips. A few drops dribbled over her dry, cracked lips, but then she parted them and drank a few sips. With a groan, she opened her eyes a sliver. The pale fog still swirled over her eyes, half obscuring the usual dark brown appearance. He'd seen her eyes go pale, but never that strange halfway mixture. "Seph," he said, squeezing her shoulder. "Drink a little more."

She pushed herself up onto her elbows, blinked at the three of them, and took a larger drink. After smacking her lips with a sigh, she waved the canteen away and laid back down. "What happened?"

"You caught us," Rylan said, half laughing. "We jumped off the top of the Watchman Manor, and you caught us."

"I did?" Sephiri asked, a dazed look on her face. "The last thing I remember is . . . looking out toward the horizon. We jumped?"

"You don't remember?" Peter asked. His heart clenched. Using the Source had weakened them all before, but never as dramatically as that. *Are we asking her to do too much?*

Sephiri felt her neck, rubbing the red marks where Razor had grabbed her. Peter swallowed to clear his dry throat. *It would've been easy for Razor to kill her. And we just made him even angrier.*

Once Sephiri drank more water and ate some of their meager food supply, the pale fog cleared from her eyes, and she climbed to her feet. She sat at the table, appearing exhausted. After starting a fire, Peter grabbed the pyramid and joined them.

"That was a smart move, Kira," Rylan said. "We never would've gotten out of there."

"At least not all of us," Peter agreed. He turned the pyramid over in his hands. "Razor was serious about killing one of us. If he finds us, he won't hesitate to finish what he started."

"How are we supposed to find the Amulet, then?" Rylan asked. "He'll have Vipers posted there at all times. They'll tear the place apart looking for it."

"Except that's not where it is," Kira said.

The three others stared at her.

"What?" Sephiri asked. "It's not?" The color had returned to her cheeks.

"Did you see the painting on the wall by the fountain?" Kira asked.

"I saw it," Peter said. "The landscape?"

She nodded. "A fortress, carved into the face of a mountain, struck by the sun, with a stone bridge leading to it. Something about it was familiar to me—like something I'd seen in a book a long time ago."

"How could you see that?" Peter said. "It was so dark."

She tapped her temple. "Source eyes, I guess. I was trying to remember where I'd seen a fortress like that before, and then I remembered what we found in the library. You remember how it said Ambrose Shepherd was buried in the Solaris Crypt, here in Palenting?"

"Yeah," Sephiri said.

"That name sounded familiar. And when I saw the painting, I remembered. Do you remember learning about the Fortress of the Sun?"

A laugh escaped Rylan's mouth. "Yeah, I remember the story." The others were quiet. Rylan's grin morphed into a look of curiosity. "Wait . . . you don't think it's real, do you?"

"Why not?" Kira said. "According to legend, it was built almost 400 years ago—by Otis Shepherd. He intended it to be a place of refuge near Palenting, for when the city was under siege. Otis supposedly lived there with his family at some point, and he was one of the early influential members of the Shepherd family. It was already long-abandoned by the time Ambrose Shepherd died."

"How do you remember that?" Rylan asked.

"I—I don't know." Kira's eyes widened in sudden confusion. "I think we covered it in Rynorian history."

"Rynorian fairy tales, more likely," Rylan muttered.

"It's strange," Kira said. "When we first saw the name Shepherd, there was something I'd learned in school niggling at my mind. But I couldn't remember. And now, it just . . . popped up."

"It's the Source," Sephiri said with a small smile. "Enhancing your strengths."

"Wow," Kira said, rubbing her forehead. "I wonder what else I only kind of remember."

"Does it exist?" Peter asked. "The fortress?"

Kira shrugged. "I'm guessing it does."

Peter held up his hands. "Wait . . . there are rumors of where this fortress supposedly is—up in the Dorthar Mountains, in the north range—"

"At the end of Dagger Path," Kira added, nodding.

"But if it's real, why hasn't anyone ever found it?"

She pursed her lips. "Maybe we know something they don't."

"We can find it," Sephiri said, nodding to Kira.

"So what does the fortress have to do with the crypt?" Rylan asked.

Kira's confidence returned. "Solaris Crypt. It means Crypt

of the Sun. And just like the story of the fortress, it faces east, so it's lit by sunrise in the morning." She spun to see them all with a grin on her face. "The Shepherds are buried in the final version of their family's home."

The hair on Peter's neck stood on end as the pieces came together. "The crypt would be their *current* home . . ."

Kira nodded her head, beaming. "We want their *ancient* home . . . the Fortress of the Sun. And *that* is where the Amulet of Power waits to test whoever would take it—in the north range of the Dorthar Mountains."

The room was silent while everyone held their breaths.

"We need to find the Fortress of the Sun," Sephiri said, breaking the silence. "Now."

"But what about the key?" Rylan asked. "'The Shepherds' Sword holds the key.' What if we get all the way to the fortress and then we can't get the Amulet because we haven't figured that out?"

A frustrated silence fell over the four of them. Peter stood and tossed the pyramid in hand as he paced the room.

"The Shepherds' Sword," he murmured to himself. "The sword isn't the key, it's the person. Vicion Shepherd had to know something." He caught the pyramid, opened it, snapped it shut, tossed it, then caught it. The repetitive motion helped him think.

Kira sighed. "We could return to the library and see if we can find any records about his belongings. That could take a while, though."

"It's too risky," Sephiri said. "The Vipers will be looking for us."

"I don't think there's anything new we can get from a book, anyway," Peter said. "We've pulled everything we could from that library. There's no secret archive. The Eanith book was the only useful text, and we already used it." He stopped, remembering the other book tucked inside his pocket. He shrugged as he tossed it to Kira. "Wynna gave me this before she handed us over to the Vipers. I doubt it has the answers we need, but you can check."

Kira gasped.

"Why would she help us if she were betraying us?" Rylan asked.

"She was a good person at heart. Yeah, she betrayed us, but —" He shook his head. "They forced her."

"And even then, she still died," Sephiri said grimly.

Kira opened the book, but her hopeful face fell. "This is in Tarphic."

"See? Nothing useful." Peter tossed the pyramid up and down again.

"Why would she give us something in Tarphic?" Kira murmured. "There has to be something in here meant to help us."

"Can you translate it?" Rylan asked.

"Maybe bits and pieces," Kira said. "It'll take me a while—I haven't studied Tarphic since school. But I can get my textbooks from home."

"Do we have that much time?" Sephiri asked.

"There has to be something we're missing." Peter turned the clue over in his mind for what felt like the thousandth time. *The Shepherds' Sword holds the key.* Vicion was the Sword, and something about him would lead them to the key . . . the key they needed to access the Amulet . . . hidden in the Fortress of the Sun.

The realization hit Peter like a bolt of lightning at the crown of his head. "Ha! We're overcomplicating the key's location."

"What do you mean?" Kira asked. "We don't have any leads on where the key is."

"Yes, we do." Peter bit back a grin as he rushed over to the table and slapped his hand on the surface. "You said it yourself, Kira. The Solaris Crypt is where the Shepherd clan is buried, right? So Vicion should be there, too."

"Okay . . ." Rylan said. "How does that help?"

"'The Shepherds' Sword holds the key!'" Peter exclaimed, grinning with his hands held out. "What if Vicion Shepherd is actually holding a key? It's not a trick. The clue means exactly what it says." Peter straightened up and pushed a hand through his hair. "Hidden in bone, remember? It's been in front of us the whole time. We've been overthinking it when it's been so simple. We need to get to the crypt."

"Grave robbing." Kira cringed. "You're talking about grave robbing."

"Grave borrowing," Rylan said. A smile spread across his face, too. "It's genius. It's so simple. Plus, what's grave robbing when we've already robbed a bank?"

"Right?" Peter said. "What do you think, Seph?"

Sephiri took the pyramid from Peter's hand and opened it. She gazed at the clue and sighed. "It's worth a shot. It's the only lead we have."

"It's better than a lead," Peter said. "It's a solution."

Kira groaned, folded her arms on the table, then dropped her head down. "I really don't want to root around a creepy graveyard."

"Aw, come on Kira, it's not a graveyard, it's an underground crypt!" Rylan said.

"We should go, now," Sephiri said. "It's still dark. Razor will be looking for us, and we need the cover."

"And we need that key," Peter said. "The sooner we have it, the sooner we can leave for the fortress."

"I think I should head home and gather some food for the trip," Kira said.

"We should stick together," Sephiri said. "If Razor somehow finds you alone, he'll kidnap you again. Or worse."

Kira sighed. "I can't believe this. You're really talking me into grave robbing?"

"Borrowing," Peter and Rylan said in unison.

"So where is the entrance to the crypt?" Sephiri asked.

"It's in the castle gardens," Kira said, sighing.

Peter raised an eyebrow. "It's not in the Palenting Cemetery?"

"The cemetery hadn't been built yet. The entrance to the crypt is in the center of the castle gardens, but no one ever goes inside there."

"Well, that's good news, isn't it?" Rylan asked. "It means no one will be lurking around, right? We'll get in like we used to always get into places. It'll be just like old times. Let's go!"

"We should hurry," Peter said. "Patrols will pick up once they discover the soldier Razor killed."

Sephiri stood. Her eyes held an eager look, but she stumbled on wobbly legs. Peter placed a comforting hand on her back. She bit her lip and said, "I want to go with you, but I don't think I have the energy. I may not be able to keep up."

"We're not leaving you by yourself in this state," Peter said. "Rylan?"

With a grin, Rylan knelt down. "Hop on."

Sephiri sighed and climbed onto Rylan's back. She hooked her legs around his waist and her arms around his neck. Rylan stood, unaffected by her weight, as if she were only a coil of rope. He beamed. "Onward!"

The four friends made their way out of the Garrison and back into the quiet streets of Palenting. They took the narrow side streets and alleyways, listening for any sounds of activity. As they'd hoped, there were no signs of the Vipers, even as they entered the town square and approached the castle.

Rylan set Sephiri down by the iron gates of the gardens, then boosted Peter. Perched on the top rail, Peter worked with Rylan as usual to help the girls over.

"Be quick," Kira whispered as she landed on the grass on the other side of the fence. "The sky's growing lighter, and the gardeners will be up and around soon."

Rylan knelt again for Sephiri. "I can walk from here," she said. "I'm feeling a bit better."

Peter had never been inside the baron's gardens. The castle waited in the distance behind its wall, large and dark in the early morning. The gardens were private, used only by the baron and his friends—the rich citizens of Palenting. They were vast, with lush green grass and topiaries shaped like birds and squirrels. Fruit trees grew along the border of the fence, blocking it from the view of the rest of the city. Paved paths wove through the grass, through flower beds exploding with color, rose bushes, and carved fountains. On one end, ivy-covered trellises surrounded a large gazebo, forming some kind of meeting space. On the other, at the top of a low rise, a small door was set into the hill, flanked by two white stone columns. "Have you been here before, Kira?" Peter asked.

"Once, for a spring ball," she said, "when I was young. I got in trouble for trying to sneak desserts out."

"Sounds about right," Sephiri murmured.

Kira pointed to the door on the hill. "That's the entrance, up there."

Peter led the way up the winding path, past the flowers and the topiaries and the occasional decorative statue. It was strange to hurry through the gorgeous scenery, thinking about what might be beneath the grasses. Peter hadn't even known about the crypt's existence. How big was it? How deep would they have to go?

He walked up the hill. The door itself looked ancient, older than the castle, made of dark stone and flanked by the white columns yellowed with dirt and wind. One tilted to the side as if a powerful gust might blow it over.

"Ugh," Kira said, "I hate this. We really have to go down there?"

"All we need to do is find Vicion Shepherd's tomb, open it, and get the key," Peter said.

"Sounds simple enough," Rylan said.

Peter grasped the heavy handle of the door and wrenched it open. Though it had no lock, secure as it was behind the garden walls, it clearly was rarely used. The hinges creaked, and the door scraped across the stone path. The noise cut through the quiet night, sending a few birds in the distant fruit trees flapping up toward the sky.

"If the gardeners weren't up yet, they might be now," Rylan murmured.

Behind the door, the corridor was pitch black, completely still, and smelled of dust and dry earth. Peter grabbed the torch mounted on the wall just inside the door and lit it. The flame flickered to life, casting shadows on the stone floor and arched hallway. The passage only extended a few paces before it opened up to a staircase leading into deeper, richer darkness. Goosebumps raised on his arms from the chill air. Peter shivered. "Ready?"

"Ready as I'll ever be," Kira muttered.

"Pull the door behind you," Peter said.

Kira balked. "Seriously?"

"You want us to leave it open?" Peter asked sarcastically. "Maybe advertise we're in here? We could put a sign out saying 'Exploring crypt. Be back soon.'"

"If we end up locked in here, I'm blaming you." Kira pulled the door closed, encasing them in darkness broken only by the flicker of the torch.

"Whoa," Rylan said. "It's dark."

"And so still," Sephiri whispered.

Peter led them down the steep staircase. It wound in a

spiral, down, down, down, so deep it made his skin crawl. The dry air turned heavy and musty, sitting thick on his tongue. He held up the torch, and when the stairs ended, he stopped so short Rylan collided into his back.

"Whoa," Rylan breathed. "Guess we're in the right place."

## 27

P eter leaned over and touched the torch in hand to the sconce built into the wall. The flame caught, and lit, and then danced down a narrow divot in the wall to another sconce a few paces away. That sconce lit as well, and the flame continued to travel down the white stone walls, lighting more as it went. Soon, warm light wreathed the entire room.

The room was enormous—larger than the Lancasters' great room, with a low ceiling supported by immense columns. Gold patterns decorated the columns, catching the torchlight and gleaming. Small recesses along each wall held labels with names and dates.

Tombs.

Some were built into the wall, and others stood freely in rows throughout the room. The tombs were made of the same heavy white stone as the wall, but each was decorated differently. Some were plain, others had ornate engravings, and still others had statues atop the lids, carved like bodies in repose.

Rylan whistled.

"It's even bigger than I thought," Kira said, the fear in her voice replaced with amazement. "It's gorgeous."

Peter set his torch in a holder by the door where two alcoves rested on either side. The four friends drifted into the room, surrounding themselves with the stone tombs.

"There are so many," Peter said, looking around. His gaze settled on a newer-looking one before him with the name Hamlin in relief across the top. "This must be the last baron."

"Yes," Kira confirmed. "Thaddeus Hamlin. Died five or so years ago . . . around this time of year, I believe."

"Wasn't he the one they say was poisoned?" Sephiri asked.

Kira nodded. "My parents never talked about it around me, but the servants would. Everyone believed it was his son, Derrik—that he couldn't wait to take over the job, so he had his father killed."

Peter shuddered. "Come on. Let's focus. Why don't we split up and search. Look for Vicion Shepherd's tomb."

Sephiri and Kira took the walls while Rylan and Peter searched the freestanding tombs. It took time to find the nameplates carved in various places. He recognized some names—former barons and lords—but most he didn't. Likely they were the various wealthy citizens of Palenting—the kind of men who lived high on the hill in Paratill View, overlooking the sea. Or they were soldiers, decorated and powerful, the ones who rose through the ranks and earned a place in the crypt with the greats of Palenting.

"Here!" Rylan cried. "It's over here!" He stood in the far corner of the crypt, waving both his hands as he jumped up and down. "I'm sure it's this one!"

Peter rushed over, with Sephiri and Kira hurrying behind him. "Whoa," Peter whispered. "This is impressive."

The tomb was the same size as the others, but its imposing display made his jaw drop. A carving of a snake wound around the entire circumference of the lower half of the tomb, and a statue adorned the lid. The actual-size rendering appeared to be of the Viper himself. The statue's eyes were closed over his large, crooked nose, and his lips twisted downward in a slight sneer. He was dressed in armor, chain mail, and a leather breastplate. His hands gripped the hilt of a sword—his sword. Even carved from white stone, it was unmistakable. It had the same carved hilt, with the snake's open mouth leading to the long, impressive blade.

"There's no name." Rylan pointed to a small plate mounted to the tomb, just under the statue's feet. "But look at this."

On the stone, where a name and date of death should be carved, there were no words at all—only a carving of a triangle.

"Do you think this is where it is?" Kira asked. She pulled her arms close to her chest, rubbing them against the cold. "Is the key in there?"

"There's only one way to find out," Rylan said. "Shall we?"

"Wait," Kira said, holding up her hand. Her head tilted oddly.

Peter leaned toward her. "What is it?"

"Shhh!"

Kira stood frozen while the other three stared. Seconds ticked by in Peter's head. He was about to ask what was wrong again when he heard it. *Voices.* His eyes grew, and he sucked in air.

"Someone's coming," Sephiri whispered.

"I thought you said no one ever comes here?" Rylan asked.

Kira threw up her hands. "I'm not an expert on this place."

The voices grew louder.

"We need to hide," Peter whispered. He crouched behind the Viper's tomb, keeping his head out of sight. His face pressed into the ancient stone. Cobwebs tickled his hair.

Rylan ducked next to him, while Kira and Sephiri tucked themselves into an alcove in the wall.

"Who's down here!" a deep male voice called across the crypt.

Peter tensed. Footsteps shuffled into the room, scraping against the stone floor.

"There's no one," a younger man with a scratchy voice said. "Did Grandston already come down to set up?"

"He must've. The lights are lit, but . . ." The wiping sound of a hand across stone filled the air. "Looks like he forgot to dust."

The younger man scoffed. "Typical. Baron Hamlin would wring our necks if we left his father's tomb in this state for his annual visit."

"Like he really cares," the man with the deep voice said. "If he killed the man, I doubt he really cares how dusty his tomb is."

"Still . . . he has to keep up appearances. How long before they all arrive?"

"A few minutes at best. We need to hurry."

A soft sound came from the girls. Peter's head shot in their direction to see Sephiri covering her mouth with her hand. He looked at Rylan. Blood drained from the larger boy's face like he'd seen a ghost.

"A few minutes?" Peter mouthed. His pulse thumped in his head.

"Set those down over there. Come on up and help me with the rest of the flowers." After some rustling sounds, the footsteps at the other end of the crypt gradually faded.

Peter peeked his head out from behind the tomb. *Empty.* He sighed and stood fully, motioning quickly for the others to come out.

"Around this time, huh?" Rylan whispered harshly toward Kira.

She threw up her arms. "I didn't know this was the *actual* day. Don't blame me!"

"He said 'before they all arrive,'" Sephiri whispered, her

face long. "These hiding places won't work if this room is filled with more than a handful of people."

"Agreed," Peter said. All four heads turned to the Viper's tomb. "Let's be quick."

"Peter!" Kira said, louder than was ideal. "We don't know when they'll—"

"Rylan, come on," Peter urged, ignoring Kira.

The two boys positioned themselves against the side and set their hands on the cool stone edge of the lid. "All right," Rylan muttered, "on three!"

They both took a breath. "One, two, three!"

Peter pushed with all his strength. He leaned his entire body into it, driving his heels onto the stone floor. Beside him, Rylan did the same, but the lid didn't budge. After a moment of effort, they both stopped, resting their arms and puffing.

"Rylan," Sephiri said, "are you using . . . ?"

"Sorry," he blurted, chuckling and shaking his head. "I've got this." He leaned forward while Peter rested. Faint sparks dotted Rylan's arms as he pushed again.

The lid moved. Stone scraped on stone, loud enough to set Peter's teeth on edge. He chanced a glance at the doorway to the crypt. *Still empty. I hope they went all the way outside.*

Rylan kept pushing until the lid dangled halfway off the tomb. Finally, he stopped with a deep sigh.

Peter leaned forward, peering into the stone coffin. "It's him," he whispered. "The Viper."

The remains of Vicion Shepherd rested inside—a replica of the statue atop it. Except where the carving was still thick with muscle and flesh, time had turned his remains into little more than bones resting beneath flat chain mail and leather armor. The Viper's skull gazed unseeing upward. One of his hands wrapped around the hilt of a plain steel sword, a placeholder for the one in the museum.

Only one of his hands.

The other hand rested at his side, palm-down—or the bones that would've made up the palm—and fingers curled inward.

"There's something here," Peter whispered. "He's holding something."

"The key?" Sephiri asked. "Is it the key?"

"Come on!" Kira urged. "They'll be back soon!"

"I'll have to . . ." Peter swallowed his nerves. All he had to do was reach out and take it. It was right there.

He reached into the tomb—closer and closer to the Viper's remains. His fingertips touched the cold bone of the skeleton's hand, and he held his breath, half expecting the remains to lurch to life and drive the sword through his chest.

The crypt was still, including his friends as they held their breaths.

He tapped the hand aside. The bones clattered against the chain mail on his body, breaking and crumbling to dust. Gleaming against the bottom of the tomb, where the Viper's hand had been, rested a long bronze key. Peter gingerly picked it up. It was heavy, as long as his palm, with three teeth at the top, and hanging from a thin metal chain. A triangle was engraved into the top of the key. "This is it," Peter said. "This is the key . . . hidden in bone."

Something in the tomb rustled. The disintegrating hand bones quivered, like they were grasping back to life. Peter leaped backward, gripping the key as his other hand flew to his hip to pull his knife. As if a knife would do any good against a sword-wielding skeleton warrior.

A fat cockroach crawled up the side of the tomb. It perched on the edge and waggled its antennae at Peter, then scuttled down the side. Kira shrieked and leaped away, flapping her arms as the bug scurried toward her. Her shrill voice echoed through the crypt, bouncing off the stone walls like there were a dozen Kiras all harassed by cockroaches. Rylan threw her a scathing look as the bug wandered away.

Kira's head retreated shamefully into her neck. "Sorry," she whispered with a grimace.

"Is that really it?" Sephiri asked, focusing on Peter. "The key?"

Peter nodded. He smoothed his thumb over the small engraving. "It is. I don't know what it unlocks, but it has to be it." He pulled the chain over his head, then tucked the key against his chest, under his clothes. The metal was cool against his skin, a reassuring presence.

Rylan pushed the lid of the tomb back into place with the same terrible scraping sound. Once the remains were encased again, he looked at Peter. "Let's get out of here."

Peter led the way across the chamber and stopped at the torch on the wall.

"What are you waiting for?" Kira asked. "Let's go!"

"What do we do if we run into those men on their way back down?" Peter asked.

A voice bounced down the stairs, and Peter froze. *Too late. They're here.* He spun, taking in their position, and pointed to the alcoves on either side. He and Sephiri ducked into one side, and Rylan and Kira hid in the other.

"I think you gave me the heavy one," the man with the scratchy voice said, his voice floating through the passage.

"Stop whining," the other said. "They're the same. Watch the last step."

Peter tried to keep his breathing steady, but the labored sound rang in his ears. In the tight space, Sephiri pressed against his back, her own chest rapidly moving. He kept an eye peering around the corner, waiting.

The men arrived. Crates with flowers and wreaths filled their arms, blocking most of their view. A lantern swung from a metal ring, dangling from one of the burdens. The men stumbled into the room, walking cautiously to make sure they didn't trip on anything.

Peter reached down and grabbed Sephiri's hand. She squeezed. When the men passed the alcoves, Peter padded out, stepping gingerly and leading Sephiri. Rylan had been peeking as well and emerged with Kira at the same moment.

The other three friends walked silently toward the stairs while Peter stopped at the torch. The men behind him lumbered their way forward, their feet scraping the stone. He winced as he lifted the torch off the wall. The light was not needed in the crypt, but they required it to get out.

Tiptoeing as fast as he could, he reached the stairs and hurried up after the others, who waited for him in the darkness. Silently, they continued up together. Peter's heart pounded in his chest, but each step brought renewed hope of making it out.

At the top of the stairs, Peter snuffed the torch, put it back in place, and pushed the heavy door open. While they were underground, the sun had crested the horizon, and its golden beam smacked him in the face. He cringed, blinking against the sudden onslaught of light, dizzying after creeping around in the dark for so long. Gradually, his eyes adjusted, and he led the way down the hill toward the fruit trees along the side of the garden.

"Walk faster," Kira whispered at his back. "Walk faster."

Peter's eyes darted around. "What is it?" he asked over his shoulder. Then he saw it.

A line of men and women emerged from the castle—twenty altogether. Their clothes were impeccable—rich and clean. Their hair was perfectly coiffed, despite the early hour. Several wore a black shawl, draped across their shoulders. They said nothing, heading in silence toward the hillside entrance to the crypt.

Peter ducked behind the tree line. The four friends peered

between the branches, watching the line of people continue, uninterrupted.

"Whew," Rylan whispered. "That was close."

Peter sighed, a grin on his face. "Yes, it was."

The regular combination of boosting succeeded in getting all four friends over the fence. Peter's pulse continued to race, despite his relieved feeling to have made it out.

The square hummed with morning activity as merchants unloaded their carts, and citizens of Palenting traveled back and forth. The fresh-baked smell of bread made Peter's mouth water.

"So what next?" Rylan asked.

"We need to get everything ready to travel," Sephiri said.

"I'll get as much food as I can sneak out of my house," Kira said.

"Me, too," Sephiri said. "Yani has some bedrolls and things I can grab hidden in an outside storage room. Don't worry, no one will see me, and she won't mind."

"Great," Peter said. "Take the morning to prep whatever you need, then we'll meet at the Garrison."

THE FOUR FRIENDS PARTED WAYS, with Sephiri headed to Yani's, Kira to Paratill View, and Peter and Rylan heading to their respective homes in Lowside. As Peter walked, the day's exhaustion weighed on him, as if iron fastened to his ankles and wrists. The adrenaline crash was nearly worse than a Source crash. He trudged through the streets, melting into the crowds.

Back in Lowside, he pushed open the front door to his parents' small house. The room was quiet. No fire burned under the cauldron, and the table was messy with the remains of the previous night's dinner. Despite his exhaustion, Peter was suddenly alert. *Something is wrong.* "Father? Mother?"

"Jason?" his mother called from the bedroom.

Peter didn't have time to ache at the realization it was one of his mother's bad days. He hurried to her. The bedroom was just as messy as the kitchen, with clothes strewn about and no water in the basin on the corner. "What happened?" Peter asked. "Where's Fa—where's Matthias?"

"In the fields, I think." His mother's eyes went glassy as she gazed toward the window. "It's been a while since he's come home. Do tell him I'd like to talk to him."

"Sure," Peter said, grimacing. He returned to the kitchen. *If Father isn't here, where is he?*

Peter walked outside to their field. He didn't see any motion or the familiar shape of his father with the plow or the scythe. But there, in the farthest field, their wagon waited alone. *Why is the wagon out here and not in the barn?* His nerves prickled as he hurried across the field. As he got closer, a collapsed figure materialized in the freshly plowed dirt, obscured by the wooden wheels of the wagon.

"Father!"

Peter rushed forward, heart pounding, and fell in the dirt to his knees at his father's side. He gripped his father's shoulders and shook. "Father! Father, wake up!"

Matthias groaned. "Peter?"

Relief crashed over Peter. "What happened?"

His father struggled to sit up. Dirt covered his clothes and arms, and the side of his face was pink from lying in the sun. *How long has he been out here?*

"Must've fallen," his father murmured. "I'm all right, Son." He pinched the bridge of his nose. Even with the dirt on his skin, a swollen angry red mark showed through on his forearm around where the brand was.

"What happened to your arm?"

"It's nothing," his father said. "Help me up, and I'll fix us some breakfast."

The skin on his father's arm was hot to the touch, and the

brand itself swelled and oozed pus. "Father. It's infected," Peter said. "How did it get this bad?"

"I just need to clean it," his father said. "We have little time to get the wiether planting done if we want to have the next harvest ready. There's work to be done."

Worry weighed like a stone in Peter's stomach. "I'll help you up. Let's get back to the house."

*If something happens to me, who's going to take care of my parents? But if I don't get the Amulet, who knows what chaos the Vipers will wreak?*

It was all too much. There was too much debt, too much work, too little pay, and no solution in sight. No solution but the Amulet. That was the only path forward for someone like Peter —he would never be a soldier, or a mason, or even a decent farmer.

*What if the Vipers figure out who my father is?* In his busyness, he had forgotten to worry about it. The walls closed in. He swallowed around the tightness in his throat and shook his head. *Now's not the time. I can't control that. Focus on getting Father inside.*

He lifted his father, helping him stagger to his feet. Matthias leaned on him as they trudged back to the house. Once they were inside, Peter helped him onto a chair at the kitchen table and cleaned up the dishes left behind from the night before. The morning was already flying by. He needed to get to the Garrison.

"Shouldn't you be at work, Son?" his father asked.

Peter cursed under his breath. *Jenkins. I hadn't even thought about him. No time to worry about that, now.*

"Here, let me start the fire—"

"Don't even think about it." Peter pushed him back down into his seat, then started the fire beneath the cauldron himself. The pot was clean, and he poured some water from the basin in to boil for tea. "I'll help you clean up, then I've got to leave for a few days."

"Days?" his father asked. "Where are you going?"

Peter sighed. He dipped a clean cloth into the basin of water, then sat at the table at his father's side. He held out his hand, and his father gave him his arm. Peter cleaned the dirt from his arm, using a gentle touch as he went over the angry, throbbing burn. His father inhaled through his teeth, but didn't move.

"Up in the Dorthar Mountains," Peter said quietly. "There's something I can do to fix all this."

"My arm's fine," his father said. "It'll be healed in a few days."

"No, I mean, all of this." Peter gestured around the house. "The farm. The loan. All of it."

"It's under control," his father said. "With a few good harvests, we'll be out of debt to the Vipers. It'll be like this never happened."

"Father . . ." Peter sighed. "The Vipers don't work like that. I don't know if they'll hold their end of the deal."

"Well, I have little choice but to hope they will," his father said gruffly.

"Father," Peter began, pausing after wrapping a bandage around his arm. He stared at his father, holding his gaze. "I'm going after . . . some treasure."

"Ha!" His father took the wet cloth and wiped the dirt from his face. "Don't get caught up in old stories of treasure, Son. You don't need to be gallivanting off in the mountains. You need to be at work. I need you here."

"I know where it is. The treasure is real. The Fortress of the Sun is real. I've got all the pieces. And once I'm back, all of this will be fixed, okay?"

"The Fortress of the Sun?" his mother said. She teetered into the doorway, gazing curiously at Peter and his father. "They say it's beautiful in the sunrise." She smiled, half-dazed.

His father leaped to his feet and ran to his mother's side. "You shouldn't be out of bed," he said. "What if you'd fallen?"

"I thought I heard your voice," she said. "Where were you last night, Matthias?"

"We'll talk more about this in a moment," his father said to Peter. "Come on, honey, let's get you back to bed, and I'll bring you some tea."

Peter watched as his parents shuffled back to their bedroom. Their movements were both stiff and small, like they were both one wrong step away from collapsing. The kitchen was still a mess, as was the bedroom. The fields were in terrible shape, not prepared at all for planting. After seeing his father collapsed, Peter doubted he would have enough strength to complete the planting at all.

*I'll be back in just a few days. Once I have the Amulet, they'll understand.*

Before his father could return to the kitchen, Peter hurried out the front door.

---

## 28

P eter made it to the Garrison, and under the mid-morning sun, immediately passed out on the fur by the hearth.

A few hours later, a gruff, familiar voice woke him up, saying, "Scoot over." Rylan slumped face-down into the fur with a groan.

Peter sat up, rubbed his eyes, and blinked at the sky. The angle of the sun proved it was early afternoon. "Where've you been?"

"My mother made me do chores before I left."

Peter laughed.

"Good morning, sleepy-head," Sephiri said, smiling and waving from the table, where she sat with Kira.

"How long have you both been here?" Peter asked, extending his arms in a stretch. "Did you get some sleep?"

"Not me," Rylan groaned.

"We both slept a bit after we got back," Sephiri replied.

"Try to get some sleep if you can, Rylan." Kira said. "We'll need to head out soon."

Rylan was already snoring on the fur before Kira even

finished her sentence. Peter rose and sat with Kira and Sephiri at the table.

"It should take about a day and a half of travel to get there," Kira whispered.

"Do we have all the stuff we need?" Peter asked.

Sephiri nodded. "Help me get everything together." She turned to Kira. "You okay to work on the translations?"

Kira nodded. "I searched forever before I found my old Tarphic language books. It may take a while though."

Peter and Sephiri packed up the bedrolls, a small tent, and all the food Kira snuck from the kitchen of the Lancaster home. Once everything was packed, Sephiri waved Peter over to the edge of the Garrison, near the swords and the bows they weren't bringing. They sat side-by-side on a bale of hay.

"Here." Sephiri pulled a sealed canteen from her pack and two small bowls. "I brought some soup from Yani's. You should eat something." She poured them each a serving from the canteen, then handed one to Peter. Only when the aroma wafted up did he realize how hungry he was, and he scarfed down the rich, meaty stew.

Sephiri laughed. "You need to take better care of yourself."

*I wish I could. If only I weren't taking care of my parents all the time.* He nodded. "I know."

A few moments passed. The only sounds were the scratch of Kira's pen as she worked on the translation, and Rylan's snores in front of the hearth. Sephiri sipped her stew. "Can I ask you something?"

"Sure," Peter said.

"Do you think this is going to work?"

Peter paused. He pressed his lips together, then rested his bowl of stew on his lap. "I think so," he said. "I have to think so."

"Razor can't get his hands on it," she said. "As long as we

keep him away from it, that's enough for me. Even if it gets destroyed in the process."

"You're not curious about it?" Peter asked. "You don't wonder about what abilities it might give you?"

Sephiri laughed, but there wasn't much humor in it. She set her bowl aside and pulled her knees up to her chest. "I've had enough of the abilities, I think."

"You don't enjoy having the Source in you?"

"I do, it's just . . . it's an enormous responsibility. That's why we can't let the Viper Syndicate get it. If someone like Razor gets the power the Amulet can provide, he could destroy this entire city. Or worse."

"What could be worse than that?" Peter asked. He was teasing, but the words made something cold settle in his gut.

Sephiri said nothing, just gazed half-focused at Kira's back, still scratching away at her translation.

"How are your parents?" she asked. "Are they okay? Is the farm recovering?"

Peter sighed. "I don't know."

"What do you mean?"

"Father was sick when I went home," Peter admitted. "He passed out in the field. I don't know what we'll do if we don't find this Amulet. I don't see a way for the farm to survive if we don't."

"I'm sorry," Sephiri murmured. "That never should've happened—the fields burning and the Viper loan. It's all so unfair."

"I'm sorry, too . . ." Peter said, looking her in the face.

Sephiri glanced up, and her brow furrowed.

". . . about your parents," he finished. "It's not fair what happened to them, either. I think they'd be proud to see you going after the Amulet like this."

A smile flickered across her face. "Thanks," she said. "Really."

Time passed quietly, with Rylan drifting in and out of sleep by the fire. Kira worked on her translations, taking breaks to stand and wander around the Garrison, stretching her arms over her head.

After a few hours, Kira sighed and closed the book. She leaned back and rubbed her hands over her eyes. "All right, that's all I can do for now. I feel like my brain is melting." She squinted up toward the sky. "It's getting late. I think we should head out. If we leave soon, we can be there the day after tomorrow."

"I wish we could take some horses," Peter said.

Kira shook her head. "I could take some from my parents' stables. But I think the terrain is going to get pretty rough."

Sephiri nodded. She finished her soup, hopped off the hay bale, and hurried over to prod Rylan's sleeping figure. He groaned and rolled over. "Five more minutes."

"Wake up," Sephiri teased. "We need you to carry the camping gear."

With some wrangling, Rylan got up, and the four of them gathered all the supplies.

They headed out of the Garrison, passed through the city, and arrived at the balds on the outskirts. Peter kept a close eye over his shoulder as they traveled, ensuring no one followed them. Once they were far enough from the city, he let his mind wander as they hiked. *What will the fortress be like? What will the Amulet do? Will we even find it? Does it even exist?*

Hours melted away as they hiked, until the sun was low in the sky. Sephiri caught a rabbit, and they roasted it over the campfire to eat with the bread and cheese Kira brought from the Lancaster kitchen. The meat was gamey but delicious, melting in Peter's mouth at the first bite. His body ached from the travel, and he knew as soon as he hit his bedroll he'd be asleep.

"I've been making some headway in translating Wynna's

book," Kira said. "It's not perfect, but it looks like it's an old story about the creation of the Amulet."

"What does it say?" Rylan asked.

"It looks like Otis Shepherd was its original owner," Kira said. "This book, written anonymously, goes into detail about *how* it was created. Apparently, Shepherd found the raw gem in the Straith Mountains, and a Tarphic gem smith shaped it into the Amulet."

"What does that mean for us?" Peter asked. "Will we need to know Tarphic to use the Amulet's powers?"

"I don't know," Kira said. "I'll work on more as we travel tomorrow. Reading and walking is not my forte, but I'll do my best."

"So, Shepherd found it, and the gem smith created it," Peter murmured. "Why would Wynna give us this book? It has to mean something."

"It won't mean anything until we get to the Fortress of the Sun," Rylan grumbled. "Now shut up and let me get some actual sleep."

Peter lay down on his bedroll by the fire and stared up at the night sky. Around him, the breeze was soft, and the moon shone, nearly full. There were no sounds but the rustle of the breeze through the tall grass and Rylan's snuffling snores. Even though his body ached from the demands of hiking, his mind still spun with possibility. What waited for them at the Fortress of the Sun? What did the Tarphic gem smith have to do with this? What would happen when—if—they found it? Would they gain more power than they already had?

*Could this really fix everything?*

At some point, between one circling thought and the next, the night air lulled him to sleep.

～

PETER AWOKE after dawn to the sounds of Kira and Rylan packing. He sat up with a groan and rubbed his eyes, blinking at his friends. "Why didn't anyone wake me?" he asked. "I could've helped."

"Looked like you needed the sleep," Sephiri said. She knelt by the recently extinguished fire and poured liquid from the small camping pot into a cup. "Tea."

"Thanks." Peter sipped the drink, letting its warmth rejuvenate him. As Sephiri packed up the remainder of the cooking items, Kira and Rylan wound up the bedrolls. Peter did the same with his own and hurried to his feet. It was still early, but the sun was over the horizon.

"Let's get a move on." Rylan heaved the pack high onto his shoulders.

Peter nodded. The Dorthar Mountains loomed to the west with the fortress supposedly sitting near the northern end. The range jutted into the sky like enormous teeth. Peter pulled his pack on, and the four of them headed across the hills.

Kira walked in the middle with Peter at her side, looking out for obstacles. She spent most of the day with her nose in the book, translating, occasionally handing it to Peter to hold open so she could review her notes and scratch new ones at the same time. As the morning melted into midday, they stopped in the shade of a large boulder to rest and eat.

"I think I've got a little more figured out." Kira leaned against the rock with the book and her notebook both open on her lap. "Listen to this. The gem smith created the Amulet from the raw mineral, right?"

"Right." Sephiri tore a hunk of bread apart and offered each of them a piece.

"There's more to the story than that. This claims that using the gem, and later the Amulet, turned Otis Shepherd into a shrewd, selfish man. The more wealth he gained—with the power given to him by the Amulet—the more paranoid he became. He believed everyone was out to steal the Amulet from him. In order to keep it a secret, he killed the gem smith who created it."

"Wow." Peter's brows pinched together. "That's . . . interesting."

"It reads here like if you use the Amulet too much, it has negative effects on you," Kira said. "Like it consumes you. I haven't gotten much more detail than that yet. It says the Shepherds tried to get rid of anyone who knew about the Amulet at all, but the rumors had already started circulating. The gem smith's son tried to find it, but the Shepherds had too much power, so he fled to Tarphan before they could kill him, too."

"What happened to him?" Rylan asked.

"I don't know. Haven't gotten that far."

"What does this have to do with the fortress?" Sephiri asked. "Is there anything about where to find it when we get there?"

"Not really. Only that the Shepherds hid it."

They ate the rest of their lunch then continued their uphill march in tired silence. Kira didn't continue the translation work until the four of them had found a place to camp in the shadow of the mountains and the sun dipped low on the horizon. As Rylan built a fire, Kira sat down on her bedroll and returned to her notes. Peter watched her with amazement. *How is she still able to do that? Doesn't her head hurt?*

"We should arrive by midday tomorrow," Sephiri said. She pointed to the steep, jagged, and snow-capped mountain overhead. Peter shuddered at the epic scale and the thought of climbing it. "Dagger Path leads up there, so the fortress should be just around that peak, in an alcove facing east."

"I sure hope it's there." Rylan plopped down on his bedroll and wrenched off his boots, then sighed with relief as he wiggled his toes in front of the flickering flame.

"Oh." Kira's eyes widened as she stared down at the final page of the book. "I think I know why Wynna gave us this."

Peter leaned forward, wide-eyed. "What do you mean? You finished?"

Kira nodded. "If I'm translating right, it says, 'The story of the Amulet of Power was told to the author by the smith's descendant Tessa Rasoir, as told to her by her parents, as told to them by theirs."

"So it's an oral history?" Rylan asked.

"Rasoir," Kira said. "It's a Tarphic name. Does it sound similar to anything?"

Peter's jaw dropped. "Rasoir. He changed his name."

"Changed it to sound Norshic," Sephiri said. "Razor."

Rylan gasped. "You think Razor is related to the gem smith? And that's why he wants the Amulet so badly?"

"It could be." Peter exhaled. "We need to get there and find it first." He placed his hand on his chest, feeling the shape of the heavy key beneath his shirt. "At least we're the ones with the key."

## 29

The next morning, the four of them set off before dawn. The sky was gray with the threat of sunlight, and the hills were silent save for the distant cries of a few birds. Peter gazed up at the imposing mountain, adjusted his pack on his shoulder, and started on his way.

Dagger Path—a narrow, overgrown trail—led up into the depths of the mountains. The way was steep and rocky, and Peter scrambled more than walked, using his hands to grasp the cool stone of the boulders as he pulled himself up the ridge. The air grew colder as they climbed higher.

Considering the narrowness of the path and the boulders they had to scramble over, the going was slow. There were more than a few close calls, with Kira's feet slipping on the slick rocks, and Rylan huffing under the weight of the pack and veering dangerously close to the edge. The drop beneath them wasn't sheer, but it'd be an unpleasant, long fall, to the hills below, which grew smaller and smaller as the path switchbacked up.

Morning melted into midday.

"Are we almost there?" Rylan asked, his voice strained.

"I believe so," Kira said. "It should be soon."

"It better be," Rylan muttered, "or else I'm going to need another break."

Peter pushed his legs, forcing them to keep stepping when the path rounded a sharp corner. He stopped, his shoulders sinking. The peaks they'd climbed between converged into a solid wall of rock.

"Where'd the path go?" Sephiri asked.

Kira sighed. "This is *supposedly* where the fortress should be."

"Great!" Rylan said, throwing a hand in the air. "Like I said, it's just a story. We're out here chasing after a fairy tale."

"It can't end here," Peter said, his voice sounding distant. A tightness formed in his chest. He walked forward, his legs suddenly unsteady as doubt rushed through him. "Maybe we have to go over it."

Rylan scoffed. "Good luck with that. Not even Sephiri's magical wind power could get you over that cliff."

Peter continued forward, refusing to believe it was a dead end. *Mother and Father need me to come through for them. It can't be just a story.* He stopped at the sheer rock wall and leaned a hand against it. The smooth stone soared above him. A dizzy spell washed over him as he looked up. He pounded his fist against the rock.

In his peripheral vision, something caught his eye. He cocked his head.

"What is it?" Kira asked. Her footsteps approached.

Peter stepped to the side and leaned forward. Hidden amongst the divots in the stone, a dark hole was carved in the wall. *A hole in the shape of a key!* His sinuses cleared in a sudden rush of adrenaline. He fumbled under his shirt and pulled out the key from the tomb. *I sure hope this is it.*

He placed the key into the hole. It slid easily, fitting snugly until it caught. *Here goes nothing.* With a flick of his wrist, he turned it.

A *clank* echoed from inside the mountain.

"This is it!" Sephiri exclaimed.

"No way!" Rylan said, his heavy steps approaching.

Peter took a step back as the wall shook. After a moment of rumbling and dust falling off the rock, a crack formed.

A giddy laugh came from Kira.

The crack grew to outline a door that swung open the width of a hand.

Peter waited while the rumbling settled. Small rocks finished skittering down the cliff face, and silence returned. With slow steps, he walked forward and pulled on the door. It pivoted open. The passage behind was dark, but a bright light shone at the end of a short tunnel. He turned to the others with a grin. "I think we found it."

The four friends walked in silence into the passage. The ceiling was low, and the walls were tight. A damp coolness filled the air.

Peter squinted as he approached the light at the end. Using his hand as a shield, he stepped into the sunlight, and his jaw dropped.

High above, across a chasm, loomed the Fortress of the Sun. Carved into the face of the mountain, the structure faced east, the midday sun beating down on the eroding exterior. The facade emerged from the mountain, half-camouflaged in the landscape. Chiseled directly from the stone, windows and doors emerged from the rock like openings into darkness. Vines and lichens covered the columns and staircases, as if nature attempted to retake the structure for itself. Across a bridge, a square courtyard stood in front of two large stone doors. On either side of the doors, two waterfalls spilled out and over the edges of the courtyard and into the deep chasm below. There was no river visible below. The water disappeared into the mist.

Gazing up at the fortress, Peter felt small. The place was ancient.

"Wow," Kira whispered. "It's really here. We made it."

"How do we get up there?" Rylan asked, his mouth hanging open.

"Looks like this is the way." Sephiri nodded to their left. A winding, shallow staircase carved into the mountainside. The polished rock ran in a steep switchback up to the bridge.

"Ready to do some climbing?" Peter asked with a grin.

Sephiri nodded. "Should be fun."

Rylan looked up toward the stone bridge. "Some definition of fun you have."

After emptying their packs of any unnecessary weight, Peter led the way up the narrow stone steps. The rock was slick under his boots. The steps sloped from age, barely wide enough for the ball of his foot. He braced his hands against the side of the mountain as he ascended the stairs, setting his fingers into narrow divots and cracks he found to maintain his balance.

As he climbed higher up the stairs, his anticipation grew. Ignoring the gaping chasm just one wrong step away, he focused only on the climb upward.

Behind him, Rylan gasped. Peter looked over his shoulder in time to see a crumble of rock break from the stairs and tumble downward, clacking against the stone. Sephiri grasped Rylan's upper arm, steadying him as he caught his footing again. He paled as she watched the rock tumble down the stairs and into the abyss below.

"Careful," Sephiri said.

Rylan chuckled. "Right. Yeah."

Peter climbed until his calves burned and sweat dripped from his temples. The stairs ended at a short ledge, where the four of them crowded together. Rylan still looked pale as he stood unsteadily, staring at the precarious-looking bridge ahead.

The mossy stone bridge was cracked and narrow, leading over the chasm to the doors of the fortress. The multiple waterfalls pouring from the fortress roared like a distant storm.

Peter pulled his pack higher onto his shoulder and nodded to his friends. Kira grinned up at the fortress. Rylan nodded with careful determination, and Sephiri's dark eyes gleamed with excitement.

*We made it. We're here.*

Peter inhaled. He took a step from the ledge onto the bridge. He half expected it to crumble as the stairs did, but the stone was sturdy. He crossed the narrow bridge in calculated steps with his friends behind him. Beneath them, the chasm gaped like a beast's hungry maw. One slip, one broken edge, and down they'd fall into the waiting mist. As he neared the waterfalls, the stone bridge grew slick, and the way became more precarious.

"Careful," Peter shouted over the tumbling water with his gaze fixed forward. His legs ached from the tension. His feet felt every crack in the stone beneath them. A light breeze forced him to extend his arms, checking his balance. He paused to take a steadying breath before moving again.

After an endless number of tense steps, he made it across the bridge into the courtyard with Sephiri, Kira, and Rylan close behind. The waterfalls plunged into the chasm below, but the roar diminished as they moved away from the edge.

"Whew," Kira whistled. "That was exciting."

Up close, the immense fortress created an overwhelming scene. The ancient and crumbling courtyard contained a mossy garden in the center, overgrown with weeds and small trees and surrounded by a crumbling stone wall. Twin warrior statues loomed overhead, flanking each side of the door. Vines crept up the stone carvings and across the walls. The cracked court-yard pavers under his feet were mossy and dotted with plants growing from the nooks and crannies. High overhead, a few large crows cawed as they took off into the sky. Their cries echoed off the mountains.

Kira walked to one of the immense statues and gazed up at it. She placed her palm flat on the stone, like she could hardly believe it was real. "It doesn't look like anyone has been here for hundreds of years."

"I don't think they have," Peter said.

"It really might be here," Sephiri said. "The Amulet of Power. I can't believe it."

Behind the overgrown garden, two immense stone doors stood sealed shut. Peter approached them with both trepidation and curiosity. There was no handle, no lock, just smooth stone. High overhead, engraved at the top of the doors, were three familiar icons: the tower, the wave, and the curved snake. A square divot met at the seam of the doors, about the size of his two hands cupped together.

Peter poked at the divot, then pulled at it, trying to push or pull the doors open. They didn't budge.

"How do we get in?" Rylan asked from behind him. "I don't think even I could push these doors open."

"Are they doors at all?" Sephiri asked. "Maybe it's a trick. There might be another way in." She gazed up toward the mountain, squinting at the stone. "A window, or a tunnel, or something like that."

"If we have to climb any higher than this, I think I'll be sick," Rylan muttered.

Peter stepped back. He traced his finger around the edge of the square divot. "No, I think this is the way." He set his pack down, opened it, and pulled out the pyramid wrapped in cloth. He tossed it once, caught it, and then held it in hand.

A smile grew on Kira's face. "I think you're right."

Peter slid the pyramid into the divot, point first, until the base set flush with the doors.

A deep, slow rumble grew under his feet.

"What is that?" Rylan asked. He jumped backward, then looked around for the source of the noise. "Do you hear that?"

Peter took a step back.

The two stone doors swung inward. Heavy stone scraped across the floor through a smooth, defined groove.

A vast room stretched beyond the doors. The floor was the same cracked stone as the courtyard, and the walls were the innards of the mountain itself. Columns stood throughout the room, looking as if someone had carved them directly from the original stone. *This must've taken ages to carve out,* Peter thought. It was dark in the chamber—hidden from the rest of the world. Peter couldn't see much further than a few paces in front of him. There were no torches on the wall, but a sconce was set by the door, low to the ground.

Peter knelt down and sparked it alight with his flint.

Flame leaped from the sconce and then rocketed throughout the chamber. Like the Solaris Crypt, the flames raced down two shallow channels carved into the floor itself, illuminating the chamber in warm light. In the center of the chamber, the two lines of flame curved and grew taller, the orange flame arcing above a deep, churning pool of water.

"Whoa," Rylan said, his deep voice bouncing through the room.

The chamber was dark, dusty, and quiet, save for the crackling flame and the rush of the water. Peter stepped forward, staring in awe.

"What is this place?" Kira whispered, stepping with him. Even her whisper echoed in the vast space.

They approached the churning water.

"You remember what the pyramid said?" Sephiri said. The

orange light reflected in her dark eyes. "The flame upon the sea."

Below the flickering fire, water flowed from the pool through two narrow channels that ran along the sides of the chamber and out through the walls. "I wonder where those flow to." Kira stared into the whirling pool as if hypnotized. "How does it do that? Where does this water even come from?"

"Deep in the mountain, I bet," Rylan said. "Probably snowmelt. Don't fall in."

"Look," Sephiri said. "It keeps going."

Peter walked around the churning pool. At the far end, a narrower rivulet flowed from the pool deeper into the chamber. It curved back and forth like a snake.

"It's the icon," Sephiri said. "It's not a snake. It's the water."

*She's right.* Water from the pool flowed in the familiar shape, all the way to a dark, narrow doorway. The flames ended suddenly, so the doorway was an abyssal rectangle at the end of the chamber. The rivulet of water flowed into the darkness and disappeared from sight.

"We need to follow it," Peter said.

"Through there?" Rylan asked. "Is there a torch or something?"

"There's got to be something," Peter said, "or maybe we're supposed to be stuck in the dark, and left to figure it out—"

"Peter Fairfield!" a deep voice roared. The sound echoed through the chamber, amplified by the space, and sent icy-cold fear racing down Peter's spine. He whipped around, one hand on the hilt of his short sword.

Garrett Razor stood in the front of the chamber, silhouetted by the sunlight through the doors behind him, the light of the flames illuminating his scowling face. Vipers stood behind him, tall and armed. Two of them had their arms around—Peter's heart dropped.

"Mother!" he cried. "Father!"

"That's right," Razor hissed as he stormed into the chamber. "I figured out who you are. You're going to do what I want, or your parents will join you and your friends in the same fate."

The Vipers followed behind him. Two of them led the way, dragging his parents. His mother was passed out, carried like a dead weight on a Viper's back while his father stumbled along with his hands bound.

"We're all right, Peter," his father said in a strained voice. The man looked exhausted, his eyes and cheeks sunken, and his limping gait looked pained.

Razor stood on the other side of the whirlpool. His cruel, stony gaze fixed upon Peter and skewered him like a blade. "You thought I wouldn't find you?" he hissed. "You thought you could get away with taking what is rightfully mine?" He wrenched Peter's father from the other Viper and shoved his sleeve up, revealing the angry red brand. "Your whole family belongs to me. Now . . . where is the Amulet?"

## 30

"We don't know where it is," Kira said.

"Don't play coy, Girl," Razor sneered. He dug his fingers into the brand on Peter's father's forearm, drawing a grunt of pain. "I could've taken your parents just as easily, Lancaster girl," Razor hissed, "but Peter's fool of a father doesn't know what's best for himself and this city. When I went to visit these Fairfield debtors, the woman was more than happy to tell us where you'd run off to." Razor laughed, a high, cruel sound.

"She didn't realize what she was saying," Peter's father said through gritted teeth.

Peter's breath caught. He remembered his mother staggering out into the hallway amid their conversation. His head hung.

"Once we knew where you were heading," Razor added, "following you through the mountains was simple."

*I was careless. And now they're paying for my mistake. Again.*

"It's not your fault," Peter's father said. "Peter, listen to me, there's nothing—"

"That's enough from you." Razor knocked the hilt of his

sword against Peter's father's head. His body slumped, and the Viper holding him grumbled as he hauled Matthias' motionless body up onto his shoulder.

"Father!"

"Take me to the Amulet," Razor hissed, "or stand here and watch as your parents drown."

The Vipers stepped closer to the edge of the whirlpool.

"All right!" Peter glanced at his friends, and they nodded, all wide-eyed and pallid with the same fear Peter felt. "All-right. We'll take you. We think it's this way."

Peter turned and stepped into the narrow, darkened hallway. Again, a sconce was placed near the floor, barely visible in the deep darkness. He knelt and lit it, sending flames dancing down the edges of the hallway. At the end, the room widened, but not to a doorway. A massive round stone—circular but flat like an immense coin—blocked the way. A handle was carved into its center.

"We have to get through there," Peter said.

"'The strength of many,'" Sephiri whispered.

"Move!" Razor shoved past Peter and gestured for his men to follow. "Push that out of the way! Now!"

Three of the biggest Vipers hustled forward. They stepped to the side of the stone and got into position to push it out of the way.

With a muted *thwack*, spears shot from the wall, digging into their flesh in their sides, backs, and necks. The men shouted in pain as the spears withdrew, disappearing back into the walls. Dark stains appeared on their clothes, and their mouths foamed. They stumbled for a moment, but after only a few stuttering breaths, all three of them slumped dead to the floor.

After a yell of frustration, even Razor was at a brief loss for words. He stared at the carnage, then turned to face Peter, eyes blazing. "Figure it out!"

Peter and his friends approached the stone cautiously.

"It must be a trigger on those sides," Kira said, pointing to faint cutouts in the stone on either side of the passage.

"There's barely room for one person to stand in the middle," Peter said.

"Remember the clue—the strength of many," Sephiri whispered. "Why wouldn't we be able to push it together?"

"Rylan has the strength of many," Kira whispered back, eyes bright. "Rylan, you can move it."

"Maybe," Rylan said. "I mean, I hope so."

The three of them backed up, and Rylan stepped forward. "All right. No pressure."

Avoiding the cutout lines on the ground with his feet, he gripped the handle carved into the stone. Pausing, his shoulders raised and lowered while he steadied his breath.

"You can do it," Peter whispered.

Rylan's muscles tensed, but the stone didn't move.

"Now!" Razor barked.

Rylan dug his heels into the floor. He tightened his grip on the handle, fixed his gaze, and then pushed again. The veins on his neck stood out, as did the ones on his arms. Every muscle in his body seemed to tense as he pushed, teeth gritted. Finally, sparks danced down his arms.

The stone rolled. Rylan grunted as he continued to push, moving it away from the collapsed bodies to the other side of the widened hallway. Another dark, narrow passage waited behind it.

"Wow," Kira said.

Rylan straightened up and shook out his arms. "Ta-da," he deadpanned, his chest heaving.

Peter stepped through the narrow passage first. Behind him, Razor snapped a command to move faster.

As Peter moved, the flames that lit the passage behind him raced through, then up and around the walls, casting dim orange light all around the chamber. There wasn't much to the new room, either. Just a wide ledge, another bridge with water rushing below, and across the bridge, two open, narrow doorways. Overhead, the roof of the chamber soared, dripping with stalactites. It was a vast cavern, so large that if Peter looked up, he expected to see stars.

"Now," Razor hissed, "where is it?" His eyes burned with anger. Behind him, the Vipers still had Peter's parents in tow. "You better know what you're doing, or it'll be your parents tossed off this bridge." The Vipers dropped Peter's unconscious parents onto the ledge, like packs they were tired of carrying.

"I know what I'm doing." Peter swallowed around the knot of fear in his throat. The bridge leading to the doors was stone, like the bridge to the fortress itself, but this one was wide enough for two people to walk side-by-side.

"Two doors," Sephiri said. "Shall we?" At his side, her gaze was determined, but her face was pale.

Peter nodded.

"The two of you stay here," Razor commanded. Swords pointed at Rylan and Kira. He looked at Peter. "If you try anything funny, they die, too."

Peter swallowed.

"Be careful," Kira whispered.

Peter nodded before he and Sephiri stepped onto the bridge. It was steady under their feet. There was no sound save for the distant roar of water. On the other side of the bridge, he paused in front of the open doorway on the left and looked at Sephiri, who waited at the other.

She squared her shoulders and nodded.

In sync, they stepped over the thresholds.

There was no rumbling. The ceiling didn't collapse onto Peter's head. No hidden door closed him into the space. There was only silence. Even with the doorway open behind him, Razor, the Vipers, and his friends faded into silence.

The stone room he'd entered was small, with dark, plain walls. A hole ran through the center of the floor, revealing a river rushing far below. To the side of the hole in the floor were two smaller indentations: a small square hole and a square divot. *Why all in the floor?* Peter wondered. *What are we supposed to do here?*

Opposite the door, a small plaque rested against the wall.

"What's it say?" Sephiri asked.

Peter blinked. She was completely visible in her own room, separated from him by an iron grate. Her room contained an identical hole in the center of the floor. She peered up toward the ceiling with her brow furrowed.

"What are you looking at?" Peter asked.

"There's a hole in the ceiling," she said. "Directly above the one in the floor."

"Any others?"

"No, just those."

Peter nodded to himself. Sephiri's room had a hole in the ceiling, and his had the smaller indentations around the hole in the floor. *We play different roles here. What are they?*

Peter peered at the plaque and read, "'To wield its power, you must be wise. Prove your worth to gain the stone. One choice will lead to your demise, but the Amulet cannot be gained alone. Two must seek its power together. The test begins when you turn the key. One alone will lose it forever. Remember naught is gained for free.'" The indent of another keyhole rested beneath the small plaque.

Sephiri knelt and peered into the hole in the floor of her side. "I see the water. We're above the river. And it's moving fast."

"One alone will lose it forever," Peter murmured. "It's going to drop."

"What? What do you mean?"

"When I turn this key. I bet the Amulet will drop from the

ceiling above you. If you're not there to catch it on the other side, then it will fall into the river." He grinned. "You ready to catch it?"

She stood up, blinking at him. "Catch it?"

"What's going on?" Kira called from above. "Are you okay?"

"We're okay." Peter tugged the key out from beneath his shirt. "It's a test for two people. We have to do this correctly." He looked at Sephiri again. "Be ready to catch it."

"No pressure, right?" she muttered. She looked up at the hole in the ceiling, then held her cupped hands beneath it.

Peter slid the Viper's key into the keyhole. He held his breath as it clicked into place. "'Hidden in rock,'" he mumbled. Slowly, he turned his hand.

Overhead, metal rumbled, groaned, and clanked, like something deep in the mountain awakened after years of dormancy. A small stone box, about half the size of a brick, dropped from the hole and landed in Sephiri's cupped hands.

She stared at the box. Then she stared at Peter with a grin on her face. The box was plain stone, lacking any decoration save for a carving of a triangle.

"We got it," she whispered.

Peter stared back, a tingle running down his spine. "This feels too easy."

A rumble sounded overhead, and another under Peter's feet.

"Uh oh."

The floor shook. Sephiri stumbled, and Peter fell backward as the shaking worsened. Then the floor dropped out beneath him.

Peter shouted as he fell, momentarily suspended in midair as the room dropped, plummeting into darkness. A loud clank pierced the air, and the rooms slammed to a stop. Then, as if they'd caught on a hinge, the rooms rotated, sending Peter tumbling. He closed his eyes as he toppled like a pebble in a cup, curled into a ball with his hands on his head, crashing against the walls.

The rooms shuddered to a stop.

Peter leaned back, dazed from the sudden drop and the tossing about. He rubbed his forehead and blinked his eyes. The iron grate that had separated him from Sephiri as a wall was now above him.

"Peter! Sephiri!" Above him, Kira peered down through the open doorway with Rylan leaning over her shoulder. She was small overhead, as if she leaned down from a second-story balcony. "Are you okay?"

"I'm okay," Sephiri said. Peter blinked. Her voice carried through the wall between them.

"Me, too." Peter stood and walked to her voice. What had been the floor was now the wall, as if the room had rotated. "Seph? Can you hear me?" He peered through the largest hole. What had shown the river before now peered into Sephiri's chamber.

Her face appeared on the other side, flushed and scratched. "What is this? What happened?"

"You still have the Amulet?"

She nodded and held up the box.

"Okay," Peter said, "the plaque said we have to prove our worth by making a choice."

"Right." Sephiri took a few breaths, brushed the stray strands of dark hair off her forehead, closed her eyes, then opened them. "There has to be a choice here."

"Hand it to me." Peter reached his arm through the passage between them.

"Why?" Sephiri set the box in his hand.

"I think it fits these indentations on my side. This must be the choice the plaque mentioned. I have to choose what to do with the box."

It was a plain, gray stone box, polished to shining—the

same type of stone as the pyramid. He smoothed his thumb over the triangle carving. There was a thin seam, but when he fiddled with it, it didn't open. He pressed his lips together. The box was heavy and cool in his hands, but unobtrusive. It felt unreal. *It's right here. It's in my hands.*

*We just have to get out of here with it.*

Peter held it up to the first hole. "It'll fit perfectly into this indentation, so it's flush against the wall.

"Okay. And the one below it is a little bigger?"

"It looks like a tunnel."

"Hang on." Sephiri looked around, on her side, and then said, "A-ha!"

"What?" Peter asked. "What is it?"

"There's another on my side, too. A bigger one, near the floor. It must be the other side of that tunnel."

"Why are there two ways to pass it to you?" Peter asked. "I can just hand it to you through here, right?"

"But that doesn't have an effect. Maybe that's the choice. You either send the Amulet to me through the tunnel, or set it into the indentation."

"That's weird," Peter said. "What will it do?"

"I don't know. I guess that's part of the test."

"'One choice will lead to your demise,'" Peter repeated.

Sephiri balked. "So if you pick the wrong one, you die?"

*Prove your worth.* The clue rattled around in his memory. "I don't know if that's the wrong choice."

"What do you mean? Peter . . . what are you planning?"

"I think it—" A shudder ran through him. "I think gaining the Amulet requires a sacrifice."

"That can't be right." Sephiri's voice pitched up in fear. "That can't be. Why would it need a sacrifice? After everything we've already figured out? Here, give it back to me. Let's think about this."

*I'm the one who has to make this choice.* Peter kept the box in hand. "Let me figure out what they do."

"Don't. Seriously. Let's talk about this."

Peter lifted the box and slid it into the divot in the wall. When it was halfway in, a great *crack* and a rumbling sounded through the rooms. Peter's chamber slid upward, the entire structure gliding as if on a pulley system up toward the door.

"Peter!"

He wrenched the box out of the divot, and the room dropped back down and rattled back to where it had sat before. Through the hole that separated them, aligned again, he could see a spiderweb of cracks splintering across the floor of Sephiri's chamber. He watched, terror cold in his veins, as the cracks spread from her side to his own.

"It's going to give out," she said in a wavering voice. "We don't have much time. Your room went up, but mine started to crumble."

*The Amulet is how I make the choice,* Peter realized. *If I go up, Sephiri's floor breaks. So that must mean . . .* he placed the stone box in the topmost hole, keeping a tight grip so it didn't fall down the slope into the other room. The same rumbling sounded, and Sephiri's chamber slid upward.

Peter wrenched the box out. Sephiri's chamber dropped back down. She gasped in fear, and the splintering cracks worsened on the floors of both of their chambers. "Peter, what's happening?"

"That's the choice," he said. "One of us goes up, and the other goes down . . . down to the river."

"You don't mean . . ."

"Yeah." He shuddered again. "That's how we prove our worth. We have to give something up." *I just didn't realize how much we'd have to give.*

"Hold on," she said. "Let me try . . ."

A gust of wind filled Peter's chamber, blowing his clothes

and hair upward. As his compartment shook, the cracks on the floor increased. "Sephiri!"

The wind died. "It's no use," she said, her voice strained.

A twisting feeling turned in Peter's gut. He'd started searching for this Amulet to make his life better. He'd wanted adventure. Excitement. Enough money for his parents to live comfortably on their farm. Maybe even a little extra for him and his friends to stop living hand-to-mouth. He'd even had thoughts of leaving Palenting with his friends, striking out into the wilderness, the mountains, the cities he longed to visit.

A life of his own.

"Peter," Sephiri said shakily.

He wouldn't get that life of adventure—but he could still keep his friends safe and save his family.

That was enough.

He took a slow, deep breath, and then an odd sense of calm fell over him. "Okay, are you ready to catch the box?"

"What? No, Peter, there has to be another way to do this. If you drop it all the way through—"

"Then your side will go up," he finished for her.

"And yours won't. Peter, you'll fall. You'll *die*."

"It's all right, Seph." His voice caught. *This is what we came here to do. We got the Amulet. We figured it out. The others will figure out how to stop Razor—they'll take care of everyone.*

"No, it's not! There has to be another way out of this. We always figure out another way. You can't—" her voice cut into a yelp as the floor cracked further.

"These floors won't last. If we don't make a choice, we're both doomed. Catch it, okay?"

"No! Peter, don't, there has to be another way, you can't—"

"This is how we prove our worth. It's what the clues led to all along." The floor splintered further, wide enough to see the river through the stone. *I can't wait any longer.*

He looked up. Kira looked down, high above the iron grate. Her face pinched. "Peter!" she called down. "What's going on?"

"Tell them I said bye, okay?" Peter said quietly, moisture pooling at the corners of his eyes.

"I won't," Sephiri said, her voice thick with tears. "You'll tell them yourself. Peter, don't you dare—"

He slid the box into the tunnel, his fingers gripping the stone edges. The rock was cool. The smooth sides pressed against the back of his hand. His fingers ran along the crisp edge. After exhaling a quiet breath, he let go.

The box slid down the slope. Sephiri gasped as it landed in her hands, then silence fell over the chamber.

After a torturous pause, the rumbling began anew. Sephiri cried out as her chamber rose, back up toward the platform and the doorways. "Peter!" she called. Her voice was muffled. "Peter, no!"

Beneath his feet, the stone floor crumbled. It started from the center, the crack breaking into dust as the pit revealed the river rushing below. Peter pressed close to the wall, staring wide-eyed as the calm dissipated, replaced by animal fear. The floor splintered, bigger chunks dropping into the raging water. He gasped, took one more look up at his friends, and then the rest of the floor dropped beneath him.

Peter plummeted, flailing, his breath coming out in a choked scream as the river surged toward him. He closed his eyes, waiting for the icy water to envelop him.

A hard impact knocked the wind out of him. He'd landed on his back on a solid surface. Around him, stone crashed into the water as the room above disintegrated. He opened his eyes to see the small faces of his friends gazing down in horror from far above. Sephiri stepped over to join them, the box in her hands.

The river rushed beneath him. The rapids spat cold droplets of water, landing like icy needles on his face. With

shaking limbs, he sat up on a dark, moss-covered wooden platform. The barrier had enough give to catch him before he'd
landed in the water. Chunks of stone from the room above had
landed in the river and protruded like boulders, but most of the
dangling chamber was gone, swept away by the river. A ladder
set into the wall of the cliff, leading up to where his friends
waited. Next to the ladder, another inscription carved into the
wall. "You have proven your worth," it read. "He who chooses
himself over others chooses death. You have chosen wisely."

Peter flopped back down, an exhausted grin on his face. *If I
had chosen to keep it, somehow we would have both died.*

He exhaled, a soft laugh bubbling from his lungs. The cold
droplets of water from the river relieved him as much as they
annoyed him. A few more breaths and he'd ascend the ladder.
Razor was still up there. As were his parents.

But they found the Amulet. It was all going to work out.

"Peter!" Kira called. "Peter, are you all right?"

"I'm okay," he called. "I'm really okay."

*I'm alive.* He could hardly believe it himself.

"We'll toss a rope down," Sephiri called. "Just wait, we'll get
you back up here!"

Razor approached from behind his friends. All Peter could
do from the platform was watch as the Viper loomed over
them, speaking words Peter couldn't hear over the roar of the
river. The wall blocked most of his sight, but he could see the
fight and hear disembodied shouts of pain. He craned his neck,
trying to see, blood pounding in his ears. "Rylan!" he cried, but
the river drowned out his voice. "Seph!"

Four Vipers stepped close to the edge of the cliff above. In
their arms, Sephiri and Kira struggled against their holds. "No!"
Peter called, as if that would do anything. As if he could stop
what was going to happen.

Razor appeared at the edge of the cliff, too, grinning.
Someone lunged at Razor. *Rylan.* The Viper kicked and spun.

After a brief scuffle, a large body flew over the edge of the shaft with Sephiri and Kira tossed just behind.

Peter rolled, relying on his Source quickness to get him out of the way, pressed against the wall just before Rylan crashed down. Then Sephiri landed, and Kira, the three of them heaped onto the wooden platform.

"Seph!" Peter cried. "Is anyone hurt? Is everyone okay?"

"He got the Amulet," Rylan groaned, rolling over and rubbing his shoulder where he'd hit the platform. "He took it."

"We're okay," Kira said. "Are you all right?"

"You jerk!" Sephiri cried. She sat up with some effort and then smacked Peter hard on the shoulder. "How could you do that?"

"What?" Peter asked. He rubbed his shoulder. "What other choice did I have?"

She rubbed her eyes hard. "I don't know! But you still shouldn't have done that!"

"If I hadn't decided, we both would've—"

A loud creaking sound cut through the argument. The platform below them shuddered. "Um," Rylan said. "Guys?"

"Again?" Peter moaned.

Beneath them, the old wooden platform splintered under their combined weight. With overlapping cries, the four of them tumbled the short distance into the raging river.

## 31

The freezing water shocked the breath from Peter's lungs. The rapids pounded over him, pulling him downstream. He sputtered and flapped his arms to keep his head above water. "Seph!" he tried to shout, only to swallow a mouthful of icy river water. He coughed and choked. The water rushed through a dark, narrow passage, where it was all Peter could do to keep breathing and avoid slapping into the rocky banks.

The rapids sent him hurtling around a corner, missing an outcropping of rocks. Sephiri crashed into him, sputtering. He grasped her upper arm, holding on as they rushed forward. Near them, Rylan and Kira held each other, too, floundering in the cold water.

Light shone ahead, and the river widened. They left the dark passage, and suddenly they were no longer within the caverns of the mountain. They were at the bottom of a deep chasm, and the bright sky was visible overhead. The sudden sunlight blinded him. A distant roar reached Peter's ears as he blinked toward the opening ahead—the opening where the water dropped. *Waterfall!* His stomach twisted.

Peter fought the strong current to the side of the river, where a narrow bank rested out of the water and a dark passage veered up and away from the river. With Sephiri in tow, he wrapped an arm around a boulder jutting out of the bank.

The water whisked Rylan past him, but with Rylan's hand wrapped around Kira's wrist, he fought his way to the banks, too. "Hold on!" Rylan shouted. He pulled Kira closer, and she grasped the rocky edge, sputtering and coughing.

Peter found a crack in the rocky bank, big enough to get a solid grip. "Here!" He hauled Sephiri closer and guided her hands to the crack.

Rylan grunted as he grasped the bank and pulled himself up. The water tried to suck him down, but Rylan wrestled his way up and onto the bank with his sheer strength. He flopped onto his belly and reached back, hand extended to Kira. "Grab on!"

"I can't!" Kira cried. "The water—it's too fast—"

"Reach for me," Rylan said. "Try, Kira!"

Kira's arm strained as she gripped the rock, reaching up with one hand. Rylan stretched down and was about to grasp her hand when a frothing wave rushed forward and slammed into Kira. She shouted and tumbled backward, off the bank and back into the rushing river, speeding toward the waterfall.

"Kira!" Peter shouted. Without thinking, he lunged off the wall and raced toward her, kicking with the current to pick up speed. He crashed into her, catching her arm a body's length from the deadly drop. "Swim!" he said, pulling in the other direction. "Come on, swim!"

Clinging to each other, they turned toward the bank. Peter used the Source to kick and pull as fast as he could, but the current was still too strong. They continued toward the falls.

The light brightened as the edge approached. The distant roar of water crashing below grew louder and louder. Peter kicked desperately, but no matter how hard he swam, he didn't get any nearer to safety.

The drop was closer. Closer.

Peter closed his eyes. Held his breath.

And then—

He didn't fall.

The cold water pushed against his body, like he clung to the banks again. Except there was no rock, no features to hold on to.

He opened his eyes. His hand still wrapped around Kira's upper arm. With her head lifted above the churning water, she stared wide-eyed and pale as a ghost.

They perched on the edge of the waterfall. Beneath them, the water plummeted into a deep, endless mist. Under their feet, the water spilled over the edge, but Peter and Kira were suspended in the air.

"It's Sephiri," Peter shouted, his jaw hanging loose.

She still gripped the boulder, one hand tight on the rock, but the other extended toward them, palm out. Her eyes were pale, and sparks of power danced over her skin, so bright and numerous they were as visible as the stars in the night sky.

"Swim, swim!" Still holding on to Kira, Peter yelled as he kicked toward the bank. With the current eased by the blocking wind, and Peter's incredible speed, it only took a moment to make it to the bank. Rylan grabbed Kira's hand, hauling her up and out of the water. She collapsed onto her hands and knees, coughing as she caught her breath.

"Get Sephiri," Peter shouted to Rylan as he held on. "I don't know how long she can keep this up!"

Rylan nodded, then rushed over to Sephiri. He dropped onto his belly again and reached, wriggling close enough to grasp her wrist where she clung to the bank. Appearing lost in a trance, she didn't react to Rylan's hold.

Kira, having caught her breath, leaned down for Peter. He

grabbed her hand and clambered out of the water, hands and feet slipping on the slick rock before he flopped onto the bank.

As soon as he exited the water, the barrier disappeared. The wind raced over him, causing a violent shiver. The river surged, leaping toward the waterfall.

Sephiri slumped.

"Whoa!" Rylan yelled. He tightened his grasp on Sephiri's wrist, then hauled her out of the freezing water and onto the bank. She was motionless, sprawled out on her back, drenched and unconscious.

Peter's heart clenched. He scrambled to his feet and rushed to Sephiri's side. He knelt down, patted her cheek, then held her shoulders. "Seph!" He shook her. "Seph, wake up!"

Kira hid her mouth behind her hand. "Is she . . . ?"

"This happened when we jumped out of the tower," Rylan said. "She just needs a minute to recover. Right? Peter, right?"

"Come on, Seph." Peter turned her onto her side and clapped her on the back. "Come on, wake up. Breathe."

Sephiri lurched, then coughed so hard her entire body jerked. Water spilled from her mouth and nose. She gasped, then flopped onto her back, chest heaving.

"Seph," Peter said. "Are you okay?"

"You saved us," Kira said, kneeling at Sephiri's side. "Again. You saved all of us."

Sephiri nodded, but her eyes were unfocused, like she couldn't quite hear Kira's words.

"We have to move," Peter said, after giving her a moment to breathe. "We have to find our way back upstairs. We can't let Razor out with the Amulet, and we need to get to my parents."

Sephiri nodded again. She tried to get up but barely made it to a seated position before she grimaced and crumpled back down.

"I'll carry her," Rylan said.

Peter nodded. He'd seen Sephiri fatigued from using the

Source, but it was never this bad. She'd never looked so sallow and exhausted—like it'd take a lot more than a quick nap and some food to restore her. *Have we pushed her too far?*

He shoved down the thought. *I can't worry about that now. We need to focus on getting out of this fortress alive.* A bleeding gash running down Rylan's arm caught his eye. "Whoa, are you all right?"

Rylan paused and flexed his arm. Finally, he dabbed it with his shirt and nodded. "I'm fine. It's only a scratch." He knelt so Sephiri could wrap her arms around his neck then stood with her on his back. She blinked, still looking dazed and only half-present, but at least she was conscious. "What now?" Rylan asked.

Peter stood, wrung out some of the water from his shirt, and got his bearings. They gathered on the rocky banks of the river, deep in the chasm. A fresh, dark tunnel of water disappeared into the sheer rock next to them, and, carved into the wall, another ladder waited. Beside the ladder, water tumbled down the cliff face, over the bank, and into the river itself. "There," he said, pointing at the ladder. "But I don't know where it leads."

"It's the courtyard," Kira said. "Remember how the whirlpool had two streams split off? I'll bet this is where they flow."

Peter nodded. "All right. Let's move. If we're lucky, we'll be able to catch up with Razor. Rylan, you're able to climb?"

Rylan grinned. "She weighs about as much as a drowned rat."

"Hey," Sephiri muttered, smacking him half-heartedly.

Peter nodded. He matched Rylan's grin, despite the exhaustion, the ache in his muscles, the freezing cold, and the long climb ahead. *This might work.*

"All right," Peter said. "I'll lead."

He climbed steadily, gripping the stone ladder so hard his knuckles turned white. The rock was slick under his hands and feet. With each step up, his awareness grew of the distance beneath him and the consequences of slipping off. He focused on the ascent, trusting his friends to do the same below him.

As they neared the end of the climb, voices echoed through the space above. Peter looked over his shoulder at the three on the ladder below him, then placed his forefinger to his lips.

He peeked over the edge of the cliff.

Kira was right. The ladder brought them to the far edge of the main chamber, and the whirlpool was straight ahead. Peter's parents leaned against a nearby wall. He fought the urge to run to them. In the flickering light of the low flames running along the floor, he saw the rise and fall of their chests. *They're alive.*

Razor stood in front of the whirlpool with his remaining dozen lackeys in a semicircle watching him. The edge of the room, where Peter peeked out, was far enough from the flames to still be shrouded in darkness.

Peter glanced back down and nodded. He moved first, creeping into the room and hustling behind a wide stone column. Kira joined him, and Rylan and Sephiri hid behind another column a stone's throw away. None of the Vipers noticed their presence—they focused on Razor. *And Razor assumes we're dead,* Peter thought.

*But how are we going to get the Amulet? There are three times as many of them, and Sephiri can hardly stand. I can't fight them all before my speed runs out.*

". . . and all that led to this moment," Razor said, in the middle of a speech. He curled his fingers around the gray stone box in his hand.

Peter set his teeth into his lower lip.

Razor continued, "When I was a boy, my father told me the stories his father told him. He told me about our forefather, a humble gem smith, who trusted a Rynorian named Otis Shepherd enough to work with him. At the Rynorian's request, my forefather turned a raw crystal from deep in the Straith Mountains into a fine piece of jewelry. It was my ancestor who honed its power and transformed it from an unwieldy, unpolished discovery into the fine Amulet of legend. Without Tristan Rasoir, there would be no Amulet at all. Do you know how they rewarded him for his work?"

Razor sneered. He wasn't waiting for an answer. He gripped the box as if he tried to smash the stone box with sheer strength. "He was murdered! The Rynorian never trusted my forefather at all. He used him, and when he was no longer useful, he killed him. He tried to kill the rest of the Rasoirs, too, but he couldn't catch us all. And so my family's work lived on.

"But what the Rynorian didn't realize is that the methods he used to protect the Amulet were not created just for him. They're Tarphic." Razor smoothed his thumb over the box. "I'm sure Shepherd thought he was being clever using this material to protect the Amulet. He never thought the Rasoir line would find it again. The fool."

Razor dipped the box into the whirlpool behind him. The stone darkened from the water, and just like the pyramid, a new seam appeared.

Kira nudged Peter. She held up a small, sharp-edged rock, then raised her eyebrows at him.

Peter nodded. He understood her plan—and with the Source, he could make it work.

Razor twisted the box, and the lid popped off.

"Now," Razor said, his voice growing in intensity, "with the Amulet in my possession, it won't be the Shepherd clan who pays for what they did to my forefather. It will be all of Palenting! And then, all of Rynor!" He reached into the box.

The Amulet of Power gleamed as Razor lifted it—a rich blue jewel fading to red at the top. *The flame upon the sea.* It was set in plain silver, hanging from a thin silver chain.

The Vipers' leader held the chain between his forefinger

and thumb. He dropped the box and focused his attention on the Amulet. The crystal caught the dim firelight, shining as it rotated. He reached to grasp it with his other hand.

Kira stepped out from behind the column and threw the rock overhand with the same speed and accuracy with which she shot arrows. It flew true, crossing the chamber and slamming into the meat of Razor's hand, between his forefinger and thumb. He barked in surprise and dropped the chain.

Time slowed down.

Source power flowed through Peter from the center of his chest and radiated out to the tips of his fingers. He exploded off the balls of his feet. The speed felt natural to him, but it appeared as if the rest of the world had slowed to the pace of dripping molasses. The dropped Amulet floated toward the ground as he crossed the room. Arriving in the blink of an eye, Peter slid and caught the jewel before it crashed to the rocks. His fingers wrapped around the crystal.

He gasped. Power surged through him—different from the Source. It was stronger, brighter. It was as if light poured into him and flowed through his veins, lighting him up with a new level of power. Sparks no longer danced down his arms— tendrils of light wrapped around them like snakes, brief and bright enough to burn his eyes before it faded.

With the Amulet in hand, he turned and faced the Vipers.

A dozen of them. Only one of Peter.

He grinned and unsheathed his short sword.

Two Vipers approached with their own swords drawn, larger and heavier than the one Peter held. They sneered at him—clearly thinking it would be easy.

The taller of the two swung his sword through the air in a high arc, bringing it down like a hammer toward Peter's skull. Peter lifted his own sword and parried. The metal-on-metal clang was earsplitting. The man gnashed his teeth as he pushed against the locked weapons. Peter held his ground for a moment, then ripped his sword away and darted to the side. He ducked low and kicked the Viper in the shin, hard enough that the man yelped and stumbled backward.

The second Viper snarled a curse, then lunged. Peter dodged from instinct—the movement as natural as breathing. He spun under the lackey's sword, then slashed at his gut. His blade bit into the man's flesh. The Viper cried out as blood spilled. He dropped his sword and pressed both hands to the gash, staggering backward.

"Get him!" Razor shrieked. "Kill him!"

Two more lackeys rushed at Peter. He blocked one strike, danced around another, then struck back with his own blade. He caught one man in the arm, and the other dodged. Peter focused on his breath as he dodged strike after strike, but the men were faster than the previous two, and they took him seriously. He wasn't just a young man they could dispatch with one well-aimed blow. He was a formidable enemy.

Two more strikes missed. Sweat beaded at his temples. His pulse pounded in his ears. Clang. Clang. Another dodge. Another spin on his heel. He nicked someone's leg and caught someone else in the gut. Blood dripped from his blade. Sweat ran into his eyes. *I can do this. I can win.*

An arrow pierced his side, and a yell tore out of his throat. Peter stumbled to the ground. Pain shot through his body. He gritted his teeth and yanked the arrow in a hard pull, tossing it to the side. Adrenaline numbed the area. He pushed the injury from his mind and jumped back to his feet.

*Surrounded.*

Vipers covered him on all sides—fewer than before, but all of them stood with weapons drawn and scowls on their faces.

Icy fear curled in his gut. He gripped the hilt of his sword and steeled himself. The Amulet's power still flowed through him, clasped in his hand, warm in his palm.

Chaos descended. Peter blocked the swords as they fell on

him like rain, relying on the Amulet to dodge strikes to his throat and the back of his head. His feet slipped on the rock, and he stumbled. His breath caught. He couldn't dodge them all. A lackey lunged close and slashed him in the waist. Bright pain burst again through his nerves, and he fell to the side. He tried to hold on to the Amulet, but the crystal spilled from his grasp, flinging to the cold rock past the Vipers and well out of reach.

He dropped his sword as his knees gave out. Without the Amulet in hand, all he felt was throbbing pain and weakness. He pressed his hands to the gash. Blood oozed through his fingers.

Above him, the remaining Vipers brandished their weapons, the sharp points pointed down at Peter's supine body. He swallowed as the fear returned anew.

"How cute," Razor said. He stood by Peter's parents, still unconscious and leaning against the walls of the whirlpool. He drummed his fingers on the crown of Mathias' head. "You thought you could get away with this little scheme? I believe I should kill your parents now, before I kill you, just so you have the privilege of watching."

Sephiri stepped out of the darkness on unsteady feet. With glassy eyes and pallid skin, she moved with careful determination.

"You—" Razor hissed.

Sephiri scooped up the Amulet from where it'd settled.

"No!" Razor cried.

Wind rushed through the chamber, sending the dust and dirt along the floor of the chamber spiraling up. The gust whipped through Peter's damp clothes and raised goosebumps on his skin.

Light burst from the Amulet in the same tendrils Peter experienced before. They wound around Sephiri's limbs, white and shimmering, glowing with the same pale light that gleamed in her eyes. She straightened, her posture steady and strong, and looked ahead at the lackeys surrounding Peter like a wolf appraising a herd of sheep.

A man dropped his sword and took a staggering step back.

"She's just a girl," a Viper said. "Let's get her!"

He leaped forward.

Sephiri stretched out her hand. Her eyes shone even brighter white, like gleaming pearls.

Wind roared in the distance. Peter gasped and tried to wriggle backward toward the whirlpool, to hang on to the edge, but he could barely move with the pain in his side. The gale entered the chamber like an oncoming stampede —unstoppable.

He squinted and waited for the torrent to blast into him, but it never happened. The wind roared in his ear as it seemed to split around him, like a river breaking around a rock. He remained in place while the wind pummeled into the men surrounding him. It knocked them backward and sent them tumbling, bumping across the dusty floor of the chamber to the farthest end. They shouted and scrabbled. Their fingers grasped fruitlessly at the edges of the stones and the weedy undergrowth as the wind drove them off the edge of the chamber, plummeting into the chasm below.

Sephiri staggered backward. She swayed unsteadily on her feet, like a tree battered by a hurricane. The wind was gone.

Only one Viper remained. From his safe distance, Razor roared in animal rage and charged at Sephiri.

"Seph!" Peter called. "Look out!"

"Take it," Sephiri said, fighting to keep her balance, her voice barely audible. With the last of her strength, she tossed the Amulet in a high arc.

Peter scrambled to his feet and snatched it from midair before it fell to the ground. Its power surged through him again, but this time, the power focused on the wounds in his side and at his waist. He gasped, swaying as the Amulet healed his injuries.

Razor caught Sephiri before she collapsed, one arm wrapped around her body, holding her up, and the other pressed a dagger to the vulnerable flesh of her throat.

She clawed at Razor's forearm, fighting against his hold. Her resistance only made Razor press the blade harder. He fixed his wild, enraged gaze on Peter. "The Amulet," he snarled. "The Amulet, or she dies."

"Don't, Peter," Sephiri choked. "Don't give it to him."

Peter took a step closer.

"That's right," Razor said. "Bring it here if you want the girl to live."

"Don't hurt her," Peter said. "Let her go, and I'll give it to you."

Razor barked a laugh. "You think I'll fall for that little ruse? Give me the Amulet *now*." He pressed the blade harder to Sephiri's neck, drawing a thin line of blood.

Sephiri closed her eyes. "Peter, please. Don't do it. It's not worth it."

"I'm not gonna let anything happen to you." Peter opened his hand, revealing the Amulet in his palm. Razor's eyes widened, and Peter took another step closer. "Fine. I'll give it to you. Just don't hurt her."

Razor's mouth broke into an evil grin. His gaze fixed on the Amulet, and its light reflected in his dark eyes. Peter stepped closer, palm outstretched. Razor kept the blade at Sephiri's throat while he extended his other hand, fingers reaching for the crystal.

Peter inhaled. *I only have one chance to do this.*

The Amulet's power still rushed through his veins.

He exhaled, closed his hand around the Amulet, and leaped forward. He moved faster than he ever had, darting forward in the space of a blink. Before Razor could react, Peter closed his hands around the knife and wrenched it out of the Viper's grasp, uncaring of the bite of the blade into his own hand. He grabbed Sephiri and dragged her away from Razor.

Off-balance, Razor whirled to face them. His roar of anger was soundless. He grasped at his waist for another blade, but before he could find one, a knife sang through the air. A blade out of the shadows buried itself in Razor's upper chest. He gasped in sudden pain as red bloomed from the wound. He staggered backward, stunned. His eyes stared out of focus when his knees knocked into the short wall surrounding the whirlpool. With a shout, he lost his balance and tumbled backward over the wall.

Peter kept his arm around Sephiri, holding her up. They took a step back as Razor thrashed in the turbulent pool, fighting against the freezing-cold rush. The water lapped over his face and body. His shouts echoed throughout the chamber before melting into gurgles as the persistent tug of the water dragged him under.

The room was still. Quiet and motionless save the flow of the water.

"Nice, Kira!" Rylan shouted. He leaped out from behind the column and threw his fist in the air. "Dead on! Great throw!"

Kira nodded. She looked dazed, staring at the whirlpool. She wiped her brow, then rushed forward. "Seph, are you okay?"

"I'm all right." Sephiri pulled away from Peter's grasp, then gasped. "Peter, your side!"

Only then did Peter remember his wounds. The pain was almost gone, nothing more than a dull ache, like a healing bruise. "I'm all right." He lifted his shirt with curiosity. What should've been a nasty gash and a deep puncture, had healed to not much more than scratches. "The Amulet healed me, I think."

Kira picked up the box from the ground, while Peter, with the Amulet still in hand, knelt by his parents.

"Are they okay?" Sephiri asked.

Peter looked at his parents, noting their breaths. "Okay?" he chuckled. "Probably not. But they're alive."

"Let's get out of here," Sephiri said.

The four of them gathered around the Amulet. Before placing it back in the box, Kira and Rylan both touched it, gasping at the sudden surge of power.

"Whoa," Rylan said. "I feel like . . . like it refilled my strength. Yeah, I can definitely carry your parents out of here, now."

"I feel like I can see for miles," Kira murmured. "This is incredible."

Rylan held out his arm where the red gash remained. "Why didn't my arm heal?"

Peter stepped closer to inspect it. Finally he shook his head. "I don't know. Maybe the power helps me to be faster— including healing. But, for you, it only focuses on strength."

"That's too bad."

"We can't keep using it, though," Sephiri said. "It's too strong. It's not like the Source." She closed the box with the Amulet inside and handed it back to Peter.

"Hey, guys?" At the back of the whirlpool, Rylan leaned down and peered at the stones surrounding it. "What's this?"

One stone in the whirlpool was engraved with a triangle. The four friends exchanged a glance.

"Remember the tower?" Kira asked. She reached out and pressed the stone. It sank. The whirlpool stilled. Something inside of it clanked and rumbled. Peter glanced around, half expecting more cracks to appear on the floor or in the ceiling, but none did. The water level in the whirlpool lowered until it was only the depth of a hand. Razor's drowned body was nowhere to be seen, but one item did emerge from the receded waters.

A large stone box.

"Whoa," Rylan said. "What's in there?"

"Let's find out," Peter said. "Can you lift it?"

Rylan grasped the handles on the sides of the box and, with a grunt of exertion, heaved it out of the whirlpool and onto the ground near them. As he did, the rumbling returned. The water rushed back into the whirlpool and resumed its churning.

"You open it," Rylan said to Peter, nodding to the latch on its side. "I feel like something's going to pop out."

Peter knelt in front of the box. He unlatched it, held his breath, and then lifted the heavy lid.

"Oh, wow," Sephiri whispered. "Oh, *wow.*"

The box glimmered in a gorgeous rainbow of colors. Gems, crystals, gold sol and silver argen filled the box. It was more wealth than Peter had ever seen in one place before—more than the bank or even the Palenting Museum.

"I guess we have some extra stuff to carry back," Peter said, smiling.

# 32

The rest of the day passed in a blur. Having divided up the treasure into each of their packs, Peter led them down the mountain while Rylan and his enhanced strength carried Peter's parents over his shoulders. They set up camp as the sun fell, and Sephiri and Peter tended more thoroughly to his parents' wounds. Peter cleaned their various cuts and scrapes, and Sephiri made a tea with dried barkleaf fungus, encouraging them to drink sips in their half-conscious state. Peter touched the Amulet to his parents' skin, but the action didn't appear to have any effect.

By the next morning, both parents were awake, albeit a bit dazed from the ordeal. The potent tea had killed the infection overnight, and Sephiri re-wrapped the healing burn.

"What happened?" Peter's father asked.

"What's the last thing you remember?" Peter asked as he packed up their things.

"Your mother and I were at home." His father's brow furrowed as he pondered. "It was late. There was a knock on the door, and Vipers rushed in. Someone hit my head . . . and then everything was a blur. There were moments, flashes of . . . caves? But I remember little else."

"The Vipers won't cause us any further problems, Father," Peter said.

"What do you mean?"

"Garrett Razor's, uh . . ." He looked at his friends for help, but the only reply was a shrug from Sephiri. He sighed. "Razor's dead. And you know that treasure I mentioned? We found it. Razor followed us to the fortress and tried to kill us, but . . . I guess we won."

Peter's father blinked in confusion. "He tried to kill you? Are you—"

"Yes, we're all right, Father. We're fine."

His father's shoulders relaxed. "What treasure?"

Peter opened his mouth to speak of the Amulet, but his voice caught. The thought of Sephiri's parents dying because of the secret they kept rushed through his head. "Uh . . . um . . ."

Rylan opened one of the packs. "This," he said, holding up a handful of coins and gems.

"Oh, my," Peter's mother said. "It's beautiful."

"That's right," Peter said, swallowing hard. He proceeded to tell his parents all that had happened over the previous weeks —leaving out any reference to the Amulet and their power from the Source. His mother and father both listened in rapt attention.

"So we're splitting up the treasure," Peter said, pointing between him and his friends as he concluded the story. "My portion will be more than enough to buy back the farm loan from the remaining Vipers, assuming they keep any semblance of order after Razor's death."

Despite the shock of hearing the events, his parents received the information well. His father looked lighter at the thought of the loan being taken care of, and his mother held a large grin on her face as the group packed up. Soon, they all continued the long hike back to Palenting.

In the early morning sun, they moved at a slower pace, with Peter's parents walking side-by-side up ahead. Rylan carried the bulk of the camping supplies, moving like he hardly even realized he carried any extra weight at all, even with the gold and the gems added. Kira bounded on her feet with a spring in her step, scratching notes about the various birds she saw with her sharpened eyes.

Peter carried the Amulet, safe in its stone box, in his pack. He sensed its weight, satisfyingly heavy amid the supplies and stash of jewels. His heart felt like a weight had been removed. *We did it. We actually found it.*

"So, what do we do, now?" Sephiri asked quietly, ". . . about the Amulet."

The four of them walked with some distance between them and Peter's parents, keeping their voices low.

"Do we tell anyone?" Rylan asked.

Peter shook his head. "I don't think so. I didn't tell my parents because it could put them in danger.

"I'm sure we could trust them, but . . . you're right," Kira said. "I agree that we should keep it to ourselves."

"Just each other," Rylan agreed. He hiked the pack higher on his shoulders. "How long do you think it'll last? Like, will the Source wear off at all?"

"I thought it was wearing off for me," Sephiri admitted. She tucked her hands in her pockets and gazed at her feet as she walked. "The last few times I used it, I thought I drained the last. Part of me wondered if that might have been better, though. If I could just be normal."

"None of us are normal now," Peter said.

"You never were, Peter," Rylan quipped, jabbing him in the shoulder.

Peter pushed back, drawing a laugh from the girls.

"So how do you feel now, Sephiri?" Peter asked. "Drained?"

"It's like the Amulet replenished the Source," Sephiri said. "I'm still tired, but not like I was before."

"Same," Rylan said. "I feel stronger. Even more than right after we first got the Source." He glanced around the rolling hills, his gaze lingering on the sparse boulders and trees. "It's making me antsy, like I haven't had a good workout in a few days. I bet I could pick up that boulder over there if I wanted to."

"Please don't," Peter said. "My parents would definitely notice."

"I've been dealing with this for my entire life," Sephiri said with a smile. "You better get used to wanting to use your power and not being able to."

"Ugh," Rylan groaned, "this is so unfair."

"Having incredible strength is unfair?" Sephiri asked.

"You know what I mean," Rylan said. "I wish we could just go to the town square and show off. I could probably pick up an entire kebab cart."

"It's not worth the risk," Kira said. "No using the Source in public. I mean it. We'll have to stick to training in the Garrison. I'm sure you can burn off some energy moving the boulders blocking the collapsed wall so we can get in a little easier."

"Sounds thrilling," Rylan griped.

"We should keep training," Kira said, "So we can learn as much as we can about these powers. Then, we can use the Amulet to recharge when needed."

"As long as we don't overuse it," Peter said. "You remember what the stories say?"

Kira nodded. "Too much use and you go mad. We don't need any of that. Rylan's mad enough as it is."

"Hey!" Rylan complained.

"But more importantly," Kira continued as if Rylan hadn't

spoken, "we need to figure out how we're going to manage our little windfall."

"I don't know if I'd call it little," Peter said. When he thought about the sheer amount of gems and gold they'd found, his head spun. "All I care about is getting my parents out of debt. I don't care after that."

"That's easy," Kira said with a dismissive wave of her hand. "Their debt will barely make a dent." She opened her notebook to a fresh page. "So . . . there are plenty of gem merchants who will buy the bulk of the haul at wholesale prices, but if we sell them all at once and flood Palenting with new inventory, the value will decrease. We should only sell a few here in Palenting, enough to free your parents from debt first, and then sell in some other cities if we can." She started scratching notes, with the tip of her tongue between her teeth as she thought. "Once we've sold maybe half, and have a good amount of coin, we should try to invest it somehow. My father has connections who should be able to help with all of this."

"I think we should buy an enormous meal." Rylan's gaze became half-focused. "At a real tavern. With an entire suckling pig. But the pig's just for me. You guys can get something else."

The conversation continued like that, with the four of them trading ideas for what to do with the money while Kira sketched out a plan to make the most of it. Rylan wanted to eat, Peter wanted to fix up the farm, and Sephiri wanted to furnish a room of her own at Yani's—all of which was within reach.

"You know," Peter said, as they walked, "I have an idea that might be better than Yani's."

Sephiri's eyebrows raised. "What are you thinking?"

The plan took shape in his mind. He grinned, drumming his fingertips against the side of his leg as he laid it out.

THE NEXT DAY, after another restful night by the campfire and a half-day of travel, they made it back to Palenting proper. Peter had never thought he'd be relieved to see the city again, with its white stone buildings high on the hill of Paratill View and the crumbling gray walls rising above them as they drew closer to Schuggec Row.

With a few murmured, exhausted goodbyes, Peter's parents headed straight toward Lowside, back to the farm. At the Garrison, Rylan dropped his pack. Then after some organization and changing out of their boots, they made their way to Brufec Heights for a huge meal at a tavern. Real food—more than they'd ever been able to afford before. Peter's mouth watered at the thought.

Peter led the way north. Palenting felt brighter, more welcoming. He didn't scan every alley for a Viper, nor was he worried about getting kicked out of the neighborhood. The coin was hefty in his pocket, and the Source still burned in his blood.

The Bitter Bat Inn bustled with activity even in the late afternoon. It was a warm brick building, with wide doors thrown open and well-dressed patrons spilling in and out, a mix of folks from Paratill View, artisans from the nearby shops, and even local bureaucrats after a day of work. A man perched on the slanted roof, painting the inn's sign a crisp shade of red —different from the faded, cracked signs Peter was used to. It was the kind of place he had never had the coin to patronize. He grinned at his friends as they approached the door.

"Hey!" a familiar voice barked.

Ashton Dunn shoved an old woman off-balance as he hurried down the cobbled street toward them. Behind him, Tanner and Hodge rushed to keep up.

Peter stepped away from the Bitter Bat and all the delicious scents wafting from the open doors. "Hi, Ashton." He threw Ashton a wave and wore a confident smile. After dealing with

Razor and the Vipers, it was a relief to face a bit of average bullying.

"What are a bunch of Lowsiders like you doing in this part of town?" Ashton sneered.

"Not this again," Rylan moaned. "Ignore him. I'm hungry."

"You think you have the money to just walk into a place like this?"

"Sephiri . . . look up," Kira whispered behind Peter's back.

Not taking his eyes off Ashton, Peter spied the painter's wooden bucket from the corner of his eye. It perched on the edge of the eaves, directly above Ashton.

Peter took a step forward. "Ashton . . . things are going to change around here. You need to get used to that."

Seemingly from nowhere, a breeze picked up, and a light rustle sounded above.

"What I will never get used to is *you* thinking you're better than *me*."

Peter's smile softened. "I don't think I'm better than you, Ashton. We're different. We're both trying to live in this city, doing the best with what we have. We just have different obstacles we're trying to overcome."

"I don't have—" Ashton cut himself off, his face turning red. "You think having obstacles makes you noble?"

Another rustle from above. "That's not what I'm saying. I—"

Ashton pointed at Peter and narrowed his eyes. "I shouldn't have stopped with your parents' fields. I should have burned your house down, too!"

A flare of anger burst inside him, but Peter fought to keep from lashing out.

"What was that?" a deep voice bellowed from the wide doorway of the Bitter Bat Inn. With his boots clumping, Constable Eastling emerged from the inn, his broad shoulders and stern countenance leveled at Ashton. "You were the one who burned the field in Lowside?"

Ashton froze with his eyes wide. His mouth hung open as he stared at the constable.

Before anyone moved, the curious bit of wind gusted, and the wooden bucket tipped. As it fell, the bucket turned and landed on Ashton's shoulder. Peter jumped back as red paint splashed in all directions.

Ashton held his dripping arms out, motionless. Only speckles of red dotted his face and hair, but paint covered his clothes.

"Sir, I'm so sorry," the painter called from the roof.

Ashton looked at Peter then back to the constable.

"Um," Tanner said, "I actually—well, I gotta get going!"

"Me, too!" Hodge agreed, and the two of them scurried off.

Ashton wasted no time. He snapped into action and hustled after Tanner and Hodge.

"Hey! Stop!" The constable ran in pursuit, disappearing after a moment in the winding streets.

"No using the Source in public, huh?" Rylan said. "Sephiri?"

An impish grin grew on Sephiri's face. Her shoulders rose in a shrug. "I don't know what you're talking about."

The four friends burst into a shared laugh.

Grinning, Peter pulled a gold sol from his pocket, tossed it, then caught it. "Come on. Dinner's on me."

# 33

"I'll take three of those," Peter said to the merchant. He
pointed to the garronts hanging from the top of the
stall. "Give me a couple legs of lamb, too."

The butcher wrapped the meat in brown paper, and Peter
paid the requisite two copper tid. He added the meat to the
basket he carried, which was already stuffed to overflowing. It
was Weekterm at the market. Visiting the few merchants who
remained open on the last day of the week, Peter had
purchased a few loaves of freshly baked bread, vegetables, and
even splurged on a few pastries filled with fruit jam. He bit into
one of the treats as he walked through the bustling square,
savoring the buttery, flaky pastry and the sweet paleno jam
exploding with flavor across his tongue.

In the three weeks since they'd returned from the Fortress
of the Sun, he'd eaten more jam pastries than he could count.
And yet, each one still tasted like the first one he'd ever had.

"Hey, Ashton," Peter said as he approached the center of the
town square. "Want a bite of pastry?"

"Beat it," Ashton grumbled. "We don't want anything from
you." The young man's typically perfect blond hair was matted

and ruffled. He attempted to look away, but it wasn't easy to do being locked in the wooden stocks.

"Tanner? Hodge?" Peter said, holding a pastry up.

The other boys obeyed Ashton's implicit requirement to not show interest, although Hodge did begin to drool.

Ashton's father fought for weeks to keep his son's trouble private after his poorly timed confession outside the inn, but the constable wouldn't give in. They finally compromised on one day in the stocks plus restitution paid to the Fairfield family, funded by Ashton's father.

"Don't worry. You'll be out of there soon," Peter said. "I've been there plenty of times. It flies by."

Ashton said nothing, just stared at Peter's feet with a sour expression.

"I know you're there for burning our farm, which was . . . awful, but I wanted you to know I'm moving on."

Ashton looked up with narrowed eyes.

"Things ended up working out for us, so . . . no hard feelings?"

"I said beat it!" Ashton snapped. He spat at Peter's feet, barely missing his nice, new boots.

"All right, all right. Fine," Peter said. "See you around whenever you're out."

He smiled as he left. It was nice to see Ashton taken down a notch. Not even the Lord of Commerce's son was invincible. *There is at least* some *justice in the world.* It gave him hope that his parents could get back on their feet.

Maybe things really were changing.

He finished his pastry and strolled with his basket back to Lowside. "I'm back!" he hollered as he hurried down the narrow road to the farm.

"Hi, Peter!" his mother called from the fields. "Go on inside. Your father's got breakfast!" She waved merrily with a hoe in hand. Her hair was tied back with a bright blue bandanna. Ever since they'd returned from the Fortress of the Sun, his mother had been clearer-minded, with more energy.

He pushed the front door open with his shoulder. Inside, his father hummed as he stirred something aromatic in the cauldron over the fire. The kitchen was clean and well-stocked, with herbs drying in the window and vegetables chopped for pickling on the counter. "Peter!" he greeted him cheerfully. "How was the market this morning?"

"Busy for a Weekterm," Peter said. "I got the last few garronts, though, since you wanted to braise them."

"Excellent, excellent." His father nodded as he poked through the basket. "You know, I don't think I'll ever get used to it. I keep expecting a Viper or someone to show up at the door." He rubbed at the healed burn on his forearm where the scar of the brand remained.

The Fairfields owned their farm completely. With Razor gone, the Vipers struggled to regain their footing in Palenting. When Peter and his father showed up with the full loan amount, plus the same amount in "interest", the Vipers didn't ask questions . . . they just handed over the deed to the farm. For the first time in all the years Peter could remember, they carried no debt.

"Did you see your mother outside?"

"Yeah, the flower garden is coming along nicely."

"She's going overboard." Matthias laughed fondly. "It's going to be an explosion of blooms in a few months. You'll be recruited into helping her harvest, I'm sure."

"That doesn't sound so bad," Peter said. "Especially since she knows who I am now."

His father's expression softened. "She hasn't called you Jason in a while, has she?"

Peter shook his head. All her days since their return had been good days, and they only seemed to get better.

"We're both doing much better," his father said. "I guess I

didn't realize how much the stress weighed on us both." Smiling, his father unpacked the basket.

Peter leaned against the doorframe. It wasn't just the alleviated stress that caused the change. *The Amulet did this.* He fought to keep from grinning. Whatever abilities his parents developed weren't clear to him, and Peter tried not to pry so they wouldn't get suspicious. He was content to know that they were doing well.

"Do you need any help with anything today?" Peter asked.

"No, no, we're not doing anything important," his father said with a wave of his hand. "Go enjoy the day. It's nice outside. Here, take this with you." He tossed a glass jar, which Peter nearly fumbled. "Pickled falend. Have your friends give some feedback. I need to know if the brine needs more peppercorn."

It'd been a long time since his father had made anything for fun. Peter nodded and tucked the jar into his rucksack. "Will do."

He made his way from the farm down to Schuggec Row. The normally quiet streets of the neighborhood hummed with activity. Peter squeezed around men carrying hefty wooden beams and masons hauling buckets of wet clay. He greeted a few of the familiar workmen as he made his way, eager to see how the progress went.

"Hey, Kira!" Peter called as he approached the Garrison. "You're here early."

Kira stood across the street from the Garrison, perched on a low wall and sipping a mug of tea. She grinned and waved Peter over. "Rylan's in there helping again," she said. "I keep telling him we're paying those guys to do this, but he can't seem to help himself."

The Garrison swarmed with workers. A group of men, including Rylan, cleared out the last of the boulders from the fire collapse. Others cleaned the ivy and vines from the front, and another group repaired the back walls. In the middle of the Garrison, Sephiri stood next to a tall woman with short hair and a severe gaze, pointing up at the exposed beams. Then they both peered at an oversized sheet of parchment in the woman's hands, then looked back up at the rafters.

"Seph!" Kira called. "Hey, Seph!"

Sephiri looked over her shoulder. She beamed, said something to the tall woman, and then hurried out of the Garrison. "Hey!" she said, jogging up. "Look at how much progress we've made!"

"What were you talking about with the architect?" Peter asked. "Also, taste this. My father made pickled falend."

"Ooh," Sephiri said. She sat next to them on the low wall.

Kira opened the jar and popped a bite into her mouth. "Ooh! Sour. I like it." She offered a bite to Sephiri.

"I was asking about the plan for adding the rooms upstairs," Sephiri said. "I think I'm annoying her with all my questions. I'm just so excited."

"You deserve to be excited," Kira said. "We all do."

Peter leaned closer and dropped his voice. "They're not going anywhere near the—" He paused to ensure no people lingered nearby. "—the stone by the hearth, are they?"

She shook her head. "They're not working there at all. The Amulet should remain well hidden."

"Good." He looked back to the building and set his hands on his hips. "I think this makes a pretty good first investment."

They'd purchased the crumbling old Berregard Garrison from the city for a pittance. No one else wanted it in its state of disrepair. Once renovated, it wouldn't just be a place for them to hang out. It'd have rooms to live in, a proper kitchen, an actual roof. There'd still be space to train, and of course the big hearth at the back, but it wouldn't just be a hangout. It'd be a home.

Sephiri couldn't stop smiling. Watching her brought a grin to Peter's face as well.

"Work is coming along well," Kira said, "right on schedule."

They sat quietly for a moment, watching the rhythmic construction, sharing pickled falend and laughing when Rylan saw them and started waving like a loon.

"So." Kira raised an eyebrow. "Once this is done, what are we doing next?"

"I don't know," Peter said. Something prickled under his skin. Things were good—things were amazing. But . . .

*The Amulet of Power is real. I wonder if there are other legends that are real, too?*

He wasn't bored. He wasn't dissatisfied. But he couldn't deny that he was a little . . . curious.

He grinned. "I bet we can think of something."

THE MAN HEAVED his pack higher onto his shoulders. Sweat dripped from his temples and stained the underarms of his heavy canvas shirt. The sun blazed overhead as he scrambled over a damp boulder. Though the mountains soared around him, they offered no respite from the heat. The sun pounded against the foliage, bleaching the stones where it snuck through the jungle canopy. Despite the sun, a thick fog remained on the ground, obscuring his vision and filling the air with a thick, palpable humidity.

He'd lost track of how long he'd walked. For years he'd searched, traveling in all directions, chasing the smallest of clues and the weakest of rumors. All he knew was the journey —the sun, the steps, then restless sleep on the hard ground, the hunger, the exhaustion. The thirst. He wiped the sweat from his brow. Thirst was his constant companion, scratching at his throat incessantly. His canteen was nearly empty. He'd have to ration what he had left until he came across another spring or a creek. He didn't know when that might be.

"Just a bit further, old man," he muttered to himself as he clambered over a boulder. "This'll be the one, I'm sure of it." His voice was scratchy from disuse. A lizard perked up at the sound where it bathed in the sun, then darted away and disappeared into a crack in the rock.

His boots hit the muddy ground. He wrestled the faded map from his pack and unfolded it. "It should be here," he said. "The doorway should be here."

He stood in a verdant, small valley, surrounded by high mountains. The rock faces surrounding him were smooth, blank, and crisscrossed with thick vines that pulled the rocks into the jungle.

"It should be here." His voice pitched up in desperation. "It has to be here."

He stared at the map. Unless it never existed at all. Unless everyone else was right—everyone who had laughed at him, ignored him, called him foolish and naïve. Unless he was on a mad quest, a doomed quest, a quest for something that was never real at all.

"No," he said aloud. "It's here. I know it's here."

The lizard reappeared. It darted across the ground, then up the rock face, and disappeared behind the thick vines. The vines shifted, and a tiny glint of gold caught the man's eye.

He pushed the vines aside. They concealed a narrow crack in the rock face, just large enough for him to squeeze through. In the walls, traces of gold gleamed. He dropped his pack onto the dirt and squeezed into the passage. The rock pressed against his body from both sides, tight enough that he could hardly breathe as he moved. He took small, shuffling steps, easing deeper into the passageway. It narrowed and narrowed, and for a moment he feared the rock might trap him there, when suddenly it widened and he stepped out.

Beams of sunlight fell through a dense canopy, dappling the ground in gold. The jungle was lush, but quiet, as if no one had been there in ages. The man inhaled deeply, savoring the earthy, grassy scent in the air.

He turned and froze. Two facing cliffs rose from the ground ahead with a path between them. At the front of the path, the light creeping through the trees illuminated a glimmering stone archway connecting the cliffs.

The man gasped.

At the top of the stone archway, in the center, embossed in gleaming gold, was a symbol—three rectangles stacked on each other from largest at the bottom to the smallest on top. From his pocket, he withdrew the small stone he'd carried all that time, over every mile and every mountainous climb. For years, he'd smoothed his thumb over it and memorized the symbol of the three rectangles carved into its surface. He stared at it. *Identical.* It had been his guide. His proof. Over all the years, he had known it was real—he'd known he'd reach that moment.

He'd made it.

He'd found it.

Past the arch, the facing cliffs formed a long path that disappeared into fog. He stumbled forward, passing under the archway. The walls of the cliffs and the stone arch shaded him. The temperature dropped, and he closed his eyes, basking in the cool relief. His steps were light and his heart felt giddy. He took a step, and then another. Here was his future. Everyone who had laughed would soon know the truth. They would remember him for his tenacity and his success.

Then he took a step, and there was no stone beneath his foot. His eyes shot open, and he gasped. He reached out desperately to catch anything, but there was nothing. Only the darkness of a pit. He plummeted, swallowed by the hole, until not even his echoing screams remained.

PETER, Sephiri, Kira, and Rylan continue their treasure-hunting adventures in Legend of the Golden City. Preorder it on Amazon to get it the day it comes out! https://mybook.to/legendgoldencity

RECEIVE a FREE digital copy of the novella, Shadow Knights: Origine, and find out more about Michael Webb by joining his newsletter. Hear about behind the scenes news, new book announcements, and get free stuff! www.subscribepage.com/michaelwebbnovels

"Hey, you with the book...did you know my dad wrote it? I keep telling all my doggie friends about it, but they want to see online reviews. I rated it five out of five dog bones, but they want more feedback. Can you help my puppy pals? Can you leave a review online?"

PLEASE leave an honest review on Amazon or wherever you got the book from. Do it for Charlie.

# ACKNOWLEDGMENTS

Leaving the Shadow Knights series behind to embark on this new one has been an exciting yet nerve-wracking journey. I've absolutely loved dreaming up treasure-hunting ideas and putting them into story form. I want to thank a few people who helped make this book happen:

- Alpha/Beta Readers - Tara, Jeff, David, Claudia, Beckham, Anna, Eli, and Cadie. You all contributed SO much, helping me fix tons of issues I didn't notice on my own.

- Mrs. Webb's ELA classes - for your help in reading and giving feedback. I appreciate the time you took. You should see some of your suggestions in the final version.

- Nicholas - for going above and beyond your beta reading assignment. Many of the ideas that give this story its rounded out edges and depth came from the discussion we had.

- Chris - In addition to your beta reading help, I'm greatly appreciative of your unwavering excitement (for years) about me writing a treasure-hunting series. It helped fuel my passion to make it a reality.

- Kate - for helping me fine tune my story ideas and brainstorm new ones. The story would not be what it is without you.

- Mom and Dad - for winning the "tell most people my son is an author" award. I feel your pride every time we talk.

- Julia and Eli - for being my greatest fans and cheerleaders and always believing in me and supporting me in my dream.

Made in the USA
Las Vegas, NV
12 July 2023

74520784R00204